silence

silence

BECCA FITZPATRICK

SIMON AND SCHUSTER

First published in the USA in 2011 by Simon & Schuster BFYR,
an imprint of Simon & Schuster Children's Publishing Division.
First published in Great Britain by Simon & Schuster UK Ltd
A CBS COMPANY

This edition published by Simon & Schuster Australia (PTY),
Suite 19A, Level 1, Building C,
450 Miller Street,
Cammeray 2062
NSW

1 3 5 7 9 10 8 6 4 2

www.simonandschuster.com.au

Simon & Schuster Australia, Sydney
Simon & Schuster India, New Delhi

A CIP catalogue copy for this book is available
from the British Library.

TPB ISBN: 978-0-85707-228-3
E-BOOK ISBN: 978-0-85707-230-6

Printed in Australia by McPherson's Printing Group

To Riley and Jace

xoxo

PROLOGUE

COLDWATER, MAINE
THREE MONTHS AGO

THE SLEEK BLACK AUDI ROLLED TO A STOP IN THE parking lot overlooking the cemetery, but none of the three men inside had any intention of paying respects to the dead. The hour burned past midnight, and the grounds were officially closed. A strange summer fog hung thin and dreary, like a string of rising ghosts. Even the moon, a slender waxing crescent, resembled a drooping eyelid. Before the road dust settled, the driver leaped out, promptly opening the two rear car doors.

Blakely exited first. He stood tall with graying hair and a hard, rectangular face—nearly thirty in human years, though markedly older by Nephilim count. He was followed by a second Nephil named Hank Millar. Hank, too, was uncommonly tall with blond hair, snapping blue eyes, and charismatic good looks. His creed was "Justice over mercy," and that, combined with his quick rise to power in the Nephilim underworld during the last few years, had earned him the nicknames the Fist of Justice, Iron Fist and, most famously, the Black Hand. He was hailed among his people as a visionary leader, a savior. But in smaller backroom circles, he was quietly referred to as the Blood Hand. Hushed voices murmured not of a redeemer, but of a ruthless dictator. Hank found their nervous chatter amusing; a true dictator had absolute power and no opposition. Hopefully, someday he could live up to their expectations.

Hank stepped out and lit a cigarette, taking a long drag. "Are my men assembled?"

"Ten men in the woods above us," Blakely answered. "Another ten in cars at both exits. Five are hiding at various points within the cemetery; three just inside the doors of the mausoleum, and two along the fence. Any more, and we'd give ourselves away. Undoubtedly, the man you are meeting tonight will come with his own backup."

Hank smiled in the darkness. "Oh, I rather doubt that."

Blakely blinked. "You brought twenty-five of your best Nephilim fighters to go against one man?"

"Not a man," Hank reminded him. "I don't want anything to go wrong tonight."

"We have Nora. If he gives you trouble, put him on the phone to her. They say angels can't feel touch, but emotions are fair game. I'm certain he'll feel it when she screams. Dagger is standing by, at the ready."

Hank turned to Blakely, giving him a slow, appraising smile. "Dagger is watching her? He's hardly sane."

"You said you wanted to break her spirit."

"I did say that, didn't I?" Hank mused. It had been four short days since he'd taken Nora captive, dragging her out of a maintenance shed inside Delphic Amusement Park, but he'd already determined precisely which lessons she needed to learn. First, never to undermine his authority in front of his men. Second, devotion to her Nephilim bloodline. And, perhaps most important, to show her own father respect.

Blakely handed Hank a small mechanical device with a button at the center that glowed an unearthly shade of blue. "Put this in your pocket. Press the blue button and your men will swarm in from every direction."

"Has it been enhanced with devilcraft?" Hank asked.

A nod. "Upon activation, it is designed to temporarily immobilize the angel. I can't say for how long. This is a prototype, and I haven't thoroughly tested it."

"Have you spoken of this to anyone?"

"You ordered me not to, sir."

Satisfied, Hank pocketed the device. "Wish me luck, Blakely."

His friend patted his shoulder. "You don't need it."

Flicking aside his cigarette, Hank descended the stone steps leading to the cemetery, a rather foggy patch of land that made his vantage point useless. He'd hoped to see the angel first, from above, but was comforted by the knowledge that he was backed by his own handpicked and highly trained militia.

At the base of the steps, Hank peered through the shadows warily. It had started to drizzle, washing out the fog. He could make out towering gravestones and trees that twisted wildly. The cemetery was overgrown and almost mazelike. No wonder Blakely had suggested the spot. The likelihood of human eyes accidentally witnessing tonight's events was negligible.

There. Ahead. The angel leaned on a gravestone but at the sight of Hank he straightened. Dressed strictly in black, including a leather motorcycle jacket, he was difficult to distinguish from the shadows. He hadn't shaved in days, his hair was unruly and unkempt, and there were lines of worry around his mouth. Mourning the disappearance of his girlfriend, then? All the better.

"You look a little worse for wear . . . Patch, is it?" Hank said, stopping a few feet away.

The angel smiled, but it wasn't pleasant. "And here I was thinking maybe you'd had a few sleepless nights yourself. After all, she's your own flesh and blood. From the looks of it, you've been getting your beauty sleep. Rixon always said you were a pretty boy."

Hank let the insult roll off. Rixon was the fallen angel who used to possess his body every year during the month of Cheshvan, and he was as good as dead. With him gone, there was nothing left in the world that frightened Hank. "Well? What do you have for me? It had better be good."

"I paid a visit to your house, but you'd skulked off into hiding with your tail between your legs and taken your family with you," the angel said in a low voice resonating with something Hank couldn't quite interpret. It was halfway between contempt and . . . mockery.

"Yes, I thought you might try something rash. An eye for an eye, isn't that the creed of fallen angels?" Hank couldn't tell if he was impressed by the angel's cool demeanor, or irritated. He'd expected to find the angel frantic and desperate. At the very least, he'd hoped to provoke him to violence. Any excuse to bring his men running. Nothing like a bloodbath to instill camaraderie. "Let's cut the pleasantries. Tell me you brought me something useful."

The angel shrugged. "Playing your rat seemed unimportant next to finding where you've stashed your daughter."

The muscles in Hank's jaw tightened. "This wasn't the deal."

"I'll get you the information you need," the angel answered, almost conversationally if it weren't for that chilling gleam in his eyes. "But first release Nora. Get your men on the phone now."

"I need insurance you'll cooperate long-term. I'm keeping her until you make good on your side of the deal."

The corners of the angel's mouth tipped up, but it was hardly a smile. There was something truly menacing in the result. "I'm not here to negotiate."

"You aren't in a position to." Hank reached into his breast pocket and retrieved his phone. "I'm out of patience. If you've wasted my time tonight, it's going to be an unpleasant night for your girlfriend. One call, and she goes hungry—"

Before he had time to carry out his threat, Hank felt himself tripping backward. The angel's arms flashed out, and all air escaped Hank in a rush. His head hit something solid, and waves of black rolled across his vision.

"This is how it's going to work," the angel hissed. Hank tried to muster a shout, but the angel's hand was clenched at his throat. Hank kicked his feet, but the gesture was pointless; the angel was too strong. He scratched for the panic button in his pocket, but his fingers fumbled uselessly. The angel had cut off his oxygen. Red lights popped behind his eyes and his chest felt as though a stone had rolled on top of it.

In a burst of inspiration, Hank invaded the angel's mind, teasing apart the threads that formed his thoughts, focusing fixedly on redirecting the angel's intentions, weakening his motivation, all the while whispering a hypnotic, *Release Hank Millar, release him now*—

"A mind-trick?" the angel scorned. "Don't bother. Make the call," he commanded. "If she walks free in the next two minutes, I'll kill you quickly. Anything longer than that, and I will rip you apart, one piece at a time. And trust me when I say I will enjoy every last scream you utter."

"Can't—kill—me!" Hank sputtered.

He felt a searing pain erupt across his cheek. He howled, but the sound never made it past his lips. His windpipe was crushed, vised in the angel's grip. The raw, burning pain intensified, and all around, Hank could smell blood mixed with his own perspiration.

"One piece at a time," the angel hissed, dangling something papery and drenched in dark liquid over Hank's whirling vision.

Hank felt his eyes widen. His skin!

"Call your men," the angel ordered, sounding infinitely less patient.

"Can't—talk!" Hank gurgled. If he could only reach the panic button . . .

Swear an oath to release her now, and I'll let you talk. The angel's threat slipped easily into Hank's head.

You're making a big mistake, boy, Hank fired back. His fingers brushed his pocket, slipping inside. He clenched the panic device.

The angel made a guttural sound of impatience, ripped the device away and hurled it into the fog. *Swear the oath or your arm goes next.*

I'll uphold our original deal, Hank returned. *I'll spare her life and bury all thought of avenging Chauncey Langeais's death if you'll bring me the information I need. Until then, I vow to treat her humanely—*

The angel slammed Hank's head against the ground. Between the nausea and pain, he heard the angel say, *I'm not leaving her with you another five minutes, let alone the time it will take me to get what you want.*

Hank tried to peer over the angel's shoulder, but all he saw was a fence of gravestones. The angel had him on the ground, blocked from view. His men couldn't see him. He didn't believe the angel could kill him—he was immortal—but he wasn't going to lie here and let himself be mutilated until he resembled a corpse.

He curled his lips and locked eyes with the angel. *I'll never forget how loud she screamed when I dragged her away. Did you know she screamed your name? Over and over. She said you'd come for her. That was the first couple of days, of course. I think she's finally starting to accept you're no match for me.*

He watched the angel's face darken as if with blood. His shoulders shook, his black eyes dilated with rage. And then it all happened in stunning agony. One moment Hank was on the verge of blacking out from the white-hot pain of his pummeled flesh, and the next he was staring at the angel's fists, painted with his blood.

A deafening howl thundered out of Hank's body. The pain exploded inside him, nearly knocking him unconscious. From some distant place, he heard the running feet of his Nephilim men.

"Get—him—off—me!" he snarled as the angel tore at his body. Every nerve ending raged with fire. Heat and agony leaked from his pores. He caught sight of his hand, but there was no flesh—only mangled bone. The angel was going to shred him to pieces.

He heard grunts of effort from his men, but the angel was still on top of him, his hands raking fire everywhere they touched.

Hank swore viciously. "Blakely!"

"Pull him off *now!*" came Blakely's gruff command to his men.

Not soon enough, the angel was dragged away. Hank lay on the ground, panting. He was wet with blood, pain stabbing him like hot pokers. Slapping aside Blakely's offered hand, Hank climbed with effort to his feet. He felt unstable, swaying and intoxicated with his own suffering. By the gaping stares of his men, Hank knew he was a horrific sight. Given the severity of the wounds, it might take him an entire week to heal—even with the enhancements of devilcraft.

"Should we take him away, sir?"

Hank dabbed a handkerchief to his lip, which was split open and hung from his face like pulp. "No. We have no use for him locked up. Tell Dagger the girl is to have nothing but water for forty-eight hours." His breathing was ragged. "If our boy here can't cooperate, she pays."

With a nod, Blakely turned from the scene, dialing on his phone.

Hank spat out a bloodied tooth, studied it quietly, then tucked it in his pocket. He fixed his eyes on the angel, whose only outward sign of fury came in the form of clenched fists. "Once again, the terms of our oath, so there's no further misunderstanding. First, you will earn back the confidence of fallen angels, rejoining their ranks—"

silence

"I'll kill you," the angel said with quiet warning. Though he was held by five men, he no longer struggled. He stood deathly still, his eyes black orbs burning with vengeance. For one moment, Hank felt a pang of fear strike like a match inside his gut.

He strove for cool indifference. "—following which, you will spy on them and report their dealings directly to me."

"I swear now," the angel said, his breathing controlled but elevated, "with these men as my witnesses, I will not rest until you are dead."

"A waste of breath. You can't kill me. Perhaps you've forgotten from whom a Nephil claims his immortal birthright?"

A murmur of amusement circled his men, but Hank waved them to silence. "When I've determined you've given me enough information to successfully prevent fallen angels from possessing Nephilim bodies this coming Cheshvan—"

"Every hand you lay on her I will return tenfold."

Hank's mouth twisted into a suggestion of a smile. "An unnecessary sentiment, don't you think? By the time I'm through with her, she won't remember your name."

"Remember this moment," the angel said with icy vehemence. "It's going to come back to haunt you."

"Enough of this," Hank snapped, making a disgusted gesture and starting back toward the car. "Take him to Delphic Amusement Park. We want him back among the fallen as soon as possible."

"I'll give you my wings."

Hank stopped his departure, not sure he'd heard the angel correctly. He barked a laugh. "What?"

"Swear an oath to release Nora right now, and they're yours." The angel sounded haggard, giving away the first hint of defeat. Music to Hank's ears.

"What use would I have for your wings?" he retorted blandly, but the angel had caught his attention. As far as he knew, no Nephil had ever torn out the wings of an angel. They did it among their own kind now and then, but the idea of a Nephil having that power was quite the novelty. Quite the temptation. Tales of his conquest would sweep through Nephilim households overnight.

"You'll think of something," the angel said with increasing weariness.

"I'll swear an oath to release her before Cheshvan," Hank countered, smothering all eagerness from his voice, knowing that to reveal his delight would be disastrous.

"Not good enough."

"Your wings might make a pretty trophy, but I have a bigger agenda. I'll release her by the end of summer, my final offer." He turned, walking away, swallowing down his greedy enthusiasm.

"Done," the angel said with quiet resignation, and Hank released a slow breath.

He turned. "How is it to be done?"

"Your men will tear them out."

Hank opened his mouth to argue, but the angel cut him off. "They're strong enough. If I don't fight, nine or ten of them together could do it. I'll go back to living beneath Delphic and make it known the archangels tore out my wings. But for this to work, you and I can't have any connection," he warned.

Without delay, Hank shook a few drops of blood from his disfigured hand to the grass at his feet. "I swear my oath to release Nora before summer's end. If I break my vow, I plead that I may die and return to the dust from which I was created."

The angel tugged his shirt over his head and braced his hands on his knees. His torso rose and fell with every breath. With a certain bravery Hank both detested and envied, the angel told him, "Get on with it."

Hank would have liked to do the honors, but his wariness won out. He couldn't be certain there weren't traces of devilcraft all over him. If the place where an angel's wings fused into his back were as receptive as rumor had it, one touch might give him away. He'd worked too hard to slip up this late in the game.

Quelling his regret, Hank addressed his men. "Tear out the angel's wings and clean up any mess. Then dump his body at Delphic's gates, where he'll be sure to be found. And take care not to be seen." He would have liked to order them to brand the angel with his mark—a clenched fist—a visible display of triumph sure to increase his stature among Nephilim everywhere, but the angel had a point. For this to work, they could leave no evidence of association.

BECCA FITZPATRICK

Back at the car, Hank gazed over the cemetery. The event was already over. The angel lay prostrate on the ground, shirtless, two open wounds running the length of his back. Though he hadn't felt an ounce of pain, his body appeared to have gone into shock from the loss. Hank had also heard a fallen angel's wing scars were his Achilles' heel. In this, the rumors appeared to be true.

"Should we call it a night?" Blakely asked, coming up behind him.

"One more phone call," Hank said with an undercurrent of irony. "To the girl's mother."

He dialed and put his cell phone to his ear. He cleared his throat, adopting a strained and worried pitch. "Blythe, darling, I just got your message. The family and I have been on vacation and I'm rushing to the airport now. I'll catch the first flight out. Tell me everything. What do you mean, kidnapped? Are you certain? What did the police say?" He paused, listening to her anguished sobs. "Listen to me," he told her firmly. "I am here for you. I'll exhaust every resource I have, if that's what it takes. If Nora is out there, we will find her."

CHAPTER

1

CHAPTER

COLDWATER, MAINE
PRESENT DAY

EVEN BEFORE I OPENED MY EYES, I KNEW I WAS IN danger.

I stirred at the soft crunch of footsteps drawing closer. A dim flicker of sleep remained, dulling my focus. I was flat on my back, a chill seeping through my shirt.

My neck was crooked at a painful angle, and I opened my eyes. Thin stones loomed out of the blue-black fog. For a strange suspended moment, an image of crooked teeth came to mind, and then I saw them for what they really were. Gravestones.

I tried to push myself up to sitting, but my hands slipped on the wet grass. Fighting the haze of sleep still curled around my mind, I rolled sideways off a half-sunken grave, feeling my way through the vapor. The knees of my jeans soaked up dew as I crawled between the haphazardly placed graves and monuments. Mild recognition hovered, but it was a side thought; I couldn't bring myself to focus through the excruciating pain radiating inside my skull.

I crawled along a wrought-iron fence, tamping down a layer of decaying leaves that had been years in the making. A ghoulish howl drifted down from above, and while it sent a shudder through me, it wasn't the sound I was most frightened of. The footsteps trampled over the grass behind me, but whether they were near or far I couldn't tell. A shout of pursuit cut through the mist, and I hurried my pace. I knew instinctively that I had to hide, but I was disoriented; it was too dark to see clearly, the eerie blue fog casting spells before my eyes.

In the distance, trapped between two walls of spindly and over-grown trees, a white stone mausoleum glowed through the night. Rising to my feet, I ran toward it.

I slipped between two marble monuments, and when I came out on the other side, he was waiting for me. A towering silhouette, his arm raised to strike. I tripped backward. As I fell, I realized my mistake: He was made of stone. An angel raised on a pediment, guarding the dead. I might have smothered a nervous laugh, but my head collided against something hard, jarring the world sideways. Darkness encroached on my vision.

I couldn't have been out for long. When the stark black of unconsciousness faded, I was still breathing hard from the exertion of running. I knew I had to get up, but I couldn't remember why. So I lay there, the icy dew mingling with the warm sweat of my skin. At long last I blinked, and it was then that the nearest headstone sharpened into focus. The engraved letters of the epitaph snapped into single-file lines.

HARRISON GREY

A DEVOTED HUSBAND AND FATHER

DIED MARCH 16, 2008

I bit down on my lip to keep from crying out. Now I understood the familiar shadow that had lurked over my shoulder since waking up minutes ago. I was in Coldwater's city cemetery. At my dad's graveside.

A nightmare, I thought. *I haven't really woken yet. This is all just a horrible dream.*

The angel watched me, his chipped wings unfurled behind him, his right arm pointing across the cemetery. His expression was carefully detached, but the curve of his lips was more wry than benevolent. For one moment, I was almost able to trick myself into believing he was real and I wasn't alone.

I smiled at him, then felt my lip quiver. I dragged my sleeve along my cheekbone, wiping away tears, though I didn't remember starting to cry. I desperately wanted to climb into his arms, feeling the beat of his wings on air as he flew us over the gates and away from this place.

The resumed sound of footsteps pulled me out of my stupor. They were faster now, crashing through the grass.

I turned toward the sound, bewildered by the bob of light twinkling in and out of the misty darkness. Its beam rose and fell to the cadence of the footsteps—*crunch . . . sweep . . . crunch . . . sweep*—

A flashlight.

I squinted when the light came to a stop between my eyes, dazzling me blind. I had the terrible realization that I definitely wasn't dreaming.

"Lookie here," a man's voice snarled, hidden behind the glare of light. "You can't be here. Cemetery is closed."

I turned my face away, specks of light still dancing behind my eyelids.

"How many others are there?" he demanded.

"What?" My voice was a dry whisper.

"How many more are here with you?" he continued more aggressively. "Thought you'd come out and play night games, did you? Hide-and-seek, I reckon? Or maybe Ghosts in the Graveyard? Not on my watch, you aren't!"

What was I doing here? Had I come to visit my dad? I fished through my memory, but it was disturbingly empty. I couldn't remember coming to the cemetery. I couldn't remember much of anything. It was as if the whole night had been ripped out from under my feet.

Worse, I couldn't remember this morning.

I couldn't remember dressing, eating, school. Was it even a school day?

Momentarily shoving my panic deep down, I concentrated on orienting myself physically and accepted the man's outstretched hand. As soon as I was sitting upright, the flashlight glared at me again. "How old are you?" he wanted to know.

Finally something I knew for certain. "Sixteen." Almost seventeen. My birthday was coming up in August.

"What in the Sam Hill are you doing out here by yourself? Don't you know it's past curfew?"

I looked around helplessly. "I—"

"You ain't a runaway, are you? Just tell me you've got someplace to go."

"Yes." The farmhouse. At the sudden recollection of home, my heart lifted, followed by the sensation of my stomach plummeting to my knees. Out after curfew? How long after? I tried unsuccessfully to shut out the image of my mom's enraged expression when I walked through the front door.

"Does 'yes' got an address?"

18   BECCA FITZPATRICK

"Hawthorne Lane." I stood, but swayed violently when blood rushed to my head. Why couldn't I remember how I'd gotten here? Surely I'd driven. But where had I parked the Fiat? And where was my handbag? My keys?

"Been drinking?" he asked, narrowing his eyes.

I shook my head.

The beam of the flashlight had slipped marginally off my face, when suddenly it was square between my eyes yet again.

"Hold on a second," he said, a note of something I didn't like slipping into his voice. "You're not that girl, are you? Nora Grey," he blurted, as if my name was a knee-jerk response.

I retreated a step. "How—do you know my name?"

"The TV. The reward. Hank Millar posted it."

Whatever he said next floated past. Marcie Millar was the closest thing I had to an archenemy. What did her dad have to do with this?

"They've been looking for you since end of June."

"June?" I repeated, a drop of panic splattering inside me. "What are you talking about? It's April." And who was looking for me? Hank Millar? Why?

"April?" He eyed me queerly. "Why, girlie, it's September."

September? No. It couldn't be. I would know if sophomore year had ended. I would know if summer vacation had come and gone. I'd woken up a mere handful of minutes ago, disoriented, yes, but not stupid.

But what reason did he have to lie?

With the flashlight lowered, I looked him over, getting my first full picture. His jeans were stained, his facial hair tufted from days without a razor, his fingernails long and black under the tips. He looked an awful lot like the vagabonds who wandered the railroad tracks and shacked up by the river during the summer months. They were known to carry weapons.

"You're right, I should be getting home," I said, backing away, brushing my hand against my pocket. The familiar bump of my cell phone was missing. Same with my car keys.

"Now just where do you think you're going?" he asked, coming after me.

My stomach cramped at his sudden movement, and I broke into a run. I raced in the direction the stone angel pointed, hoping it led to the south gate. I would have used the north gate, the one I was familiar with, but it would have required me to run toward the man, instead of away. The ground cut away beneath my feet, and I stumbled downhill. Branches scraped my arms; my shoes slapped against the uneven and rocky ground.

"Nora!" the man shouted.

I wanted to shake myself for telling him I lived on Hawthorne Lane. What if he followed me?

His stride was longer, and I heard him tramping behind me, closing in. I flung my arms wildly, beating back the branches that sank like claws into my clothes. His hand clamped my shoulder, and I swung around, batting it away. "Don't touch me!"

BECCA FITZPATRICK

"Now hold on a minute. I told you about the reward, and I aim to get it."

He lunged for my arm a second time, and on a shot of adrenaline, I drove my foot into his shin.

"Uuhn!" He doubled over, clutching his lower leg.

I was shocked by my violence, but I didn't have any other choice. Staggering back a few steps, I cast a hasty look around, trying to get my bearings. Sweat dampened my shirt, slinking down my backbone, causing every hair on my body to stand tall. Something was off. Even with my groggy memory, I had a clear map of the cemetery in my head—I'd been here countless times to visit my dad's grave—but while the cemetery felt familiar, down to every last detail including the overwhelming smell of burning leaves and stale pond water, something about its *appearance* was off.

And then I put my finger on it.

The maple trees were speckled with red. A sign of impending autumn. But that wasn't possible. It was April, not September. How could the leaves be changing? Was the man possibly telling the truth?

I glanced back to see the man limping after me, pressing his cell phone to his ear. "Yeah, it's her. I'm sure of it. Leaving the cemetery, heading south."

I plunged ahead with renewed fear. *Hop the fence. Find a well-lit, well-populated area. Call the police. Call Vee—*

Vee. My best and most trusted friend. Her house was closer

than mine. I'd go there. Her mom would call the police. I'd describe to them what the man looked like, and they'd track him down. They'd make sure he left me alone. Then they'd talk me back through the night, retracing my steps, and somehow the gaps in my memory would stitch back together and I'd have something to work with. I'd shake off this detached version of myself, this feeling of being suspended in a world that was mine but rejecting me.

I stopped running only to hoist myself over the cemetery fence. There was a field one block up, just on the other side of Wentworth Bridge. I'd cross it and weave my way up the tree streets—Elm and Maple and Oak—cutting through alleys and side yards until I was safe inside Vee's house.

I was hurrying toward the bridge when the sharp sound of a siren wailed around the corner, and a pair of headlights pinned me in place. A blue Kojak light was attached to the roof of the sedan, which screeched to a halt on the far side of the bridge.

My first instinct was to run forward and point the police officer in the direction of the cemetery, describing the man who'd grabbed me, but as my thoughts came around, I was filled with dread.

Maybe he wasn't a police officer. Maybe he was trying to look like one. Anyone could get their hands on a Kojak light. Where was his squad car? From where I stood, squinting through his windshield, he didn't appear to be in uniform.

All these thoughts tumbled through me in a hurry.

BECCA FITZPATRICK

I stood at the foot of the sloping bridge, gripping the stone wall for support. I was sure the maybe-officer had seen me, but I moved into the shadows of the trees bowing over the river's edge anyway. From my peripheral vision, the black water of the Wentworth River glinted. As kids, Vee and I had crouched under this very bridge, catching crayfish from the riverbank by inserting sticks speared with hotdog pieces into the water. The crayfish had fastened their claws to the hotdog, refusing to let go even when we lifted them out of the river and shook them loose in a bucket.

The river was deep at the center. It was also well hidden, snaking through undeveloped property where no one had forked out money to install streetlights. At the end of the field, the water rushed on toward the industrial district, past retired factories, and out to sea.

I briefly wondered if I had it in me to jump off the bridge. I was terrified of heights and the sensation of falling, but I knew how to swim. I only had to make it into the water . . .

A car door shut, yanking me back to the street. The man in the maybe-police car had stepped out. He was all mob: curly dark hair, and dressed formally in a black shirt, black tie, black slacks.

Something about him slapped my memory. But before I could truly grasp it, my memory slammed shut and I was as lost as ever.

An assortment of twigs and branches littered the ground. I

bent down, and when I straightened, I was holding a stick half as thick as my arm.

The maybe-officer pretended not to see my weapon, but I knew he had. He pinned a police badge to his shirt, then raised his hands level with his shoulders. *I'm not going to hurt you,* the gesture said.

I didn't believe him.

He sauntered a few steps forward, taking care not to make any sudden movements. "Nora. It's me." I flinched when he spoke my name. I'd never heard his voice before, and that made my heart pound hard enough that I felt it clear up around my ears. "Are you hurt?"

I continued to watch him with growing anxiety, my mind darting in multiple directions. The badge could easily be fake. I'd already decided the Kojak light was. But if he wasn't police, who was he?

"I called your mom," he said, climbing the gradual slope of the bridge. "She's going to meet us at the hospital."

I didn't drop the stick. My shoulders rose and fell with every breath; I could feel air panting between my teeth. Another bead of sweat slicked beneath my clothes.

"Everything's going to be okay," he said. "It's all over. I'm not going to let anybody hurt you. You're safe now."

I didn't like his long, easy stride or the familiar way he spoke to me.

"Don't come any closer," I told him, the sweat on my palms making it hard to grip the stick properly.

BECCA FITZPATRICK

His forehead creased. "Nora?"

The stick wobbled in my hand. "How do you know my name?" I demanded, not about to let him know how scared I was. How much *he* scared me.

"It's me," he repeated, gazing straight into my eyes, as if he expected lights to coming blazing on. "Detective Basso."

"I don't know you."

He said nothing for a moment. Then tried a new approach. "Do you remember where you've been?"

I watched him warily. I moved deeper in my memory, looking down even the darkest and oldest corridors, but his face wasn't there. I had no recollection of him. And I *wanted* to remember him. I wanted something—anything—familiar to cling to, so I could make sense of a world that, from my vantage point, had been twisted to distortion.

"How did you get to the cemetery tonight?" he asked, tilting his head ever so slightly in that direction. His movements were cautious. His eyes were cautious. Even the line of his mouth was politic. "Did someone drop you off? Did you walk?" He waited. "I need you to tell me, Nora. This is important. What happened tonight?"

I'd like to know myself.

A wave of nausea rolled through me. "I want to go home." I heard a brittle clatter near my feet. Too late, I realized I'd dropped the stick. The breeze felt cold on my empty palms. I wasn't supposed to be here. The whole night was a huge mistake.

No. Not the whole night. What did I know of it? I couldn't remember the whole of it. My only starting point was a slice back in time, when I'd woken on a grave, cold and lost.

I drew up a mental picture of the farmhouse, safe and warm and real, and felt a tear trickle down the side of my nose.

"I can take you home." He nodded sympathetically. "I just need to take you to the hospital first."

I squeezed my eyes shut, hating myself for being reduced to crying. I couldn't think of a better or faster way to show him just how frightened I really was.

He sighed—the softest of sounds, as if he wished there were a way around the news he was about to deliver. "You've been missing for eleven weeks, Nora. Do you hear what I'm saying? Nobody knows where you've been the past three months. You need to be looked at. We need to make sure you're okay."

I stared at him without really seeing him. Tiny bells pealed in my ears but sounded very far off. Deep in my stomach I felt a lurch, but I tried to stuff the queasiness away. I'd cried in front of him, but I wasn't going to be sick.

"We think you were abducted," he said, his face unreadable. He'd closed the distance between us and now stood too close. Saying things I couldn't grasp. "Kidnapped."

I blinked. Just stood there and blinked.

A sensation grabbed my heart, tugging and twisting. My body went slack, tottering in the air. I saw the gold blur of the street-

BECCA FITZPATRICK

lights above, heard the river lapping under the bridge, smelled the exhaust from his running car. But it was all in the background. A dizzy afterthought.

With only that brief warning, I felt myself swaying, swaying. Falling into nothing.

I was unconscious before I hit the ground.

CHAPTER

I WOKE IN A HOSPITAL.

The ceiling was white, the walls a serene blue. The room smelled of lilies, fabric softener, and ammonia. A cart on wheels pushed up beside my bed balanced two flower arrangements, a bouquet of balloons that cheered GET WELL SOON! and a purple foil gift bag. The names on the note cards seesawed in and out of focus. DOROTHEA AND LIONEL. VEE.

There was movement in the corner.

"Oh, baby," a familiar voice whispered, and the person behind it flung herself out of her chair and at me. "Oh, sweetheart." She sat on the edge of my bed and drew me into a suffocating hug. "I love you," she choked into my ear. "I love you so much."

"Mom." The mere sound of her name scattered the nightmares I'd just pulled myself out of. A wave of calm filled me, loosening the knot of fear in my chest.

I knew she was crying by the way her body shook against mine, little tremors at first and then great racking heaves. "You remember me," she said, nothing short of deliverance welling up in her voice. "I was so scared. I thought—Oh, baby. I thought the worst!"

And just like that, the nightmares crept back under my skin. "Is it true?" I asked, something greasy and acidic churning in my stomach. "What the detective said. Was I . . . for eleven weeks . . ." I couldn't bring myself to say the word. Kidnapped. It was so clinical. So impossible.

She made a sound of distress.

"What—happened to me?" I asked.

Mom dragged her fingertips under her eyes to dry them. I knew her well enough to know she was only trying to appear self-composed for my benefit. I immediately braced myself for bad news.

"The police are doing everything they can to piece together answers." She put on a smile, but it wavered. As if she needed something to anchor herself to, she reached for my hand and squeezed it.

"The most important thing is that you're back. You're home. Everything that happened—it's over. We're going to get through this."

"How was I kidnapped?" The question was directed more at myself. How had this happened? Who would want to kidnap me? Had they pulled up in a car while I was leaving school? Stuffed me in the trunk while I was crossing the parking lot? Had it been that easy? Please no. Why hadn't I run? Why hadn't I fought? Why had it taken me so long to escape? Because clearly that's what had happened. Wasn't it? The shortage of answers pecked away at me.

"What do you remember?" Mom asked. "Detective Basso said even a small detail might be helpful. Think back. Try to remember. How did you get to the cemetery? Where were you before that?"

"I don't remember anything. It's like my memory . . ." I broke off. It was like part of my memory had been stolen. Snatched away, with nothing left in its place but a hollow panic. A feeling of violation swayed inside me, making me feel as if I'd been shoved off a high platform without warning. I was falling, and I feared the sensation far more than hitting bottom. There was no end; just a constant sense of gravity having its way with me.

"What is the last thing you remember?" Mom asked.

"School." The answer rolled off my tongue automatically. Slowly my shattered memories began to stir, fragments shifting back together, locking against one another to form something solid. "I had a biology test coming up. But I guess I missed it," I added, the reality of those eleven missing weeks sinking in deeper.

I had a clear picture of sitting in Coach McConaughy's biology class. The familiar smells of chalk dust, cleaning supplies, stuffy air, and the ever-present tang of body odor rose up from memory. Vee was beside me, my lab partner. Our textbooks were open on the black granite table in front of us, but Vee had stealthily slid a copy of US Weekly into hers.

"You mean chemistry," Mom corrected. "Summer school."

I fastened my eyes to hers, unsure. "I've never gone to summer school."

Mom brought her hand to her mouth. Her skin had blanched. The only sound in the room was the methodical tick of the clock above the window. I heard each tiny chime echo through me, ten times, before I found my voice.

"What day is it? What month?" My mind spun back to the cemetery. The composting leaves. The subtle chill in the air. The man with the flashlight insisting it was September. The only word repeating over and over in my mind was no. No, it wasn't possible. No, this wasn't happening. No, months of my life couldn't have just walked off unnoticed. I shoved my way back through my memories, trying to grasp anything that could help me bridge this moment to sitting in Coach's biology class. But there was nothing to build on. Any memory of summer was completely and utterly gone.

"It's okay, baby," Mom murmured. "We're going to get your memory back. Dr. Howlett said most patients see marked improvement over time."

I tried to sit up, but my arms were a tangle of tubes and medical monitoring equipment. "Just tell me what month it is!" I repeated hysterically.

"September." Her crumpled face was unbearable. "September sixth."

I sank back down, blinking. "I thought it was April. I can't remember anything past April." I threw up walls to block the outbreak of fear banging inside me. I couldn't deal with it in one great flood. "Is summer really—is it over? Just like that?"

"Just like that?" she echoed in a detached voice. "It dragged on. Every day without you ... Eleven weeks of knowing nothing ... The panic, the worry, the fear, the hopelessness never ending ..."

I mulled this over, doing the math. "If it's September, and I was gone for eleven weeks, then I went missing—"

"June twenty-first," she said blandly. "The night of summer solstice."

The wall I'd built was cracking faster than I could mentally repair it. "But I don't remember June. I don't even remember May."

We watched each other, and I knew we were sharing the same terrible thought. Was it possible my amnesia stretched further than the missing eleven weeks, all the way back to April? How could something like this even happen?

"What did the doctor say?" I asked, moistening my lips, which felt papery and dry. "Did I have a head injury? Was I drugged? Why can't I remember anything?"

BECCA FITZPATRICK

"Dr. Howlett said it's retrograde amnesia." Mom paused. "It means some of your preexisting memories are lost. We just weren't sure how far back the memory loss went. April," she whispered to herself, and I could see all hope fading from her eyes.

"Lost? How lost?"

"He thinks it's psychological."

I plowed my hands through my hair, leaving an oily residue on my fingers. It suddenly dawned on me that I hadn't considered where I'd been all those weeks. I could have been chained in a dank basement. Or tied in the woods. Clearly I hadn't showered in days. A glance at my arms revealed smudges of dirt, small cuts, and bruises all over. What had I gone through?

"Psychological?" I forced myself to shut out the speculations, which only made the hysteria clamp down harder. I had to stay strong. I needed answers. I couldn't fall apart. If I could force my mind to focus despite the spots popping across my vision . . .

"He thinks you're blocking it to avoid remembering something traumatic."

"I'm not blocking it." I closed my eyes, unable to control the tears leaking from the corners. I sucked in a shaky breath and clamped my hands into tight balls to stop the awful trembling in my fingers. "I would know if I was trying to forget five months of my life," I said, speaking slowly to force a measure of calm into my voice. "I want to know what happened to me."

If I glared at her, she ignored it. "Try to remember," she urged gently. "Was it a man? Were you with a male this whole time?"

Was I? Up until this point, I hadn't put a face to my kidnapper. The only picture in my head was of a monster lurking beyond the reach of light. A terrible cloud of uncertainty loomed over me.

"You know you don't have to protect anyone, right?" she continued in that same soft tone. "If you know who you were with, you can tell me. No matter what they told you, you're safe now. They can't get you. They did this horrible thing to you, and it's their fault. Their fault," she repeated.

A sob of frustration rose in my throat. The term "blank slate" was nauseatingly accurate. I was about to voice my hopelessness, when a shadow stirred near the doorway. Detective Basso stood just inside the room's entrance. His arms were folded over his chest, his eyes alert.

My body reflexively tensed. Mom must have felt it; she looked beyond the bed, following my gaze. "I thought Nora might remember something while it was just the two of us," she told Detective Basso apologetically. "I know you said you wanted to question her, but I just thought—"

He nodded, signaling that it was okay. Then he walked over, staring down at me. "You said you don't have a clear picture, but even fuzzy details might help."

"Like hair color," Mom interjected. "Maybe it was . . . black, for instance?"

I wanted to tell her there was *nothing*, not even a lingering snapshot of color, but I didn't dare with Detective Basso in the room. I didn't trust him. Instinct told me something about him was . . . off. When he stood close, the hairs on my scalp tingled, and I had the brief but distinct feeling of an ice cube slithering down the back of my neck.

"I want to go home," was all I said.

Mom and Detective Basso shared a look.

"Dr. Howlett needs to run a few tests," Mom said.

"What kind of tests?"

"Oh, things related to your amnesia. It'll be over in no time. And then we'll go home." She waved a hand dismissively, which only made me more suspicious.

I faced Detective Basso, since he seemed to have all the answers. "What aren't you telling me?"

His expression was as unfaltering as steel. I supposed years as a cop had perfected that look. "We need to run a few tests. Make sure everything is fine."

Fine?

What part of any of this seemed *fine* to him?

CHAPTER

3

MY MOM AND I LIVE IN A FARMHOUSE NESTLED between Coldwater's city limits and the remote outback regions of Maine. Stand at any window, and it's like a glimpse back in time. Vast unadulterated wilderness on one side, flaxen fields framed by evergreen trees on the other. We live at the end of Hawthorne Lane and are divided from our nearest neighbors by a mile. At night, with the fireflies lighting up the trees in gold, and the fragrance of warm, musky pine overwhelming the air, it's not hard to trick my mind into believing I've transported myself into a completely different century. If I slant my vision just so, I can even picture a red barn and grazing sheep.

Our house has white paint, blue shutters, and a wraparound porch with a slope grade visible to the naked eye. The windows are long and narrow, and protest with an obnoxiously loud groan when pushed open. My dad used to say there was no need to install an alarm in my bedroom window, a secret joke between us, since we both knew I was hardly the kind of daughter to sneak out.

My parents moved into the farmhouse-slash-money-pit shortly before I was born on the philosophy that you can't argue with love at first sight. Their dream was straightforward: to slowly restore the house to its charming 1771 condition, and one day hammer a bed-and-breakfast sign in the front yard and serve the best lobster bisque up and down Maine's coast. The dream dissolved when my dad was murdered one night in downtown Portland.

This morning I'd been released from the hospital, and now I was alone in my room. Hugging a pillow to my chest, I eased back on my bed, my eyes nostalgically tracing the collage of pictures tacked to a corkboard on the wall. There were snapshots of my parents posing at the top of Raspberry Hill, Vee modeling a spandex Catwoman disaster she sewed for Halloween a few years back, my sophomore yearbook picture. Looking at our smiling faces, I tried to fool myself into believing I was safe now that I was back in my world. The truth was, I'd never feel safe and I'd never have my life back until I could remember what I'd gone through during the last five months, particularly the last two and a half. Five months seemed insignificant held up against seventeen years (I'd missed my seventeenth birthday during those eleven unaccountable weeks), but the missing gap was all I could see. A huge hole standing in my path, blocking me from seeing beyond it. I had no past, no future. Only a huge void that haunted me.

The tests Dr. Howlett had ordered had come back fine, just fine. As far as anyone could tell, except for a few healing cuts and bruises, my physical health was as stellar as it had been on the day I'd gone missing.

But the deeper things, the invisible things, those parts of me that lay under the surface out of reach of any test—with those things I found my resilience wavering. Who was I now? What had I undergone during those missing months? Had the trauma shaped me in ways I would never understand? Or worse, never recover from?

Mom had imposed a strict no-visitors policy while I was in the hospital, and Dr. Howlett had backed her up. I could understand their concern, but now that I was home and slowly settling back into the familiarity of my world, I wasn't going to let Mom seal me up with the well-meant but misguided intention of protecting me. Maybe I was changed, but I was still me. And the only thing I wanted right now was to talk everything out with Vee.

Downstairs, I swiped Mom's BlackBerry off the counter and

took it back to my room. When I'd woken up in the cemetery, I hadn't had my cell phone with me, and until I picked up a replacement, her phone would have to do.

IT'S NORA. CAN U TALK? I texted Vee. It was late, and Vee's mom enforced lights-out at ten. If I called, and her mom heard the ring, it could mean a lot of trouble for Vee. Knowing Mrs. Sky, I didn't think she'd be lenient, even with the special nature of the circumstances.

A moment later the BlackBerry chimed. BABE?!?!!!!!! AM FREAKING OUT. AM A TOTAL WRECK. WHERE R U?

CALL ME AT THIS NUMBER.

I set the BlackBerry in my lap, chewing the tip of my nail. I couldn't believe how nervous I felt. This was Vee. But best friends or not, we hadn't talked in months. It didn't feel that long in my mind, but there it was. Thinking of the two sayings, "Absence makes the heart grow fonder" versus "Out of sight, out of mind," I was definitely hoping for the former.

Even though I was expecting Vee's call, I still jumped when the BlackBerry rang.

"Hello? Hello?" Vee said.

Hearing her voice caused my throat to thicken with emotion. "It's me!" I choked.

"'Bout time," she huffed, but her voice sounded thick and emotional too. "I was at the hospital all day yesterday, but they wouldn't let me see you. I bolted past security, but they called a code ninety-nine and chased me down. They escorted me out in handcuffs, and by escorted I mean there was a lot of kicking and bad language being slung in both directions. The way I see it, the only criminal here is your mom. No visitors? I'm your best friend, or did she not get the memo every year for the past eleven? Next time I'm over, I am going to lay into that woman."

In the darkness, I felt my trembling lips crack into a smile. I clutched the phone to my chest, torn between laughing and crying. I should have known Vee wouldn't let me down. The memory of everything that had gone horribly wrong since I'd woken up in the cemetery three nights ago was quickly eclipsed by the mere fact that I had the best friend in the world. Maybe everything else had changed, but my relationship with Vee was rock solid. We were unbreakable. Nothing could change that.

"Vee," I breathed, a sigh of relief. I wanted to bask in the normality of this moment. It was late, we were supposed to be sleeping, and here we were, chatting with the lights off. Last year Vee's mom had trashed Vee's phone after catching her talking to me after lights-out. The next morning, in front of the whole neighborhood, Vee went dumpster diving for it. To this day, she uses that phone. We call it Oscar, as in Oscar the Grouch.

"Are they giving you quality drugs?" Vee asked. "Apparently Anthony Amowitz's dad is a pharmacist, and I could probably score you some good stuff."

My eyebrows lifted in surprise. "What's this? You and Anthony?"

"Heck, no. Not like that. I've sworn off guys. If I need romance, that's what Netflix is for."

I'll believe it when I see it, I thought with a smirk. "Where is my best friend and what have you done with her?"

"I'm doing boy detox. Like a diet, only for my emotional health. Never mind that, I'm coming over," Vee continued. "I haven't seen my best friend in three months, and this phone reunion is crap. Girl, I'm gonna show you the bear in hug."

"Good luck getting past my mom," I said. "She's the new spokes-woman for helicopter parenting."

"That *woman*!" Vee hissed. "I'm making the sign of the cross right now."

We could debate my mom's status as a witch another day. Right now, we had more important things to discuss. "I want a rundown of the days leading up to my kidnapping, Vee," I said, taking our con-versation to a far more serious level. "I can't shake the feeling that my kidnapping wasn't random. There had to have been warning signs, but I can't remember any of them. My doctor said the memory loss is temporary, but in the meantime I need you to tell me where I went, what I did, and who I was with that last week. Walk me through it."

Vee was slow to answer. "You sure this is a good idea? It's kind of soon to stress about that stuff. Your mom told me about the amnesia—"

"Seriously?" I interjected. "You're going to side with my mom?"

"Stuff it," Vee muttered, relenting.

For the next twenty minutes, she recounted every event during that final week. The more she talked, however, the more my heart sank. No bizarre phone calls. No strangers skulking unexpectedly into my life. No unusual cars following us around town.

"What about the night I disappeared?" I asked, interrupting her mid sentence.

"We went to Delphic Amusement Park. I remember taking off to buy hot dogs . . . and then all hell broke loose. I heard gunfire and people started stampeding out of the park. I circled back to find you, but you were gone. I figured you'd done the smart thing and bolted. Only I didn't find you in the parking lot. I would have gone back inside the park, but the police came and kicked everybody out. I tried to tell them that you might still be in the park, but they weren't in the mood. They forced everyone home. I called you a zillion times, but you didn't answer."

It felt like someone had punched me in the stomach. Gunfire? Delphic had a reputation, but still. Gunfire? It was so bizarre—so completely outrageous—that had anyone other than Vee been telling me, I wouldn't have believed it.

Vee said, "I never saw you again. I found out later about the whole hostage situation."

"Hostage situation?"

"Apparently the same psychopath who shot up the park held you hostage in the mechanical room under the fun house. Nobody knows why. He eventually let you go and bolted."

I opened my mouth, shut it. At last I managed a shocked, "What?"

"The police found you, got your statement, and took you home around two in the morning. That was the last anybody saw you. As for the guy who took you hostage . . . nobody knows what happened to him."

Right then, all the threads converged into one. "I must have been taken from my house," I concluded, working it out as I went. "After two a.m., I was probably sleeping. The guy who held me hostage must have followed me home. Whatever he hoped to accomplish at Delphic was interrupted, and he came back for me. He must have broken in."

"That's the thing. There was no sign of a struggle. Doors and windows were all locked."

I kneaded the heel of my hand into my forehead. "Did the police have any leads? This guy—whoever he was—couldn't have been a complete ghost."

"They said he was most likely using a phony name. But for what it's worth, you told them his name was Rixon."

"I don't know anyone named Rixon."

Vee sighed. "That's the problem. Nobody does." She was quiet a moment. "Here's another thing. Sometimes I think I recognize his name, but when I try to remember how, my mind goes blank. Like the memory is there, but I can't retrieve it. Almost like . . . there's a hole where his name should be. It's the freakiest feeling.

silence

I keep telling myself maybe it's just that I *want* to remember him, you know? Like if I remember him—bingo! We have our bad guy. And the police can arrest him. Too simple, I know. And now I'm just babbling," she said. Then, softly, "Still . . . I could have sworn . . ."

My bedroom door creaked open, and Mom ducked her head inside. "I'm going to turn in for the night." Her eyes traveled to the BlackBerry. "It's getting late, and we both need our sleep." She waited expectantly, and I caught her hidden message.

"Vee, I have to go. I'll call you tomorrow."

"Send the witch my love." And she hung up.

"Do you need anything?" Mom asked, casually taking the Black-Berry from me. "Water? Extra blankets?"

"No, I'm good. 'Night, Mom." I forced a quick but reassuring smile.

"Did you double-check your window?"

"Three times."

She crossed the room and rattled the lock anyway. When she found it secure, she gave a weak laugh. "Doesn't hurt to check one last time, right? Good night, baby," she added, smoothing my hair and kissing my forehead.

After she backed out, I scrunched under my covers and mulled over everything Vee had said. A shoot-out at Delphic, but *why?* What had the shooter hoped to accomplish? And why, of the presumably thousands of people at the park that night, had he chosen me as his hostage? Maybe it was sheer bad luck on my side, but it didn't feel right. The unknown spun through my head until I was exhausted. If only—

If only I could remember.

Yawning, I settled in for sleep.

Fifteen minutes ticked away. Then twenty. Flopping onto my back, I stared slightly cross-eyed at the ceiling, trying to sneak up on my memory and catch it off guard. When that failed to produce results, I tried a more direct approach. I banged my head against my pillow, trying to knock loose an image. A line of dialogue. A scent that might spark ideas. Anything! But it quickly became apparent that rather than anything, I was going to have to settle for nothing.

When I'd checked out of the hospital this morning, I was convinced my memory was lost forever. But with my head cleared and the worst of the shock over, I was beginning to think otherwise. I sensed, acutely, a broken bridge in my mind, the truth on the far side of the gap. If I was responsible for tearing down the bridge as a defense mechanism against the trauma I'd suffered during my kidnapping, then surely I could rebuild it again. I just needed to figure out how.

Starting with the color black. Deep, dark unearthly black. I hadn't told anyone yet, but the color kept streaking across my mind at the oddest moments. When it did, my skin shivered pleasantly, and it was as if I could feel the color tracing a finger tenderly along my jaw, tipping my chin up to face it directly.

I knew it was absurd to think a color could come to life, but once or twice, I was sure I'd caught a flash of something more sub-stantial behind the color. A pair of eyes. The way they studied me cut to the heart.

But how could something lost in my memory during this time cause me pleasure instead of pain?

I let go of a slow breath. I felt a desperate urgency to follow the color, no matter where it led me. I longed to find those black eyes, to stand face-to-face with them. I longed to know who they belonged to. The color tugged at me, beckoning me to follow it. Rationally, it made no sense. But the thought stuck in my brain. I felt a hypnotic, obsessive desire to let the color guide me. A power-ful magnetism that even logic couldn't break.

I let this desire build up inside me until it vibrated powerfully under my skin. Uncomfortably hot, I wrestled out of my blankets. My head buzzing, I tossed and turned. The intensity of the buzzing increased until I shivered with heat. A strange fever. *The cemetery*, I thought. *It all started in the cemetery.*

The black night, the black fog. Black grass, black gravestones. The glittering black river. And now a pair of black eyes watching me. I couldn't ignore the flashes of black, and I couldn't sleep them away. I couldn't rest until I acted on them.

I swung out of bed. I stretched a knit shirt over my head, zipped myself into a pair of jeans, and threw a cardigan over my shoulders. I paused at my bedroom door. The hall outside was quiet except for the reverberating tick of the grandfather clock carrying up from the main level. Mom's bedroom door was not quite shut, but no light spilled from the crack. If I listened hard enough, I could just make out the soft purr of her snoring.

I moved silently down the stairs, grabbed a flashlight and house key, and let myself out through the back door, fearing the creaky boards on the front porch would give me away. That, and there was a uniformed officer stationed at the curb. He was there to divert reporters and cameras, but I had a feeling that if I strolled out front at this hour, he'd speed-dial Detective Basso.

A small voice at the rear of my mind protested that it probably wasn't safe to go out, but I was propelled by a strange trance. Black night, black fog. Black grass, black gravestones. Glittering black river. A pair of black eyes watching me.

I had to find those eyes. They had the answers.

Forty minutes later I'd walked to the arched gates leading inside Coldwater's cemetery. Under the breeze, leaves twirled down from their branches like dark pinwheels. I found my father's grave without difficulty. Shuddering against the damp chill in the air, I used trial and error to find my way back to the flat headstone where it had all begun.

Crouching down, I ran my finger over the aged marble. I shut my eyes and blocked out the night sounds, concentrating on finding the black eyes. I threw my question out there, hoping they'd hear. How had I gotten to the point of sleeping in a cemetery after spending eleven weeks in captivity?

I let my eyes travel a slow circle around the graveyard. The decaying smells of approaching autumn, the rich tang of cut grass, the pulse of insect wings rubbing together—none of it illuminated the answer I so desperately wanted. I swallowed against the thickness in my throat, trying hard not to feel defeated. The color black, teasing me for days, had failed me. Shoving my hands inside the pockets of my jeans, I turned to go.

From the edge of my vision, I noticed a smudge on the grass. I picked up a black feather. It was easily the length of my arm, shoulder to wrist. My eyebrows pulled together as I tried to envision what kind of bird could have left it. It was much too big for a crow. Much too big for *any* bird, as far as I was concerned. I ran my finger over the feather's vane, each satiny barb snapping back into place.

A memory stirred inside me. *Angel,* I seemed to hear a smooth voice whisper. *You're mine.*

Of all the ridiculous, confusing things, I blushed. I looked around, just to make sure the voice wasn't real.

I haven't forgotten you.

With my posture rigid, I waited to hear the voice again, but it faded into the wind. Whatever flicker of memories it left behind dived out of reach before I could grasp them. I felt torn between wanting to fling the feather away, and the frantic impulse to bury it where no one would find it. I had the intense impression that I'd stumbled across something secret, something private, something that could cause a great deal of harm if discovered.

A car revved into the parking lot just up the hill from the cemetery, blaring music. I heard shouts and spurts of laughter, and I wouldn't have been surprised if they belonged to people I went to school with. This part of town was dense with trees, far from the hub of downtown, and made a good place to hang out unsupervised on weekends and nights. Not wanting to stumble across anyone I knew, especially since my sudden reappearance was being splashed across local news, I tucked the feather under my arm and speed-walked along the gravel path leading back to the main road.

Shortly after two thirty a.m. I let myself inside the farmhouse and, after locking up, tiptoed upstairs. I stood, indecisive, in the middle of my bedroom a moment, then hid the feather in my middle dresser drawer, where I also stashed my socks, leggings, and scarves. In hindsight, I didn't even know why I'd carried it home. It wasn't like me to collect scrappy items, let alone tuck them inside my drawers. But it had sparked a memory. . . .

Stripping off my clothes and stretching out a yawn, I turned toward bed. I was halfway there when my feet came to a halt. A sheet of paper rested on my pillow. One that hadn't been there when I left.

I whipped around, expecting to see my mom in the doorway, angry and worked up that I'd sneaked out. But given everything that had happened, did I really think she would simply leave a note upon finding my bed empty?

I picked up the paper, realizing that my hands were shaking. It was lined notebook paper, just like I used in school. The message appeared to have been hastily scribbled in black Sharpie.

JUST BECAUSE YOU'RE HOME
DOESN'T MEAN YOU'RE SAFE.

CHAPTER

4

I CRUMPLED THE PAPER, FLINGING IT AT THE WALL OUT
of fear and frustration. Striding to the window, I rattled the
lock to make sure it was secure. I wasn't feeling gutsy enough
to open the window and have a look out, but I cupped my hands
around my eyes and peered into the shadows stretched across the
lawn like long, lean daggers. I had no idea who could have left the
note, but one thing was certain. I'd locked up before leaving. And
earlier, before we'd headed upstairs for the night, I'd watched my

mom walk through the house and check every window and door at least three times.

So how had the intruder gotten in?

And what did the note even mean? It was cryptic and cruel. A twisted joke? Right now, that was my best guess.

Down the hall, I pushed on my mom's bedroom door, opening it just far enough to see inside. "Mom?"

She sat up ramrod straight in the darkness. "Nora? What is it? What happened? A bad dream?" A pause. "Did you remember something?"

I clicked on the bedside lamp, suddenly fearful of the dark and what I couldn't see. "I found a note in my room. It told me not to fool myself into believing I'm safe."

She blinked against the sudden brightness, and I watched her eyes absorb my words. Suddenly she was wide awake. "Where did you find the note?" she demanded.

"I—" I was nervous about how she'd react to the truth. In hindsight, it had been a terrible idea. Sneaking out? After I'd been abducted? But it was hard to fear the possibility of a second abduction when I couldn't even remember the first. And I'd needed to go to the cemetery for my own sanity. The color black had led me there. Stupid, unexplainable, but nonetheless true. "It was under my pillow. I must not have noticed it before bed," I lied. "It wasn't until I shifted in my sleep that I heard the paper crinkle."

She pulled on her bathrobe and jogged to my bedroom. "Where's the note? I want to read it. Detective Basso needs to know about this right away." She was already dialing on her phone. She punched in his number from memory, and it occurred to me that they must have worked closely together during the weeks I was missing.

"Does anyone else have a key to the house?" I asked.

She held her finger up, signaling for me to wait. *Voice mail*, she mouthed. "It's Blythe," she told Detective Basso's message system. "Call me as soon as you get this. Nora found a note in her bedroom tonight." Her eyes cut briefly to mine. "It may be from the person who took her. I've had the doors locked all night, so the note had to have been placed under her pillow before we got home."

"He'll call back soon," she told me, hanging up. "I'm going to give the note to the officer out front. He might want to search the house. Where is the note?"

I pointed at the crumpled paper ball in the corner, but I didn't move to pick it up. I didn't want to see the message again. Was it a joke . . . or was it a threat? *Just because you're home doesn't mean you're safe.* The tone suggested a threat.

Mom flattened the paper on the wall, ironing out the wrinkles with her hand. "This paper is blank, Nora," she said.

"What?" I walked over for a closer look. She was right. The writing had vanished. I hastily flipped the paper over, but the back side was also blank.

"It was right here," I said, confused. "It was right here."

"You might have imagined it. A projection of a dream," Mom said gently, drawing me against her and rubbing my back. The gesture didn't do anything to comfort me. Was there any way I might have invented the message? Out of what? Paranoia? A panic attack?

"I didn't imagine it." But I didn't sound so sure.

"It's okay," she murmured. "Dr. Howlett said this might happen."

"Said what might happen?"

"He said there was a very good chance you'd hear things that aren't real—"

"Like what?"

She regarded me calmly. "Voices and other sounds. He didn't say anything about seeing things that aren't real, but anything could happen, Nora. Your body is trying to recover. It's under a lot of stress, and we have to be patient."

"He said I might hallucinate?"

"Shh," she commanded softly, taking my face between her hands. "These things might have to happen before you can recover. Your mind is doing its best to heal, and we have to give it time. Just like any other injury. We're going to get through this together."

I felt the sting of tears, but I refused to cry. Why me? Of all the billions of people out there, why me? Who did this to me? My mind was spinning in circles, trying to point a finger at someone, but I didn't have a face, a voice. I didn't have one shred of an idea.

"Are you scared?" Mom whispered.

I looked away. "I'm angry."

I crawled into bed, falling asleep surprisingly fast. Caught in that woozy, topsy-turvy place between awareness and a full-on dream, my mind aimlessly wandered down a long, dark tunnel that narrowed with each step. Sleep, blissful sleep, and given the night I'd had, I vigorously welcomed it.

A door appeared at the end of the tunnel. The door opened from within. The light inside cast a faint glow, illuminating a face so familiar, it almost knocked me over. His black hair curled around his ears, damp from a recent shower. Sun-bronzed skin, smooth and tight, stretched over a long, lean body that towered at least six inches over me. A pair of jeans hung low on his hips, but his chest and feet were bare, and a bath towel was slung over his shoulder. Our gazes locked, and his familiar black eyes bored into mine with surprise . . . followed by instant wariness.

"What are you doing here?" he said low.

Patch, I thought, my heart beating faster. It's Patch.

I couldn't remember how I knew him, but I did. The bridge in my mind was as broken as ever, but at the sight of him, little pieces snapped together. Memories that put a swarm of butterflies in my stomach. I saw a flash of sitting beside him in biology. Another flash as he stood very close, teaching me how to play pool. A white-hot flash as his lips brushed mine.

I'd been searching for answers, and they'd led me here. To Patch. I'd found a way to get around my amnesia. This wasn't merely a dream; it was a subconscious passageway to Patch. I now understood the great feeling crashing around inside me that never seemed satisfied. On some deep level I knew what my brain couldn't grasp. I *needed* Patch. And for whatever reason—fate, luck, sheer willpower, or for reasons I might never understand—I'd found him.

Through my shock, I somehow found my voice. "You tell me."

He stuck his head out the door, looking down the tunnel. "This is a dream. You realize that, don't you?"

"Then who are you worried followed me?"

"You can't be here."

My words came out stiff, frozen. "Looks like I found a way to communicate with you. I guess the only thing left to say is I'd hoped for a cheerier reception. You have all the answers, don't you?"

He steepled his fingers over his mouth. All the while, his eyes never wavered from my face. "I'm hoping to keep you alive."

My mind lagged, unable to understand enough of the dream to read a deeper message. The only thought pounding through me was, *I found him. After all this time, I found Patch. And instead of matching my excitement, the only feeling he harbors is . . . cold detachment.*

"Why can't I remember anything?" I asked, swallowing the lump in my throat. "Why can't I remember how or when or—or why you left?" Because I was sure that was what had happened. He'd left. Otherwise we'd be together now. "Why haven't you tried to find me? What happened to me? What happened to us?"

Patch hung his hands on the back of his neck and closed his eyes. He went deathly still, except for the tremble of emotion that rippled under his skin.

"Why did you leave me?" I choked.

He straightened. "You really believe I left you?"

That only thickened the lump in my throat. "What am I supposed to think? You've been gone for months, and now, when I finally find you, you can barely look me in the eye."

"I did the only thing I could. I gave you up to save your life." His jaw worked, clenching and unclenching. "It wasn't an easy decision, but it was the right one."

"Gave me up? Just like that? How long did it take you to make your decision? Three seconds?"

His eyes turned cold with recollection. "That's about as long as I had, yes."

More pieces snapped together. "Someone forced you to leave me? Is that what you're telling me?"

He didn't speak, but I had my answer.

"Who forced you to leave? Who scared you that much? The Patch I knew didn't run from anyone." The pain bursting inside me forced my volume higher. "I would have fought for you, Patch. I would have fought!"

"And you would have lost. We were surrounded. He threatened your life, and he would have made good on that threat. He had you, and that meant he had me, too."

"He? Who is he?"

I received another brittle silence.

"Did you even try to find me once? Or was it that easy"—my voice caught—"to let me go?"

Whipping the towel off his shoulder, Patch flung it aside. His eyes flared, his shoulders rising and falling with every breath, but I got the feeling his anger wasn't directed at me.

"You can't be here," he said, his voice rough. "You have to stop looking for me. You have to go back to your life, and make do the best you can. Not for me," he added, as if guessing my next resentful barb. "For you. I've done everything to keep him away from you, and I'm going to continue doing everything I can, but I need your help."

"Like I need your help?" I shot back. "I need you *now*, Patch. I need you back. I am lost and I'm scared. Do you know I can't remember one single thing? Of course you know," I said bitterly, as realization dawned. "That's why you haven't come looking for me. You know I can't remember you, and it lets you off the hook. I never thought you'd take the easy way out. Well, I haven't forgotten you, Patch. I see you in everything. I see flashes of black—the color of your eyes, your hair. I feel your touch, I remember the way you held me. . . ." I trailed off, too choked up to continue.

"It's better if you don't know," Patch said flatly. "That's the worst explanation I've given you yet, but for your own safety, there are things you can't know."

I laughed, but the sound was thick and anguished. "So this is it?"

He closed the distance between us, and just when I thought he'd draw me against him he stopped, holding himself in check. I exhaled, trying not to cry. He leaned his elbow on the doorjamb, just above my ear. He smelled so devastatingly familiar—of soap and spice—the heady scent bringing back a rush of memories so pleasurable, it only made the current moment that much more difficult to bear. I was seized by the desire to touch him. To trace my hands over his skin, to feel his arms tighten securely around me. I wanted him to nuzzle my neck, his whisper to tickle my ear as he said private words that belonged only to me. I wanted him near, so near, with no thought of letting go.

"This isn't over," I said. "After everything we've been through, you don't get the right to brush me off. I'm not letting you off that easily." I wasn't sure if it was a threat, my last stab at defiance, or irrational words spoken straight from my splintered heart.

"I want to protect you," Patch said quietly.

He stood so close. All strength and heat and silent power. I couldn't escape him, now or ever. He'd always be there, consuming my every thought, my heart locked in his hands. I was drawn to him by forces I couldn't control, let alone escape.

"But you didn't."

He cupped my chin, his touch unbearably tender. "Do you really think so?"

I tried to pull free, but not hard enough. I couldn't resist his touch; back then, now, or ever. "I don't know what to think. Can you blame me?"

"My history is long, and not much of it is good. I can't erase it, but I'm determined not to make another mistake. Not when the stakes are this high, not when it comes to you. There's a plan in all this, but it's going to take time." This time he gathered me into his arms, stroking hair off my face, and something inside me broke at his touch. Hot, wet tears tumbled down my cheeks. "If I lose you, I lose everything," he murmured.

"Who are you so afraid of?" I asked again.

Resting his hands on my shoulders, he tilted his forehead against mine. "You're mine, Angel. And I won't let anything change that. You're right—this isn't over. It's only the beginning, and nothing about what lies ahead will be easy." He sighed, a tired sound. "You're not going to remember this dream, and you won't be coming back. I don't know how you found me, but I have to make sure you don't do it again. I'm going to erase your memory of this dream. For your own safety, this is the last you'll see of me."

Alarm shot through me. I pulled away, flinching at Patch's face, horrified by the determination I found there. I opened my mouth to protest—

And the dream crashed down around me, as though made of sand.

CHAPTER

5

I WOKE UP THE FOLLOWING MORNING WITH A KINK IN my neck and a distant memory of strange, colorless dreams. After showering, I buttoned myself into a zebra-print shirt-dress and pulled on cropped tights and ankle boots. If nothing else, at least I appeared put together on the outside. Smoothing out the mess on the inside was a bigger project than I could tackle in forty-five minutes.

I breezed into the kitchen to find Mom making old-fashioned

oatmeal in a pot on the stove. It was the first time I could remember since my dad's death that she'd made it from scratch. Following last night's drama, I wondered if this fell in the ballpark of a pity meal.

"You're up early," she said, and paused in her slicing of strawberries near the sink.

"It's after eight," I pointed out. "Did Detective Basso call back?" I tried to act like I didn't care what her answer was, and got busy brushing nonexistent lint off my dress.

"I told him it was a mistake. He understood."

Meaning they'd agreed that I'd hallucinated. I was the girl who cried wolf, and from now on, everything I said would be brushed off as an exaggeration. *Poor thing. Just nod and humor her.*

"Why don't you head back to bed and I'll bring up breakfast when it's finished?" Mom suggested, resuming her slicing.

"I'm fine. I'm already up."

"Given everything that's happened, I thought you might want to take things easy. Sleep in, read a good book, maybe take a nice long bubble bath."

I couldn't remember my mom *ever* suggesting I play it lazy on a school day. Our typical breakfast conversation usually included rushed exchanges along the lines of, *Did you finish your essay? Did you pack your lunch? Is your bed made? Can you drop off the electricity bill on your way to school?*

"How about it?" Mom tried again. "Breakfast in bed. Doesn't get better than that."

BECCA FITZPATRICK

"What about school?"

"School can wait."

"Until when?"

"I don't know," she said lightly. "A week, I guess. Or two. Until you're feeling back to normal."

Clearly she hadn't thought this through, but in just a few short seconds, *I* had. I might have been tempted to take advantage of her leniency, but that wasn't the point. "I guess it's good to know I have a week or two to get back to normal."

She set down the knife. "Nora—"

"Never mind that I can't remember anything from the past five months. Never mind that from now on, every time I see a stranger watching me in a crowd, I'll wonder if it's him. Better yet, my amnesia is all over the news, and he must be laughing. He knows I can't identify him. And I guess I should be comforted that because all the tests Dr. Howlett ran came back fine, just fine, probably nothing bad happened to me during those weeks. Maybe I can even make myself believe I was soaking up rays in Cancún. Hey, it could've happened. Maybe my kidnapper wanted to set himself apart from the pack. Do the unexpected and pamper his victim. The truth is, normal might take years. Normal might never happen. But it's definitely not going to happen if I lounge around here watching soaps and avoiding life. I'm going to school today, end of story." I said it matter-of-factly, but my heart did one of those dizzy spins. I pushed the feeling aside, telling myself this was the only way I knew to get any semblance of my life back.

"School?" Mom was fully turned around now, the strawberries and oatmeal long forgotten.

"According to the calendar on the wall, it's September ninth." When Mom said nothing, I added, "School started two days ago."

She pressed her lips together in a straight line. "I realize that."

"Since school is in session, shouldn't I be there?"

"Yes, eventually." She wiped her hands on her apron. It looked to me like she was stalling or debating her word choice. I wished that whatever it was, she'd just spit it out. Right now, hot argument felt better than cool sympathy.

"Since when do you condone truancy?" I said, prodding her.

"I don't want to tell you how to run your life, but I think you need to slow down."

"Slow down? I can't remember anything from the past several months of my life. I'm not going to slow down and let things slip even further out of reach. The only way I'm going to start feeling better about what happened is by reclaiming my life. I'm going to school. And then I'm going out with Vee for doughnuts, or whatever junk food she happens to crave today. And then I'm coming home and doing homework. And then I'm going to fall asleep listening to Dad's old records. There's so much I don't know anymore. The only way I'm going to survive this is by clinging to what I do know."

"A lot changed while you were gone—"

"You think I don't know that?" I didn't mean to keep pouncing on her, but I couldn't understand how she could stand there and lecture me. Who was she to give me advice? Had she ever been through anything remotely similar? "Trust me, *I get it*. And I'm scared. I know I can't go back, and it terrifies me. But at the same time—" How was I supposed to explain it to her, when I couldn't even explain it to myself? Back *there* was safe. Back *then* I was in control. How was I supposed to jump forward, when the platform beneath my feet had been yanked out?

She blew out a deep, frazzled breath. "Hank Millar and I are dating."

Her words drifted through me. I stared at her, feeling my forehead crease in confusion. "Sorry, what?"

"It happened while you were gone." She braced a hand on the counter, and it looked to me like it was the only thing holding her up.

"Hank Millar?" For the second time in days, my mind was slow to throw a net around his name.

"He's divorced now."

"Divorced? I was only gone three months."

"All those endless days of not knowing where you were, if you were even alive, he was all I had, Nora."

"Marcie's dad?" I blinked at her, bewildered. I couldn't seem to push through the haze strung ear to ear inside my brain. My mom was dating the father of the only girl I'd ever hated? The girl who'd keyed my car, egged my locker, and nicknamed me Nora the Whore-a?

"We dated. In high school and college. Before I met your dad," she added hastily.

"You," I said, finally pushing some volume into my voice, "and Hank Millar?"

She started speaking very quickly. "I know you're going to be tempted to judge him based on your opinion of Marcie, but he's actually a very sweet guy. So thoughtful and generous and romantic." She smiled, then blushed, flustered.

I was outraged. This was what my mom was doing while I was missing?

"Right." I snatched a banana from the fruit bowl, then headed for the front door.

"Can we talk about this?" Her bare feet thumped on the wood floor as she followed after me. "Can you at least hear me out?"

"Sounds like I'm a little late to the let's-talk-it-over party."

"Nora!"

"What?" I snapped, spinning around. "What do you want me to say? That I'm happy for you? I'm not. We used to make fun of the Millars. We used to joke that Marcie's attitude problem was mercury poisoning due to all the expensive seafood their family eats. And now you're dating him?"

"Yes, him. Not Marcie."

"It's all the same to me! Did you even wait until the ink on the divorce papers was dry? Or did you make your move while he was still married to Marcie's mom, because three months is awfully fast."

"I don't have to answer that!" Apparently realizing how red in the face she was, she composed herself by kneading the back of her neck. "Is this because you think I'm betraying your dad? Believe me, I've already tortured myself enough, questioning if anything short of eternity is too soon to move on. But he would have wanted me to be happy. He wouldn't have wanted me to mope around feeling sorry for myself forever."

"Does Marcie know?"

She flinched at my sudden transition. "What? No. I don't think Hank has told her yet."

In other words, for the time being, I didn't have to live in fear of Marcie taking our parents' decisions out on me. Of course, when she did figure out the truth, I could guarantee the retribution would be swift, humiliating, and brutal. "I'm late for school." I rummaged through the dish on the entryway table. "Where are my keys?"

"They should be in there."

"My house key is. Where's the Fiat key?"

She applied pressure to the bridge of her nose. "I sold the Fiat."

I directed the full weight of my glare at her. "Sold it? Excuse me?" Granted, in the past I'd expressed just how much I hated the Fiat's peeling brown paint, weather-beaten white leather seats, and untimely habit the car's stick shift had of popping out of the shifter. But still. It was *my* car. Had my mom given up on me so quickly after my disappearance that she'd started hocking my belongings on Craigslist? "What else?" I demanded. "What else did you sell while I was gone?"

"I sold it before you went missing," she murmured, eyes lowered.

A swallow caught in my throat. Meaning once upon a time I'd known she'd sold my car, only I couldn't remember it now. It was a painful reminder of just how defenseless I really was. I couldn't even conduct a conversation with my mom without looking like an idiot. Rather than apologize, I flung open the front door and stomped down the porch steps.

"Whose car is that?" I asked, coming up short. A white convertible Volkswagen sat on the cement slab where the Fiat used to reside. From the look of it, it had taken up permanent residence. It might have been there yesterday morning when we'd pulled in from the hospital, but I'd hardly been in the frame of mind to soak up my surroundings. The only other time I'd left the house was last night, and I'd gone out through the back door.

"Yours."

"What do you mean, mine?" I shielded my eyes from the morning sun as I glowered back at her.

"Scott Parnell gave it to you."

"Who?"

"His family moved back to town at the beginning of summer."

"Scott?" I repeated, thumbing through my long-term memory, since the name provoked a vague recollection. "The boy in my kindergarten class? The one who moved to Portland years ago?"

Mom nodded wearily.

"Why would he give me a car?"

"I never got the chance to ask you. You disappeared the night he dropped it off."

"I went missing the night Scott mysteriously donated a car to me? Didn't that set off any alarm bells? There's nothing normal about a teenage guy giving a car to a girl he hardly knows and hasn't seen in years. Something about this isn't right. Maybe—maybe the car was evidence of something, and he needed to get rid of it. Did that ever cross your mind?"

"The police searched the car. They questioned the previous owner. But I think Detective Basso had ruled out Scott's involvement after hearing your side of the night's events. You'd been shot earlier, before you went missing, and while Detective Basso originally thought Scott was the shooter, you told him it was—"

"Shot?" I shook my head in confusion. "What do you mean shot?"

She closed her eyes briefly, exhaling. "With a gun."

"What?" How had Vee left this out?

"At Delphic Amusement Park." She shook her head. "I hate even thinking about it," she whispered, her voice breaking. "I was out of town when I got the call. I didn't make it back in time. I never saw you again, and I've regretted nothing in my life more. Before you disappeared, you told Detective Basso that a man named Rixon shot you in the fun house. You said Scott was there too, and Rixon also shot him. The police looked for Rixon, but it was like he vanished. Detective Basso was convinced Rixon wasn't even the shooter's real name."

"Where was I shot?" I asked, my skin crawling with an unpleasant tingle. I hadn't noticed a scar, or any indication of a wound.

"Your left shoulder." It seemed to pain my mom just to say it. "The shot was in and out, hitting only muscle. We're very, very lucky."

I tugged my collar down over my shoulder. Sure enough, I could see scar tissue where the skin had healed.

"The police spent weeks looking for Rixon. They read your diary, but you'd ripped out several pages, and they didn't find his name in the rest of it. They asked Vee, but she denied ever having heard his name. He wasn't in the records at school. There was no record of him at the DMV—"

"I ripped out pages in my diary?" I cut in. It didn't sound like me at all. Why would I do such a thing?

"Do you remember where you put the pages? Or what they said?"

I shook my head absently. What had I gone to such great lengths to hide?

Mom made a deflated sound. "Rixon was a ghost, Nora. And wherever he went, he took all the answers with him."

"I can't accept that," I said. "What about Scott? What did he say when Detective Basso questioned him?"

"Detective Basso put all his energy into hunting down Rixon. I don't think he ever spoke to Scott. The last time I talked to Lynn

Parnell, Scott had moved on. I think he's in New Hampshire now, selling pest control."

"That's it?" I said in disbelief. "Detective Basso never tried to track down Scott and hear his side?" My mind cranked at full speed. Something about Scott wasn't sitting right. According to my mom's account, I'd told the police he'd been shot by Rixon too. He was the only other witness that Rixon existed. How did that fit with the donated Volkswagen? It seemed to me that at least one crucial piece of information was missing.

"I'm sure he had a reason for not talking to Scott."

"I'm sure he did too," I said cynically. "Like maybe he's incompetent?"

"If you'd give Detective Basso a chance, you'd see he's actually very sharp. He's very good at his job."

I didn't want to hear it.

"What now?" I said tersely.

"We do the only thing we can. Do our best to move on."

For one moment, I pushed aside my doubts about Scott Parnell. There was still so much to deal with. How many other hundreds of things was I in the dark on? Was this what I had in store? Day upon day of humiliation as I relearned my life? I could already envision what would be waiting for me inside the walls of school. Discreet looks of pity. The awkward averting of eyes. The shuffling of feet and drawn-out silences. The safe option of shying away from me altogether.

I felt indignation boil up inside me. I didn't want to be a spectacle. I didn't want to be the object of rabid speculation. What kinds of shameful theories involving my abduction had already spread? What did people think about me *now*?

"If you see Scott, be sure to point him out so I can thank him for the car," I said bitterly. "Right after I ask him why he gave it to me in the first place. Maybe you and Detective Basso are convinced he's innocent, but too many things about his story aren't adding up."

"Nora—"

I thrust my hand out. "Can I have the key?"

After a moment's pause, she unhooked a key from her own key chain and laid it in my palm. "Be careful."

"Oh, not to worry. The only thing I'm in danger of is making a fool of myself. Know of any other people I might smack into today and not recognize? Fortunately, I remember the way to school. And would you look at that," I said, tugging open the car door and dropping inside. "The Volkswagen is a five-speed. Good thing I learned how to drive five-speed pre-amnesia."

"I know now isn't the best time, but we've been invited to dinner tonight."

I met her eyes coldly. "Have we."

"Hank would like to take us to Coopersmith's. To celebrate your return."

"How thoughtful of him," I said, ramming the key into the ignition and revving the engine. By the noisy sputtering, I assumed the car hadn't budged since the day I'd vanished.

"He's trying," she called above the whine of the engine. "He's trying really hard to make this work."

I had a snide retort on the tip of my tongue, but decided to go for more impact. I'd worry about the repercussions later. "What about you? Are you trying to make it work? Because I'll be up front. If he stays, I go. Now if you'll excuse me, I have to figure out how to live my life again."

CHAPTER

6

AT THE HIGH SCHOOL, I FOUND A PARKING SPACE at the back of the student lot and hiked across the lawn to a side entrance. I was running late, thanks to the fight with my mom. After peeling away from the farmhouse, I'd had to pull to the side of the road for fifteen minutes just to calm down. *Dating Hank Millar.* Was she sadistic? Out to ruin my life? Both?

One glance at my mom's pilfered BlackBerry proved I'd missed all but the tail end of first period. The dismissal bell would ring in ten minutes.

Intending to leave a message, I dialed Vee's cell.

"Hellooo. That you, angel?" she promptly answered in her best temptress's voice. She was trying to be funny, but I nearly tripped.

Angel.

The mere sound of the word caused heat to lick up my skin. Once again, the color black raced furiously around me like a hot ribbon, but this time there was more. A physical touch so real I stopped in my tracks. I felt an enticing brush along my cheek-bone, as if an invisible hand caressed me, followed by a soft, utterly seductive pressure against my lips. . . .

You're mine, Angel. And I'm yours. Nothing can change it.

"This is crazy," I muttered out loud. Seeing the color black was one thing, but making out with it was taking it to a whole 'nother level. I had to stop haunting myself this way. If I kept it up any longer, I was genuinely going to doubt my sanity.

"Come again?" Vee said.

"Uh, parking," I covered up quickly. "All the good spots are taken."

"Guess who has PE first hour? This is so unfair. I start the day off perspiring like an elephant in heat. Don't the people who make up our schedules understand body odor? Don't they understand frizzy hair?"

"Why didn't you tell me about Scott Parnell?" I asked evenly. We'd start there and work our way forward.

Vee's silence hung sharp between us, only confirming my suspicions: She hadn't given me the whole story. Intentionally.

"Oh, yeah, Scott," she faltered at last. "About that."

"The night I disappeared, he dropped an old Volkswagen off at my house. That detail slipped your mind last night, did it? Or maybe you didn't think it qualified as interesting or suspicious? You're the last person I would have expected to give me a watered-down version of what led to my kidnapping, Vee."

I heard her chewing her lip. "I might have omitted a few things."

"Like the fact that I was shot?"

"I didn't want to hurt you," she said in a rush. "What you went through was traumatic. More than traumatic. A million times worse. What kind of friend am I if I just heap it on higher?"

"And?"

"Okay, okay. I heard Scott gave you the car. Probably to apologize for being a chauvinistic pig."

"Explain."

"Remember in middle school how our moms always taught us that if a boy teases you, it means he likes you? Well, when it came to relationships, Scott never outgrew seventh grade."

"He liked me." I sounded doubtful. I didn't think she'd lie to me again, not when I'd just confronted her, but clearly my mom had gotten to her first and brainwashed her into thinking I was too fragile for the truth. This sounded like a beat-around-the-bush answer if I'd ever heard one.

"Enough to buy you a car, yeah."

"Did I have any contact with Scott the week before I was kidnapped?"

"The night before you disappeared, you snooped around in his bedroom. But you didn't find anything more interesting than a wilted marijuana plant."

Finally we were getting somewhere. "What was I looking for?"

"I never asked. You told me Scott was a whack job. That was all the evidence I needed to help you bust in."

I didn't doubt it. Vee never needed a reason to do something stupid. Sad thing was, most of the time I didn't either.

"That's all I know," Vee insisted. "I swear it, up and down."

"Don't hold out on me again."

"Does this mean you forgive me?"

I was irritated, but much to my dismay, I could see Vee's point in wanting to protect me. It's *what best friends do*, I reasoned. Under other circumstances, I might even have admired her for it. And in her shoes, I probably would have been tempted to do the same. "We're square."

Inside the main office, I expected to have to talk myself out of a tardy slip, so I was surprised when the secretary saw me approaching and, after completing a double take, said, "Oh! Nora. How *are* you?"

Ignoring the buttery sympathy in her tone, I said, "I'm here to pick up my class schedule."

"Oh. Oh, my. So soon? Nobody expects you to jump right back into things, you know, hon. Some of the staff and I were just talking this morning about how we thought you should take a couple of weeks to—" She struggled for an acceptable word, since there was no right word for what I had ahead of me. Recover? Adapt? Hardly. "Acclimatise." She was practically flashing a neon sign that read, *What a pity! Poor girl! I'd better use my kid gloves with this one.*

I propped an elbow on the counter and leaned close. "I'm ready to be back. And that's what matters, right?" Because I was already in a bad mood, I tacked on, "I'm so glad this school has taught me not to value any other opinion but my own."

She opened her mouth, closed it. Then she went to work paging through several manila folders on her desk. "Let me see, I know I've got you in here somewhere. . . . Ah! Here we are." She pulled a sheet of paper from one of the folders and passed it over to me. "Everything look okay?"

I scanned my schedule. AP U.S. history, honors English, health, journalism, anatomy and physiology, orchestra, and trig. Clearly I'd had a death wish for my future self when I'd registered for classes last year.

"Looks good," I said, throwing my backpack over my shoulder and pushing through the office door.

The hall outside was dim, the overhead fluorescent lights casting a dull gleam on the waxed floors. In my head, I told myself this was my school. I belonged here. And even though it was jarring every time I reminded myself I was now a junior, despite the fact that I couldn't remember finishing sophomore year, eventually the strangeness would wear off. It had to.

The bell rang. In an instant doors everywhere opened and the hall flooded with the student body. I fell into step with the current of students fighting their way to the restrooms, locker bays, and soda machines. I kept my chin tilted slightly up and leveled my gaze straight ahead. But I felt the eyes of my classmates when they looked my way. Everyone took a surprised second look. They had to know I was back by now—my story was the highlight of local news. But I supposed seeing me in the flesh cemented the fact. Their questions danced front and center in their curious stares. *Where was she? Who kidnapped her? What kinds of icky, unspeakable things happened to her?*

And the biggest speculation by far: *Is it true she can't remember any of it? I bet she's faking. Who just forgets months of their life?*

I fingered through the notebook I'd been hugging to my chest, pretending to search for something highly important. *I don't even notice you,* the gesture implied. Then I threw back my shoulders and faked a look of indifference. Maybe even aloofness. But under it all, my legs were shaking. I hurried down the hall with only one goal driving me forward.

Pushing my way inside the girls' bathroom, I locked myself in the last stall. I dragged my back down the wall until I was sitting on my bottom. I could taste bile rising in my throat. My arms and legs felt numb. My lips felt numb. Tears dripped off my chin, but I couldn't move my hand to wipe them away.

No matter how hard I squeezed my eyes shut, no matter how dark I forced my vision, I could still see their leering, judgmental faces. I wasn't one of them anymore. Somehow, without any effort of my own, I'd become an outsider.

I sat in the stall several minutes longer, until my breathing calmed and the urge to cry faded. I didn't want to go to class, and I didn't want to go home. What I really wanted was the impossible. To travel back in time and get a second chance. A do-over, starting with the night I disappeared.

I'd just climbed to my feet when I heard a voice whisper past my ear like a cold current of air.

Help me.

The voice was so small, I almost didn't hear it. I even considered the possibility that I'd invented it. After all, imagining things was all I was good for lately.

Help me, Nora.

At my name, goosebumps popped out on my arms. Holding still, I strained to hear the voice again. The sound hadn't come from inside the stall—I was alone in here—but it didn't appear to have come from the larger area of the bathroom either.

When he finishes with me, it will be like I'm dead. I'll never go home again.

This time the voice sounded much stronger and more urgent.

BECCA FITZPATRICK

I looked up. It seemed to have floated down from the ceiling vent.

"Who's there?" I called up warily.

At the lack of a reply, I knew this had to be the start of another hallucination. Dr. Howlett had predicted it. My thoughts turned anxious. I needed to remove myself from the setting. I had to distract my current train of thought and break the spell before it overtook me.

I reached for the door lock, when a sudden image burst across my mind, eclipsing my sight. In a terrifying twist of scenery, I could no longer see the bathroom. Instead of tiles, the floor under my feet became concrete. Overhead, metal rafters crisscrossed the ceiling like giant spider legs. A row of truck bay doors ran along one wall.

I'd hallucinated myself inside a—

Warehouse.

He sawed off my wings. I can't fly home, the voice whimpered.

I couldn't see who the voice belonged to. There was a stripped lightbulb overhead, illuminating a conveyor belt at the center of the warehouse. Aside from it, the building was empty.

A drone reverberated all around as the conveyor belt turned on. A clanging, mechanical noise carried out of the darkness at the end of the belt. It was carrying something toward me.

"No," I said, because it was the only thing I could think to say. I swept my hands in front of me, trying to feel the bathroom stall door. This was a hallucination, just like my mom had warned. I had to push through it and find a way back to the real world. All the while, the awful metallic scraping grew louder.

I backed away from the conveyor belt until I was pressed up against a cement wall.

With nowhere to run, I watched as a metal cage rattled and clanged out of the shadows, moving to the edge of the light. The bars glowed a ghostly electric blue, but that wasn't what seized my attention. A person was hunched inside. A girl, bent to fit the confines of the cage, her hands grasping the bars, her blue-black hair tangled in front of her face. Her eyes peered through the screen of hair, and they were colorless orbs. There was a length of rope emitting the same eerie blue light tied around her neck.

Help me, Nora.

I wanted to run for an exit. I was afraid to try the bay doors, fearing they'd only lead me deeper into the hallucination. What I needed was my own door. One I created *right now* that I could escape through to the inside of the school bathroom.

Don't give him the necklace! The girl shook the bars of the cage fiercely. *He thinks you have it. If he gets the necklace, he can't be stopped. I won't have a choice. I'll have to tell him everything!*

My skin was damp at my lower back and my underarms. Necklace? What necklace?

There is no necklace, I told myself. *Both the girl and the necklace are wild concoctions of your imagination. Force them out. Force. Them. Out!*

A bell shrilled.

Just like that, I was jolted out of the hallucination. The keyed-up door of the bathroom stall was inches from my nose. MR. SARRAF SUCKS. B.L. + J.F. = LOVE. JAZZ BAND ROCKS. I reached a hand out, tracing the deep grooves. The door was real. I slumped in relief.

Voices carried into the bathroom. I flinched, but they were normal, happy, chatty. Through the door crack, I watched three girls line up in front of the mirrors. They fluffed their hair and touched up their lip gloss.

"We should order pizza and watch movies tonight," one of them said.

"No can do, girls. It's just me and Susanna tonight." I recognized the voice as belonging to Marcie Millar. She was in the middle of the lineup, tidying her strawberry blond side ponytail, pinning it in place with a pink plastic flower.

"You're ditching us for your mom? Um, ouch?"

"Um, yes. Deal with it," Marcie said.

The two girls on either side of Marcie made a big show of pouting. Odds were they were Addyson Hales and Cassie Sweeney. Addyson was a cheerleader like Marcie, but I'd once overheard Marcie confess that the only reason she was friends with Cassie was because they lived in the same neighborhood. Their bond was due to the simple fact that they could afford the same lifestyle. Peas in a pod—a very affluent pod.

"Don't even start," Marcie said, but the smile in her voice clearly stated she was flattered by their disappointment. "My mom needs me. Girls' night out."

"Is she . . . you know . . . depressed?" the girl I believed to be Addyson asked.

"Seriously?" Marcie laughed. "She got to keep the house. She's still a member of the yacht club. Plus she made my dad buy her a Lexus SC10. It's sooo cute! And I swear half the single guys in town have already called or stopped by." Marcie ticked each item off on her fingers so fluidly it made me think she'd been rehearsing this speech.

"She's so beautiful." Cassie sighed.

"Exactly. Whoever my dad hooks up with will be a major downgrade."

"*Is* he seeing anybody?"

"Not yet. My mom has friends all over. Somebody would have seen something. So," she transitioned with a gossipy voice, "did you guys see the news? About Nora Grey?"

My knees went a little soft at the mention of my name, and I flattened a hand to the wall for support.

"They found her in the cemetery, and they're saying she can't remember anything," Marcie went on. "I guess she's so messed up she even ran from the police. She thought they were trying to hurt her."

"My mom said she was probably brainwashed by her kidnapper," Cassie said. "Like some skeezy guy could have made her think they were married."

"Ew!" they all said in unison.

"Whatever happened, she's damaged goods now," Marcie said. "Even if she says she can't remember anything, she knows what happened subconsciously. She's going to be dragging around that baggage for the rest of her life. She might as well wrap herself in yellow tape that says, 'Stay out and do not cross.'"

They giggled. Then Marcie said, "Back to class, girlies. I'm clean out of late passes. The secretaries keep locking them in their drawers. Whores."

I waited long after they had filed out, just to be sure the bathroom and halls would be empty. Then I hustled through the door. I speed-walked all the way to the end of the hall, shoved through the outside exit, and broke into a jog toward the student parking lot.

I flung myself inside the Volkswagen, wondering why I'd ever believed I could waltz back into my life and expect to pick up right where things had left off.

Because that was exactly it. Things hadn't left off.

They'd moved on without me.

I PREPPED FOR DINNER WITH HANK AND MY MOM by changing into flats and a billowy bohemian dress that fell above the knee.

It was nicer than Hank deserved, but I had an ulterior motive. Tonight's goal was twofold. First, make my mom and Hank wish they'd never invited me. Second, make my stance on their relationship crystal clear. I was already mentally rehearsing my discourse, which I'd deliver on my feet at top volume, and it would end when I doused Hank with his own glass of wine. I intended to usurp Marcie's Diva Queen throne tonight, my own propriety be damned.

But first things first. I had to lull Mom and Hank into believing I was in the right frame of mind to be taken out in public. If I exited my bedroom foaming at the mouth and dressed in a black LOVE SUCKS tee, my plan would never get off the ground.

I'd spent thirty minutes in the shower, hot water beating every inch of my body, and after vigorously scrubbing and shaving, I'd pampered my skin with baby oil. The tiny cuts crisscrossing my arms and legs were healing fast, as were the bruises, but both shed a crack of unwanted light on what life had been like during my abduction. Combined with the filthy skin I'd arrived at the hospital with, my best guess was that I'd been held deep in the woods. Somewhere so remote, it would have been impossible for a passerby to stumble across me. Somewhere so godforsaken that my chances of escaping and surviving would be to next to nothing.

But I must have escaped. How else could I explain making it back home? Adding to this speculation, I envisioned the dense forests spanning northern Maine and Canada. Though I had no evidence to prove I had been held there, it was my best guess. I'd escaped, and against all odds, I'd survived. It was my only working theory.

On my way out of my bedroom, I hesitated in front of the mirror long enough to scrunch my hair. It was longer now, falling halfway down my spine, with natural caramel highlights, thanks to summer's sun. I'd definitely been someplace outdoors. My skin held a kiss of bronze, and something told me I hadn't been hiding out in a tanning salon all those weeks. I had the aimless thought to buy new makeup, then scratched it. I didn't want new makeup to match the new me. I just wanted the old me back.

Downstairs, I met Hank and my mom in the foyer. I vaguely noted that Hank looked like a life-size Ken doll with icy blue eyes, a golden skin tone, and an impeccable side parting. The only discrepancy was Hank's lithe build. In a brawl, Ken would have won, hands down.

"Ready?" Mom asked. She was all dressed up too, in lightweight wool pants, a blouse, and a silk wrap. But I was more aware of what she wasn't wearing. For the first time, her wedding band was missing, leaving a pale stripe around her ring finger.

"I'll drive separately," I said brusquely.

Hank squeezed my shoulder playfully. Before I could squirm away, he said, "Marcie is the same way. Now that she has her license, she wants to drive everywhere." He raised his hands as if offering no argument. "Your mother and I will meet you there."

I debated telling Hank that my wanting to drive separately had nothing to do with a piece of plastic in my wallet. And a lot more to do with the way being around him made my stomach roll.

I swiveled to face my mom. "Can I have money for gas? Tank's low."

"Actually," Mom said, aiming a *help me with this* look at Hank, "I was really hoping to use this time for the three of us to talk. Why don't you drive with us, and I'll give you money to fill up the car tomorrow?" Her tone was polite, but there was no mistaking. She wasn't offering me a choice.

"Be a good girl and listen to your mother," Hank told me, flashing a perfectly straight, perfectly white smile.

"I'm sure we'll have plenty of time to talk at dinner. I don't see the big deal in driving by myself," I said.

"True, but you're still going to have to ride with us," Mom said. "Turns out I'm all out of cash. The new cell phone I bought you today wasn't cheap."

"I can't pay for gas with your credit card?" But I already knew her answer. Unlike Vee's mom, my mom never loaned me her credit card, and I didn't have the moral flexibility to "borrow" it. I supposed I could have used my own money, but I'd taken a stand and I wasn't backing down now. Before she could shoot me down, I added, "Or what about Hank? I'm sure he'll spot me twenty dollars. Right, Hank?"

Hank tipped his head back and laughed, but I didn't miss the lines of irritation forming around his eyes. "You've got quite the negotiator on your hands, Blythe. Instinct tells me she didn't inherit your sweet, unassuming nature."

Mom said, "Don't be rude, Nora. Now you're making a big deal out of nothing. Carpooling for one night isn't going to kill you."

I looked at Hank, hoping he could read my mind. *Don't be so sure.*

"We'd better get going," Mom said. "We have reservations for eight and we don't want to lose our table."

Before I could roll out another argument, Hank opened the front door and motioned my mom and me out. "Ah, so that's your car, Nora? The Volkswagen?" he asked, looking across the driveway. "Next time you're in the market, stop by my dealership. I could have hooked you up with a convertible Celica for the same price."

"It was a gift from a friend," Mom explained.

Hank let out a low whistle. "That's some friend you've got."

"His name is Scott Parnell," Mom said. "Old friend of the family."

"Scott Parnell," Hank mused, dragging a hand over his mouth. "The name rings a bell. Do I know his parents?"

"His mom, Lynn, lives over on Deacon Road, but Scott left town over the summer."

"Interesting," Hank murmured. "Any idea where he ended up?"

"Somewhere in New Hampshire. Do you know Scott?"

Hank dismissed her inquiry with a shake of his head. "New Hampshire is God's country," he murmured appreciatively. His voice was so smooth, it instantly grated.

Equally as irritating was the fact that he could have passed as Mom's younger brother. Really and truly. He had facial hair, a fine scruff that covered most of his face, but where I could see, he had excellent skin tone and very few wrinkles. I'd considered the possibility that my mom would eventually start dating again, and maybe even remarry, but I wanted her husband to look distinguished. Hank Millar came off as a frat boy hiding under a shark-gray suit.

At Coopersmith's, Hank parked in the rear lot. As we climbed out, my new cell phone chirped. I'd texted Vee my new number before leaving, and it appeared she'd received it.

BABE! I'M @ UR HOUSE. WHERE R U?

"I'll meet you inside," I told Mom and Hank. "Text," I explained, jiggling my cell.

Mom sent me a black look that said, *Make it fast*, then took Hank's arm and let him escort her toward the restaurant doors.

I keyed in a response to Vee.

GUESS WHERE I AM.

CLUE? she texted back.

SWEAR U WON'T TELL A SOUL?

U HAVE 2 ASK?

I reluctantly texted, @ DINNER W. MARCIE'S DAD.

#?@#$?!&

MY MOM IS DATING HIM.

TRAITOR! IF THEY GET MARRIED, U & MARCIE . . .

COULD USE A LITTLE CONSOLATION HERE!

DOES HE KNOW UR TEXTING ME? Vee asked.

NO. THEY R INSIDE. I'M IN THE PARKING LOT—COOPERSMITH'S.

THE PIMP. 2 GOOD 4 APPLEBEE'S, I SEE.

I'M GOING 2 ORDER THE MOST EXPENSIVE THING ON THE MENU. IF ALL GOES WELL, I'M GOING TO THROW HANK'S DRINK IN HIS FACE 2.

HA! DON'T BOTHER. I'LL COME PICK U UP. WE NEED 2 HANG OUT. BEEN 2 LONG. DYING 2 SEE U!

silence

THIS SUCKS SO BAD! I texted back. I HAVE 2 STAY. MOM IS ON THE WARPATH.

TURNING ME DOWN?!

PAYING FAMILY DUES. CUT ME SOME SLACK.

DID I MENTION I'M DYING 2 SEE U?

ME 2. UR THE BEST, U KNOW THAT, RIGHT?

WORD.

MEET @ ENZO'S TOMORROW 4 LUNCH? NOON?

DEAL.

Hanging up, I crossed the gravel parking lot and let myself inside. The lights were dim, the decor masculine and rustic with brick walls, red leather booths, and antler chandeliers. The smell of sizzling meat overwhelmed the air, and the TVs over the bar blared the day's sports highlights.

"My party just came in a minute ago," I told the hostess. "The reservation is under the name Hank Millar."

She beamed. "Yes, Hank just came in. My dad used to golf with him, so I know him really well. He's like a second father to me. I'm sure the divorce has just devastated him, so it's really nice to see him dating again."

I recalled Marcie's earlier comment that her mom had friends everywhere. I prayed Coopersmith's wasn't on her radar, fearing how fast news of this date might travel. "I guess it depends on who you ask," I mumbled.

The hostess's smile turned flustered. "Oh! How thoughtless of me. You're right. I'm sure his ex-wife would disagree. I shouldn't have said anything. Right this way, please."

She'd missed my point, but I left it alone. I followed her past the bar, down a short flight of steps, and into the sunken dining area. Black-and-white photos of famous mobsters hung on both brick walls. The tabletops were constructed from old ship hatch covers. Rumor had it the slate floor had been imported from a ruined castle in France and dated back to the sixteenth century. I made a mental note that Hank was fond of old things.

Hank rose from his chair when he saw me approach. Ever the gentleman. If only he knew what I had in store for him.

"Was that Vee texting you?" Mom asked.

I dropped into a chair and propped up the menu to obstruct my view of Hank. "Yes."

"How is she?"

"Fine."

"Same old Vee?" she teased.

I made a consenting noise.

"The two of you should get together this weekend," she suggested.

"Already covered."

After a moment, my mom picked up her own menu. "Well! Everything looks wonderful. It's going to be hard to decide. What do you think you'll have, Nora?"

I scanned the price column, looking for the most exorbitant figure.

Suddenly Hank coughed and loosened his tie, as though he'd swallowed water down the wrong tube. His eyes went a little wide in disbelief. I followed his gaze and saw Marcie Millar stroll into the restaurant with her mom. Susanna Millar hung her cardigan on the antique coatrack just inside the front doors, then both she and Marcie followed the hostess to a table four down from ours.

Susanna Millar took a chair with her back to us, and I was pretty sure she hadn't noticed. Marcie, on the other hand, who was seated opposite her mom, did a double take in the middle of picking up her ice water. She paused with the glass inches from her mouth. Her eyes mimicked her dad's, growing wide with shock. They traveled from Hank, to my mom, finally stopping at me.

Marcie leaned across the table and whispered a few words to her mom. Susanna's posture stiffened.

A tight feeling of impending disaster slid through my stomach and didn't stop until it settled in my toes.

Marcie pushed out of her chair abruptly. Her mom grabbed for her arm, but Marcie was faster. She marched over.

"So," she said, stopping at the edge of our table. "Y'all having a nice little dinner out?"

Hank cleared his throat. He glanced at my mom once, shutting his eyes briefly in silent apology.

"Can I give an outsider's opinion?" Marcie continued in a bizarrely cheerful voice.

"Marcie," Hank said, warning creeping into his tone.

"Now that you're eligible, Dad, you're going to want to be careful who you date." For all her bravado, I noticed that Marcie's arms had adopted a fine tremble. Maybe out of anger, but oddly, it looked more like fear to me.

With his lips barely moving, Hank murmured, "I'm asking you politely to go back to your mother and enjoy your meal. We can talk about this later."

Not about to be deterred, Marcie continued, "This is going to sound harsh, but it will save you a lot of pain in the end. Some women are gold diggers. They only want you for your money." Her gaze locked solidly on my mom.

I stared at Marcie, and even I could feel my eyes flashing with hostility. Her dad sold cars! Maybe in Coldwater that amounted to an impressive career choice, but she was acting like her family had a pedigree and so many trust funds they were tripping on them! If my mom was a gold digger, she could do much—much—better than a sleazy car salesman named Hank.

"And Coopersmith's, of all places," Marcie went on, a note of disgust overshadowing her cheery tone. "Low blow. This is our restaurant. We've had birthdays here, work parties, anniversaries. Could you be any tackier?"

Hank squeezed between his eyes.

Mom said quietly, "I picked the restaurant, Marcie. I didn't realize it had special meaning to your family."

"Don't talk to me," Marcie snapped. "This is between me and my dad. Don't act like you get any say in this."

"Okay!" I said, pushing up from my chair. "I'm going to the restroom." I sent my mom a quick look, hinting for her to join me. This wasn't our problem. If Marcie and her dad wanted to go at it, and in public, fine. But I wasn't going to sit here and make a spectacle of myself.

"I'll join you," Marcie said, catching me off guard.

Before I could figure out my next move, Marcie looped her arm through mine and propelled me toward the front of the restaurant.

"Mind telling me what this is all about?" I asked when we were out of earshot. I shifted my eyes between our linked arms.

"A truce," Marcie stated pointedly.

Things were getting more interesting by the minute.

"Oh? And how long is it going to last?" I asked.

"Just until my dad breaks up with your mom."

"Good luck with that one," I said with a snort.

She let go of my arm so we could pass single file into the ladies' room. When the door fell shut at our backs, she did a quick check under the stalls to make sure we were alone. "Don't pretend like you don't care," she said. "I saw you sitting with them. You looked like you were going to vomit out your eyes."

"Your point?"

"My point being we have something in common."

I laughed, but my laugh was of the dry, humorless variety.

"Scared of taking sides with me?" she asked.

"More like wary. I'm not particularly fond of getting stabbed in the back."

"I wouldn't stab you in the back." She flicked her wrist impatiently. "Not on something this serious."

"Note to self: Marcie is only a backstabber on trivial things."

Marcie boosted herself onto the sink's ledge. She was now half a head taller, looking down on me. "Is it true you can't remember anything? Like, your amnesia is real?"

Stay cool. "Did you drag me in here to talk about our parents, or are you really that interested in me?"

Lines of concentration formed on her forehead. "If something happened between us . . . you wouldn't remember, right? It would be like it didn't happen. In your mind, anyway." She watched me closely, clearly intent on my answer.

I rolled my eyes. I was growing more irritated by the minute. "Just spit it out. What happened between us?"

"I'm being completely hypothetical here."

I didn't believe that for a second. Marcie had probably humiliated me in some grand way before I'd vanished, but now that she needed my cooperation, she hoped I'd forgotten. Whatever she'd done, I was almost glad I couldn't remember. I had a lot more on my mind than worrying about Marcie's latest offensive strike.

"It's true then," Marcie said, not exactly smiling, but not frowning either. "You really can't remember."

I opened my mouth, but I didn't have a comeback. Lying, and getting caught in the act, would say a lot more about my insecurities than just being up-front.

"My dad said you can't remember anything from the last five months. Why does the amnesia stretch back that far? Why not just from when you were kidnapped?"

My tolerance had reached its limit. If I was going to discuss this with anyone, Marcie wasn't first on the list. She wasn't on the list, period. "I don't have time for this. I'm going back to the table."

"I'm just trying to get information."

"Ever consider it's none of your business?" I said, my parting shot.

"Are you telling me you don't remember Patch?" she blurted.

Patch.

As soon as his name fell from Marcie's lips, the same haunting shade of black eclipsed my vision. It vanished as quickly as it came, but left an impression. Hot, unaccountable emotion. Like an unexpected slap to the face. I momentarily lost the ability to draw breath. The sting radiated all the way to the bone. I knew the name. There was something about him. . . .

"What did you say?" I asked slowly, turning back.

"You heard me." Her eyes studied mine. "Patch."

I tried but failed to keep a blush of bewilderment and uncertainty from trickling into my expression.

"Well, well," Marcie said, not looking as pleased as I would have expected for catching me stripped and defenseless.

I knew I should walk out, but that elusive flare of recognition caused me to hold my place. Maybe, if I kept talking to Marcie, it would return. Maybe this time it would hang around long enough for me to make something of it. "Are you going to stand there and 'well, well' me, or are you going to give me a hint?"

"Patch gave you something earlier in the summer," she said without preamble. "Something that belongs to me."

"Who's Patch?" I managed at last. The question seemed redundant, but I wasn't about to let Marcie race on ahead until I was caught up—at least as much as I could be. Five months was a lot of ground to cover in a quick trip to the bathroom.

"A guy I dated. A summer fling."

Another potent stirring within that felt eerily close to jealousy, but I shoved the impression away. Marcie and I would never be interested in the same guy. Attributes she valued, such as being shallow, unintelligent, and egotistical, didn't pique my interest.

"What did he give me?" I knew I was missing a lot, but it was a *really* far stretch to think Marcie's boyfriend would have given me anything. Marcie and I shared none of the same friends. We weren't involved in any of the same clubs. None of our extra-curricular activities overlapped. In short, we had nothing in common.

"A necklace."

Savoring the fact that for once I didn't have to play defense, I gave her a gold-medal smirk. "Why, Marcie, I could have sworn giving another girl jewelry is a sign that your boyfriend is a cheat."

She tilted her head back and laughed so convincingly, I felt that same uneasiness settle back into my gut. "I can't decide if it's sad that you're so completely in the dark, or funny."

I folded my arms across my chest, aiming for a subtle show of annoyance and impatience, but the truth was, I was cold on the inside. A cold that didn't have to do with temperature. I was never going to escape this. I had a quick and terrible feeling that my run-in with Marcie was only the beginning, a subtle foreshadowing of what lay ahead. "I don't have the necklace."

"You think you don't have it, because you can't remember it. But you have it. It's probably sitting inside your jewelry box right now. You promised Patch you'd pass it along to me." She held out a scrap of paper for me to take. "My number. Call me when you find the necklace."

I took the paper, but I wasn't going to be bought that easily. "Why didn't he just give you the necklace himself?"

"We were both friends with Patch." At my look of deep skepticism, she added, "There's a first time for everything, isn't there?"

"I don't have the necklace," I repeated with finality.

"You have it, and I want it back."

Could she be any more persistent? "This weekend, when I have some free time, I'll look around for it."

"Sooner rather than later would be nice."

"My offer, take it or leave it."

She flapped her arms. "Why do you have a stick up your derriere?"

I kept my smile pleasant, my way of giving her the finger. "I might not be able to remember the last five months, but the sixteen years before that are crystal clear. Including the eleven we've known each other."

"So this is about a grudge. Very mature."

"This is a matter of principle. I don't trust you, because you've never given me a reason to. If you want me to believe you, you're going to have to show me why I should."

"You're such an idiot. Try to remember. If there was one good thing Patch did, it was bring us together. Did you know you came to my summer party? Ask around. You were there. As my friend. Patch made me see a different side of you."

"I came to one of your parties?" I was instantly skeptical. But why would she lie? She was right—I could ask around. It seemed foolish to make such a claim when the truth was so easy to prove.

Apparently reading my thoughts, she said, "Don't take my word for it. Really. Call around and see for yourself." Then she pushed the strap of her purse up onto her shoulder and sashayed out.

I hung behind a few moments, gathering my cool. I had one equally bewildering and aggravating idea bouncing around in my head. Was there any possible way Marcie was telling the truth? Had her boyfriend—Patch?—cracked years' worth of accumulated ice between us and brought us together? The idea was almost laughable. The phrase I'd have to see it to believe it danced in my head. More than ever, I resented my faulty memory, if for no other reason than it placed me at a disadvantage with Marcie.

And if Patch was both her summer fling and our mutual friend, where was he now?

Leaving the restroom, I noticed Marcie and her mother were nowhere in sight. I assumed they'd asked to be reseated, or made a statement to Hank by leaving altogether. Either way, I wasn't complaining.

As our table came into view, my stride slowed. Hank and my mom were holding hands across the table and gazing into each other's eyes in a deeply private way. He reached out to tuck a runaway strand of hair behind her ear. She blushed with pleasure.

I backed away without realizing it. I was going to be sick. The biggest cliché, but painfully accurate. So much for dousing Hank with his wine. So much for morphing into a diva of epic proportions.

Changing course, I ran for the front doors. I asked the hostess to relay the message to my mom that I'd called Vee for a ride, then hurried into the night.

I swallowed several deep breaths. My blood pressure stabilized, and I stopped seeing double. A few stars glinted overhead, even though the western horizon still glowed from the recent sunset. It was just cool enough to make me wish I was wearing an extra layer, but in my rush to leave, I'd left my jean jacket hanging on the back of my chair. I wasn't going back for it now. I was more tempted to go back for my cell, but if I'd survived the past three months without one, I was pretty sure I could handle one more night.

There was a 7-Eleven a handful of blocks away, and while I considered the possibility that it wasn't wise to be out alone at night, I also knew that I couldn't spend the rest of my life cowering in fear. If shark attack victims could get back in the ocean again, surely I could walk a few blocks by myself. I was in a very safe, well-lit part of town. If I wanted to force myself to break through my fear, I couldn't have selected a better location.

Six blocks later I entered the 7-Eleven, the door chiming as I did. I was so caught up in my own thoughts, it took me a few beats to figure out that something was wrong. The store was eerily quiet. But I knew I wasn't alone; I'd seen heads through the plate-glass window as I'd crossed the parking lot. Four guys, from what I'd been able to tell. But they'd all vanished, and fast. Even the front counter was left unattended. I couldn't remember *ever* walking into a convenience store to find the front counter neglected. It was asking to be robbed. Especially after dark.

"Hello?" I called out. I walked along the front of the store, glancing down the aisles, which stocked everything from Fig Newtons to Dramamine. "Is anyone here? I need change for the pay phone."

A muffled sound came from the hallway at the rear. It was unlit, presumably leading to the restrooms. I strained to hear the sound again. Given all the false alarms lately, I was afraid this was the beginning of another hallucination.

Then I heard a second sound. The faint squeak of a door closing. I was pretty sure this sound was real, which meant someone could be hiding back there, just out of sight. Anxiety pinched my stomach, and I hustled outside.

Rounding the building, I located the pay phone and punched in 9-1-1. I heard only one ring before a hand reached over my shoulder, clicked the receiver, and ended the call.

CHAPTER
8

I SWUNG AROUND.

He had a good six inches and fifty pounds on me. The lights from the parking lot did a poor job of reaching back here, but I ran down a quick list of identifying features: reddish-blond hair gelled and spiked, watery blue eyes, studs in both ears, a shark-tooth necklace. Light acne on the lower half of his face. A black tank top that showed off a muscley bicep inked with a fire-breathing dragon.

"Need help?" he asked with a twist of his lips. He offered me his cell phone, then braced an arm on the pay phone, leaning into my private space. His smile was a little too sweet, a little too superior. "Hate to see a pretty girl waste money on a call."

When I didn't answer, he frowned slightly. "Unless you were placing a *free* call." He scratched his cheek, a show of deep contemplation. "But the only free call you can make from a pay phone is . . . to the police." Any hint of the angelic vanished from his tone.

I swallowed. "There was no one inside at the front counter. I thought something was wrong." And now I *knew* something was wrong. The only reason he'd care if I was calling the police was if it was in his best interest to keep them far, far away. *A robbery, then?*

"Let me make this simple for you," he said, slouching down and putting his face close to mine, as if I were five years old and needed slow, clear instruction. "Get back in your car and keep driving."

It dawned on me that he didn't realize I'd walked here. But the thought became a moot point when I heard scuffling coming from the alley just around the corner. There was a slew of curse words, and a grunt of pain.

I considered my options. I could take Shark Tooth Necklace's advice and leave quickly, pretending I'd never been here. Or I could run to the next gas station down the road and call the police. But by then, it might be too late. If they were robbing the store, Shark Tooth and his friends weren't going to take their sweet time. My

BECCA FITZPATRICK

only other option was to stay put and make an either very brave, or very stupid, attempt to stop the robbery.

"What's going on back there?" I asked innocently, signaling to the rear of the building.

"Look around," he replied, his voice soft and silky. "This place is empty. Nobody knows you're here. Nobody's ever going to remember you were here. Now be a good girl and get back in your car and drive away."

"I—"

He pressed his finger to my lips. "I'm not going to ask again." His voice was gentle, flirtatious even. But his eyes were icy pits.

"I left my keys on the counter inside," I said, using the first excuse that came to mind. "When I first walked in."

He took me by the arm and hauled me around to the front of the building. His stride was twice as long as mine, and I found myself half jogging to keep up. All the while I was mentally shaking myself, ordering my ingenuity to think up an excuse for when he figured out I was lying. I didn't know how he'd react, but I had a general idea, and it made my stomach flip upside down.

The door chimed on our way in. He forced me over to the cash register and flicked aside a cardboard display of ChapStick and a plastic bin of key chains for sale, clearly hunting for my lost keys. He moved to the next register and repeated his rushed hunt. Suddenly he stopped. His eyes drifted idly over me. "Want to tell me where your keys really are?"

I wondered if I could outrun him to the street. I wondered what the chances were that a car would drive by when I needed it most. And why, oh why, had I left Coopersmith's without grabbing my jacket and cell phone?

"What's your name?" he asked.

"Marcie," I lied.

"Let me tell you something, Marcie," he said, tucking a curl behind my ear. I tried to take a step back, but he pinched my ear in warning. So I stood there, enduring his touch as his finger trailed over the curve of my ear and along my jaw. He tipped my chin up, forcing me to meet his pale, almost translucent eyes. "Nobody lies to Gabe. When Gabe tells a girl to run along, she'd better run along. Otherwise it makes Gabe angry. And that's a bad thing, because Gabe has a short temper. In fact, short is a generous way of putting it. You get me?"

I found it eerie that he referred to himself in the third person, but I wasn't about to make an issue of it. Instinct told me Gabe didn't like to be corrected, either. Or questioned. "I'm sorry." I didn't dare turn away from him, afraid he might mistake such a movement for a sign of disrespect.

"I want you to go now," he said in that deceptively velvet voice.

I nodded, backing up. My elbow bumped the door, letting in a rush of cool air.

As soon as I was outside, Gabe called through the glass door, "Ten." He was slouched against the front counter, a warped smile on his face.

I didn't know why he'd said the word, but I held my expression in check as I continued to back away, faster now.

"Nine," he called next.

That's when I figured out he was counting backward.

"Eight," he said, pushing up from the counter and taking a few lazy steps toward the door. He placed his palms on the glass, then drew an invisible heart with his finger. Seeing the stricken look on my face, he chuckled. "Seven."

I turned and ran.

I heard a car approaching on the main road, and I began shouting and flagging my arms. But I was still too far away, and the car zipped past, the drone of its engine vanishing around the bend.

When I made it to the road, I glanced right, then left. On a hasty decision, I turned toward Coopersmith's.

"Ready or not, here I come," I heard Gabe call out behind me.

I pumped my arms harder, hearing the obnoxious slap of my ballet flats on the pavement. I wanted to throw a look over my shoulder and see how far back he was, but forced myself to concentrate on the bend in the road ahead. I tried to keep as much distance as possible between me and Gabe. A car would come soon. It had to.

"Is that as fast as you can go?" He couldn't have been more than twenty feet behind. Worse, his voice didn't sound fatigued. I was struck by the horrible thought that he wasn't even trying. He was enjoying the cat-and-mouse, and while I grew more and more tired with every step, he grew more and more excited.

"Keep going!" he singsonged. "But don't wear yourself out. It won't be any fun if you can't put up a fight when I catch you. I want to play."

Ahead, I heard the deep rumble of an approaching engine. Headlights swung into view, and I moved into the middle of the road, frantically waving my arms. Gabe wouldn't hurt me with a witness looking on. Would he?

"Stop!" I yelled, continuing to hail what I could now see was a pickup truck rolling closer.

The driver slowed beside me, cracking his window. He was middle-aged with a flannel shirt and smelled strongly of the fish docks.

"What's the matter?" he asked. His gaze shifted over my shoulder, where I felt Gabe's presence like a cold crackle in the air.

"Just playing hide-and-seek," Gabe said, slinging his arm around my shoulders.

I shrugged him off. "I've never seen this guy before," I told the man. "He threatened me at the 7-Eleven. I think he and his friends are trying to rob the store. When I walked in, the store was empty and I heard a struggle in the back. We need to call the police."

I paused, about to ask the man if he had a cell phone, when I watched with confusion as he turned to face forward, ignoring me. He cranked his window all the way up, locking himself inside the cab of the truck.

"You have to help!" I said, rapping his window. But his forward

BECCA FITZPATRICK

fixed stare didn't waver. A little chill danced over my skin. The man wasn't going to help. He was going to leave me out here with Gabe.

Gabe mimicked me, knocking obnoxiously on the man's window. "Help me!" he cried in a shrill voice. "Gabe and his friends are robbing the 7-Eleven. Oh, mister, you have to help me stop them!" When he finished, he flung his head back, choking on his own laughter.

Almost robotically, the man in the truck looked over at us. His eyes were slightly crossed and unblinking.

"What's the matter with you!" I said, rattling the truck's door handle. I smacked the window again. "Call the police!"

The man stepped on the gas. The truck accelerated slowly, and I jogged beside it, still clinging to the hope that I could open the door. He fed the truck more gas, and I tripped over my feet to keep up. Suddenly he took off like a shot, and I was flung off into the road.

I whirled to Gabe. "What did you do to him?"

This.

I flinched, hearing the word echo inside my head like a phantom presence. Gabe's eyes blackened into hollows. His hair started visibly growing, first on top of his head, and then everywhere. It tufted out from his arms, down to the tips of his fingers, until he was covered in fur. Matted, reeking brown fur. He lumbered toward me on his hind legs, gaining height until he towered over me. He swiped his arm, and I saw a flash of claws. Then he crashed down on all fours, put his wet black nose in my face, and roared—an angry, reverberating sound. He had transformed into a grizzly bear.

In my terror, I tripped backward and went down. I scuttled backward, blindly sweeping the roadside for a rock. Catching one in my hand, I hurled it at the bear. It hit him in the shoulder and bounced aside. I grabbed another rock, aiming for his head. The rock flew into his snout, and he snapped his head to the side, saliva trailing from his mouth. He roared again, then came at me faster than I could scramble backward.

Using his paw, he flattened me against the pavement. He was pushing too hard; my ribs creaked in pain.

"Stop!" I tried to shove his paw off, but he was much too strong. I didn't know if he could hear me. Or understand. I didn't know if any part of Gabe was left inside the bear. Never before in my life had I witnessed anything so inexplicably horrifying.

The wind picked up, tangling my hair across my face. Through it, I watched the wind carry off the bear's fur. Little tufts of it drifted up into the night. When I looked again, it was Gabe leaning over me. His sadistic grin implied, *You're my puppet. And don't you forget it.*

I wasn't sure which terrified me more: Gabe or the bear.

"Up you go," he said, hoisting me to my feet.

He propelled me back along the road until the lights of 7-Eleven came into view. My mind staggered. Had he—hypnotized me? Made me believe he'd turned himself into a bear? Was there any other explanation? I knew I had to get out of here and call for help, but I hadn't come up with the *how* yet.

BECCA FITZPATRICK

We rounded the building to the alley, where the others were congregated.

Two were dressed in street clothes, similar to Gabe's. The third was wearing a lime-green polo with 7-ELEVEN and the name P.J. embroidered on the pocket.

P.J. was on his knees, clutching his ribs, moaning inconsolably. His eyes were squeezed shut, and saliva trickled from the corner of his mouth. One of Gabe's friends—he wore an oversize gray hoodie—stood over P.J. with a tire iron, raised and ready to swing, presumably again.

My mouth went dry, and my legs seemed to be made of straw. I couldn't unglue my eyes from the dark red stain seeping through the midsection of P.J.'s shirt.

"You're hurting him," I said, aghast.

Gabe held his hand out for the tire iron, and it was readily given to him.

"You mean this?" Gabe asked with mock sincerity.

He swung the tire iron down square against P.J.'s back, and I heard a grotesque crunch. P.J. screamed, collapsed onto his side, and writhed in pain.

Gabe stretched the tire iron across the back of his shoulders, hanging his arms over it like it was a baseball bat. "Home run!" he hollered.

The other two laughed. I was dizzy with the need to be sick.

"Just take the money!" I said, my voice rising toward a shout.

Clearly this was a robbery, but they were taking it five steps too far. "You're going to kill him if you keep hitting him!"

A snicker moved through the group, as if they knew something I did not.

"Kill him? Unlikely," Gabe said.

"He's already bleeding heavily!"

Gabe raised an uncaring shoulder. And that's when I knew he wasn't just cruel, but insane. "He'll heal."

"Not if he doesn't get to a hospital soon."

Gabe used his shoe to nudge P.J., who had rolled over and planted his forehead on the cement apron spreading out from the back entrance. His whole body trembled, and I thought it looked like he was going into shock.

"Did you hear her?" Gabe yelled down at P.J. "You need to get to a hospital. I'll drive you there myself and dump you in front of the ER. But first you got to say it. Swear the oath."

With great effort, P.J. lifted his head to fix a withering stare on Gabe. He opened his mouth, and I thought he was going to say whatever it was they all wanted him to, but instead he spat, hitting Gabe in the leg. "You can't kill me," he sneered, but his teeth chattered and his eyes rolled back to whites, clearly showing he was on the brink of fainting. "The—Black—Hand—told—me."

"Wrong answer," Gabe said, tossing the tire iron up and catching it like a baton. When the trick ended, he swooped the tire iron down in a violent arc. The metal smashed over P.J.'s spine, causing him to jerk rod-straight and cry out in a hair-raising yowl.

I drew both hands over my mouth, transfixed by horror. Horror from both the gruesome picture in front of me, and from a word screaming inside my head. It was as though the word had snapped free from deep in my subconscious and smacked me head-on.

Nephilim.

That's what P.J. is, I thought, even though the word meant nothing to me. *And they're trying to force him to swear an oath of fealty.*

It was a frightening revelation, because I didn't know what any of it meant. Where was I getting this from? How could I know anything about what was happening, when I'd never seen anything like it before?

I was torn from any further thought on the matter when a white SUV swung into the alley ahead, the beam of its headlights causing all of us to freeze. Gabe discreetly lowered the tire iron, hiding it behind his leg. I prayed that whoever was behind the wheel would reverse out of the alley and call the police. If the driver came much closer, well, I'd already seen what Gabe could do to convince people not to help.

I began drafting ideas in my mind of how to drag P.J. from the scene while Gabe and the others were distracted, when one of the guys—the one in the gray hoodie—asked Gabe, "Do you think they're Nephilim?"

Nephilim. That word. Again. Spoken out loud this time.

silence

Instead of comforting me, the word only ratcheted up my terror another few notches. I knew the word, and now it seemed Gabe and his friends did too. How could we possibly have it in common? How could we have *anything* in common?

Gabe shook his head. "They'd bring more than one car. The Black Hand wouldn't go up against us with less than twenty of his guys."

"Police, then? Could be an unmarked car. I can go convince them they've made a wrong turn."

The way he said it made me wonder if Gabe wasn't the only one capable of his powerful brand of hypnotism. Maybe his two friends were as well.

The guy in the gray hoodie started forward, when Gabe put his arm out, catching him in the chest. "Wait."

The SUV rumbled closer, gravel popping under its wheels. My legs hummed with nervous adrenaline. If a fight broke out, Gabe and the others might get so wrapped up in it, I could grab P.J. under his armpits and haul him out of the alley. A slim chance, but a chance nonetheless.

Suddenly Gabe boomed with laughter. He slapped his friends on the back, his teeth gleaming.

"Well, well, boys. Look who came to the party after all."

CHAPTER

THE WHITE SUV ROLLED TO A STOP AND THE
engine cut off. The driver's-side door opened, and
through the grainy darkness, someone stepped out.
Male. Tall. Loose-fit jeans and a white-and-navy baseball tee
pushed up to his elbows. His face was concealed under the brim
of a ball cap, but I saw the strong line of his jaw and the shape of
his mouth, and the picture jolted me like a current of electricity.

The flash of black bursting at the back of my mind was so intense, the color completely stained my vision for several seconds.

"Decided to join us after all?" Gabe called to him.

The newcomer didn't answer.

"This one's offering resistance," Gabe continued, driving the toe of his shoe into P.J., who was still coiled in a ball on the ground. "Doesn't want to swear fealty. Thinks he's too good for me. And this, coming from a crossbreed."

Laughter circled through Gabe and his two friends, but if the driver of the SUV got the joke, he didn't show it. Sliding his hands into his pockets, he studied us in silence. I thought his gaze lingered a little long on me, but I was strung so tight, I could have seen something that wasn't really there.

"Why is she here?" he asked quietly, lifting his chin at me.

"Wrong place, wrong time," Gabe said.

"Now she's a witness."

"I told her to keep driving." Was it just me, or did Gabe sound defensive? It was the first time all night anyone, however subtly, had questioned his authority, and I could practically feel the air around him sizzle with a negative charge.

"And?"

"She wouldn't leave."

"She's going to remember everything."

Gabe swung the tire iron agilely in his hand, round and round. "I can convince her not to talk."

The driver's eyes shifted to P.J.'s balled-up form. "Just like you convinced this one to talk?"

Gabe frowned. His grip on the tire iron tightened. "Got a better idea?"

"Yeah. Let her go."

Gabe thumbed his nose and gave a snort of laughter. "Let her go," he repeated. "What'll stop her from running straight to the police? Huh, Jev? Thought that one through?"

"You're not afraid of the police," Jev said calmly, but I thought I detected a hint of challenge. His second indirect threat to Gabe's power.

Taking a risk, I decided to insert myself into their argument. "If you let me go, I promise I won't talk. Just let me take him with me." I motioned at P.J.'s crumpled figure, and I said the words like they came from the very bottom of my soul. But I entertained the scary realization that I would have to talk. I couldn't let this kind of violence go unpunished. If Gabe was free, nothing was stopping him from torturing and terrorizing another victim. I shielded those thoughts from my eyes, suddenly worried that Gabe would see through me.

"You heard her," Jev said.

Gabe's jaw clenched. "No. He's mine. I've been waiting months for him to turn sixteen. I'm not walking away now."

"There'll be others," Jev said, looking uncannily relaxed as he laced his fingers on top of his head. He shrugged. "Walk away."

"Yeah? And be like you? You don't have a Nephil vassal. It's going to be a long, lonely Cheshvan, pal."

"Cheshvan is still weeks away. You've got time. You'll find someone else. Let the Nephil and the girl go."

Gabe stepped up to Jev. Jev was taller and smarter and knew how to keep his cool—I'd gathered that in all of three seconds—but Gabe had the advantage of bulk. Where Jev was long and lean like a cheetah, Gabe was built like a bull. "You turned us down earlier. Said you had other business tonight. Far as I'm concerned, this isn't your call. I'm sick of you strolling in at the last minute and calling the shots. I'm not leaving until the Nephil swears his oath of fealty."

There was that phrase again, "oath of fealty." Vaguely familiar, and yet distant. If on some deeper level I knew what it meant, the memory wasn't resurfacing. Either way, I knew it would have terrible consequences for P.J.

"This is my night," Gabe added, punctuating the fact by spitting at his feet. "I'm ending it on my terms."

"Wait a minute," the guy in the gray hoodie interrupted, sounding stupefied. His eyes swiveled in both directions down the alley. "Gabe! Your Nephil. He's gone!"

We all turned toward the spot where P.J. had lain inert only moments ago. An oily stain on the gravel was the only sign he'd been there.

"He couldn't have gone far," Gabe snapped. "Dominic, go that way," he ordered the guy in the gray hoodie, pointing down the alley. "Jeremiah, check the store." The other guy, the one in a white graphic T-shirt, took off jogging around the corner.

"What about her?" Jev asked Gabe, nodding at me.

"Why don't you make yourself useful and go bring me back my Nephil?" Gabe shot back.

Jev raised his hands level with his shoulders. "Have it your way."

I felt my stomach tumble to my knees as I realized that this was it. Jev was leaving. He was friends with, or at least an acquaintance of, Gabe, and that alone was enough to make me nervous of him, but at the same time, he was my only shot at getting out of here. Up until this point, he'd appeared to take my side. If he left, I was on my own. Gabe had made it clear he was the alpha male, and I wasn't going to pretend I thought his remaining two friends would stand up to him.

"You're going to walk away, just like that?" I yelled after Jev. But Gabe rammed his shoe into the back of my leg, forcing me to collapse to my knees, and before I could say more, my breath was knocked out of me.

"It'll be easier if you don't watch," Gabe told me. "One solid hit, and it'll be the last thing you feel."

I lunged forward to escape, but Gabe grabbed a fistful of my hair, jerking me back. "You can't do this!" I screamed. "You can't just kill me."

"Hold still," he growled.

silence

"Don't let him do this, Jev!" I yelled, unable to see Jev, but certain he could still hear me, since I hadn't heard the SUV start up yet. I was rolling in the gravel, trying to turn around so I could see the tire iron and try to dodge it. I wrapped my fist around a scoop of rocks, twisted violently just long enough to spot Gabe, and flung them.

His big hand came down, grinding my forehead into the ground. My nose was bent at a painful angle, rocks biting into my chin and cheeks. There was a sickening crunch, and Gabe collapsed on top of me. Through a haze of panic, I wondered if he was trying to smother me. Killing me quickly wasn't enough, was it? Had to draw out the pain as long as possible? Gasping for breath, I clawed my way out from under him.

I scrambled to my feet and flipped around. I braced myself in a defensive position, expecting to find Gabe prepping to take a second shot at me. My gaze dropped. He was facedown on the ground, the tire iron jutting out of his back. He'd been stabbed with it.

Jev wiped his sleeve across his face, which glistened with sweat. At his feet, Gabe twitched and shuddered, swearing violently and incoherently. I couldn't believe he was still alive. The tire iron had to be straight through his spine.

"You—stabbed him," I blurted, horror-struck.

"And he's not going to be happy about it, so I'd suggest you get out of here," Jev said, twisting the tire iron deeper. He glanced over at me and did an eyebrow raise. "Sooner rather than later."

I backed away. "What about you?"

He watched me for an absurdly long moment, considering the circumstances. A brief expression of regret flicked across his features. Once again, I felt a powerful tug to my memory that threatened to mend the bridge holding everything out of reach. I opened my mouth, but the conduit between my mind and my words had been destroyed. I was at a loss as to how to connect the two. I had something to say to him, but I couldn't nail down *what*.

"You can sit tight, but I'm guessing P.J. already put a call in to the cops," Jev said, screwing the tire iron deeper, causing Gabe's body to spring taut at one moment, and fall limp the next.

As if on cue, the distant wail of sirens shrilled across the night.

Jev grabbed Gabe under his arms, dragging him into the weeds on the far side of the alley. "On the back roads, at the right speed, you can put a couple miles between you and this place in no time."

"I don't have a car."

His eyes sliced into mine.

"I walked here," I explained. "I'm on foot."

"Angel," he said in a way that sounded like he sincerely hoped I was joking.

A few moments together hardly qualified us for pet names, but nonetheless, my heartbeat went a little erratic at the endearment. *Angel.* How could he possibly know that name had haunted me for days now? How could *I* possibly explain the eerie flashes of black that intensified the closer he came?

Most unnerving of all, if I connected the dots . . .

Patch, a voice whispered from my subconscious, a quiet syllable that dashed itself against a cage deep within. *The last time you felt this way was when Marcie mentioned Patch.*

The single syllable of his name opened me up to a swarm of black; maddening, consuming black that flooded from every direction. I concentrated through it, eyes intent on Jev, trying to make sense of a feeling I couldn't put words to. He knew something I didn't. Maybe about the mysterious Patch, maybe about me. Definitely about me. His presence cut me with emotions too deep to be a coincidence.

But how were Patch, Marcie, Jev, and I connected?

"Do I—know you?" I asked him, unable to come up with any other explanation.

He gazed at me, unflinching. "No car?" he confirmed, ignoring my question.

"No car," I repeated, my voice considerably thinner.

He arched his neck back, as though to ask the moon, *Why me?* Then he jerked his thumb at the white SUV he'd pulled up in. "Get in."

I shut my eyes, trying to think. "Wait. We have to stay and testify. If we run, we might as well be confessing our guilt. I'll tell the police you killed Gabe to save my life." Further inspiration struck me. "We'll find P.J. and get him to testify too."

Jev opened the driver's-side door of the SUV. "All of the above would be true if the police could be relied on."

"What are you talking about? They're the police. It's their job to catch criminals. We're not in the wrong here. Gabe would have killed me if you hadn't stepped in."

"That part I don't doubt."

"Then what?"

"This isn't the kind of case local law enforcement is set up to handle."

"I'm pretty sure murder falls under the jurisdiction of the law!" I argued.

"Two things," he said patiently. "First, I didn't kill Gabe. I stunned him. Second, believe me when I say Jeremiah and Dominic will not go into custody willingly and without a lot of bloodshed."

I opened my mouth to argue when, from the corner of my eye, I saw Gabe twitch again. Miraculously, he wasn't dead. I remembered the way he'd manipulated my sight with what I could only guess was a powerful form of hypnotism or a magician's sleight of hand. Was he using another trick to somehow evade death? I had the eerie sensation that something bigger than I understood was going on. But—

What, exactly?

"Tell me what you're thinking," Jev said quietly.

I hesitated, but there wasn't time for it. If Jev knew Gabe as well as I suspected, he had to know about his . . . abilities. "I saw Gabe do—a trick. A magic trick." When Jev's grim expression confirmed that he wasn't surprised, I added, "He made me see something that wasn't real. He turned himself into a bear."

"That's the tip of the iceberg when it comes to what he's capable of."

I swallowed against the sticky film lining my mouth. "How did he do it? Is he a magician?"

"Something like that."

"He used magic?" I'd never given two moments' thought that such convincing magic might actually exist. Until now.

"Close enough. Listen, time's running a little thin."

My gaze traveled to the weeds partially concealing Gabe's body. Magicians could create illusions, but they could not defy death. There was no logical way he could have survived.

The sirens blared closer, and Jev ushered me toward the SUV. "Time's up."

I didn't move. I couldn't. I had a moral responsibility to stay—

Jev said, "If you hang around to talk to the police, you'll be dead before the week is over. And so will every cop involved. Gabe will stop the investigation before it starts."

I took another two seconds to think it through. I didn't have to trust Jev. But in the end, for reasons too complicated to untangle on the spot, I did.

I strapped myself in beside him, my heart thundering behind my rib cage. He put what I could now see was a Tahoe in gear. With one arm braced behind my seat, he craned his neck to see out the back window.

Jev reversed down the alley, backed onto the street, then gunned forward toward the intersection ahead. There was a stop sign on the corner, but the Tahoe wasn't slowing. I was just wondering if Jev would at least yield for the stop sign, as I clutched the granny handle above my door with both hands and hoped he would, when a dark silhouette staggered into our lane. The tire iron projecting out of Gabe's back was wrenched at a gruesome angle, and in the hazy light, it resembled a broken appendage. A battered wing.

Jev stepped on the gas and threw the SUV into higher gear. It pitched forward, increasing in speed. Gabe was too far away to read his expression, but he showed no sign of moving. He crouched, tucking his legs beneath him, his hands up in front of him as though he thought he could block us.

I gripped the seat-belt strap. "You're going to hit him!"

"He'll move."

My foot stomped an imaginary brake pedal. The distance between Gabe and the Tahoe rapidly narrowed. "Jev—stop—right—now!"

"This won't kill him either."

He forced the Tahoe into another burst of speed. And then it all happened too quickly.

Gabe lunged, hurtling through the air toward us. He struck the windshield, the glass cracking into a latticelike web. An instant later he flew out of sight. A scream filled the car, and I realized it was mine.

"He's on top of the car," Jev said. He floored it over the curb, plowing through a sidewalk bench and driving under a low-hanging tree. Jerking the steering wheel a hard left, he steered back onto the street.

"Did he fall off? Where is he? Is he still up there?" I pressed my face to my window, trying to see above me.

"Hang on."

"To what?" I shouted, grasping for the granny handle again.

I never felt the brake. But Jev must have stepped on it, because the Tahoe spun a full rotation before squealing to a stop. My shoulder was slammed up against the door frame. Out of the corner of my eye I saw a dark mass fly through the air and land with catlike grace on the ground. Gabe stayed there a moment, crouching, his back to us.

Jev threw the Tahoe into first gear.

Gabe looked back over his shoulder. His hair clung to the sides of his face, a sheen of sweat holding it in place. His eyes locked with mine. His mouth tipped up diabolically. He said something just as the Tahoe lunged into motion, and even though I couldn't decipher a single word from the movement of his lips, the message was clear. *This isn't over.*

I pressed back in my seat, swallowing gulps of air as Jev peeled away in a manner I was sure left tire treads tattooed on the street.

EV DROVE ONLY FIVE BLOCKS. IT DAWNED ON ME A little late that I should have asked him to take me to Coopersmith's, but he'd opted for the obscurity of the back roads. He steered the Tahoe to the shoulder of a peaceful country road, lined by acres of trees and cornfields.

"Can you find your way home from here?" he asked.

"You're just going to dump me here?" But the real question

framed in my mind was this: Why had Jev, presumably one of them, alienated himself to save me?

"If you're worried about Gabe, trust me, he's got more on his mind right now than tracking you down. He won't be doing much of anything until he gets the tire iron out. I'm surprised he had the strength to chase us as far as he did. Even after he gets it out, he'll have what I can only describe as a killer hangover. He's not going to be in the mood to do much other than sleep for the next several hours. If you're waiting for the perfect moment to make a break for it, you aren't going to get a better one."

When I didn't budge, he jerked his thumb back the way we'd come. "I need to make sure Dominic and Jeremiah clear out."

I knew he wanted me to take a hint, but I wasn't convinced. "Why are you really protecting them?" Maybe Jev was right, and Dominic and Jeremiah would fight the police. Maybe it would end in a bloodbath. But wasn't the risk better than letting them walk free?

Jev's eyes were fixed on the darkness beyond the windshield. "Because I'm one of them."

I immediately shook my head. "You're not like them. They would have killed me. You came back for me. You stopped Gabe."

Instead of answering, he angled out of the Tahoe and came around to my side. He yanked my door open and pointed into the night. "Head that way to town. If your cell phone doesn't work, keep walking until the trees clear. Sooner or later you'll get reception."

"I don't have my cell."

He paused only a beat. "Then when you get to Whitetail Lodge, ask the front desk for their phone. You can call home from there."

I slid out. "Thanks for saving me from Gabe. And thanks for the ride," I said civilly. "But for future reference, I don't appreciate being lied to. I know there's a lot you aren't telling me. Maybe you think I don't deserve to know. Maybe you think you hardly know me, and I'm not worth the trouble. But given what I just went through, I think I've earned the right to the truth."

To my surprise, he nodded. Not eagerly; a reluctant inclination of his head that said, *Fair enough*. "I'm protecting them because I have to. If the police see them in action, it will blow our cover. This town isn't ready for Dominic, Jeremiah, or any of us." He watched me, his razor-sharp eyes softening to a velvety black. There was something so consuming about the way his eyes took me in, I almost felt his gaze like a real touch. "And I'm not ready to leave town yet," he murmured, his eyes still holding mine.

He stepped closer, and I felt my breath come a little faster. His skin was darker than mine, more rugged. He wasn't beautiful enough to be handsome. He was all hard, prominent angles. And he was telling me that he was different. Not because he was unlike any other guy I'd ever known, but because he was something else entirely. I clung to the one strange new word that had stayed with me all night. "Are you Nephilim?"

Almost as if he'd been shocked, he jerked back. The whole

moment snapped apart. "Go home and get on with your life," he said. "Do that, and you'll be safe."

With his blunt brush-off, I felt tears spring to my eyes. He saw them and shook his head in apology. "Look, Nora," he tried again, resting his hands on my shoulders.

I stiffened in his embrace. "How do you know my name?"

The moon broke briefly through the clouds, allowing me a glimpse of his eyes. The soft velvet was gone, replaced by a hard and hooded black. His were the kind of eyes that held secrets. The kind that lied without flinching. The kind that once you looked into them, it was hard to break away.

We were both damp from the exertion of our earlier escape, and what I assumed was the lingering scent of his shower gel hung between us. It held the slightest trace of mint and black pepper, and the memory of it rushed through me so fast I was left dizzy. I had no way to trace it, but I knew the scent. Even more unsettling, I *knew* I knew Jev. Somehow, whether it was in a trivial way, or something much larger and therefore much more disconcerting, Jev had been a part of my life. There was no other way to explain the searing flashbacks that came from being near him.

It crossed my mind that maybe he was my kidnapper, but the idea didn't have a lot of conviction behind it. I didn't believe it. Maybe because I didn't want to.

"We knew each other, didn't we?" I said, my extremities tingling. "Tonight isn't the first time we've met."

When Jev stayed quiet, I was pretty sure I had my answer. "Do you know about my amnesia? Do you know I can't remember the last five months? Is that why you thought you could get away with pretending not to know me?"

"Yes," he said wearily.

My heart beat faster. "Why?"

"I didn't want to pin a target on your back. If Gabe thought we had a connection, he could use you to hurt me."

Fine. He'd answered that question. But I didn't want to talk about Gabe. "How did we know each other? And after we left Gabe behind, why did you still pretend not to know me? What are you keeping from me?" I waited restlessly. "Are you going to fill in the gaps?"

"No."

"No?"

He merely looked at me.

"Then you're a selfish jerk." The accusation flew out before I could stop it. But I wasn't going to take it back. He may have saved my life, but if he knew something about those missing five months, and refused to tell me, anything he'd done to redeem himself was lost in my eyes.

"If I had anything good to tell you, trust me, I'd start talking."

"I can handle bad news," I said curtly.

He shook his head and sidestepped me, heading back to the driver's side. I grabbed his arm. His eyes dropped to my hand, but he didn't pull free.

"Tell me what you know," I said. "What happened to me? Who did this to me? Why can't I remember those five months? What was so bad that I'm choosing to forget?"

His face was a mask, all emotion compartmentalized away. The only sign that he heard me was a muscle flexing in his jaw. "I'm going to give you some advice, and for once, I want you to take it. Go back to your life and move on. Start over if you have to. Do whatever it takes to leave this all behind. This will end badly if you keep looking back."

"This? I don't even know what this is! I can't move on. I want to know what happened to me! Do you know who kidnapped me? Do you know where they took me and why?"

"Does it matter?"

"How dare you," I said, not bothering to swallow away the choked-up quality of my voice. "How dare you stand here and make light of what I've been through."

"If you find out who took you, is it going to help? Will it be the closure you need to pick yourself up and start living again? No," he answered for me.

"Yes, it will." What Jev didn't understand was that anything was better than nothing. Half-full was better than empty. Ignorance was the lowest form of humiliation and suffering.

He let go of a troubled sigh, raking his fingers through his hair. "We knew each other," he relented. "We met five months ago, and I was bad news from the moment you laid eyes on me. I used you and hurt you. Fortunately, you had the good sense to kick me out of your life before I could come back for round two. The last time we spoke, you swore that if you ever saw me again, you'd do your best to kill me. Maybe you meant it, maybe not. Either way, there was a lot of strong emotion behind it. Is that what you were looking for?" he finished.

I blinked. I couldn't imagine myself making such a malicious threat. The closest I'd ever come to hating someone was Marcie Millar, and even then, I'd never fantasized about her death. I was human, but I wasn't heartless. "Why would I say that? What did you do that was so horrible?"

"I tried to kill you."

I met his eyes sharply. The line of his mouth, grim but steady, told me he wasn't in the slightest way joking.

"You wanted the truth," he said. "Deal with it, Angel."

"Deal with it? It doesn't make any sense. Why did you want to kill me?"

"For fun, because I was bored, does it matter? I tried to kill you."

No. Something wasn't right. "If you wanted to kill me back then, why did you help me tonight?"

"You're missing the point. I could have ended your life. Do yourself a favor and run as far and as fast from me as you can." He turned away with a dismissive gesture, signaling for me to walk in the opposite direction. This was the last we'd see of each other.

"You're a liar."

He turned around, his black eyes snapping. "I'm also a thief, a gambler, a cheat, and a murderer. But this happens to be one of the rare times when I'm telling the truth. Go home. Consider yourself lucky. You've got a chance to start fresh. Not everyone can say the same."

I'd wanted the truth, but I was more confused than ever. How had I, a straitlaced, straight-A student, *ever* crossed paths with him? What could we possibly have had in common? He was abominable . . . and the most alluring, tortured soul I'd ever met. Even now, I could feel a war brewing inside me. He was nothing like me, quick and caustic and dangerous. Maybe even a little scary. But from the moment he'd stepped out of the Tahoe tonight, my heart hadn't been able to find a steady rhythm. In his presence, every last nerve ending in my body felt wired with electricity.

"One last thing," he said. "Stop looking for me."

"I'm not looking for you." I scoffed.

He touched his index finger to my forehead, my skin absurdly warming under his touch. It didn't escape me that he couldn't seem to stop finding reasons to touch me. Nor did I miss that I didn't want him to stop. "Under all the layers, a part of you remembers. It's that part that came looking for me tonight. It's that part that's going to get you killed, if you're not careful."

We stood face-to-face, both of us breathing hard. The sirens were so close now.

"What am I supposed to tell the police?" I said.

"You're not going to talk to the police."

"Oh, really? Funny, because I plan on telling them *exactly* how you rammed that tire iron into Gabe's back. Unless you answer my questions."

He gave an ironic snort. "Blackmail? You've changed, Angel."

Another strategic stab to my blind side, making me feel even more unsure and self-conscious. I would have squeezed my memory, trying to place him one last time, but I knew it was wrung dry. Since I couldn't rely on my memory, I'd just have to cast my nets elsewhere and hope for the best.

I said, "If you know me as well as you claim to, you know I'm not going to stop looking for whoever it was who kidnapped me until I either find them, or hit rock bottom."

"And let me tell you where rock bottom will be," he returned with a gravelly edge. "Your grave. A shallow backwoods grave where no one will find you. No one will come to your graveside and mourn for you. As far as humanity is concerned, you'll vanish off the grid. It will wear on your mom. That constant menacing sense of the unknown. It will peck away at her, driving her closer to the edge until it shoves her over. And instead of being buried in some green-lawned cemetery beside you, where loved ones can visit you until the end of time, she'll be alone. And so will you. For eternity."

I stood taller, determined to show him I wasn't going to be scared off that easily, but I felt a queasy little flutter of premonition in my belly. "Tell me, or I'll rat you out to the cops, that's a promise. I want to know where I've been. And I want to know who took me."

He dragged a hand down his mouth, laughing to himself. It was a tense, tired sound.

"Who kidnapped me?" I snapped, running out of patience. I wasn't moving from this spot until he confessed what he knew. I suddenly resented him for saving my life earlier. I wanted to view him with nothing short of hot contempt and hatred. I'd point him out to the police without a moment's hesitation if he refused to tell me what he knew.

He raised those impenetrable eyes to mine, his mouth crooking down on one side. Not a frown. Something infinitely more bewildering and frightening.

"You're not supposed to be in this anymore. Even I can't keep you safe."

Then he walked away, having said all he was going to, but I couldn't accept it. This was my one chance to make sense of the part of my life that was missing.

I stomped after him and grabbed the back of his shirt so hard it tore. I didn't care. I had bigger things to worry about. I said, "What am I not supposed to be involved in anymore?"

Only the words didn't come out right. They were sucked away from me at the exact same time that a hook seemed to latch behind my stomach and yank me inside out. I felt myself being hurled through the air, and every muscle in my body tensed, bracing for the unknown.

The last thing I remembered was the roar of air past my ears and the world crashing to black.

BECCA FITZPATRICK

WHEN I OPENED MY EYES, I WASN'T ON THE
street anymore. The Tahoe, the cornfields, the
starry night—it was all gone. I stood inside a
concrete building that smelled of sawdust and something slightly
metallic, like rust. I was shivering, but not from cold.

I'd grabbed Jev's shirt. I'd heard fabric ripping. I might have
touched his back. And now . . . I was in what appeared to be a vacant
warehouse.

Ahead, I saw two figures. Jev and Hank Millar. Relieved that I wasn't in this place alone, I strode toward them, hoping they could tell me where I was, and how I'd gotten here.

"Jev!" I called out.

Neither one so much as looked in my direction, but surely they'd heard me. In this vast space, voices carried.

I was about to open my mouth a second time, when I came to a startled halt. Behind them, the evenly spaced bars of a cage peeked out from under a canvas. In a great wave, it all came back to me. The cage. The girl with icy-black hair. The high school bathroom. When I'd blacked out momentarily. My palms tingled with sweat. It could mean only one thing. I was hallucinating.

Again.

"You brought me here to show me this?" Jev told Hank with quiet disgust. "Do you understand the risk I take every time we meet? Don't call me here to chat. Don't call me here for a shoulder to cry on. Don't *ever* call me here to show off your latest conquest."

"Patience, boy. I showed you the archangel because I need your help. Obviously we both have questions." He looked meaningfully at the cage. "Well, she has answers."

"My curiosity for that life died a long time ago."

"Whether you want it or not, this life is still yours. I've tried everything to persuade her to talk, but she's cagey, pardon the pun." He smiled mildly. "Get her to tell me what I need to know, and I'll turn

her over to you. I doubt I need to remind you the trouble the archangels have caused for you. If there were a way to seek revenge . . .
well, surely I don't need to say more."

"How have you managed to keep her caged?" Jev asked coolly.

Hank's mouth twisted with amusement. "Sawed off her wings.
Just because I can't see them doesn't mean I don't have a pretty
good idea where they are. You put the idea in my head. Before you,
I never would have imagined a Nephil could un-wing an angel."

Something dark stirred in Jev's eyes. "An ordinary saw couldn't
cut through her wings."

"I didn't use an ordinary saw."

"Whatever you're messed up in, Hank, I'd advise you to get out.
Fast."

"If you knew what I was messed up in, you'd beg me to let you
in on it. The archangels' empire won't last forever. There are powers out there that surpass even theirs. Powers waiting to be harnessed, if you know where to look," he said cryptically.

With a disgusted gesture, Jev turned to go.

"Our agreement, boy," Hank called after him.

"This wasn't part of it."

"Perhaps we can come to a new arrangement, then. Rumor has
it you haven't forced a Nephil to swear fealty. Cheshvan is only
weeks away. . . ." He let the sentence hang.

Jev stopped. "You'd offer me one of your own men?"

"For the greater good, yes." Hank spread his hands, chuckling softly. "You'd have your pick. Am I making this offer too good to refuse yet?"

"I wonder what your men would think if they knew you were selling them off to the highest bidder."

"Swallow your pride. Pushing my buttons won't settle the score. Let me tell you why I've made it as far as I have in this life. I don't take things personally. You shouldn't either. Don't let this be about you and me, and past differences. We both have something to gain. Help me, and I'll help you. It's as simple as that."

He paused, giving Jev time to think.

"Last time you walked away from an offer of mine, it ended disastrously," Hank added with a certain curl of his lips.

"I'm done making deals with you," Jev answered in measured tones. "But I'll give you some advice. Let her go. The archangels are going to notice she's missing. Kidnapping might be your strong suit, but this time you're pushing your luck. We both know how this is going to end. The archangels don't lose."

"Ah, but they do," Hank corrected. "They lost when your kind fell. They lost again when you created the Nephilim race. They can lose again, and they will. All the more reason you should act now. We have one of their own, giving us the upper hand. Together, you and I can turn the tables. Together, boy. But we must act now."

I sat against the wall and hugged my knees to my chest. I let my head tip back until it rested on concrete. *Deep breaths.* I'd gotten myself out of a hallucination before, and I could do it again. Wiping away the sweat beading my forehead, I concentrated on what I'd been doing before the hallucination started. *Go back to Jev—the real Jev. Open a door in your mind. Walk through it.*

"I know about the necklace."

At Hank's words, my eyes flew open. I looked between the two men standing in front of me, ultimately focusing on Hank. He knew about the necklace? The one Marcie was looking for? Was there any way the two necklaces were one and the same?

No, they're not, I reasoned. Nothing in this hallucination is valid. You're creating every detail of this scene with your subconscious. Focus instead on creating an exit.

Jev raised his eyebrows in inquiry.

"I'd rather not reveal my source," Hank replied dryly. "Obviously all I need now is an actual necklace. You're smart enough to know this is where you come in. Help me find an archangel's necklace. Any one will do."

"Try your source," Jev said simply, but with a trace of derision.

Hank's mouth compressed into a severe line. "Two Nephilim. Your choice, of course," he bargained. "You could alternate between them—"

Jev waved him off. "I don't have my archangel's necklace anymore, if that's where you're going. The archangels confiscated it when I fell."

"That's not what my source tells me."

"Your source lied," he said blandly.

"A second source confirms seeing you wearing it as recently as this past summer."

A moment ticked by before Jev wagged his head at the floor. He tipped his head back and laughed, almost disbelievingly. "You didn't." His laughter died abruptly. "Tell me you didn't drag your daughter into the middle of this."

"She saw a silver chain around your neck. This past June."

Jev's eyes sized up Hank. "How much does she know?"

"About me? She's learning. I don't like it, but my back's against the wall. Help me, and I won't use her again."

"You're assuming I care about your daughter."

"You care about one of them," Hank said with a sardonic twist of his lips. "Or used to."

A muscle in Jev's jaw twitched, and Hank laughed. "After all this time, you're still stoking the fire. A pity she doesn't know you exist. Speaking of my other daughter, I also heard she was seen wearing your necklace in June. She has it, doesn't she," he stated rather than inquired.

Jev returned Hank's even stare. "She doesn't have it."

"It would have been a genius plan," Hank said, not sounding in the least like he believed Jev. "It's not like I can torture its where-abouts out of her—she doesn't know anything." He laughed, but the sound didn't ring true. "Now that would be ironic. The one piece of information I need is buried deep in a mind I effectively erased."

"A shame."

With a flourish, Hank yanked the canvas off the cage. He kicked the metal box into the light, the base scraping over the floor. The girl's hair was tangled across her face, her eyes ringed in black and darting wildly around the warehouse, as though trying to memorize every detail of her prison before the canvas blinded her again.

"Well?" Hank asked the girl. "What do you think, my pet? Do you think we can find you an archangel's necklace in time?"

She turned toward Jev, and there was no mistaking the recognition widening her eyes. Her hands squeezed the bars of the cage so tightly her skin turned translucent. She snarled a word that sounded like "traitor." She glared between Hank and Jev, then her mouth snapped open with a piercing, howling scream.

The force of the scream hurled me backward. My body smashed through the walls of the warehouse. I flew through darkness, tumbling over and over. My stomach roiled, a great wave of nausea crashing over me.

And then I was sprawled facedown on the shoulder of the road, my hands curling into the gravel. I scrambled into a sitting position. The air was thick with the smell of cornfields. Night insects droned all around. Everything was exactly as it had been.

I didn't know how long I'd been out. Ten minutes? Half an hour? My skin was covered in a sheen of sweat, and this time my shivers were from the cold.

"Jev?" I called out hoarsely.

But he was gone.

CHAPTER

FOLLOWING JEV'S INSTRUCTIONS, I WALKED TO Whitetail Lodge. From the reception desk, I called a taxi. Even if I hadn't known my mom was at dinner, I might not have called her. I wasn't in any condition to talk. My head was filled with too much noise. Thoughts whizzed past, but I made no effort to pin them down. I felt myself shutting down, too overwhelmed to sort through everything that had happened tonight.

At the farmhouse, I climbed the stairs to my bedroom. I

stripped down. I stretched a nightshirt over my head. I curled into a fetal position under my blankets and fell asleep.

I was snapped awake by the sound of shoes moving at a brisk clip outside my door. I must have been dreaming of Jev, because my first foggy thought was, *It's him*, and I clutched the sheet to my chin, bracing myself for his entrance.

My mom flung the door open so hard it slapped the wall. "She's here!" she called over her shoulder. "She's in bed!" She crossed to me, clutching a fist over her heart as though to keep it from leaping out of her chest. "Nora! Why didn't you tell me where you'd gone? We've been driving all over town looking for you!" She was panting, her eyes wild and frantic.

"I told the hostess to tell you I called Vee for a ride," I stammered. Thinking back, it had been an irresponsible move. But caught up in the moment, seeing how my mom glowed in Hank's company, all I could think of was how my presence was an intrusion.

"I called Vee! She didn't know what I was talking about."

Of course she didn't. I'd never made it that far. Gabe had come along before I'd had a chance.

"You can't do that again," Mom said. "You can't ever do that again!"

Even though I knew it wouldn't help, I started crying. I hadn't meant to frighten her or send her chasing randomly after me. It was just that when I saw her with Hank . . . I'd *reacted*. And as much as I wanted to believe Gabe was out of my life for good, his implied threat that he wasn't finished with me was fresh in my thoughts. What had I gotten myself into? I considered how different the night would have turned out if I'd kept quiet and left the 7-Eleven when Gabe had given me the chance.

No. I'd done the right thing. If I hadn't stepped in, P.J. might not have survived.

"Oh, Nora."

I let my mom gather me against her and pressed my face into her blouse.

"This was just a bad scare, that's all," she said. "We'll be more careful next time."

The boards in the hall creaked, and I looked over to see Hank leaning on the door frame. "You gave us quite a fright, young lady." His voice was light and calm, but there was something almost wolfish in his eyes that caused a chill to tiptoe up my back.

"I don't want him here," I whispered to my mom. Even though I was sure there was no validity to my most recent hallucination, it haunted me. I couldn't stop picturing Hank tugging the canvas off the cage. I couldn't shut out the words he'd said. Logically, I knew I was projecting my own fears and anxieties on him, but either way, I wanted him to leave.

"I'll call you later, Hank," Mom said reassuringly over the top of my head. "After I tuck Nora in. Thank you again for dinner, and I'm sorry about the false alarm."

He gestured it off. "Don't fret, darling. You forget I have my own hormonal drama queen under my roof, though at least I can say she's never done anything this rash." He chuckled, as if he genuinely found any word he'd said amusing.

I waited until I heard his footsteps retreat down the hall. I wasn't sure how much to tell my mom, especially since Jev said the police couldn't be counted on and I feared that everything I said now would reach Detective Basso's ears, but too much had happened tonight not to tell anyone.

"I met someone tonight," I told my mom. "After I left Coopersmith's. I didn't recognize him, but he said we knew each other. I must have met him sometime in the last five months, but I can't remember."

Her hold on me grew taut. "Did he tell you his name?"

"Jev."

She'd been holding her breath, but now a little slip of air escaped. I wondered what it meant. Had she expected a different name?

"Do you know him?" I asked. Maybe she would be able to shed light on my history with Jev.

"No. Did he say how he knew you? From school, maybe? Or when you worked at Enzo's?"

I'd worked at Enzo's? This was news to me, and I was about to get clarification, when her eyes snapped back to mine. "Wait. What was he wearing?" She gestured impatiently. "What did his clothes look like?"

I felt my forehead crease in confusion. "Why does it matter?"

She stood, then paced to the door and back to the bed. As if suddenly aware of how anxious she looked, she parked herself in front of my dresser and nonchalantly examined a perfume bottle. "Maybe he was wearing a uniform with a logo? Or maybe he was dressed entirely in one color? Like . . . black?" She was clearly leading me, but why?

"He was wearing a white-and-navy baseball shirt with jeans."

Worry lines formed clear parentheses around her mouth, which was tightly pursed in thought.

"What aren't you telling me?" I asked.

The worry lines spread to her eyes.

"What do you know?" I demanded.

"There was a boy," she began.

I sat up a little taller. "What boy?" I couldn't help but wonder if she was talking about Jev. And I found myself hoping she was. I wanted to know more about him. I wanted to know everything about him.

"He came around a few times. He always dressed in black," she said with obvious distaste. "He was older and—please don't take this the wrong way, but I couldn't figure out what he saw in you. He'd dropped out of school, he had a gambling problem, and he worked clearing tables at the Borderline. I mean, for goodness' sake! I have nothing against clearing tables, but it was almost laughable. As if he thought you were going to stay in Coldwater forever. He couldn't begin to relate to your dreams, let alone keep up with them. I'd be very surprised if he had the determination to go to college."

"Did I like him?" Her description didn't sound like Jev, but I wasn't ready to give up just yet.

"Hardly! You had me make excuses every time he called. Eventually he got the picture and left you alone. The whole thing was very short-lived. A couple of weeks at most. I only brought him up because I always thought something about him was off. And I always wondered if he might have known something about your abduction. Not to be dramatic, but it seemed like a dark cloud settled over your life the day you met him."

"What happened to him?" I realized my heart was pounding in double time.

"He left town." She shook her head. "See? It couldn't have been him. I panicked, that's all. I wouldn't worry about him," she added, coming over and patting my knee. "He's probably halfway across the country by now."

"What was his name?"

She hesitated only a moment. "You know, I don't remember. Something with a P. Peter, maybe." She laughed louder than necessary. "I guess that proves just how insignificant he was."

I smiled absently at her joke, all the while hearing Jev's voice rumble through my mind.

We knew each other. We met five months ago, and I was bad news from the moment you laid eyes on me.

If Jev and this mysterious boy from my past were one and the same, someone wasn't giving me the full story. Maybe Jev *was* trouble. Maybe it was in my best interest to sprint in the opposite direction.

But something told me it wasn't because he was the hardened and indifferent person he was trying so hard to convince me he was. Right before the hallucination, I'd heard him say, *You're not supposed to be in this anymore. Even I can't keep you safe.*

My safety meant something to him. His actions tonight proved it. And *actions speak louder than words,* I told myself grimly.

Which left only two questions. What wasn't I supposed to be involved in anymore? And given the two—Jev and my mom—who was lying?

If they thought I was quite content to sit with my hands in my lap, the perfect model of a sweet, uninformed little girl, they weren't as smart as they thought.

CHAPTER

13

SATURDAY MORNING I WOKE EARLY, TUGGED ON cotton shorts and a tank, and went running. It felt strangely empowering to pound my feet against the pavement and sweat out all my immediate troubles. I was doing my best not to think about last night. So much for testing my courage by wandering around alone at night—as far as I was concerned, from now on, I'd be perfectly happy to stay locked up in my house the moment the moon showed its face. And if I never had to visit that particular 7-Eleven again, so much the better.

Strangely enough, it wasn't Gabe who was haunting my thoughts, though. That job belonged to a pair of sinfully black eyes that had lost their edge when they studied me, turning as soft and sultry as silk. Jev had told me not to go looking for him, but I couldn't stop fantasizing about all the different ways we might bump into each other again. In fact, the last dream I recalled before waking up this morning was of going to Ogunquit Beach with Vee, only to discover that Jev was the on-duty lifeguard. I'd pulled out of the dream with my heart thumping, and the strangest ache shredding me up inside. I could interpret the dream well enough myself: Despite the infuriated, tangled way he'd left me feeling, I wanted to see Jev again.

The sky was overcast, keeping the air cool, and after my stopwatch beeped to signal three miles, I gave it a smug smile and challenged myself to one more, not quite ready to give up my private thoughts about Jev. That, and I was enjoying myself immeasurably. I'd gone to spinning classes and Zumba at the gym with Vee, but out in the clean air, saturated with the smells of pine and dewy tree bark, I decided that hands down, I preferred sweating outdoors. After a while, I even tugged out my earbuds, allowing me to concentrate on the peaceful sounds of nature rising out of dawn.

At home I took a long, luxurious bath, then stood in front of my closet, biting the tip of my fingernail as I studied my wardrobe. In the end, I zipped myself into skinny jeans and tugged on knee-high boots and a turquoise silk camisole. Vee would remember the outfit, since she was the one who'd persuaded me to buy it during last summer's sidewalk sales. Scrutinizing myself in the mirror, I decided I passed as the same old Nora Grey. One step in the right direction, only a thousand or so more to go. I was a little worried what Vee and I would talk about, especially given the glaring issue of my kidnapping, but I reassured myself that that was what made Vee and me so compatible. I could strategically steer our conversation by raising certain subjects, and Vee could blather on forever about them. I just had to make sure I got her talking about what I wanted.

There was only one thing missing, I concluded, as I checked over my reflection. My outfit needed an accessory. Jewelry. No, a scarf.

I pulled out my dresser drawer, a sick feeling sweeping through me when I saw the long black feather. I'd forgotten about it. It was probably dirty. I made a mental note to throw it away as soon as I got back from lunch, but there wasn't much conviction behind the thought. I was wary of the feather—but not enough to give it up just yet. First I wanted to know what kind of bird had shed it, and I wanted an explanation for why I felt like it was my responsibility to keep it safe. It was a ridiculous thought and didn't make sense, but nothing had since I'd woken in the cemetery. Pushing the feather deeper to the back of the drawer, I grabbed the first scarf I saw.

Then I jogged downstairs, pocketed a ten-dollar bill from the freshly stocked petty cash drawer, and folded myself behind the wheel of the Volkswagen. I had to bang my fist on the dash four times before the engine caught, but I told myself it wasn't necessarily a sign of a dud. It meant this car was aged like, well, fine cheese. This car had seen the world. Chances are, it had hauled around at least a few interesting people. It was seasoned and experienced and held all the charm of 1984. Best of all, I hadn't paid a cent for it.

After pumping a few dollars' worth of gas into the tank, I motored over to Enzo's. Tidying my hair in the storefront window, I let myself inside.

I took off my sunglasses, soaking in the impressive setting. Enzo's had undergone a major makeover since I last remembered. A wide set of stairs led down to the front counter and a circular dining pit. Two catwalks spread out from either side of the hostess station, scattered with industrial aluminum tables that were part vintage, part chic. Big-band-style music played through the stereo system, and for a moment, I felt like I'd stumbled through time and landed in a speakeasy.

Vee was kneeling on her chair for height advantage, whipping her arm over her head like a propeller. "Babe! Over here!"

She met me halfway down the catwalk to my right and squeezed me into a hug. "I ordered iced mochas and a plate of sprinkled doughnuts for us. Man, we have so much to talk about. I wasn't going to tell you, but the heck with surprises. I lost three pounds. Can you tell?" She twirled in front of me.

"You look amazing," I told her, and I meant it. After all this time, we were finally together. She could have gained ten pounds, and I'd have thought she was absolutely beautiful.

"*Self* magazine said curves are a fall trend, so I'm feeling really confident," she said, plopping down into her chair. We were at a table set for four, but instead of taking the chair across from Vee, I slipped into one directly beside her. "So," she said, leaning forward conspiratorially, "tell me about last night. Holy freak show. I can't believe your mom and Hanky Panky."

I raised my eyebrows. "Hanky Panky?"

"We are so calling him Hanky Panky. It's so accurate it hurts."

"I think we should call him Frat Boy."

"That's what I'm talking about!" Vee said, slapping her palm down on the table. "How old do you think he is? Twenty-five? Maybe he's really Marcie's older brother. Maybe he has an Oedipus complex, and Marcie's mom is his mom *and* his wife!"

I was laughing so hard I accidentally snorted. Which only sent us into deeper hysterics.

"Okay, stop," I said, flattening my hands to my thighs and trying to muster a serious face. "This is mean. What if Marcie walked in and heard us?"

"What's she going to do? Poison me with her secret stash of Ex-Lax?"

Before I could respond, the two available chairs at our table scraped back, and Owen Seymour and Joseph Mancusi sat down. I knew both boys from school. Owen had been in Vee's and my biology class last year. He was tall and wiry, and wore studious-looking black glasses and Ralph Lauren polos. In sixth grade he'd beaten me out as our grade's representative in the citywide spelling bee. Not that I had hard feelings. I hadn't had a class with Joseph, or Joey, in years, but we'd known each other since elementary school, and his dad was Coldwater's only chiropractor. Joey bleached his hair, wore flips-flops even in the winter, and played drums in the marching band. I knew for a fact that in junior high, Vee had a crush on him.

Owen pushed his glasses up his nose and smiled benignly. I braced myself for a barrage of questions concerning my kidnapping, but he simply said in a slightly nervous voice, "We saw you guys sitting over here and thought we'd, uh, amble over."

"Gee, what a coincidence." Vee's curt tone startled me. Not typical for Vee, who was a self-proclaimed flirt, but maybe she was going for deadpan? "And what do you mean 'amble over'? Who talks like that anymore?"

"Er, have any plans for the rest of the weekend?" Joey asked, folding his hands on the table, where they rested a few inches from Vee's.

She drew back, stiffening her spine. "Plans that don't include you."

Okay, not deadpan. I peeked sideways at her, trying to catch her eye long enough to nonverbally articulate, *What's wrong?* but she was too busy evil-eyeing Owen.

"If you don't mind," she said, clearly implying that it was time for them to leave.

Owen and Joey exchanged brief, perplexed looks.

"Remember when we had PE together in seventh grade?" Joey asked Vee. "You were my badminton partner. You totally rocked at badminton. If memory serves, we won the class tournament." He raised his hand to give her a high five.

"Not in the mood to stroll down memory lane."

Joey slowly dropped his hand beneath the table. "Er, right. Uh, you sure you don't want us to buy you guys a lemonade or something?"

"So you can spike it with GHB? Pass. Besides, we've already got drinks, something you might have noticed if you were actually looking higher than our chests." She rattled her iced mocha in his face.

"Vee," I said under my breath. First of all, neither Owen nor Joey had been looking anywhere remotely close to where Vee insinuated, and second of all, *what was the matter with her?*

"Um . . . okay . . . sorry to bother," Owen said, rising awkwardly to his feet. "We just thought—"

"You thought wrong," Vee snapped. "Whatever evil schemes you two have in mind? Ain't gonna happen."

"Evil what?" Owen repeated, pushing up his glasses again and blinking owlishly.

"We get it," Joey said. "We shouldn't have butted in. Private girl conversation. I have sisters," he said knowingly. "Next time we'll, uh, ask first?"

"There isn't going to be a next time," Vee said. "Consider Nora and me"—she jerked her thumb between the two of us—"closed to your business."

I cleared my throat, trying but failing to figure out how to salvage this long enough to end on a positive note. Clean out of ideas, I did the only thing I could. With an apologetic smile, I told Owen and Joey, "Um, thanks, guys. Have a nice day." It sounded like a question.

"Yeah, thanks for nothing," Vee called after them as they backed away, their whole faces screwed up in bewilderment.

When they were out of hearing range, she said, "What is up with guys today? They think they can just stroll over, flash a pretty smile, and we'll melt in their hands? Uh-uh. No way. Not us. We're wiser than that. They can take their romance scam somewhere else, thank you very much."

I cleared my throat. "Wow."

"Don't wow me. I know you saw right through those guys too."

I scratched my eyebrow. "Personally, I think they were just making conversation . . . but what do I know," I quickly added when she cast a withering glare at me.

"When a guy shows up out of nowhere and instantly turns on

the charm, it's a front. There's always a deeper motive. This much I know."

I sucked on my straw. I wasn't sure what else to say. I'd never be able to look Owen or Joey in the eye again, but maybe Vee was having a day. Maybe she was in a mood. When I watched Lifetime original movies, it took me a day or two to get over the idea that the cute boy next door is actually a serial killer. Maybe Vee was going through a similar fade-back-to-reality phase.

I was about to ask her directly, when my cell phone chirped.

"Let me guess," Vee said. "That would be your mom checking up on you. I was surprised she let you out of the house. It's no secret she doesn't like me. For a while there, I think she even thought I was some-how mixed up in your disappearance." She made a grunt of contempt.

"She likes you, she just doesn't understand you," I said, opening what appeared to be a text message from none other than Marcie Millar.

BTW, THE NECKLACE IS A MAN'S SILVER CHAIN. DID U FIND IT?

"Give it a rest," I muttered out loud.

"Well?" Vee said. "What lame excuse did that woman give to drag you home?"

HOW DID U GET MY NUMBER? I texted Marcie.

OUR PARENTS SWAP MORE THAN SPIT, DUMB-A.

Right back at you, I thought.

I shut my phone and gave my attention back to Vee. "Can I ask a stupid question?"

"My favorite kind."

"Did I go to a party at Marcie's over the summer?"

I braced myself for a round of over-the-top laughter, but Vee simply chewed off a bite of doughnut and said, "Yeah, I remember that. You dragged me along too. You still owe me for that, by the way."

Not the response I'd anticipated. "Weirder question. Was I" — here goes nothing—"friends with Marcie?"

Now came the reaction I'd been expecting. Vee nearly coughed her doughnut onto the table. "You and the ho, friends? Did I hear that right? I know you've got the whole temporary memory loss thing going on, but how could you forget eleven years' worth of Little Miss Pain in the You Know What?"

Now we were getting somewhere. "What am I missing? If we weren't friends, why did she invite me to her party?"

"She invited everybody. She was fund-raising for new cheerleading costumes. She wanted twenty bucks from us at the door," Vee explained. "We almost left right then, but you just had to spy on—" She snapped her mouth shut.

"Spy on who?" I prodded.

"Marcie. We went to spy on Marcie. That's how it was." She was nodding a little too vigorously.

"And?"

"We wanted to nab her diary," Vee said. "We were going to print all the juicy parts in the eZine. Pretty epic, right?"

I observed her, knowing something was wrong with this picture, but failing to figure out what. "You realize how made-up that sounds, right? We'd never get permission to publish her diary."

"Never hurts to try."

I pointed a finger at her. "I know you're keeping something from me."

"Who, me?"

"Spill it, Vee. You promised not to hold out on me again," I reminded her.

Vee flapped her arms. "All right, all right. We went to spy on"—dramatic pause—"Anthony Amowitz."

Anthony Amowitz and I had shared the same PE class last year. Average height, average looks. The personality of a pig. Not to mention Vee had already sworn there was nothing between them. "You lie."

"I—had a crush on him." She blushed furiously.

"You had a crush on Anthony Amowitz," I repeated doubtfully.

"A lapse in judgment. Can we not talk about it, please?"

After eleven years, Vee could still surprise. "First, swear that you aren't holding anything back. Because this whole story sounds shaky."

"Girl Scout's honor," Vee said, eyes clear, expression determined. "We went to spy on Anthony, end of story. Just please keep the verbal abuse to a minimum. I'm humiliated enough as it is."

Vee wouldn't lie to me again, not after we'd just been over this, so despite a few rocky details that I chalked up to embarrassment, I was content with the knowledge I'd been given.

silence

"Okay," I relented, "back to Marcie, then. She cornered me at Coopersmith's last night and told me her boyfriend, Patch, gave me a necklace that I was supposed to pass on to her."

Vee choked on her drink. "She said Patch was her boyfriend?"

"I believe the exact term she used was 'summer fling.' She said Patch was friends with both of us."

"Huh."

I tapped my finger impatiently on the table. "Why do I feel like I'm in the dark all over again?"

"I don't know any Patches," Vee said. "Anyhow, isn't that a dog's name? Maybe she made him up. If Marcie is good at one thing, it's messing with people's minds. Best to forget all about Patch and Marcie. Boy, oh, boy, aren't these doughnuts to die for?" She thrust one at my face.

I took the doughnut, set it aside. "Does the name Jev ring a bell?"

"Jev? Just Jev? Is that short for something?"

By the sound of it, Vee had never heard his name before.

"I ran into a guy," I explained. "I think we knew each other, maybe from over the summer. His name is Jev."

"Can't help you, babe."

"Maybe it is short for something. Jevin, Jevon, Jevro . . ."

"No, no, and nope."

I opened my cell.

"What are you doing now?" Vee asked.

"Sending Marcie a text."

"What are you going to ask her?" She scooted up taller. "Listen, Nora—"

I shook my head, guessing Vee's thoughts. "This isn't the start of a long-term thing, trust me. I believe you, not Marcie. This will be the last text I ever send to her. I'm going to tell her *nice try* on her big fat lies."

Vee's expression lost its tension. She nodded sagely. "You tell her, babe. Tell that cheat her lies are futile with me watching your back."

I keyed in my text and hit send.

LOOKED EVERYWHERE. NO NECKLACE. BUMMER.

Less than a minute later, her response bounced back.

LOOK HARDER.

"Cheery as ever," I muttered.

"Here's what I think," said Vee. "Your mom and Hanky Panky might not be such a bad thing. If it gives you a leg up on Marcie, I'd say promote the relationship full force."

I gave her a sly look. "Of course you would."

"Hey now, none of that. You know I don't have one evil bone in my body."

"Only two hundred and six of them?"

Vee grinned. "Have I mentioned how good it is to have you back?"

CHAPTER

14

AFTER LUNCH, I DROVE HOME. LESS THAN A MINUTE after I'd parked the Volkswagen on the cement slab beside the driveway, my mom bounced her Taurus into the drive. She'd been home when I left earlier, and I wondered if she'd slipped out for lunch with Hank. I hadn't stopped smiling since leaving Enzo's, but my mood cooled suddenly.

Mom pulled into the garage and came out to meet me. "How was lunch with Vee?"

"Same old, same old. What about you? Hot lunch date?" I inquired innocently.

"More like work." She released a long-suffering sigh. "Hugo asked me to travel to Boston this week."

My mom works for Hugo Renaldi, owner of an auction company of the same name. Hugo conducts high-end estate auctions, and it's my mom's job to make sure the auctions run smoothly, something she can't do long distance. She's constantly on the road, leaving me home alone, and we both know it's not an ideal situation. She'd considered quitting in the past, but it always came down to money. Hugo paid her more—quite a bit more—than she'd make anywhere inside Coldwater's city limits. If she quit, several sacrifices would have to be made, starting with selling the farmhouse. Since every memory I had of my dad was wrapped up in the house, you could say I was sentimental about it.

"I turned him down," Mom said. "I told him I'm going to need to find a job that doesn't require me to leave home."

"You told him *what*?" My surprise wore off quickly, and I felt alarm creep into my tone. "You're quitting? Have you found a new job? Does this mean we're going to have to move?" I couldn't believe she'd made this decision without me. In the past, we had always taken the same stance: Moving was out of the question.

"Hugo said he'd see what he can do about giving me a local position, but not to get my hopes up. His secretary has been working for him for years and does her job well. He's not going to let her go just to keep me happy."

I stared at the farmhouse, stunned. The thought of another family living inside its walls made my stomach roll. What if they remodeled? What if they gutted my dad's study and tore out the cherry floors we'd installed together? And what about his bookshelves? They weren't perfectly straight, but they'd been our first genuine attempt at woodworking. They had character!

"I'm not worried about selling yet," Mom said. "Something will come up. Who knows? Maybe Hugo will realize he needs two secretaries. If it's meant to be, it'll happen."

I turned on her. "Are you so casual about quitting because you're counting on marrying Hank and having him bail us out?" The cynical observation sprang out before I could stop it, and I immediately felt a wrench of guilt. This kind of rudeness was beneath me. But I'd spoken from that hollow place of fear that hid deep in my chest and overruled all.

Mom's entire posture went stiff. Then she clicked off through the garage, punching the button that automatically lowered the door behind her.

I stood in the driveway a moment, torn between wanting to go straight inside and apologize, and growing fear over her easy avoidance of my question. So that was that. She was dating Hank with every intention of marrying him. She was doing the very thing Marcie had accused her of: thinking of the money. I knew our finances were tight, but we'd survived, hadn't we? I resented my mom for stooping so low, and I resented Hank for giving her a choice other than making do with me.

Dropping back into the Volkswagen, I drove across town. I was going fifteen over, but for once, I didn't care. I didn't have a destination in mind—I simply wanted to put distance between me and my mom. First Hank, and now her job. Why did I feel like she kept making decisions without consulting me?

When the entrance to the highway appeared in the lane ahead, I hung right and followed it to the coast. I took the last exit before Delphic Amusement Park and followed signs to the public beaches. This stretch of coast saw far less traffic than the southern beaches of Maine. The coastline was rocky, and evergreens sprang up just out of reach of high tide. Instead of tourists with beach towels and picnic baskets, I saw a lone hiker and a dog chasing seagulls.

Which was exactly what I wanted. I needed time alone to cool down.

I jerked the Volkswagen curbside. In the rearview mirror, a souped-up red car glided in behind me. I vaguely remembered seeing it on the highway, always hanging a few cars back. The driver probably wanted to squeeze in one last trip to the beach before the weather changed for the worse.

I jumped the guardrail and climbed down the rocky embankment. The air was cooler than it had been in Coldwater, and a steady wind pummeled my back. The sky was more gray than blue, and hazy. I stayed above the reach of the waves, scaling the higher rocks. The terrain grew increasingly difficult to navigate, and I kept my concentration glued on careful foot placement rather than my latest fight with my mom.

My boot slipped on a rock, and I went down, landing awkwardly on my side. Muttering under my breath, I regained my footing, and that was when a large shadow fell over me. Taken by surprise, I flipped around. I recognized the driver from the red car. He was taller than average and had a year or two on me. His hair was cut utilitarian short, with sandy-brown eyebrows and a touch of hair at his chin. By the fit of his sweatshirt, he hit the gym regularly.

"About time you left your house," he said, glancing around. "I've been trying to get you alone for days."

I pushed to my feet, balancing on a rock. I searched his face for familiarity, but the lights didn't come on. "I'm sorry, do we know each other?"

"Do you think you were followed?" His eyes continued to rove the coastline. "I tried to keep tabs on all the cars, but I might have missed one. It would have helped if you'd circled the block before parking."

"Uh, I honestly have no idea who you are."

"That's a strange thing to say to the guy who bought the car you drove here in."

A moment ticked by before I wrapped my head around his

words. "Wait. You're—Scott Parnell?" Even though it had been years, the similarities were there. The same dimple in his cheek. The same hazel eyes. More recent additions included the scar across his cheekbone, the five o'clock shadow, and the juxtaposition of a full, sensuous mouth with sculpted, symmetrical features.

"I heard about your amnesia. Rumors are true, then? Looks like it's as bad as they say."

My, my, wasn't he optimistic. I crossed my arms over my chest and said coolly, "While we're on the subject, maybe now's a good time to tell me why you ditched the Volkswagen at my house the night I disappeared. If you know about my amnesia, surely you've heard I was kidnapped."

"The car was an apology for being a jerk." His eyes still flicked over the trees. Who was he so worried had followed us?

"Let's talk about that night," I stated. Out here all alone didn't seem like the best place to have this conversation, but my determination to get answers won out. "It seems we were both shot by Rixon earlier that night. That's what I told the police. You, me, and Rixon alone in the fun house. If Rixon even exists. I don't know how you pulled it off, but I'm starting to think you invented him. I'm starting to think you shot me and needed someone else to blame. Did you force me to give Rixon's name to the police? And next question, did you shoot me, Scott?"

"Rixon's in hell now, Nora."

I flinched. He'd said it without any hesitation and with just the right amount of melancholy. If he was lying, he deserved an award.

"Rixon's dead?"

"He's burning in hell, but yeah, same basic idea. Dead works, as far as I'm concerned."

I scrutinized his face, watching for the slightest false movement. I wasn't going to argue specifics of the afterlife with him, but I needed confirmation that Rixon was gone for good. "How do you know? Have you told the police? Who killed him?"

"I don't know who we get to thank, but I know he's gone. Word travels fast, trust me."

"You're going to have to do better than that. You might have the rest of the world fooled, but I'm not bought that easily. You dumped a car in my driveway the night I was kidnapped. Then you ran off into hiding—New Hampshire, was it? Forgive me if the last word that comes to mind when I see you is 'innocent.' I think it goes without saying: I don't trust you."

He sighed. "Before Rixon shot us, you convinced me that I really am Nephilim. You're the one who told me I can't die. You're part of the reason I ran away. You were right. I was never going to end up like the Black Hand. No way was I going to help him recruit more Nephilim to his army."

The wind pierced my clothes, breathing like frost against my skin. Nephilim. That word again. Following me everywhere. "I told you that you're Nephilim?" I asked nervously. I closed my eyes briefly, praying he would correct himself. Praying that he'd been

BECCA FITZPATRICK

using the words "can't die" figuratively. Praying this was where he explained that he was the final stop in an elaborate hoax that had started last night, with Gabe. A big hoax, and the joke was on me.

But the truth was there, stirring in that murky place where my memory had once been intact. I couldn't rationalize it in my head, but I could *feel* it. Inside me. Burning in my chest. Scott wasn't making this up.

"What I want to know is why you can't remember any of this," he said. "I thought amnesia wasn't permanent. What gives?"

"I don't know why I can't remember!" I snapped. "Okay? *I don't know.* I woke up a few nights ago in the cemetery with nothing. I couldn't even remember how I'd gotten there." I wasn't sure why I felt the sudden urge to spill everything to Scott, but there it was. My nose began to run, and I could feel tears forming behind my eyes. "The police found me and took me to the hospital. They said I'd been missing for nearly three months. They said I have amnesia because my mind is blocking the trauma to protect myself. But you want to know what's crazy? I'm starting to think I'm not blocking anything. I got a note. Someone broke into my house and left it on my pillow. It said even though I'm home, I'm not safe. Someone is behind this. They know what I don't. They know what happened to me."

Right then, I realized I'd divulged too much. I had *no* evidence the note existed. Worse, logic proved it didn't. But if the note was a figment of my imagination, why did the thought of it refuse to fade?

Why couldn't I accept that I'd invented, contrived, or hallucinated it?

Scott studied me with a deepening frown. "They?"

I threw my hands up. "Forget it."

"Did the note say anything else?"

"I said drop it. Do you have a Kleenex?" I could feel the skin under my eyes growing puffy, and I was past the point where sniffling was helping to keep my nose dry. As if that weren't bad enough, two tears tumbled down my cheek.

"Hey," Scott said gently, grasping me by the shoulders. "It's going to be okay. Don't cry, all right? I'm on your side. I'll help you figure out this mess." When I didn't resist, he pulled me against his chest and patted my back. Awkwardly at first, and then he settled into a soothing rhythm. "The night you went missing, I went into hiding. It's not safe for me here, but when I saw on the news you were back and couldn't remember anything, I had to come out of hiding. I had to find you. I owe you that much."

I knew I should pull away. Just because I wanted to believe Scott didn't mean I should trust him completely. Or let down my guard. But I was tired of throwing up walls, and I let my defenses slip. I couldn't remember the last time it had felt so good just to be held. In his embrace, I could almost make myself believe I wasn't in this alone. Scott had promised we'd get through this together, and I wanted to believe him on that count as well.

Plus, he *knew* me. He was a link to my past, and that meant more to me than I could put into words. After so many discouraging attempts at remembering any fragment my memory saw fit to throw at me, he'd appeared without any effort on my part. It was more than I could have asked for.

Wiping my eyes on the back of my arm, I said, "Why isn't it safe for you here?"

"The Black Hand is here." As if remembering that the name meant nothing to me, he said, "Just to make sure we're clear, you remember nothing of this? I mean, nothing as in *nothing*?"

"Nothing." With that one word, I felt as though I were standing at the opening of a forbidding labyrinth that stretched to the horizon.

"Sucks to be you," he said, and despite his word choice, I believed he sincerely meant he was sorry. "The Black Hand is the nickname of a powerful Nephil. He's building an underground army, and I used to be one of his soldiers, for lack of a better word. Now I'm a deserter, and if he catches me, it won't be pretty."

"Back up. What is a Nephil?"

Scott's mouth quirked up on one side. "Get ready to feel your mind blow, Grey. A Nephil," he explained patiently, "is an immortal." His smile tipped even higher at my dubious expression. "I can't die. None of us can."

"What's the catch?" I asked. He couldn't really mean immortal as in *immortal*.

He gestured to the ocean shattering itself against the rocks far below. "If I jump, I'll live."

Okay, so maybe he'd been stupid enough to make the jump

before. And survived. That didn't prove anything. He wasn't immortal. He simply believed he was because he was a typical teenage guy who'd done a few reckless things, lived to talk about them, and now he believed he was invincible.

Scott arched his eyebrows in mock offense. "You don't believe me. Last night I spent a good two hours in the ocean, diving for fish, and I didn't freeze to death. I can hold my breath down there for eight, nine minutes. Sometimes I pass out, but when I come around, I've always floated to the surface, and all my vital signs are up and working."

I opened my mouth, but it took a minute for words to form. "That doesn't make sense."

"It makes sense if I'm immortal."

Before I could stop him, Scott whipped out a Swiss Army knife and drove it into his thigh. I gave a strangled scream and leaped for him, unsure if I should pull out the knife or stabilize it. Before I'd made up my mind, he yanked it out himself. He swore in pain, his jeans seeping blood.

"Scott!" I shrieked.

"Come back tomorrow," he said in a more subdued voice. "It will be like it never happened."

"Oh, yeah?" I snapped, still worked up. Was he completely out of his mind? Why would he do such a stupid thing?

"It's not the first time I've done it. I've tried to burn myself alive. My skin was torched—gone. A couple days later, I was as good as new."

Even now I could see the blood on his jeans drying. The wound had stopped bleeding. He was . . . healing. In seconds rather than weeks. I didn't want to trust my eyes, but seeing *was* believing.

All of a sudden, I remembered Gabe. More clearly than I wanted to, I summoned up a visual of a tire iron projecting from his back. Jev had sworn the injury wouldn't kill Gabe. . . .

Just like Scott swore his wound would heal without so much as a scratch.

"Okay, then," I whispered, even though I was anything but okay.

"You sure you're convinced? I could always throw myself in front of a car if you need more proof."

"I think I believe you," I said, failing to keep the dazed bewilderment out of my tone.

I forced myself to snap out of my stupor. For now, I was going to go with the flow as much as I could. *Focus on one thing at a time*, I told myself. *Scott is immortal. Okay. What's next?*

"Do we know who the Black Hand is?" I asked, suddenly hungry to get my hands on any information Scott might have. What else was I missing? How many more of my beliefs could he send spinning on their heads? And highest priority: Could he help mend my memory?

"Last we spoke, we both wanted to know. I spent the summer following leads, which wasn't easy, given that I'm living on the run, clean out of cash, working solo, and the Black Hand isn't what you'd call careless. But I've narrowed it down to one man." His eyes swept to mine. "You ready for this? The Black Hand is Hank Millar."

"Hank is *what*?"

We were sitting on two tree stumps in a cave, about a quarter mile up the coast, tucked around a jutting cliff, and far out of view of the road. The cave was semi-dark with a low ceiling, but it offered protection from the wind and, as Scott had insisted, concealed us from any potential spies of the Black Hand. He'd refused to say another word until he was certain we were alone.

Scott struck a match on the bottom of his shoe and lit a fire in a pit of rocks. Light glinted off the jagged walls, and I got my first good look around. There was a backpack and a sleeping bag against the back wall. A cracked mirror was propped against a rock that jutted out like a shelf, along with a razor, a can of shaving cream, and a stick of deodorant. Closer to the mouth of the cave was a large toolbox. On it rested a few dishes, silverware, and a frying pan. Beside it lay a fishing pole and an animal trap. The cave both impressed and saddened me. Scott was anything but helpless, clearly able to survive on his own knowledge and fortitude. But what kind of life did he have, hiding and running from one place to the next?

"I've been watching Hank for months," Scott said. "This isn't a stab in the dark."

"Are you sure Hank is the Black Hand? No offense, but he

doesn't fit my picture of an underground militarist or—" An *immortal man*. The thought seemed unreal. No, absurd. "He runs the most successful car dealership in town, he's a member of the yacht club, and he single-handedly supports their fund-raising. Why would he care what's going on in the world of Nephilim? He already has everything he could possibly want."

"Because he's Nephilim too," Scott explained. "And he doesn't have everything he wants. During the Jewish month of Cheshvan, all Nephilim who've sworn an oath of fealty have to give up their body for two weeks. They don't have a choice. They give it up and someone else possesses it—a fallen angel. Rixon was the fallen angel who used to possess the Black Hand, and that's how I came to hear he's burning in hell. The Black Hand might be free, but he hasn't forgotten and he's not about to forgive. That's what the army is for. He's going to try to overthrow the fallen angels."

"Back up. Who are the fallen angels?" A gang? That's what it sounded like. I was increasingly doubtful. Hank Millar was the last person in Coldwater who'd lower himself to associate with gangs. "And what do you mean 'possesses'?"

Scott's mouth twitched with a disparaging smile, but to his credit, he answered with patience. "Definition of a fallen angel: heaven's rejects and a Nephil's worst nightmare. They force us to swear fealty, and then possess our bodies during Cheshvan. They're parasites. They can't feel anything in their own bodies, so they invade ours. Yeah, Grey," he said at the look of abhorrence I was sure was frozen on my face. "I mean they literally come inside us and use our bodies like their own. A Nephil is mentally there while they do it, but doesn't have any control."

I tried to swallow Scott's explanation. More than once, I imagined the theme song of The Twilight Zone playing in the background, but the truth of the matter was, I knew he wasn't lying. It was all coming back. The memories were splintered and damaged, but they were there. I'd learned this all before. When or how, I didn't know. But I knew this—all of it. I said, "The other night I saw three guys beating up a Nephil. That's what they were doing? Trying to force him to give up his body for two weeks? That's inhumane. It's—repulsive!"

Scott had dropped his eyes, stirring the fire with a stick. My mistake hit me too late. Shame swept through me and I whispered, "Oh, Scott. I wasn't thinking. I'm so sorry you have to go through that. I can't imagine how hard it must be to give up your body."

"I haven't sworn fealty. And I'm not going to." He tossed the stick on the fire, and gold sparks showered into the dark, smoky air of the cave. "If nothing else, that's what the Black Hand taught me. Fallen angels can try any mind-trick on me they want. They can chop my head off, cut out my tongue, and burn me to ash. But I'll never swear that oath. I can handle pain. But I can't handle the consequences of that oath."

"Mind-trick?" The skin at the back of my neck tingled, and my thoughts turned once more to Gabe.

"A perk of being a fallen angel," he said bitterly. "You get to mess with people's minds. Make them see things that aren't real. Nephilim inherited the trick from fallen angels."

It seemed I'd been right about Gabe after all. But he hadn't used a magician's sleight of hand to create the illusion of turning himself into a bear, as Jev had let me believe. He'd used a Nephilim weapon—mind control.

"Show me how it's done. I want to know exactly how it works."

"I'm out of practice," was all he said, rocking back on his stump and lacing his hands behind his head.

"Can't you at least try?" I said with a playful shot to his knee, hoping to lighten the mood. "Show me what we're up against. Come on. Surprise me. Make me see something I'm not expecting. Then teach me how it's done."

When Scott continued to stare at the fire, the light illuminating the hard edges of his features, the smile slipped from my face. This was anything but a joke to him.

"Here's the thing," he said. "Those powers are addictive. When you get a taste of them, it's hard to stop. When I ran away three months ago and realized what I was capable of, I used my powers every chance I got. If I was hungry, I'd walk into a store, throw what I wanted into a cart, and mind-trick the clerk into bagging my stuff and letting me walk out without paying. It was easy. It made me feel superior. It wasn't until I was spying on the Black Hand one night, and saw him do the same thing, that I quit cold turkey. I'm not going to live the rest of my life like that. I'm not going to be like him." He pulled a ring out of his pocket, holding it up in the light. It appeared to be made of iron, and the crown of the ring was stamped with a clenched fist. For one fleeting moment, a strange blue halo of light seemed to radiate from the metal. But it immediately vanished, and I wrote it off as a trick of the light.

"All Nephilim have heightened strength, making us physically more powerful than humans, but when I wear this ring, it takes that strength to a whole different level," Scott said solemnly. "The Black Hand gave me the ring after he tried to recruit me to his army. I don't know what kind of curse or enchantment is on the ring, or if it's even one of those. But there's *something*. Anyone with one of these rings is almost physically unstoppable. Before you disappeared in June, you stole the ring from me. The pull to get it back was so intense I didn't sleep, eat, or rest until I found it. I was like a junkie searching for the one thing that could give me my next high. I broke into your house one night after you were kidnapped. I found it in your bedroom in your violin case."

"Cello," came my murmured correction. Faint recollection stirred inside me, a sensation of having seen the ring before.

"I'm not the smartest guy, but I know this ring isn't harmless. The Black Hand did something to it. He wanted a way to give every member of his army an advantage. Even when I'm not wearing the ring, and just relying on my natural strength and powers, the pull for more of both is strong. The only way to beat

BECCA FITZPATRICK

it is to lay off using my powers and abilities as much as I can."

I tried to sympathize with Scott, but I was a little disappointed. I needed to gain a better understanding of how Gabe had tricked me in case I found myself face-to-face with him again. And if Hank really was the Black Hand, the leader of an underground and nonhuman militia, I had to wonder if he was in my life for reasons darker than met the eye. After all, if he was so busy battling fallen angels, how did he have time to run his dealership, be a father, and date my mom? Maybe I was suspicious, but given everything Scott had just told me, I was pretty sure it was warranted.

I needed someone on my side who could go up against Hank, if it came to that. Right now, the only person I knew of was Scott. I wanted him to keep his integrity, but at the same time, he was the only person I knew of who stood a chance against Hank.

"Maybe you could try using the ring's powers for good," I suggested softly after a minute.

Scott scrubbed a hand through his hair, obviously ready to drop the subject. "Too late. I've made my decision. I won't wear the ring. It connects me to him."

"Don't you ever worry that if you don't wear the ring, it will give Hank a dangerous advantage?"

His eyes caught mine, but he avoided answering. "You hungry? I can catch us some bass. It tastes decent pan-seared over the fire." Without waiting for my response, he grabbed the fishing pole and descended the rocks leading down from the cave.

I followed after him, suddenly wishing I could swap my boots for tennis shoes. Scott navigated the rocks in strides and jumps, whereas I was forced to take one cautious step after another.

"Fine, I'll put all talk of your powers on hold," I called after him, "but I'm not finished. There are still way too many gaps. Let's go back to the night I disappeared. Do you have any guesses as to who kidnapped me?"

Scott took a seat on a rock, threading his line with bait. By the time I caught up to him, he was almost finished.

"At first I thought it had to be Rixon," he said. "That was before I learned he's in hell. I wanted to come back and look for you, but it wasn't that simple. The Black Hand has spies everywhere. And given what happened in the fun house, I figured I'd have the cops on my tail too."

"But?"

"But I didn't." He looked sideways at me. "Don't you find it a little strange? The cops had to have known I was in the fun house that night with you and Rixon. You would have told them. You probably told them I was shot, too. So why didn't they ever come looking for me? Why'd they let me off the hook? It's almost like—" He caught himself.

"Like what?"

"Like someone came in after and cleaned up. And I'm not talk-ing about physical evidence. I'm talking about mind-tricks. Erasing memories. Someone powerful enough to make the police look the other way."

"A Nephil, you mean."

A shrug. "It makes sense, doesn't it? Maybe the Black Hand didn't want the police looking for me. Maybe he wanted to find me himself and take care of me off the record. If he finds me, trust me, he's not handing me over to the police for questioning. He'll lock me in one of his prisons and make me regret the day I ran out on him."

So we were looking for someone strong enough to tamper with minds, or as Scott put it, erase memories. The correlation to my own lost memory didn't slip past me. Could a Nephil have done this to me? A knot tightened in my stomach as I pondered the possibility.

"How many Nephilim have that kind of power?" I asked.

"Who knows? Definitely the Black Hand."

"Have you ever heard of a Nephil named Jev? Or a fallen angel, for that matter?" I added, increasingly aware that Jev was most likely one or the other. Not that the realization made me feel the least bit consoled.

"No. But that's not saying much. Almost as soon as I found out about Nephilim, I had to go into hiding. Why?"

"The other night I met a guy named Jev. He knew about Nephilim. He stopped the three guys—" I caught myself. No need to be vague, even though it was easier on my state of mind. "He stopped the fallen angels I told you about from forcing a Nephil named P.J. into swearing fealty. This is going to sound crazy, but Jev gave off some kind of energy. I felt it like electricity. It was a lot stronger than anything the others gave off."

"Probably a good indicator of his power," Scott said. "Taking on three fallen angels speaks for itself."

"He's that powerful, and you've never heard of him?"

"Believe it or not, I know about as much as you when it comes to this stuff."

I remembered Jev's words to me. I tried to kill you. What did that mean? Was he mixed up with my kidnapping after all? And was he strong enough to erase my memory? Based on the intensity of the power radiating from him, he was capable of more than a few simple mind-tricks. A lot more.

"Knowing what I do about the Black Hand, I'm surprised I'm still a free man," Scott said. "He must hate that I've made a fool of him."

"About that. Why did you desert Hank's army?"

Scott sighed, dropping his hands heavily on his knees. "This is a conversation I didn't want to have. There's no easy way to say this, so I'm just going to put it out there. The night your dad died, I was supposed to keep an eye on him. He was on his way to a dangerous meeting, and the Black Hand wanted to make sure he was safe. The Black Hand said if I succeeded, it proved he could count on me. He wanted me in his army, but it wasn't what I wanted."

A chill of premonition tingled up my spine. The last thing I'd expected was for Scott to bring my dad into this. "My dad—knew Hank Millar?"

"I blew off the Black Hand's order. Figured I'd give him the finger and make my point. But all I really succeeded in doing was letting an innocent man die."

I blinked, Scott's words cascading over me like a bucket of ice water. "You let my dad die? You let him walk into danger and did nothing to help him?"

Scott spread his hands. "I didn't know it was going to be like that. I thought the Black Hand was crazy. I had him pegged as an egotistical freak. I never got the whole Nephilim thing. Not until it was too late."

I set my eyes straight ahead, staring steadfastly at the ocean. An unwanted sensation clenched my chest, squeezing relentlessly. My dad. All this time, Scott had known the truth. He hadn't given it to me until I'd dragged it out of him.

"Rixon pulled the trigger," Scott said, his voice breaking quietly into my thoughts. "I let your dad walk into a trap, but it was Rixon who stood at the end of it."

"Rixon," I repeated. In bitter pieces, it was all coming back. One awful glimpse at a time. Rixon leading me into the fun house. Rixon admitting matter-of-factly that he'd killed my dad. Rixon leveling his gun at me. I couldn't remember enough to paint the full picture, but the flashes were enough. I was sick to my stomach.

"If Rixon didn't kidnap me, who did?" I asked.

"Remember how I said I spent the summer following the Black Hand? At the beginning of August, he made a trip out to White Mountain National Forest. He drove to a remote cabin and stayed less than twenty minutes. A long drive for such a short visit, right? I didn't dare get close enough to look in the windows, but I overheard a conversation he had on his phone a couple days later, back in Coldwater. He told the person on the other line that the girl was still at the cabin, and he needed to know she was a clean slate. Those were his words. He said there was no room for error. I'm starting to wonder if the girl he was referring to—"

"Was me," I finished for him, stunned. Hank Millar, an immortal. Hank Millar, the Black Hand. Hank, possibly my kidnapper.

"There's one dude who could probably get answers," Scott said, tugging his eyebrow. "If anyone knows how to get information, it's him. Tracking him down could get tricky. I wouldn't know where to start. And given the circumstances, he might not jump to help us, especially since the last time I saw him, he nearly broke my jaw for trying to kiss you."

I flinched. "Kiss *me*? What? Who is this guy?"

Scott frowned. "That's right. I guess you wouldn't remember him, either. Your ex—Patch."

15

"BACK UP," I ORDERED. "PATCH WAS MY EX?" This didn't match with Marcie's story. Or Vee's, for that matter.

"The two of you broke up. Something to do with Marcie, I think." He flipped his palms up. "That's all I know. I moved back to town in the middle of the drama."

"Are you sure he was my boyfriend?"

"Your words, not mine."

"What did he look like?"

"Scary."

"Where is he now?" I asked more forcefully.

"Like I said, finding him won't be easy."

"Do you know anything about a necklace he might have given me?"

"You ask a lot of questions."

"Marcie said Patch was her boyfriend. She said he gave me a necklace that belongs to her, and now she wants it back. She said he made me see the good in her and brought us together."

Scott stroked his chin. His eyes laughed at me. "And you bought it?"

My mind reeled. Patch was my boyfriend? Why had Marcie lied? To get the necklace? What could she possibly want with it?

If Patch was my boyfriend, it explained the flashes of déjà vu every time I heard his name, but—

If he was my boyfriend, and I'd meant something to him, where was he now?

"Anything else you can give me on Patch?"

"I hardly knew the guy, and what I knew scared the crap out of me. I'll see if I can hunt him down, but I can't make any promises. In the meantime, let's focus on a sure thing. If we can get enough dirt on Hank, maybe we can figure out why he's taken an interest in you and your mom and what he's planning next, and come up with a way to bring him down. We've both got something to gain from this. You in, Grey?"

"Oh, I'm in," I said fiercely.

I stayed with Scott until the sun dipped into the horizon. I left my half-eaten fish dinner behind and hiked back along the shoreline. Scott and I said our good-byes at the guardrail. He didn't want to make a habit of showing his face in public, and judging by what he'd told me about Hank and his Nephilim spies, I understood his caution. I promised to visit again soon, but he shot down the idea. Routine traffic toward the cave was too risky, he claimed. Instead he'd find me.

On the drive home, I reflected. I walked myself through everything Scott had told me. A strange feeling simmered inside me. Revenge, maybe. Or hatred in its purest form. I didn't have enough evidence to say for sure that Hank was behind my kidnapping, but I'd given Scott my word that I would do everything in my power to get to the bottom of this. And by "bottom," I meant if Hank had *anything* to do with it, I would make him pay.

And then there was Patch. My supposed ex-boyfriend. A guy who radiated mystery, left a strong impression on both Marcie and me, and had vanished without a trace. I couldn't picture myself with a boyfriend, but if I had to, I envisioned a nice normal guy who turned in his math homework on time and maybe even played rec baseball. A squeaky-clean description at odds with everything I knew about Patch. Which wasn't much.

I'd have to find a way to change that.

At the farmhouse, I found a sticky note on the counter. My

mom was out with Hank for the evening. Dinner, followed by the symphony orchestra in Portland. The thought of her alone with Hank caused my insides to free-fall, but Scott had been watching Hank Millar long enough to know he was dating my mom, and had given me a clear warning: I couldn't, under any circumstances, let on what I knew. To *either* of them. Hank believed he had us all fooled, and it was best to keep it that way. I had to trust that, for now, my mom was safe.

I debated calling Vee, making it clear I knew she'd lied about Patch, but I was feeling passive-aggressive. Give her a day of silent treatment, and let her stew over what she'd done. I'd confront her once I knew she was panicked enough to start telling the truth— for real this time. Her betrayal hurt, and for her sake, I hoped she had a *very* good explanation.

I cracked open a cup of chocolate pudding and ate it in front of the TV, using sitcom reruns to fill up the night. At last the clock slipped past eleven, and I padded upstairs to my room. Peeling out of my clothes, it wasn't until I returned my scarf to its proper place in the drawer that I noticed the black feather again. It had a silky sheen that reminded me of the color of Jev's eyes. A black so endless, it absorbed every last particle of light. I remembered riding beside him in the Tahoe, and even though Gabe was *right there*, I wasn't scared. Jev made me feel safe, and I wished I had some way to bottle the feeling, pulling it out whenever I needed it.

Most of all, I wished I'd see Jev again.

BECCA FITZPATRICK

I'd been dreaming of Jev when my eyes snapped open. The creak of wood had penetrated my sleep, jerking me awake. A shadowy figure crouched in my window, blocking out the moonlight. The figure jumped inside, landing in my bedroom as quietly as a cat.

I shot into a sitting position, and all breath left me in a *whoosh.*

"Shh," Scott murmured, finger to his lips. "Don't wake your mom."

"Wh-what are you doing here?" I finally managed to stammer.

He pulled the window shut behind him. "I told you I'd pay a visit soon."

I flopped back on my bed, trying to recover a normal heart-beat. I hadn't exactly seen my life flash before my eyes, but I'd come embarrassingly close to screaming at the top of my lungs. "You failed to mention that it would involve breaking into my bedroom."

"Is Hank here?"

"No. He's out with my mom. I fell asleep, but I haven't heard them come in yet."

"Get dressed."

I gave the clock a look. Then I gave him a look. "It's almost midnight, Scott."

"Very observant, Grey. As it turns out, we're going someplace that will be a lot easier to break into after hours."

Oh boy. "Break into?" I echoed a little testily, still not recovered from being woken so abruptly. Especially if Scott was serious about doing something potentially illegal.

My eyes were finally adjusting to the blurry darkness, and I caught him grinning. "Not afraid of a little B and E, are you?"

"Not at all. What's one felony? It's not like I have high hopes of going to college or getting a job someday," I quipped.

He ignored my sarcasm. "I found one of the Black Hand's warehouses." Crossing the room, he ducked his head into the hall. "You sure they're not back yet?"

"Hank probably has a lot of warehouses. He sells cars. He has to store them somewhere." I rolled over, pulled my covers up to my chin, and shut my eyes, hoping he'd take a hint. What I really wanted was to insert myself back into the dream with Jev. I could taste his kiss lingering on my lips. I wanted to live the fantasy a little longer.

"The warehouse is in the industrial district. If Hank is storing cars there, he's begging to get robbed. This is big-time. I'm feeling it, Grey. He's keeping something a lot more valuable than cars there. We need to find out what. We need all the dirt on him we can get."

"Breaking and entering is illegal. If we're going to nail Hank, we have to do it legitimately."

Scott came around the bed. He pulled the covers down until he could see my face. "He doesn't play by the rules. The only way this is going to work is if we level the playing field. Aren't you a little bit curious about what he's keeping in the warehouse?"

BECCA FITZPATRICK

I thought about the hallucination, the warehouse and the caged angel, but I said, "If it could get me arrested, no."

He sat back, frowning. "What happened to helping me bury the Black Hand?"

That was the thing. A few hours alone to reason things out, and I felt my confidence slipping. If Hank was everything Scott claimed, how could the two of us go up against him alone? We needed a better plan. A smarter plan.

"I want to help, and I will, but we can't just jump into this," I said. "I'm too tired to think. Go back to the cave. Come back at a reasonable hour. Maybe I can talk my mom into visiting Hank at his warehouse and ask her what's inside."

"If I bring down Hank, I get my life back," Scott said. "No more hiding. No more running. I'd get to see my mom again. Speaking of moms, yours would be safe. We both know you want this as much as I do," he murmured in a voice I didn't like. It was a voice that hinted at knowing me more than I was comfortable with. I didn't want Scott to have that kind of insight into me. Not at midnight, anyway. Not when I was this close to slipping back into the dream with Jev. "I'm not going to let anything happen to you," he said softly, "if that's what's got you worried."

"How do I know that?"

"You don't. This is your chance to put my intentions to the test. Find out what I'm really made of."

I snagged my lower lip between my teeth, thinking. I wasn't the kind of girl who sneaked out at night. And here I was, about to do it twice in one week. I was beginning to think I was one hundred eighty degrees from the person I liked to believe I was. *Not so good after all?* the devil on my shoulder seemed to taunt.

The idea of going out after dark to spy on one of Hank's warehouses didn't exactly send a warm, fuzzy feeling through me, but I rationalized that I'd be with Scott the entire time. And if there was one thing I wanted, it was to get Hank out of my life for good. Maybe, if Scott was right about him being Nephilim, Hank was capable of mind-tricking one or two cops, but if he was doing something highly illegal, there was no way he could evade the entire police force. Right now, getting the police to breathe down his neck seemed like a good start to unraveling his plans, whatever they were.

"Is this even safe?" I asked. "How do we know we won't get caught?"

"I've been watching the building for days. Nobody's there at night. We'll take a few pictures from the windows. Level of risk is low. You in or not?"

I gave a relenting sigh. "Fine! I'll throw on some clothes. Turn around. I'm in my pj's." Pj's that consisted of nothing but a tank and boy shorts—an image I didn't want to sear into Scott's mind.

Scott smiled. "I'm a guy. That's like asking a kid not to glance at the candy counter."

Ugh.

The dimple in his cheek deepened. And it was *not* in any way cute.

Because I wasn't going down this road with Scott. I made the decision instantly. Our relationship was complicated enough. If we were going to work together, platonic was the only way to go.

With a wry smile, he raised his arms in defeat and gave me his back. I scrambled out of bed, loped across the room, and shut myself in the closet.

Since the doors were slatted, I left the light off just to be safe and felt my way down the rack of clothes. I tugged on a pair of skinny jeans, a layering tee, and a hoodie. I opted for tennis shoes, fearing we might have to run at a moment's notice.

Buttoning the top of my jeans, I opened the closet door. "You know what I'm thinking right now?" I asked Scott.

His eyes scanned me. "That you look cute in that girl-next-door way?"

Why did he have to say things like that? I felt a blush spring to my cheeks and hoped Scott missed it in the dim light.

I said, "That I'd better not regret this."

CHAPTER

16

SCOTT'S MODE OF TRANSPORTATION WAS A 1971 Dodge Charger, not the quietest of cars for a guy who insisted we keep a low profile. Add on the fact that the tailpipe sounded like it had developed a crack, and I was pretty sure we could be heard rocketing around from several blocks away. Even though I thought we were only piling on the suspicion by thundering through town with our hoods up, Scott was adamant.

"The Black Hand has spies everywhere," he informed me yet

again. As if to punctuate his point, his eyes flicked to the rearview mirror. "If he catches us together . . ." He let the sentence dangle.

"I get it," I said. Brave words, considering they sent a shudder right through me. I preferred not to think about what Hank would do if he suspected Scott and I were spying on him.

"I shouldn't have taken you to the cave," Scott said. "He'd do just about anything to find me. I wasn't thinking about how this would impact you."

"It's okay," I said, but that ominous chill hadn't vanished. "You were surprised to see me. You weren't thinking. Neither was I. I'm still not thinking," I added with a shaky laugh. "Otherwise I wouldn't be snooping around one of his warehouses. Is the building under video surveillance?"

"No. My guess is the Black Hand doesn't want any extra evidence proving what goes on there. Video can leak," he added meaningfully.

Scott parked the Charger by the Wentworth River, under the low-hanging branches of a tree, and we swung out. By the time we'd walked a block, I couldn't see the car when I glanced over my shoulder. I supposed that was what Scott had been going for. We crept alongside the river, the moon too thin to cast our shadows.

We crossed Front Street, weaving between old brick warehouses, slender and tall, built one right after another. The original architect clearly hadn't wanted to waste space. The buildings' windows were greased over, barred with iron, or covered from the inside with newsprint. Trash and tumbleweeds crammed the foundations.

"That's the Black Hand's warehouse," Scott whispered. He pointed in the direction of a four-story brick structure with a rickety fire escape and arched windows. "He's gone inside it five times in the past week. He always comes just before dawn, when the rest of town is sleeping. He parks several blocks away and walks the rest of the way on foot. Sometimes he'll circle a block twice just to make sure he's not being followed. You still think he's storing cars?"

I had to admit, the chances of Hank taking that kind of precaution over Toyota inventory was pretty low. If anything, it sounded like he was using the building as a chop shop, but I didn't really believe that, either. Hank was one of the wealthiest and most influential men in town. He wasn't desperate to make a little cash on the side. No, something else was going on. And by the way the hairs on the back of my neck stood on end, I predicted it wasn't good.

"Are we going to be able to see inside?" I asked, wondering if the windows on Hank's building were blacked out like the others. We were still too far away to tell.

"Let's move up another block and find out."

We hugged each building along the way so closely the bricks snagged my hoodie. At the end of the block, we were close enough to Hank's building to see that while the windows on the bottom two floors were covered in newspaper, those on the top two floors had been left unobstructed.

"You thinking what I'm thinking?" Scott asked with a mischievous gleam in his eyes.

"Climb the fire escape and have a look inside?"

"We could draw lots. Loser goes up."

"No way. This was your idea. You should go up."

"Chicken." He grinned, but sweat glistened on his forehead. He pulled out a cheap disposable camera. "It's dark, but I'll try to get a few clean pictures."

Without another word, we ran in a crouch across the street. We hurried down the alley behind Hank's building and didn't stop until we were hidden behind a Dumpster splashed with graffiti. I braced my hands on my knees and swallowed air. I couldn't tell if my shortness of breath was due to the running or anxiety. Now that we'd come this far, I suddenly wished I'd stayed behind in the Charger. Or stayed home, period. My greatest fear at this point was being discovered by Hank. How certain was Scott that we weren't being caught on surveillance tape at this very moment?

"Are you going up?" I asked, secretly hoping he'd developed cold feet too and would make an executive decision to retreat to the car.

"Or in. What are the chances the Black Hand forgot to lock up?" he asked, jerking his head in the direction of a row of truck bay doors.

I hadn't noticed the bay doors until Scott pointed them out. They were raised off the ground and set back in an alcove. Perfect for loading and unloading cargo privately. There were three in a row, and something clicked in my head when I saw them. They looked a lot like the bay doors I'd pictured during my hallucination in the school bathroom. The warehouse also had a creepy resemblance to the other hallucination I'd had with Jev by the side of the road. I found the coincidences eerie, but wasn't sure how to raise the issue with Scott. Telling him, *I think I saw this place during one of my hallucinations* wasn't going to earn me a lot of credibility.

While I was still pondering the spooky connection, Scott leaped up on the cement ledge and tried the first bay door. "Locked." He moved to the keypad. "What do you think the code is? Hank's birthday?"

"Too obvious."

"His daughter's birthday?"

"Doubtful." Hank didn't strike me as stupid.

"Back to plan A, then." Scott sighed.

He jumped, catching the bottom rung of the fire escape. A layer of rust sprinkled down and the metal gave a low groan of protest, but the pulley worked, the chain fed through it, and the ladder lowered.

"Catch me if I fall," was all he said before going up. He tested the first couple of rungs, bouncing his weight against them. When they didn't give, he continued up, one cautious step at a time to minimize the creaking metal. I watched him all the way to the first landing.

BECCA FITZPATRICK

Figuring I should keep watch while Scott climbed, I poked my head around the side of the building. Ahead, at the adjacent corner, a long, knifelike shadow spread across the sidewalk, and a man stepped into view. I pulled back.

"Scott," I whispered up, my voice the barest sound.

He was too high to hear.

I glanced around the edge of the building a second time. The man stood on the corner with his back to me. Between his fingers burned the orange glow of a cigarette. He leaned into the street, glancing both ways down it. I didn't think he was waiting for a ride, and I didn't think he'd stepped out of work for a smoke. Most of the warehouses in this district had been retired years ago, and it was past midnight. Nobody was working at this hour. If I had to bet, the man was guarding Hank's building.

Further proof that whatever Hank was hiding had value.

The man ground his cigarette beneath his boot, glanced at his watch, and started a bored amble toward the alley.

"Scott!" I hissed, cupping my mouth. "We have a problem."

Scott was well past the second level, only a few steps away from the third-storey landing. The camera was in his hand, ready to take pictures the minute he had a clear shot.

Realizing he wasn't going to hear me, I grabbed a piece of gravel and threw it at him. Instead of hitting him, however, the rock hit the fire escape, ringing out with a clang, clang, clang as it bounced back down.

I covered my mouth, paralyzed by fear.

Scott looked down and froze. I jabbed my finger urgently at the side of the building.

Then I ran to the Dumpster, crouching behind it. Through the crack between the Dumpster and the building, I watched Hank's guard jog into view. He must have heard the pebble I'd thrown, because his eyes immediately traveled up, trying to pinpoint the sound.

"Hey!" he yelled at Scott, jumping onto the bottom rung of the fire escape and hauling himself up with a speed and agility that very few humans could match. He was tall, too, one of the easiest ways Scott had taught me I could spot a Nephil.

Scott clambered up the fire escape, taking the rungs two at a time. In his hurry, the camera slipped from his hand, sailing down to the alley, where it shattered. He gave it one brief glance of disbelief before resuming his rushed ascent. At the fourth-storey landing, he hauled himself up the ladder that hooked onto the rooftop and disappeared above.

I ran down my options in a hurry. The Nephil guard was only a flight behind Scott, moments away from cornering him on the roof. Would he rough up Scott? Haul him back down for questioning? My stomach lurched. Would he call Hank here, to deal with Scott directly?

I hustled out to the front of the building and craned my neck, trying to locate Scott. As I did, a shadow streaked overhead. Not along the edge of the rooftop, but in the air between this building and the one across the street. I blinked, clearing my vision just in time to see a second comet race across the sky, arms and legs pinwheeling athletically.

My jaw dropped. Scott and the Nephil were jumping buildings. I didn't know how they were doing it, and there wasn't time to dwell on the impossibility of what I was seeing. I sprinted toward the Charger, trying to anticipate Scott's mind. If we could both beat the Nephil to the car, we stood a chance of getting away. Pumping my arms harder, I followed the sound of their shoes ringing and scuffing far overhead.

Halfway to the car, Scott veered suddenly to the right, and the Nephil followed. I heard the last of their impossibly fast footsteps sprint into the darkness. As they did, a metallic chime rang out on the sidewalk just ahead. I scooped up the car key. I knew what Scott was doing: diverting the Nephil long enough to give me a chance to get to the car before they did. They were faster—much faster—and without an extra few minutes, I'd never make it. Still, Scott couldn't take the Nephil on a wild-goose chase forever. I had to hurry.

At Front Street, I put on one final burst of speed and sprinted the last block to the Charger. I was light-headed, blackness crowding my vision. Clutching my side, I leaned against the car, catching my breath. I scanned the rooftops intently, hunting for any sign of Scott or the Nephil.

A figure streaked off the side of the building straight ahead, legs and arms revolving through air as he dead-dropped. At the bottom of four storeys, Scott hit the ground, stumbled, and rolled. The Nephil was right on his tail, but nailed the landing. He yanked Scott off the ground and delivered a fierce blow to the side of his head. Scott staggered, but remained conscious. I wasn't sure he'd be able to manage as much with a second well-aimed punch.

With no time to think, I threw myself into the Charger. I shoved Scott's key into the ignition. Flipping on the headlights, I floored it straight for Scott and the Nephil. My hands gripped the steering wheel, bloodless. *Please let this work.*

Both Scott and the Nephil spun to face me, their complexions washed out in the headlights. Scott shouted at me, but I couldn't make out the words. The Nephil shouted too. At the last moment, he released Scott and dodged away from the car's bumper. Scott wasn't as lucky; he flew up and over the hood. I didn't have time to wonder if he'd been injured before he hurled himself into the seat beside me.

"Go!"

I stomped the gas. "What was that back there?" I shrieked. "You were jumping buildings like they were hurdles!"

"I told you I'm stronger than your average guy."

"Yeah, well, you didn't mention flying! And you told me you didn't like using those strengths!"

"Maybe you changed my outlook." A cocky smile. "So you were impressed?"

"That Nephil back there nearly captured you and *that's* all you care about?"

"Thought so." He sounded self-satisfied, clenching and unclenching his hand, where the Black Hand's ring fitted snugly around his middle finger. I didn't think now was the time to press for an explanation. Especially given the relief I felt over his decision to start wearing it again. With it, Scott stood a chance against Hank. And I did as well, by association.

"Thought what?" I said, frazzled.

"You're blushing."

"I'm *sweating*." When I realized what he was getting at, I rushed on, "I am *not* impressed! What you did back there— What could have happened—" I shoved some stray hairs off my face and collected myself. "I think you're reckless and careless, and you've got some nerve making this all sound like a big joke!"

His smile turned into a full-on grin. "No further questions. I have my answer."

CHAPTER

17

SCOTT DROVE ME HOME AND WAS FAR MORE LIBERAL with the speed limit than I'd ever been. He parked a distance from the farmhouse, at my insistence. The entire ride home, I'd juggled two kinds of fear. First, that the Nephil guard had somehow followed us, despite Scott's careful measures, and second, that my mom would beat us home. Chances were, she would have speed-dialed my cell the moment she found my bed empty, but then again, maybe her seething rage at my second count of reckless disobedience in less than a week had rendered her speechless.

"Well, that was exciting," I told Scott, my voice pale.

He thumped his hand on the steering wheel. "Thirty more seconds. That's all I needed. If I hadn't dropped the camera, we'd have pictures of the warehouse." He wagged his head in disbelief.

I was about to tell him that if he had thoughts of going back, he should find another sidekick, when he said soberly, "If the guard got a good look at me, he's going to tell Hank. Even if he didn't see my face, he could have seen my brand. Hank will know it was me. He'll send a team out to search the area." His eyes flicked to mine. "I've heard rumors of Nephilim being locked away in reinforced prisons for life. Underground chambers in the woods, or beneath buildings. You can't kill a Nephil, but you can torture him. I'm going to have to lie low for a while."

"What brand?"

Scott stretched the collar of his shirt down, revealing a small circle of skin that had been seared with the mark of a clenched fist identical to the one on his ring. The flesh had healed, but I could only imagine how raw and painful it had once been. "The Black Hand's mark. It's how he forced me into his army. On the bright side, he wasn't smart enough to embed a tracking device."

I wasn't in the mood to joke, and didn't return his half smile. "Do you think the guard saw your brand?"

"Can't say."

"Do you think he saw me?"

Scott shook his head. "We couldn't see anything through the headlights. I only knew it was you because I recognized the Charger."

This should have made me breathe easier, but I was wound so tight, a sigh of relief was out of the question.

"Hank could drop your mom off at any minute." Scott jerked his thumb at the road. "I've got to roll. I'm going to keep my head down for a few weeks. Hopefully the guard didn't see my mark. Hopefully he thinks I'm a common thug."

"Either way, he knows you're Nephilim. Last I checked, humans don't jump buildings. When Hank finds out, I don't think he's going to brush this off as a coincidence."

"All the more reason to back off. If I disappear off the grid, Hank might think I got scared and left town. When this blows over, I'll find you. We'll draft a different plan and take him down from a new angle."

I felt my patience shredding. "What about me? You're the one who put this whole idea into my head. You can't bail now. He's dating my mom. I don't get the luxury of lying low. If he was involved in my kidnapping, I want him to pay. If he's planning even worse things, I want him stopped. Not in a few weeks or months but now."

"And who is going to get rid of him?" His voice was gentle, but there was an underlying firmness. "The police? He's got half of them on his payroll. And the other half he could mind-trick into submission. Listen to me, Nora. Our plan is to ride this out. We have to let the dust settle and make the Black Hand think he's in charge again. Then we'll regroup and try a different attack when he's least expecting it."

"He is in charge. It's not a coincidence he's suddenly dating my mom. She isn't his top priority—building his Nephilim army is. Cheshvan starts next month, in October. So why her, why now? How does she fit into his plans? I have to figure this out before it's too late!"

Scott tugged on his ear irritably. "I shouldn't have told you anything. You're going to crumble. The Black Hand is going to call you out from a mile away. You're going to talk. You're going to tell him about me and the cave."

"Don't worry about me," I snapped. I pushed out of the Charger and gave him one parting shot before slamming the door. "Lie low, fine. But you're not the one whose mom is falling more in love with that monster by the day. I'm going to out him with or without you."

Of course, I had no idea how. Hank had embedded himself so deeply in this town, he was at its very core. He had friends, allies, and employees. He had money, resources, and his own private army. Most worrisome of all, he had my mom clenched in his fist.

Two days passed with little excitement. True to his word, Scott vanished. In hindsight, I regretted blowing up at him. He was doing what he had to, and I couldn't blame him for that. I'd accused him of bailing, but that wasn't the case at all. He knew when to push and when to pull back. He was smarter than I'd given him credit for. And patient.

And then there was me. I didn't like Hank Millar, trusted him even less, and the sooner I figured out his endgame, the better. Cheshvan hung like a black cloud at the back of my thoughts, a constant reminder that Hank was planning something. I didn't have hard proof that my mom was part of that plan, but there were red flags. Given everything Hank was trying to accomplish before Cheshvan, including building and training an entire Nephilim army to win back possession of their bodies from fallen angels, why was he devoting so much time to my mom? Why did he need her trust? Why did he need her, period?

It wasn't until I was sitting in AP history, listening halfheartedly to my teacher describe the events leading up to the English Protestant Reformation, that a lightbulb blazed on. Hank knew Scott. Why hadn't I thought of it before? If Hank suspected that Scott was the Nephil responsible for snooping around his building two nights ago, he knew Scott wouldn't risk a second pass so soon after getting caught. In fact, Hank probably assumed Scott had scrambled straight into hiding, which he had. Never in a million years would Hank expect another trespasser as early as tonight.

Never in a million years . . .

BECCA FITZPATRICK

Evening came and went. At ten Mom kissed me good night and retreated to her bedroom. An hour later her light clicked off. I waited an extra minute or two to be sure, then flung off my covers. Fully dressed, I grabbed a duffel packed with a flashlight, a camera, and my car keys from under my bed.

As I pushed the Volkswagen soundlessly down Hawthorne Lane, I inwardly thanked Scott for buying me a light vehicle. I never could have done this with a truck. It wasn't until I was a good quarter mile from the farmhouse, and far out of my mom's hearing range, that I started the engine.

Twenty minutes later I parked the Volkswagen a few blocks from where Scott had left the Charger two nights ago. The scenery hadn't changed. Same boarded-up buildings. Same streetlights in disrepair. In the distance, a train blew a forlorn whistle.

Since Hank's building was guarded, I discarded the idea of going anywhere near it. I was going to have to find another way to look inside. An idea struck me. If there was one thing I could use to my advantage, it was the construction—the buildings were built one right next to the other. I could probably see inside Hank's building from the one directly behind it.

Sticking to the route Scott and I had taken, I jogged closer to Hank's building. Crouching in the shadows, I settled in for my first stab at surveillance. I noticed that the fire escape had been promptly removed. Hank was being careful, then. There was fresh newsprint covering the third-floor windows, but whoever had started the job

silence

hadn't made it to the fourth floor yet. Every ten minutes, like clock-work, a guard exited the building and walked the perimeter.

Convinced I had enough information to go on, I circled the block, coming out near the building that backed to Hank's. As soon as the guard finished his walk-around and retreated inside Hank's building, I sprinted into the open. Only this time, instead of hiding in the alley behind Hank's building, I hid one alley down.

Standing on top of an overturned trash can, I tugged the fire escape down to ground level. I was afraid of heights, but I wasn't about to let that fear get in the way of finding out what Hank was hiding. Taking some shallow breaths, I climbed to the first landing. I told myself not to look down, but the temptation was too strong. My eyes swept the alley below, seeing it through the iron latticework of the fire escape. My stomach cramped and my vision blurred.

I climbed to the second level. Up to the third. A little nauseated, I tried the windows. The first few were locked, but finally I jimmied one loose, and it opened with a gritty whine. Camera in hand, I stuffed myself through the window.

I'd just come to a full stand inside when I was blinded by lights. I threw my arm over my eyes. All around, I heard the sounds of stirring bodies. When I opened my eyes again, I gazed at row upon row of cots. One sleeping body in each cot. All male, all exceptionally tall.

Nephilim.

Before I could form a follow-up thought, an arm hooked my waist from behind.

"Move!" a low voice ordered, hauling me back toward the window I'd come through.

Snapping out of my daze, I felt the pair of strong arms drag me back through the window and onto the fire escape. Jev gave me a hasty look-over, his eyes brimming with aggravation. Wordlessly, he pushed me toward the rungs. As we clambered down the fire escape, shouts echoed from the front of the building. Any minute now, we were going to find ourselves trapped from above and below.

Making an impatient sound, Jev scooped me into his arms, holding me flush against him. "Whatever you do, don't let go."

I'd barely fastened my grip when we were flying. Straight down. Without bothering to use the fire escape, Jev had jumped over the railing. Air ripped past us as gravity pulled us toward the alley below. It was over before I could scream, my body jolting with the impact of landing, and just like that I was back on my own two feet.

Jev grabbed my hand and yanked me toward the street. "I'm parked three blocks away."

We rounded the corner, ran a block, cut up an alley. Ahead, parked at the curb, I saw the white Tahoe. Jev key-fobbed the doors open, and we flung ourselves inside.

Jev drove fast and hard, screeching around corners and flooring it down the straightaways, until he'd put miles between us and the Nephilim. At last he bounced the Tahoe into a little two-pump gas station halfway between Coldwater and Portland. A closed sign hung in the window, with only a few dim lights burning inside.

Jev cut the engine. "What were you doing back there?" His volume was low, his tone furious.

"Climbing the fire escape, what did it look like?" I shot back. My cords were torn, my knees were scuffed, my hands were scraped, and getting angry was the only thing stopping me from bursting into tears.

"Well, congratulations, you climbed it. And nearly got yourself killed. Don't tell me you were there by coincidence. Nobody hangs out in that neighborhood after dark. And that was a Nephilim safe house you barged into, so again, I'm not buying that it was by accident. Who told you to go there?"

I blinked. "A Nephilim safe house?"

"You're going to play dumb?" He shook his head. "Unbelievable."

"I thought the building was vacant. I thought the building next to it was the Nephilim warehouse."

"Both are owned by a Nephil—a very powerful Nephil. One is a decoy and the other sleeps about four hundred Nephilim on any given night. Guess which one you walked into?"

A decoy. How smart of Hank. Too bad I hadn't thought of it twenty minutes ago. He'd have the entire operation relocated by tomorrow morning, and I'd lose my only lead. At least now I knew what he was hiding. The warehouse was the sleeping quarters for at least a portion of his Nephilim army.

"I thought I told you to stop looking for trouble. I thought I told you to try normal for a while," Jev said.

"Normal didn't last very long. Right after I last saw you, I bumped into an old friend. An old Nephil friend." I'd let the words fly out without thinking, but I didn't see the harm in telling Jev about Scott. After all, Jev had taken my side when I'd argued with Gabe to release P.J., so he couldn't hate Nephilim the way Gabe clearly did.

Jev's eyes hardened. "What Nephil friend?"

"I don't have to answer that."

"Forget it. I already know. The only Nephil you'd be gullible enough to call a friend is Scott Parnell."

I wasn't fast enough to hide my surprise. "You know Scott?"

Jev didn't answer. But I could tell by the quiet, killer look in his eyes that he didn't think highly of Scott. "Where's he staying?" he asked.

I thought of the cave, and how I'd promised Scott I wouldn't tell anyone. "He—didn't tell me. I bumped into him when I was out running. It was a brief conversation. We didn't even have time to exchange phone numbers."

"Where were you running?"

"Downtown," I lied easily. "He stepped out of a restaurant as I was passing and recognized me, and we talked for a minute."

"You're lying. Scott wouldn't be out in the open like that, not when the Black Hand has a price on his head. I'm betting you saw him somewhere more remote. The woods by your house?" he guessed.

"How do you know where I live?" I asked nervously.

"You've got an untrustworthy Nephil shadowing you. If you're going to worry about something, worry about that."

"Untrustworthy? He filled me in on Nephilim and fallen angels, which is more than I can say about you!" I gathered my cool. I didn't want to talk about Scott. I wanted to talk about us and force Jev to open up on our past connection. I'd been fantasizing about seeing him for days, and now that I had what I wanted, I wasn't about to let him slip away again. I needed to know who he'd been to me.

"And what did he tell you? That he's the victim? That fallen angels are the bad guys? He can blame fallen angels for the existence of his race, but he isn't a victim and he isn't harmless. If he's hanging around, it's because he needs something from you. Everything else is a pretense."

"Funny you should say that, since he hasn't asked me for a single favor. So far, it's been all about me. He's trying to help me get my memory back. Don't look so surprised. Just because you're a closed-off jerk doesn't mean the rest of the world is too. After shedding light on Nephilim and fallen angels, he told me Hank Millar is building an underground Nephilim army. Maybe that name means nothing to you, but it means a lot to me, since Hank is dating my mom."

The scowl faded from his face. "What did you just say?" he asked in a genuinely menacing voice.

"I called you a closed-off jerk, and I meant every word."

He narrowed his gaze beyond the window, clearly thinking, and I got the distinct impression he'd found something I'd said important. A muscle in his jaw clenched, a dark and frightening look bringing a cold edge to his eyes. Even from where I sat, I sensed the tightening of his body, a current of underlying emotion—none of it good—flexing under his skin.

"How many people have you told about me?" he asked.

"What makes you think I've told anyone about you?"

His eyes pinned me in place. "Does your mom know?"

I debated another snide comment, but was too exhausted to put in the effort. "I might have mentioned your name, but she didn't recognize it. So we're back at square one. How do I know you, Jev?"

"If I asked you do to something for me, I don't suppose you'd listen?" When he had my attention, he continued, "I'm going to take you home. Try to forget tonight happened. Try to act normal, especially around Hank. Don't mention my name."

By way of an answer, I shot him a black look and swung out of the Tahoe. He followed suit, coming around to my side.

"What kind of answer is that?" he asked, but his voice wasn't nearly so gruff.

I stalked away from the Tahoe, in case he thought he could use force to stuff me back into the car. "I'm not going home. Not yet.

Ever since the night you saved me from Gabe, I've been thinking of all the ways I could run into you again. I've spent way too much time speculating how you knew me before, how you knew me at all. I might not remember you or anything else from the past five months, but I can still *feel*, Jev. And when I first saw you the other night, I felt something that I've never felt before. I couldn't look at you and breathe at the same time. What does that mean? Why don't you want me to remember you? Who *were* you to me?"

At that, I stopped walking and turned back to face him. His eyes were dilated to full black, and I suspected all kinds of emotion hid there. Regret, torment, wariness.

"The other night, why did you call me Angel?" I asked.

"If I were thinking straight, I'd take you home right now," he said quietly.

"But?"

"But I'm tempted to do something I'll probably regret."

"Tell me the truth?" I hoped.

Those black eyes flicked over me. "First I need to get you off the streets. Hank's men can't be far behind."

AS IF ON CUE, THE SCREECH OF TIRES RANG OUT BEHIND us. Hank would be proud; his men didn't give up easily. Jev yanked me behind a crumbling brick wall. "We can't outrun them to the Tahoe, and even if we could, I'm not dragging you into a car chase with Nephilim. They'll walk away from a rolled or totaled car, but you might not. Better to take our chances on foot and circle back to the car after they've given up. There's a nightclub a block from here. Not the cleanest place, but we can hide there." He took my elbow, propelling me forward.

"If Hank's men check the club, and they'd be stupid not to since they'll see the Tahoe and know we're on foot, they'll recognize me. The lights in the warehouse were on for a full five seconds before you dragged me out. Someone in that room had to have gotten a good look at me. I can try to hide in the bathroom, but if they start asking around, I won't stay hidden long."

"The warehouse you broke into is for new recruits. Sixteen or seventeen in human years and newly sworn, making them less than one in Nephilim years. I'm stronger than they are, and I've had a lot more practice when it comes to toying with minds. I'm going to put a trance on you. If they look at us, they're going to see a guy in black leather chaps with a spiked choker, and a platinum blond girl in a corset and combat boots."

Suddenly I felt a little light in the head. A trance. Was that how the mind-tricks worked? By enchantment?

Jev tipped my chin up, searching my eyes. "Do you trust me?"

Whether or not I trusted him didn't matter. The hard truth was, I had to. The alternative was facing down Hank's men alone, and I could guess how that would end.

I nodded.

"Good. Keep walking."

I followed Jev into a retired factory that now served as Bloody Mary's nightclub, and he handled the cover charge. It took my eyes a moment to adjust to the strobe light pulsing my vision between

BECCA FITZPATRICK

black and white. The interior walls had been knocked down, allowing for open space that at the moment was crammed with gyrating bodies. Ventilation was poor, and I was immediately hit by a wave of body odor mingled with perfume, cigarette smoke, and vomit. The clientele was a good fifteen years older than me, and I was the only person dressed in cords and sporting a ponytail, but Jev's mind-tricks must have been working, because amid the sea of chains, leather, spikes, and fishnets, no one batted an eye in my direction.

We fought our way to the center of the crowd, where we could hide and still keep watch on the doors.

"Plan A is to stay here and wait them out," Jev yelled at me over the throb of music. "Eventually they'll have to give up and go back to the warehouse."

"And plan B?"

"If they follow us in here, we'll leave through the back exit."

"How do you know there's a back exit?"

"I've been here before. Not my top choice, but it's a favorite when it comes to my kind."

I didn't want to think about what his kind was. Right now, I didn't want to think about anything but making it home alive.

I glanced around. "I thought you said you could mind-trick everyone. So why do I get the feeling people are staring?"

"We're the only two people in the room not dancing."

Dancing. Men and women who bore an impressive resemblance

to Kiss band members were head-banging, shoving, and licking each other. A guy with chain suspenders holding up his jeans climbed a ladder affixed to the wall and hurled himself into the crowd. To each his own, I thought.

"May I have this dance?" Jev asked with a sympathetic tug of his mouth.

"Shouldn't we be finding a way out of here? Devising a couple more backup plans?"

He clasped my right hand, drawing me against him in a slow dance that was at odds with the racing music. As if reading my mind, he said, "They'll stop staring soon. They're too busy competing for most extreme dance move of the night. Try to relax. Sometimes the best offense is a good defense."

My heart rate picked up then, and not because I knew Hank's men had to be close by. Dancing this way with Jev tore down any chance I had at holding my feelings in check. His arms were strong, his body warm. He wasn't wearing cologne, but there was an intriguing hint of fresh-cut grass and rainwater when he pulled me close. And those eyes. Deep, mysterious, unfathomable. Despite everything, I wanted to lean into him and . . . just let go.

"Better," he murmured into my ear.

Before I could respond, he spun me out. I'd never danced like this before, and Jev's skill at it surprised me. Street dancing I might have guessed, but not this. The way he danced reminded me of another time and place. He was confident and elegant . . . smooth and sexy.

"Do you think they're going to buy that a guy in tacky leather chaps dances like this?" I scoffed when he twirled me back into his embrace.

"Keep it up, and I'll put you in the chaps." He didn't smile, but I sensed an undercurrent of amusement. Glad one of us found something about the situation remotely funny.

"How do the trances work? Like a glamour?"

"It's more complicated than that, but same end result."

"Could you teach me?"

"If I taught you everything I know, we'd need a considerable amount of time alone together."

Unsure if he was suggesting anything, I said, "I'm sure we could keep it . . . professional."

"Speak for yourself," he said in that same steady tone that made it hard to guess his intentions.

His hand was on my back, holding me against him, and I realized I was more nervous than I'd originally thought. I found myself wondering if the connection between us had been this electric before. Had being near him always felt like playing with fire? Warm and bright, intense and dangerous?

To keep our conversation from treading further into uncomfortable territory, I laid my head against his chest, even though I knew it wasn't safe. Nothing about him felt safe. My entire body hummed under his touch, a completely foreign and riveting sensation. The sensible part of me wanted to dissect my emotions, overthinking and overcomplicating my reaction to Jev. But a more physical and immediate part was tired of allowing logic to chase me in circles, constantly wondering about that gap in time, and just like that, I shut off the switch to my brain.

Piece by piece, I let Jev break down my defenses. I swayed and dipped against him, letting him set the rhythm. I was overly warm, my head clogged with smoke, and the moment began to feel unreal, only making it easier to believe that later, if guilt or regret haunted me, I could pretend it never happened. While I was here, trapped in the club, trapped in Jev's eyes, he made it too easy to succumb.

His mouth grazed my ear. "What are you thinking?"

I closed my eyes briefly, drowning in sensation. *How warm I feel. How incredibly alive and vibrant and heedless every last inch of me feels next to you.*

His mouth twisted into a perceptive, sexy smile. "Hmm."

"Hmm?" I looked away, flustered, automatically using irritation to cover my discomfort up. "What does 'hmm' have to do with anything? Could you ever use more than five words? All this grunting and minced words makes you come across as—primal."

His smile tipped higher. "Primal."

"You're impossible."

"Me Jev, you Nora."

"Stop it." But I nearly smiled in spite of myself.

"Since we're keeping it primal, you smell good," he observed. He moved closer, making me acutely aware of his size, the rise and fall of his chest, the warm burn of his skin on mine. Electricity tingled along my scalp, and I shuddered with pleasure.

"It's called a shower . . . ," I began automatically, then trailed off. My memory snagged, taken aback by a compelling and forceful sense of undue familiarity. "Soap, shampoo, hot water," I added, almost as an afterthought.

"Naked. I know the drill," Jev said, something unreadable passing over his eyes.

Unsure how to proceed, I attempted to wash away the moment with an airy laugh. "Are you flirting with me, Jev?"

"Does it feel that way to you?"

"I don't know you well enough to say either way." I tried to keep my voice level, neutral even.

"Then we'll have to change that."

Still uncertain of his motives, I cleared my throat. Two could play this game. "Running from bad guys together is your idea of playing getting-to-know-you?"

"No. This is."

He dipped my body backward, drawing me up in a slow arc until he raised me flush against him. In his arms, my joints loosened, my defenses melting as he led me through the sultry steps. His muscles flexed under his clothes, holding me, leading me. Never letting me stray far.

My knees felt rubbery, but not from dancing. My breathing came faster, and I knew I was treading down a slippery slope. Being this close to Jev, skin brushing, legs touching lightly, gazes connecting briefly in the dark, it was all blind sensation and intoxicating heat. A strange jumble of nervous exhilaration, I pulled away, but not too hard.

"I don't have the body for this," I quipped, lifting my chin at a voluptuous woman nearby who shook her hips zealously to the beat. "No curves."

Jev's eyes held mine. "Are you asking my opinion?"

I flushed. "I asked for that."

He tipped his head down, his breath warming my skin. His lips grazed my forehead with featherweight pressure. I shut my eyes, trying to hold back the absurd desire for him to move his mouth lower, until it found my own.

"Jev—," I wanted to say. Only his name didn't escape. Jev, Jev, Jev, I thought in perfect cadence to my heightened pulse. I repeated his name, a silent request, until it spun me dizzy.

The sliver of air between our mouths was a vivid presence, teasing and tempting. He was so close, my body attuned to his in a way that both frightened and marveled. I waited, leaning into his embrace, my breath light with anticipation.

Suddenly his body grew taut. The spell broke, the gap between us irrevocably widening, and I stepped back.

"We've got company," Jev said.

I tried to pull completely away, but Jev tightened his hold on me, forcing me to keep up the pretense of dancing. "Stay calm," he murmured, his cheek brushing my forehead. "Remember, if they look at you, they're going to see blond hair and combat boots. They're not going to see the real you."

"Won't they expect you to tamper with their minds?" I tried to catch a glimpse of the doorway, but several taller men in the crowd blocked me. I couldn't tell if Hank's men were advancing or lingering by the doors, watching.

"They didn't get a good look at me, but they saw me jump from the third floor of the warehouse, which will tell them I'm not human. They'll be looking for a guy and a girl together, but that could be any number of couples in here."

"What are they doing now?" I asked, still unable to see past the crowd.

"Having a look around. Dance with me and keep your eyes off the doors. There are four of them. They're spreading out." Jev swore. "Two are heading this way. I think we've been spotted. The Black Hand trained them well. I've never met a Nephil who could see through a trance within the first year of swearing fealty, but they just might pull it off. Walk toward the bathrooms and take the exit at the end of the hall. Don't walk too fast, and don't look back. If anyone tries to stop you, ignore them and keep walking. I'm going to head them off to buy us time. I'll meet you in the alley in five."

Jev went one way and I went the other—with my heart in my throat. I elbowed my way through the crowd, the heat of too many bodies and my own nervous adrenaline making my skin moist. I veered into the hallway leading to the bathrooms, which, judging by the rancid smell and the swarm of flies, were anything but sanitary. There was a long line, and I had to edge sideways around each person, muttering a hurried, "Excuse me."

As Jev promised, a door appeared at the end of the hallway. I pushed through it and found myself outside. Wasting no time, I broke into a jog. I didn't think it was a good idea to stand in the open, choosing instead to hide behind the dumpsters until Jev came for me. I was halfway down the alley when the door swung open behind me.

"Over there!" a voice shouted. "She's getting away!"

I looked back only long enough to confirm they were Nephilim. Then I took off. I didn't know where I was going, but Jev would have to find me elsewhere. I raced across the street, heading back to where we'd abandoned the Tahoe. When Jev didn't find me in the alley, hopefully his car was the next place he'd think to look.

The Nephilim were too fast. Even at a full sprint, I could hear them closing in. Everything came ten times easier to them, I realized with increasing panic. When they were only moments away from seizing me, I whirled around.

The two Nephilim slowed, instantly wary of my intentions. I shifted my eyes between them, breathing heavily. I could keep running and draw out the inevitable. I could put up a fight. I could scream bloody murder and hope Jev heard. But every option felt like grasping at straws.

BECCA FITZPATRICK

"Is it her?" the shorter one asked with a formal accent that sounded British. He eyed me shrewdly.

"It's her," the taller, an American, confirmed. "She's using a trance. Focus on one detail at a time, the way the Black Hand taught us. Her hair, for instance."

The shorter Nephil squinted at me so intently I wondered if he could see all the way through to the bricks on the building behind me. "Well, well," he said after a moment. "Red, is it? I preferred you blond."

With inhuman speed, they were at my sides, each gripping an elbow so hard I winced. "What were you doing in the warehouse?" the taller Nephil asked. "How did you find it?"

"I—," I began. But I was too terrified to think up a plausible lie. They weren't going to believe me if I said sheer dumb luck was responsible for my stumbling through their window in the middle of the night.

"Cat got your tongue?" the shorter said, tickling under my chin.

I jerked away.

"We have to take her back to the warehouse," the taller one said. "The Black Hand or Blakely will want to question her."

"They won't be back till tomorrow. Might as well get some answers now."

"What if she doesn't talk?"

The shorter Nephil licked his lips, something frightening lighting up his eyes. "We'll make sure she does."

The taller Nephil frowned. "She'll tell them everything."

"We'll wipe her memory when we're done. She won't know the difference."

"We're not strong enough yet. Even if we could erase half of it, it wouldn't be enough."

"We could try devilcraft," the shorter suggested with a disturbing gleam in his eyes.

"Devilcraft is a myth. The Black Hand made that clear."

"Oh yeah? If the angels in heaven have powers, it makes sense the demons in hell should too. You say myth, I say potential gold mine. Imagine what we could do if we got our hands on it."

"Even if devilcraft exists, we wouldn't know where to start."

The shorter Nephil wagged his head in irritation. "Always one for fun, you are. Fine. We make sure our stories match. Our word against hers." He counted down his suggested version of the night's events on his fingers. "We chased her from the warehouse, found her hiding in the club, and while dragging her back, she got scared and spilled everything. It won't matter what she says happened. She already broke into the warehouse. If anything, the Black Hand will expect her to lie again."

The taller Nephil didn't look fully convinced, but he didn't argue, either.

"You're coming with me," the shorter one grunted, forcing me roughly into the tight space between the buildings at our rear. He paused only to tell his friend, "Stay here and make sure nobody bothers us. If we can extract information from her, it just might earn us extra privileges. Maybe even move us up a rank."

My whole body went into a slow freeze at the idea of being interrogated by the Nephil, but I'd quickly come to accept that I didn't stand a fighting chance against both of them. Maybe I could press my advantage. My only hope—and even I knew it was a thin one—was to level the playing field by going one on one. Letting the shorter Nephil drag me deeper into the narrow breezeway, I hoped the gamble would pay off.

"You're making a big mistake," I told him, putting all the threat I possessed behind my words.

He rolled up his sleeves, exposing knuckles decorated with various sharp rings, and my courage suddenly felt slippery. "Been in America six months now, waking up at the crack of dawn, training all day under a tyrant, and locked up in the barracks at night. After six months of that prison, let me tell you, it's going to feel good to take it out on someone." He licked his lips. "I'm going to enjoy this, sweetheart."

"You stole my line," I said, and shoved my knee up between his legs.

I'd seen enough guys at school take a similar hit during sports games or PE class to know the injury wouldn't completely immobilize him, but I wasn't expecting him to be ready to lunge at me after nothing more than a pained moan.

He came at me in a blur. There was a discarded two-by-four

near my feet, and I snatched it up. Several rusty nails protruded from it, making it a useful weapon.

The Nephil eyed the block of wood and shrugged. "Go ahead. Try and hit me. Won't hurt."

I gripped the two-by-four like a bat. "It might not permanently injure you, but trust me, it will hurt."

He faked to his right, but I was expecting it. When he jumped to his left, I swung down hard. There was an awful puncturing sound, and the Nephil yelped.

"That's gonna cost you." He kicked high before I had time to register the movement, his boot sending the wood out of my grasp. He wrestled me to the ground, pinning my arms over my head.

"Get off me!" I yelled, twisting under his weight.

"Sure thing, sweetheart. Just tell me what you were doing at the safe house."

"Get—off—me—now."

"You heard her."

The Nephil's eyes widened in impatience. "What now?" he snapped, whipping his head around to see who dared interrupt us.

"It was an easy enough request," Jev said, smiling slightly, but it was all lethality at the edges.

"I'm a little busy at the moment, mate," the Nephil barked, raking his eyes over me for emphasis. "If you don't mind."

"Turns out I do." Jev grabbed the Nephil by the shoulders and flung him against the building. He splayed his hand across the Nephil's throat, shutting off his airway.

"Apologize." With a flick of his head, Jev gestured in my direction.

The Nephil clawed at Jev's hand, his face flaring with color. His mouth opened and closed like a fish's, trying to draw oxygen.

"Tell her how deeply sorry you are, or I'll make sure you have nothing to say for a good while longer." With his free hand, Jev waved a switchblade, and I realized he meant to cut out the Nephil's tongue. For what it was worth, I didn't feel a shred of sympathy. "What's it going to be?"

The Nephil's eyes burned with rage as he glanced between me and Jev.

Sorry, his infuriated voice spat into my mind.

"It won't win an Oscar, but it'll do," Jev told him with a vicious smile. "That wasn't so hard, was it?"

Wrenching free, the Nephil gulped air and massaged his throat. "Do I know you? I know you're a fallen angel—I can feel your power rolling off you like a stench, which makes me think you must have been pretty high up before you fell, maybe even an archangel—but what I want to know is if we've crossed paths before." It seemed like a trick question, meant to help the Nephil track Jev down at some future point, but Jev wasn't baited.

"Not yet," he said. "I'll keep the introduction short." He plowed his fist into the Nephil's gut. The Nephil's mouth was still in the shape of an O when he sank to his knees and went slack.

Jev turned to me. I expected him to demand why I hadn't stayed in the alley like we'd agreed, and how I'd wound up with the present company, but he simply wiped a smudge of dirt off my cheek and buttoned the top two buttons on my blouse.

"You okay?" he asked quietly.

I nodded, but felt tears swell at the back of my throat.

"Let's get out of here," he said.

For once, I didn't protest.

CHAPTER

19

AS JEV DROVE, I LEANED MY HEAD AGAINST THE window, staying quiet. He kept to side roads and back roads, but I had a rough idea of where we were. Another few turns, and I knew exactly where we were. The entrance to Delphic Amusement Park loomed ahead, imposing and skeletal. Jev pulled into the vacant lot. Four hours ago, he would have been lucky to find a place half this close to the gates.

"What are we doing here?" I asked, sitting up straighter.

He shut off the engine, arching a dark brow. "You said you wanted to talk."

"Yeah, but this place is . . ." *Empty.*

A hard smile touched his mouth. "Still don't know if you can trust me? As for why Delphic, call me sentimental."

If I was supposed to catch his meaning, I didn't. I followed him to the gates, watching him vault up and over them with ease. On the other side, he pushed the gate open just wide enough to allow me entrance.

"Could we go to jail for this?" I asked, knowing it was a stupid question. If we were caught, how could we not?

But because Jev looked like he knew what he was doing, I followed. Above the lamplight, a roller coaster towered over the park. An image blazed across my mind, momentarily halting me. I saw myself hurtling off the tracks into a free fall. I swallowed, brushing the image off as having to do with my terror of heights.

I was growing more uneasy by the minute. Just because Jev had saved my skin three times didn't mean it was a good idea to be alone with him. I supposed I'd been lulled here by the idea of answers. Jev had promised we'd talk, and the temptation had been too appealing to resist.

At last Jev slowed, veering off the walkway and coming to a stop before a ramshackle maintenance shed. It was overshadowed by the roller coaster on one side and a giant spinning wheel on the other. The squat gray structure was the last place anyone's eyes would travel.

"What's in the shed?" I asked.

"Home."

Home? Either he had a sense of humor, or he was redefining simple living. "Glamorous."

A shrewd smile crept to his mouth. "I sacrificed style for safety."

I eyed the weathered paint, sloped awning, and paper-thin construction. "Safe? I could probably kick down the door."

"Safe from the archangels."

At the word, I felt a jab of panic. I remembered my last hallucination. *Help me find an archangel's necklace,* Hank had said. The coincidence tingled unpleasantly under my skin.

Inserting his key, Jev opened the shed door and held it for me.

"When do I get to find out about the archangels?" I asked. I sounded glib, but nerves were making a wreck of my stomach. Just how many different angel spin-offs were there?

"All you need to know is that right now, they're not on our side."

I read deeper into his tone. "But they might be later?"

"I'm an optimist."

I stepped over the threshold, thinking there had to be more to the shed than met the eye. If the walls would be spared by a gusty wind, I'd be amazed. The floorboards creaked under my weight, and I breathed in the smell of stale air. The shed was small—about fifteen by ten feet. No windows. The space fell to total darkness when Jev let the door shut behind us.

"You live here?" I asked, just to be sure.

"This is more like the antechamber."

Before I could ask what that meant, I heard him cross the shed. There was the low whine of a door opening. When he spoke again, his voice was much lower to the ground.

"Give me your hand."

I shuffled over, wading through blackness, until I felt him grasp my hand. It seemed he was standing below me, in a recessed area. His hands moved to my waist. He lifted me down—

Into a space beneath the shed. We stood face-to-face in the darkness. I felt him breathing, low and steady. My own breathing was less regular. *Where was he taking me?*

"What is this place?" I whispered.

"There's a labyrinth of tunnels beneath the park. Layer upon layer of mazes. Years ago, fallen angels didn't mingle with humans. They separated themselves, living out here on the coast, going into towns and villages only during Cheshvan to possess their Nephilim vassals' bodies. A two-week vacation, and those towns were like their resorts. They did what they wanted. Took what they wanted. Filled their pockets with their vassals' money.

"These cliffs by the ocean were remote, but fallen angels built their cities underground as a precaution. They knew that over time things would change. And they did. Humans expanded. The boundary between human and fallen angel territory blurred. Fallen angels built Delphic on top of their city to hide it. When they opened the amusement park, they used the revenue to sustain themselves."

His voice was so measured, so steady, I didn't know how he felt about what he'd just told me. In return, I didn't know what to say. It was like hearing a dark fairy tale, late at night, with heavy eyes. The whole moment felt dreamlike, fluttering in and out of focus, yet so very real.

I knew Jev was telling the truth, not because his history of fallen angels and Nephilim matched Scott's, but because every last word rattled me, shaking loose fragments of my memory I'd thought were gone forever.

"I almost brought you here once," Jev said. "The Nephil whose safe house you broke into tonight interfered."

I didn't have to be honest with Jev, but I decided to take the risk. "I know Hank Millar is the Nephil you're talking about. He's the reason I went to the safe house tonight. I wanted to know what he was hiding inside. Scott told me if we got enough dirt on him, we could figure out what he's planning and devise a way to bring him down."

Something I interpreted as pity flashed across Jev's eyes. "Hank isn't an ordinary Nephil, Nora."

"I know. Scott told me he's building an army. He wants to overthrow fallen angels so they can't possess Nephilim bodies anymore. I know he's powerful and connected. What I don't understand is how you're involved. Why were you at the safe house tonight?"

Jev said nothing for a moment. "Hank and I have a business arrangement. It's not unusual for me to pay him a visit." He was being deliberately vague. I didn't know whether even after my gesture of honesty he was unwilling to be open with me, or whether he was trying to protect me. He let go of a long sigh. "We need to talk."

He took my elbow, leading me deeper into the perfect darkness beneath the shed. We moved downward, twisting through corridors and around bends. At last Jev slowed, opened a door, and picked up something from the ground.

A match hissed to life, and he held it against the wick of a candle. "Welcome to my place."

Compared to utter darkness, the candlelight was surprisingly bright. We stood at the opening of a black granite foyer that led to a vast room beyond, also carved from black granite. Silk rugs in chromatic shades of navy, gray, and black decorated the floors. The furniture was sparse, but the pieces Jev had selected were sleek and contemporary, with clean lines and artistic appeal.

"Wow," I said.

"I don't bring many people down here. It's not something I want to share with everyone. I like the privacy and seclusion."

He definitely had both, I thought, looking around the cavelike studio. Under the candlelight, the granite walls and floors glittered as though flecked with diamonds.

As I continued my slow exploration, Jev walked the room, lighting candles.

"Kitchen to the left," he said. "Bedroom in the back."

I tossed a coy glance over my shoulder. "Why, Jev, are you flirting with me?"

He watched me with dark eyes.

"I'm starting to wonder if you're trying to distract me from our previous conversation." I trailed my finger over the only heirloom piece in the room, a full-length silver-plated mirror that looked like it belonged in a medieval French château. My mom would be truly impressed.

Jev dropped into a French Deco–inspired black leather sofa, spreading his arms along the back. "I'm not the distraction in the room."

"Oh? And what might that be?"

I felt his eyes devour me as I moved around the room. He assessed me head to toe without blinking, and a hot ache shivered through me. A kiss would have been less intimate.

Shoving down the warmth his gaze stirred inside me, I stopped to take in a breathtaking oil painting. The colors were so vivid, the detail so violent.

"*The Fall of Phaeton*," he informed me. "The Greek sun god Helios had a son, Phaeton, by a mortal woman. Each day Helios drove a chariot across the sky. Phaeton tricked his father into letting him drive the chariot, even though Phaeton wasn't strong enough or skilled enough to handle the horses. As expected, the horses ran wild and fell to Earth, burning everything in their path." He waited, drawing my eyes to him. "Surely you're aware of the effect you have on me."

"Now you're teasing me."

"I enjoy teasing you, true. But there are some things I never joke about." All banter left him, and his eyes turned serious.

Trapped in Jev's gaze, I accepted what had so plainly been laid out before me. He was a fallen angel. The power that vibrated off him was different from what I felt around Scott. Stronger and sharper. Even now, the air whipped with energy. Every molecule in my body was ultrasensitive to his presence, aware of his movements.

"I know you're a fallen angel," I said. "I know you force Nephilim to swear an oath of fealty. You possess their bodies. In this war that's going on, you're on the opposite side from Scott. No wonder you don't like him."

"You're remembering."

"Not nearly enough. If you're a fallen angel, why do business with Hank, a Nephil? Aren't you supposed to be mortal enemies?" I sounded more sharp than I intended; I wasn't sure how to feel about the idea of Jev as a fallen angel. A bad guy. To keep this revelation from pushing me over the edge, I reminded myself I'd figured this all out before, once upon a time. If I'd handled it then, I could handle it now.

Once again, pity flashed across his expression. "About Hank." He dragged his hands down his face.

"What about him?" I stared at him, trying to figure out what he was having such a difficult time telling me. His features carried such deep sympathy, I automatically stiffened, bracing for the worst.

Jev stood, walked to the wall, leaned an arm against it. His sleeves were pushed to his elbows, his head bowed.

"I want to know everything," I told him. "Starting with you. I want to remember us. How did we meet? What did we mean to each other? After that, I want you to tell me everything about Hank. Even if you're worried I won't like what you have to say. Help me remember. I can't go on like this. I can't move forward until I know what I left behind. I'm not afraid of Hank," I added.

"I'm afraid of what he's capable of. He doesn't draw the line. He pushes as far as he can. Worst of all, he can't be trusted. With anything." He hesitated. "I'll come clean. I'll tell you everything, but only because Hank double-crossed me. You're not supposed to be in this anymore. I did everything I could to leave you out of it. Hank gave me his word he'd stay away from you. Imagine my surprise, then, when you told me earlier tonight that he's putting the moves on your mom. If he's back in your life, it's because he's up to something. Which means you're not safe, we're back to square one, and coming clean doesn't put you in any more danger."

My pulse hammered through my veins, my alarm running deeper than bone. Hank. Just as I'd suspected, everything led back to him. "Help me remember, Jev."

"Is that what you want?" He searched my face with the need to know that I was absolutely certain.

"Yes," I said, sounding braver than I felt.

Jev lowered himself onto the edge of the sofa. He unbuttoned his shirt carefully. Even though I was taken aback, instinct told me to be patient. Bracing his elbows on his knees, Jev hung his head between his naked shoulders. Every muscle in his body was rigid. For one moment, he looked like Phaeton from his painting, each sinew etched and chiseled. I took one step closer, then two. The guttering candlelight flickered across his body.

I sucked in a breath. Two jagged stripes of torn flesh marred his otherwise flawless back. The wounds were raw and red, and wrung my stomach into a knot. I couldn't imagine the pain he was in. I couldn't imagine what had happened to create such brutal gouges.

"Touch them," Jev said, looking up at me with nervousness rising to the surface of those unreadable black eyes. "Concentrate on what you want to know."

"I—don't understand."

"The night I drove you away from the 7-Eleven, you ripped my shirt and touched my wing scars. You saw one of my memories."

I blinked. That wasn't a hallucination? Hank, Jev, the caged girl—they were from Jev's memory?

Any doubt I'd been dragging around vanished. Wing scars. Of course. Because he was a fallen angel. And even though I didn't know the physics behind it, when I touched his scars, I saw things no one else could possibly know. Except Jev. I finally had what I wanted, a window to the past, and fear threatened to get the better of me.

"I should warn you that if you go inside a memory that includes you, things will get complicated," he said. "You might see a double of yourself. You and my memory of you could be there at the same time, and you'd be forced to watch the events as an invisible bystander. The other scenario is that you'll transfer into your own version of the memory. Meaning you might experience my memory from your own point of view. You won't see a double if that happens. You'll be the only version of yourself in the memory. I've heard of both happening, but the first is more common."

My hands trembled. "I'm scared."

"I'll give you five minutes. If you haven't come back, I'll pull your hand off my scars. That will break the connection."

I bit my lip. *This is your chance*, I told myself. *Don't run away, not when you've made it this far. The truth is scary, but knowing nothing is crippling. You of all people understand that.*

"Give me a half hour," I told Jev firmly.

Then I cleared my mind, trying to calm my racing thoughts. I didn't have to understand everything right now. I only had to take a leap of faith. I held my hand out, part of the way. I squeezed my eyes shut, summoning courage. I was grateful when Jev's hand closed over mine, guiding me the rest of the way.

M Y FIRST CONSCIOUS THOUGHT WAS OF BEING nailed down. No. Nailed *inside*. Locked in the snuggest of coffins. Tangled in a net. Defenseless and dictated by another body. A body that looked like my own— same hands, same hair, identical down to the finest detail—but one I had no control over. A strange phantom body that acted against my will, dragging me into its tide.

My second thought was *Patch*.

Patch was kissing me. Kissing me in a way that terrified me even more than the phantom body and its unbreakable hold over me. His mouth, everywhere. The rain, warm and sweet. The swell of distant thunder. And his body, taking up space, standing so very close, radiating heat.

Patch.

Astonished and shaken, I clawed at the memory. I begged to be let out.

I gasped as if coming up from a lengthy and punishing stay under water. At the same time, my eyes flew open.

"What is it?" Jev asked, grasping me protectively by the shoulders as I slumped against him.

We were back in his granite studio, the same candles flickering along the walls. The familiarity of it flooded me with relief. I was terrified of being trapped down there. Terrified of the sensation of being held captive in a body that I couldn't command.

"Your memory was of me," I choked. "But there wasn't a double. I was trapped inside my body, but I couldn't control it. I couldn't move it. It was—terrifying."

"What did you see?" he asked, his body tense enough to be made of stone. One hard push in the wrong direction, and he might well shatter.

"We were above here. In the shed. When I said your name, I didn't say Jev. I called you Patch. And you were—kissing me." I was too shocked to think about blushing.

Jev smoothed hair off my face, stroking my cheek. "Nothing is wrong," he murmured. "Back then you knew me as Patch. That was the name I was going under when we met. I dropped the name when I lost you. I've been going by Jev ever since."

I felt stupid for crying, but I couldn't stop myself. Jev was Patch. My old boyfriend. It suddenly made sense. No wonder no one had recognized Jev's name—he'd changed it after I disappeared.

"I kissed you back," I said, still crying softly. "In the memory."

The tightness in his face softened. "That bad?"

I wondered if I could ever tell him just what his kiss had done to me. It was so pleasurable it had single-handedly frightened me out of his memory.

To avoid having to answer him, I said, "You told me earlier that you tried to bring me here to your home once before, but Hank stopped us. I think that was the memory I saw. But I didn't see Hank. I didn't make it that far. I broke the connection. I couldn't handle being inside my body but not being able to control it. I wasn't prepared for just how real it would feel."

"The girl in control of your body was you," he reminded me. "You in the past. Before you lost your memory."

I jumped up, pacing the room. "I have to go back."

"Nora—"

"I have to face Hank. And I can't face him here until I've faced him in there," I said, thrusting my finger at Jev's scars. And *face yourself,* I thought. *You have to face the part of you that knows the truth.*

Jev gave me a measured look. "Do you want me to pull you out?"

"No. This time I'm going all the way."

The moment I arrived back inside Jev's memory, I felt a switch being thrown, and the next thing I knew, I was reliving the flashback through the eyes of the girl I'd been before my memory was damaged. Her body overtook mine, and her thoughts overshadowed my own. I breathed through the panic, opening myself up to her—to *me.*

Outside, the rain made a metallic *ping* as it pattered the shed. Patch and I were both wet from it, and he sucked a drop of rainwater from my lip. I hung my fingertips on the waistband of his jeans and tugged him closer. Our mouths slipped over each other, a warm distraction from the chill in the air.

He nuzzled my neck affectionately. "I love you. I'm happier right now than I ever remember being."

I was about to answer when a man's voice, unaccountably familiar, carried out of the darkest part of the shed. "How very touching. Seize the angel."

A handful of overly tall young men, undoubtedly Nephilim, rushed out of the shadows and surrounded Patch, twisting his arms behind his back.

I hardly had time to absorb what was happening when Patch's voice broke into my thoughts as clearly as if he'd spoken in my ear.

When I start fighting, run. Take the Jeep. Don't go home. Stay in the Jeep and keep driving until I find you.

The man who lingered at the back of the shed, commanding the others, stepped forward into the eerie carnival light slicing through the shed's many cracks. He was unnaturally young for his age, with crisp blue eyes and a ruthless curl to his mouth.

"Mr. Millar," I whispered.

How could he possibly be here? After everything I'd gone through this night, a near-fatal attempt on my life, learning the sordid truth about my heritage, and overcoming it all to be with Patch, now this? It didn't seem real.

"Let me introduce myself properly," he said. "I'm the Black Hand. I knew your father Harrison well. I'm glad he's not here now to see you debasing yourself with one of the devil's brood." He wagged his head at me. "You're not the girl I thought you'd grow up to be, Nora. Fraternizing with the enemy, making a mockery of your heritage. But I can forgive that." He paused with significance. "Tell me, Nora. Was it you who killed my dear friend and associate, Chauncey Langeais?"

My blood ran cold. I was caught between the impulse to lie and the knowledge that it wouldn't do any good. He knew I'd killed Chauncey. The cold twist of his mouth frowned at me in judgment.

Now! Patch shouted, cutting into my thoughts. *Run!*

I bolted for the shed door. But I only made it a few steps before a Nephil hooked my elbow. Just as fast, he yanked my other arm

BECCA FITZPATRICK

behind my back. I tried to wrench free, every movement a desperate lunge for the shed door.

Hank Millar's footfalls crossed the shed behind me. "I owe this to Chauncey."

Any chill I'd felt from the rain had vanished; rivulets of sweat trickled beneath my shirt.

"We shared a vision. One we intended to see through to the end," Hank continued. "Who would've guessed you of all people would be the one to nearly destroy it?"

A slew of spiteful responses sprang to mind, but I didn't dare set off Hank. My only asset was time, and I needed to keep it on my side. The Nephil spun me around just as Hank retrieved a long, thin dagger from the waist of his pants.

Touch my back.

Patch's voice cut through the panic clanging between my ears. Frantically, I looked sideways at him.

Go inside my memory. Touch the place where my wings fuse into my back. He nodded, urging me to act.

Easier said than done, I thought at him, even though I knew he couldn't hear me. A span of five or six feet separated us, and both of us were held captive by Nephilim.

"Let go of me," I snapped at the Nephil pinning my arms. "We both know I'm not going anywhere. I can't outrun all of you."

The Nephil glanced at Hank, who confirmed my request with a slight nod. Then he sighed, almost bored. "I'm sorry to do this,

Nora. But justice must be served. Chauncey would have done the same for me."

I rubbed the insides of my elbows, my skin burning from where the Nephil had gripped me. "Justice? What about family? I'm your daughter by blood." *And nothing more.*

"You're a blight on my heritage," he dismissed. "A turncoat. A humiliation."

I gave him the blackest look I had inside me, even though my stomach roiled in fear. "Are you here to avenge Chauncey, or is this an attempt to save face? Couldn't handle your daughter dating a fallen angel and embarrassing you in front of your little Nephilim army? Am I getting warm?" So much for not setting him off.

Hank frowned slightly.

Think you could get inside my memory before he snaps your neck? Patch hissed to my mind.

I didn't look at Patch, afraid I'd lose my resolve if I did. We both knew escaping into his memory wasn't going to get me out of here. It would merely transport my mind into his past. And I supposed that was what Patch wanted; for me to be in some other place when Hank killed me. Patch knew this was the end, and he was saving me the pain of being conscious at my own execution. A ridiculous image of an ostrich with its head in the sand came distinctly to mind.

If I was going to die in the next few moments, it wouldn't be before I said the words that I hoped would haunt Hank for the rest of eternity.

"I guess it's a good thing you chose to keep Marcie as your daughter instead of me," I said. "She's cute, popular, dates the right boys, and is too dumb to question anything you do. But I know for a fact the dead can come back. I saw my dad earlier tonight—my real dad."

The frown on Hank's face deepened.

"If he can visit me, there's nothing preventing me from visiting Marcie—or your wife. And I won't stop there. I know you're dating my mom on the sly again. I'll tell her the truth about you, dead or alive. How many dates do you think you can squeeze in before I let her know you killed me?"

That was all I had time to say before Patch rammed his knee into the gut of the Nephil holding his right arm. The Nephil slumped, and Patch swung his free fist at the nose of the Nephil pinning his left arm. There was an awful crunch, and a blubbering yowl.

I ran for Patch, throwing myself against him.

"Hurry," he said, forcing my hand up the back of his shirt.

I splayed my hand blindly on Patch's back, hoping I'd make contact with the place where his wings fused into his skin. His wings were made of spiritual matter and I couldn't see or feel them, but it only made sense that they'd span a good portion of his back and be hard to miss.

Someone—Hank or one of the other Nephilim—tore at my shoulders, but I only slipped a little; Patch's arms were around me, locking me against him. With no time to spare, I plunged my hand a second time up the smooth, toned skin of Patch's back. *Where were his wings?*

He kissed my forehead roughly and murmured something unintelligible. There was no time for more. A searing white light exploded at the back of my mind. The very next moment, I was suspended in a dark universe speckled with pricks of colorful light. I knew I had to move toward any of the millions of light pricks—each one a stored memory—but they seemed miles away.

I heard Hank shouting, and I knew it meant I hadn't fully crossed over. Maybe my hand was close to the base of Patch's wings, but not close enough. I couldn't block out the flashing images of all the horrible, painful ways Hank could end my life, and I fought my way through the darkness, determined to see Patch in his memories one last time before it was all over.

Tears stained my vision. *The end.* I didn't want this to be that moment, stealing up behind me with no warning. I had so much more I wanted to tell Patch. Did he know how much he meant to me? What we had together—it had barely started. Everything could not come crashing down now.

I summoned a picture of Patch's face. The image I chose was of the very first time we met. His hair was long, curling over his ears, and his eyes looked like they didn't miss a thing, perceiving the secrets and desires of my soul. I remembered the startled expression on his face when I'd stormed into Bo's Arcade, upsetting his pool game, and demanded that he help me finish our biology assignment. I remembered his wolfish smile, daring me to play along, as he'd moved to kiss me that very first time in my kitchen. . . .

Patch was shouting too. Not ahead of me in his memories, but far below me, in the shed. Two words rose above the others, sounding distorted in my ears, as though they had traveled a great distance.

Deal. Compromise.

I frowned, straining to hear more. What was Patch saying? I suddenly feared that whatever it was, I wouldn't like it.

No! I shouted, needing to stop Patch. I tried to propel myself back to the shed, but I was in a vacuum, floating idly. Patch! What are you telling him?

I felt a strange tug to my body, as if I'd been latched behind my spine. The sound of shouting voices swirled shut behind me as I hurtled toward a blinding light and inside the corridors of Patch's memory.

Again.

I arrived inside the second memory in an instant.

I stood once again in the damp chill of the shed crowded with Hank, his Nephilim men, and Jev, and I could only gather that this second memory was beginning precisely where the last one had ended. I felt that familiar switch being thrown, but this time I wasn't locked inside a version of myself from the past. My thoughts and actions belonged to the present me. I was now a double, an invisible bystander, watching Jev's version of this moment as he remembered it.

Jev held a sluggish version of my body. My body was limp except for my hand, which was splayed on his back. My eyes were rolled back to whites and I vaguely wondered if I would remember both memories when I pulled out entirely.

"Ah, yes. I'd heard about that trick," Hank said. "It's true, I gather? She's inside your memory as we speak, and all this by simply touching your wings?"

Looking at Hank, I felt a surge of helplessness. Had I just said he was my father? I had. I felt a compulsion to beat my fists against his chest until he denied it, but the truth burned like a fever inside me. I could loathe him all I wanted, but it didn't change the fact that his vile blood coursed through my veins. Harrison Grey might have given me all the love of a parent, but Hank Millar had given me life.

"I'll make a deal," Jev said roughly. "Something you want, in exchange for Nora's life."

Hank's lips twitched. "What could you possibly have that I want?"

"You're building a Nephilim army with the hope of overthrowing fallen angels as early as this Cheshvan. Don't look surprised. I'm not the only angel who knows what you're up to. Bands of

BECCA FITZPATRICK

fallen angels are forming alliances, and they're going to make their Nephilim vassals regret thinking they could ever break free. It's not going to be a pretty Cheshvan for any Nephil who bears the Black Hand's mark of allegiance. And that's only the tip of the iceberg when it comes to what they have in store. You're never going to pull this off without a man on the inside."

Hank gestured to dismiss his men. "Leave me alone with the angel. Take the girl outside."

"You're kidding if you think I'm letting her out of my sight," Jev said.

Hank relented with an amused snort. "Very well. Keep her while you can."

As soon as the Nephilim exited, Hank said, "Keep talking."

"Let Nora live, and I'll spy for you."

Hank's blond eyebrows swept up. "My, my. Your feelings for her run deeper than I thought." His gaze raked my unconscious figure. "I daresay she's not worth it. Sadly, I don't care what you and your guardian angel friends think of my plans. I'm far more interested in fallen angels, what they're thinking, any countermeasures they might attempt. You're not one of them anymore. So how do you plan to be privy to their dealings?"

"Let me worry about that."

Hank considered Jev with a discriminating eye. "All right," he said at last. "I'm intrigued." A careless shrug. "I'm not the one who stands to lose. I take it you'd have me swear an oath?"

"Wouldn't have it any other way," Jev said coolly.

Drawing the dagger once again from the waist of his pants, Hank made a slash across the palm of his left hand. "I swear my oath to let the girl live. If I break my vow, I plead that I may die and return to the dust from which I was created."

Jev accepted the blade and sliced his hand next. Making a fist, he shook loose a few drops of a bloodlike substance. "I swear to feed you all the information I can on what fallen angels are planning. If I break my vow, I will voluntarily lock myself in the chains of hell."

The two of them clasped hands, mingling their blood. By the time they pulled free, their wounds had healed perfectly.

"Keep in touch," Hank said with irony, dusting his shirt as though being in the shed had somehow sullied him. He raised his cell phone to his ear, and when he caught Jev watching, he explained, "Making sure my car is ready."

However, when he spoke into the phone, his words adopted a hardened undertone. "Send my men in. All of them. I want the girl taken away."

Jev went still. Even as the sound of running feet approached the shed he said, "What's this?"

"I swore an oath to let her live," Hank informed him. "When I release her is up to me—and you. She's yours after you've given me enough information to guarantee I can overthrow fallen angels by Cheshvan. Consider Nora insurance."

Jev's eyes flicked to the shed door, but Hank interjected smoothly, "Don't go down that road. You're outnumbered twenty to one. We'd both hate to see Nora needlessly injured in a scuffle. Play this smart. Hand her over."

Jev grabbed Hank's sleeve, jerking him close. "If you take her away, I will see to it that your corpse fertilizes the ground we're standing on," he said, his voice more venomous than I'd ever heard it.

Nothing in Hank's expression hinted at fear. If anything, he appeared almost smug. "My corpse? Is that my cue to laugh?"

Hank opened the shed door, and his Nephilim men thundered in.

Just like a dream, Jev's memories ended almost before they began. There was a moment of disorientation, and then the granite studio came into focus. Jev stood silhouetted against the candlelight. The flame gave just enough illumination to bring a severe glint to his eyes. A dark angel indeed.

"Okay," I whispered, haunted by a sensation of lingering vertigo. "Okay . . . then."

He smiled, but his expression was uncertain. "Okay then? That's it?"

I turned my face up to his. I could hardly look at him the same way. I was crying without realizing I'd started. "You made a deal with Hank. You saved my life. Why would you do that for me?"

"Angel," he murmured, clasping my face between his hands. "I don't think you understand the lengths I would go to if it means keeping you here with me."

My throat choked with emotion. I couldn't find words. Hank Millar, a man who'd stood quietly in the shadows for years, was now revealed to have given me life, only to try to end it, and Jev was the reason I was alive. Hank Millar. The man who'd stood in my house on numerous occasions, as if he belonged. Who'd smiled and kissed my mom. Who'd spoken to me with warmth and familiarity—

"He kidnapped me," I said, piecing it all together. I'd suspected it before, but Jev's memories filled in the gaps with shocking clarity. "He swore the oath not to kill me, but he held me hostage to make sure you were motivated to spy for him. Three whole months. He strung everyone along for *three whole months*. All to get his hands on information about fallen angels. He let my mom believe I was as good as dead."

Of course he had. He'd proven he had no qualms when it came to getting his hands dirty. He was a powerful Nephil, capable of an arsenal of mind-tricks. And after dumping me in the cemetery, he'd used them to keep my memories far, far away. After all, he couldn't release me and have me shouting his diabolical deeds to the world.

"I hate him. Words can't express how angry I am. I want him to pay. I want him dead," I said with hardened resolution.

"The mark on your wrist," Jev said. "It's not a birthmark. I've seen it twice before. On my old Nephil vassal, a man named Chauncey Langeais. Hank Millar also has the mark, Nora. The mark links you to their bloodline, like an outward expression of a genetic marker or DNA sequence. Hank is your biological father."

"I know," I said, shaking my head with bitterness.

He laced his hand in mine, brushing a kiss across my knuckles. I was acutely aware of the pressure of his mouth, little tingles swimming under my skin. "You remember?"

"I heard myself say it in the memory, but I must have already known. I wasn't surprised; I was *angry*. I don't remember when I first knew it." I pressed my thumb into the mark slashing my inner wrist. "But I feel it. There's a disconnect between my mind and my heart, but I feel the truth. They say when people lose their vision, their hearing becomes sharper. I've lost part of my memory, but maybe my intuition is stronger."

We considered this in silence. What Jev didn't know was that my true parentage wasn't the only piece of information my intuition was making a judgment on.

"I don't want to talk about Hank. Not right now. I want to talk about something else I saw. Or rather, I should say something I discovered."

He regarded me with equal parts curiosity and wariness.

A deep breath. "I learned that I was either crazy in love with you, or putting on the best performance of my life."

His eyes remained carefully guarded, but I thought I saw a flicker of hope. "Which one are you leaning toward?"

Only one way to find out. "First, I need to know what happened between you and Marcie. This is one of those times when giving me full disclosure is in your best interest," I warned. "Marcie said you were her summer fling. Scott told me she played a role in our breakup. All that's missing is your version."

Jev stroked his chin. "Do I look like a summer fling?"

I tried to picture Jev playing Frisbee at the beach or lathering up in sunscreen. I tried to imagine him buying Marcie ice cream on the boardwalk and patiently listening to her endless chatter. Any way I tried it, the image brought a smile to my face. "Point taken," I said. "So spill."

"Marcie was an assignment. I hadn't gone rogue yet; I still had my wings, which made me a guardian angel, taking orders from the archangels, and they wanted me to keep an eye on her. She's Hank's daughter, which equates to danger by association. I kept her safe, but it wasn't a pleasant experience. I've done my best to put the memory behind me."

"So nothing happened?"

His mouth tipped up slightly. "I almost shot her once or twice, but the excitement ends there."

"Missed opportunity."

He shrugged. "There's always next time. Still want to talk about Marcie?"

I held his steady gaze, shaking my head no. "I don't feel like talking," I confessed quietly.

I rose to my feet, pulling him up with me, a little dizzy from the audacity of what I was about to do. I was all slippery emotions inside, able to grasp only two of them. Curiosity, and desire.

He held perfectly still. "Angel," he said roughly. He stroked his thumb across my cheek, but I pulled back slightly.

"Don't rush this. If there's any memory of being with you left inside me, I can't force it." That was half the truth. The other half I kept to myself. I'd been secretly fantasizing about this moment since I'd first seen Jev. I'd created a hundred variations of it in my head since then, but my imagination had never come close to making me feel the way I did right now. I felt an irresistible draw, luring me closer, closer.

No matter what happened, I didn't ever want to forget how it felt with Jev. I wanted to imprint his touch, his taste, event the scent of him so solidly inside me that no one—*no one*—could take them away from me.

I slid my hands up his torso, memorizing every ripple of muscle. I inhaled the same scents I had that first night in the Tahoe. Leather, spice, mint. I traced the planes of his face with my fingers, curiously exploring his sharp, almost Italian features. All through this Jev didn't move, enduring my touch with his eyes closed. "Angel," he repeated in a strained voice.

"Not yet."

I spread my fingers through his hair, feeling it flutter through them. I committed every last detail to memory. The bronzed shade of his skin, the confident line of his posture, the seductive length of his eyelashes. He wasn't clean lines and perfect symmetries, and I found him even more interesting for it.

Done stalling, I told myself at last. Leaning in, I closed my eyes.

His mouth opened under mine, his tightly reined control shuddering through his body. His arms wrapped around me, securing me against him. He kissed me harder, and the depth of my response unnerved me.

My legs felt wobbly and heavy. I sank into Jev, and he backed us slowly down the wall until I came to straddle his lap. Brightness lit up inside me, and the heat of it consumed every hollow corner. A hidden world opened between us, one that was as frightening as it was familiar. I knew it was real. I'd kissed like this before. I'd kissed Patch like this before. I couldn't remember calling him anything but Jev, but somehow Patch just felt . . . right. The hot delicious-ness of being with him came roaring back, threatening to swallow me whole.

I pulled away first, trailing my tongue along my lower lip.

Patch made a low, questioning sound. "Not bad?"

I bent my head toward his. "Practice makes perfect."

CHAPTER

MY EYES FLUTTERED OPEN AND THE ROOM took shape. The lights were off. The air was cool. The most luxurious and delicious fabric caressed my skin. The memory of last night came back to me in a whirl-wind. Patch and I had made out.... I vaguely recollected muttering something to him about being too exhausted to drive....

I'd fallen asleep at Patch's.

I wrestled myself up to sitting. "My mom is going to kill me!" I blurted to no one in particular. For one thing, it was a school night. For another, I'd missed curfew by a mile and never bothered to call and explain why.

Patch sat in a chair in the corner, his chin propped on his fist. "Already taken care of. I called Vee. She agreed to vouch for you. The story she gave your mom is that the two of you were at her house watching the five-hour version of *Pride and Prejudice*, you lost track of time, you fell asleep first, and rather than wake you up, Vee's mom agreed to let you sleep over."

"You called Vee? And she agreed, no questions asked?" It didn't sound like Vee at all. Especially the new Vee, who'd developed a death wish for the male race in general.

"It might have been slightly more difficult than that."

His enigmatic tone clicked in my brain. "You *mind-tricked* her?"

"Between asking permission and begging forgiveness, I lean toward the latter."

"She's my best friend. You can't mind-trick her!" Even though I was still angry at Vee for lying about Patch, she must have had her reasons. And while I didn't approve, and intended to get to the bottom of it very, very soon, she meant the world to me. Patch had crossed a line.

"You were exhausted. And you looked peaceful sleeping in my bed."

"That's because your bed has some kind of spell on it," I said, less testily than I intended. "I could sleep here forever. Satin sheets?" I guessed.

"Silk."

Black silk sheets. Who knew how much they'd cost? One thing was certain, they had a hypnotic quality I found very distracting. "Swear you won't *ever* mind-trick Vee again."

"Done," he said easily, now that he'd gotten away with it. Beg forgiveness sounded about right.

"I don't suppose you have an explanation for why both Vee and my mom have consistently denied knowing you exist? In fact, the only two people who've confessed to remembering you at all are Marcie and Scott."

"Vee dated Rixon. After Hank kidnapped you, I erased her memory of Rixon. He used her and put her through a lot of pain. He put everyone through a lot of pain. It was easier in the long run if I did my best to make everyone forget him. The alternative was letting your friends and family hang their hopes on an arrest that was never going to happen. When I went to wipe Vee's mind, she put up a fight. To this day, she's angry. She doesn't know why, but it's rooted inside her. Erasing someone's memory isn't as easy as it sounds. It's like trying to pick all the chocolate chips out of a cookie. It's never going to be perfect. Pieces get left behind. Unexplainable beliefs that feel compelling and familiar. Vee can't remember what I did to her, but she knows not to trust me. She can't remember Rixon, but she knows there's a guy out there who caused her a lot of grief."

It explained Vee's suspicion toward guys and my instant aversion to Hank. Our minds might have been wiped clean, but a few crumbs got left behind.

"Might want to cut her some slack," Patch suggested. "She has your back. Honesty is a good thing, but so is loyalty."

"In other words, let her off the hook."

He shrugged. "Your call."

Vee had looked me in the eye and lied without reservation. It wasn't a light offense. But the thing was, I knew how she felt. She'd had her memory tampered with, and it wasn't a good feeling. Vulnerable didn't begin to describe it. Vee lied to protect me. Was I that different? I hadn't told her a thing about fallen angels or Nephilim, and I'd used the same excuse. I could either hold Vee to a double standard, or I could take Patch's advice and let it go.

"And my mom? Going to vouch for her, too?" I asked.

"She thinks I had something to do with your abduction. Better me than Hank," he said, his tone cooling. "If Hank thought she knew the truth, he'd do something about it."

He was putting it lightly. I wouldn't put it past Hank to hurt her if it meant getting what he wanted. All the more reason to keep her in the dark . . . for the time being.

I didn't want to feel a shred of empathy for Hank, to humanize him in any way, but I found myself wondering what kind of man he'd been when he first fell in love with my mom. Had he always been evil? Or, in the beginning, had he cared about us . . . and over time, he'd built his entire world around his Nephilim mission, and it had taken precedence?

I abruptly ended my speculations. Hank was evil now, and that was what mattered. He'd kidnapped me, and I was going to make certain he was held accountable.

I said, "You mean the arrest was never going to happen because Rixon's in hell now." *Literally in hell, by the sound of it.*

He confirmed this with a nod, but his eyes darkened a shade. I supposed Patch didn't like to talk about hell. I doubted any fallen angel did.

"In your memory, I saw you agree to spy on fallen angels for Hank," I said.

Patch nodded. "What they're planning and when. I meet weekly with Hank to share information."

"What if fallen angels find out you're selling secrets behind their backs?"

"I'm hoping they don't."

I wasn't comforted by his casual attitude. "What would they do to you?"

"I've been in worse situations and managed to pull through." The edges of his mouth tilted higher. "All this time and you still don't have any faith in me."

"Could you be serious for two seconds?"

He leaned over and kissed my hand, and spoke to me with sincerity. "They'd cast me into hell. They're supposed to let the archangels handle that, but it doesn't always work that way."

"Explain," I said firmly.

He slouched back with a certain lazy arrogance. "Humans are forbidden from killing each other; it's the law. But people are murdered every day. My world isn't much different. For every law, there's someone out there willing to break it. I won't pretend to be innocent. Three months ago I chained Rixon in hell, even though I had no authority other than my own sense of justice."

"You chained Rixon in hell?"

Patch eyed me with curiosity. "He had to pay. He tried to kill you."

"Scott told me about Rixon, but he didn't know who chained him in hell, or how it was done. I'll let him know he has you to thank."

"I'm not interested in the half-breed's gratitude. But I can tell you how it's done. When the archangels banish a fallen angel from heaven and rip out his wings, they keep one feather for themselves. The feather is meticulously filed and preserved. If the occasion arises where a fallen angel needs to be chained in hell, the archangels retrieve his feather and burn it. It's a symbolic act with inescapable results. The term 'burn in hell' isn't a figure of speech."

"You had one of Rixon's feathers?"

"Before he went behind my back, he was the closest thing I had to a brother. I knew he had a feather, and I knew where he kept it. I knew everything about him. And because of it, I didn't give him an impersonal send-off." Though I suspected he meant to remain impassive, Patch's jaw contracted. "I dragged him down to hell and burned the feather in front of him."

His recounting of the story raised every hair on my scalp. Even if Vee betrayed me so blatantly, I wasn't sure I had it in me to make her suffer the way he had clearly made Rixon suffer. Suddenly I understood why Patch had taken the subject so personally.

Breaking away from the gruesome picture Patch had painted in my mind, I recalled the feather I'd found in the cemetery. "Are these feathers floating around everywhere? Can anyone stumble across one?"

Patch shook his head. "The archangels keep one feather on record. A few fallen angels like Rixon make it to Earth with a feather or two intact. When that happens, the fallen angel makes damn sure his feather doesn't fall into the wrong hands." The suggestion of a smile lifted the corners of his mouth. "And you thought we weren't sentimental."

"What happens to the rest of the feathers?"

"They rapidly deteriorate on the way down. Falling from heaven isn't a smooth ride."

"What about you? Any secret feathers locked away?"

He cocked an eyebrow. "Plotting my downfall?"

I smiled back, despite the seriousness of the subject. "A girl's got to keep her options open."

"Hate to disappoint, but no feathers. I came to Earth stripped naked."

"Mm," I said as casually as I could, but I felt my face growing warm at the picture that one little word had planted in my brain. Naked thoughts were not good thoughts to have while I was locked away in Patch's ultrasecret, ultraswanky bedroom.

"I like you in my bed," Patch said. "I rarely pull down the covers. I rarely sleep. I could get used to this picture."

"Are you offering me a permanent place?"

"Already put a spare key in your pocket."

I patted my pocket. Sure enough, something small and hard was snug inside. "How charitable of you."

"I'm not feeling very charitable now," he said, holding my eyes, his voice deepening with a gravelly edge. "I missed you, Angel. Not one day went by that I didn't feel you missing from my life. You haunted me to the point that I began to believe Hank had gone back on his oath and killed you. I saw your ghost in everything. I couldn't escape you and I didn't want to. You tortured me, but it was better than losing you."

"Why didn't you tell me everything that night in the alley with Gabe? You were so angry." I shook my head, remembering every caustic word he'd directed at me. "I thought you hated me."

"After Hank released you, I spied on you to make sure you were okay, but I swore to end my involvement with you for your own safety. I'd made my decision and I thought I could deal with it. I tried to convince myself there was nothing left for us. But when I saw you that night in the alley, my argument fell apart. I wanted you to remember me the way I couldn't stop thinking about you. But you couldn't. I'd made sure of it." His gaze dropped to his hands, clasped loosely between his knees. "I owe you an apology," he said quietly. "Hank erased your memory to keep you from remembering what he did to you, but I agreed to it. I told him to erase it back far enough that you wouldn't remember me, either."

I snapped my eyes to Patch's. "You agreed to *what?*"

"I wanted to give you your life back. Before fallen angels, before Nephilim, before me. I thought that was the only way you'd get through the worst of what happened. I don't think either of us will deny that I've complicated your life. I've tried to make it better, but things haven't always gone my way. I thought it through and came to the difficult decision the best thing for your recovery and your future was for me to walk away."

"Patch—"

"As for Hank, I refused to watch him destroy you. I refused to watch him ruin any chance you had at happiness by making you carry around those memories. You're right—he kidnapped you because he thought he could use you to control me. He took you away at the end of June, and didn't bring you back until September. Every day during those months you were locked up and left by yourself. Even the most hardened soldiers can break in solitary confinement, and Hank knew that was my greatest fear. He demanded I show my willingness to spy for him, even though I'd sworn an oath. He dangled you over me every minute of those months." Patch's eyes glittered with a hardened edge. "He'll pay for that, and on my terms," he said in a low, deadly voice that sent a chill up my spine.

"That night in the shed, he had us surrounded," he continued. "The only thing on my mind was keeping him from killing you on the spot. If I'd been alone in the shed, I would have fought. I didn't trust you to handle a fight, and I've regretted it ever since. I couldn't handle seeing you hurt, and it blinded me. I underestimated everything you've already been through and grown stronger because of. Hank knew that, and I played right into his hands.

"I laid a deal on the table. I told him I'd be his spy if he'd let you live. He accepted, then called in his Nephilim men to take you away. I fought as hard as I could, Angel. They were mangled by the time they managed to drag you away. I met Hank four days later and offered to let him tear out my wings if he'd release you. It was the last thing I had to bargain with, and he agreed to hand you over, but the best I could get out of him was by the end of summer. During the next three months, I searched tirelessly for you, but Hank had planned for that as well. He went to great lengths to keep your location secret. I caught and tortured several of his men, but none of them could tell me where you were. I'd be surprised if Hank told more than one or two handpicked men he assigned to make sure your basic needs were met.

"A week before Hank released you, he sent one of his Nephilim messengers to find me. The messenger smugly informed me that Hank intended to erase your memory once he let you go, and did I have any objections? I wiped the smirk off his face. Then I dragged him, bloody and battered, to Hank's home.

"We were waiting for Hank when he left for work the next morning. I told him if he wanted to avoid looking like his messenger, he would erase your memory far back enough that you'd never have flashbacks. I didn't want you to have a single memory of me, and I didn't want you waking up with nightmares of being locked up and completely alone for days on end. I didn't want you screaming out in the night without knowing why. I wanted to give you back as much of a life as I could. I knew the only way to keep you safe was to keep you out of everything. Then I told Hank to never lay eyes on you again. I made it clear that if he crossed paths with you, I would hunt him down and mutilate his body beyond recognition. And then I would find a way to kill him, no matter the cost. I thought he was smart enough to hold up his end of the bargain until you told me he's hooked up with your mom. Instinct tells me this isn't just about his amorous affections. He's up to something, and whatever it is, he's using your mom, or more likely you, to accomplish it."

My heart pounded in double time. "That snake!"

Patch laughed grimly. "I would have used a stronger word, but that works too."

How could Hank do those things to me? Obviously he'd chosen not to love me, but he was still my father. Didn't blood mean anything? How did he have the audacity to look me in the eye these past few days and smile? He'd ripped me away from my mom. He'd held me captive for weeks, and now he dared step inside my home and act as though he cared about my family?

"He has an endgame in all of this. I don't know what it is, but it can't be harmless. Instinct tells me he wants his plan put into motion before Cheshvan." Patch's eyes sliced to mine. "Cheshvan begins in less than three weeks."

"I know what you're thinking," I said. "That you're going after him alone. But don't rob me of the satisfaction of bringing him down. I deserve that much."

Patch hooked his elbow around my neck and pressed his lips fiercely to my forehead. "I wouldn't dream of it."

"So what now?"

"He's had a head start, but I plan on evening the score. Your enemy's enemy is your friend, and I have an old friend who might be useful to us." Something about the way he said "friend" implied that the person in question was anything but. "Her name is Dabria, and I think it's time I gave her a call."

It seemed Patch had decided his next move, and so had I. I swung out of bed and scooped up my shoes and pullover, which he'd laid out on the dresser. "I can't stay here. I have to go home. I can't let Hank use my mom this way and not tell her what's going on."

Patch let out a troubled sigh. "You can't tell her anything. She won't believe you. He's doing the same thing to her that I did to

Vee. Even if she didn't want to trust him, she has to. She's under his influence, and for now, we have to leave it that way. A little longer, until I can figure out what he's planning."

My resentment boiled up, flaring at the very thought of Hank controlling and manipulating my mom. "Can't you march over there and tear him to shreds?" I demanded. "He deserves a lot worse, but at least it would solve our problems. And give me some satisfaction," I added bitterly.

"We need to bring him down for good. We don't know who else is helping him and how far his plan extends. He's assembling a Nephilim army to go against fallen angels, but he knows as well as I do that once Cheshvan starts, no army is strong enough to defy an oath sworn under heaven. Fallen angels will sweep in by the droves and possess his men. He must be planning something else. But where do you fit in?" he pondered aloud. Suddenly his eyes narrowed. "Whatever he's planning, it all hangs on information he needs from the archangel. But to get her to talk, he needs an archangel's necklace."

Patch's words seemed to smack me. I'd been so caught up in the rest of the night's revelations, I'd completely forgotten the hallucination of the caged girl, which I now knew was a real memory. She wasn't a girl, but an archangel.

Patch sighed. "I'm sorry, Angel, I'm getting ahead of myself. Let me explain."

But I cut him off. "I know about the necklace. I saw the caged archangel in one of your memories. And I'm pretty sure she tried to tell me to make sure Hank doesn't get it, but at the time I thought I was hallucinating."

Patch watched me in silence for a moment, then spoke. "She's an archangel and powerful enough to insert herself into your conscious thought. Clearly she felt it necessary to warn you."

I nodded. "Because Hank thinks I have your necklace."

"You don't have it."

"Try telling him that."

"That's what this is about," Patch said slowly. "Hank thinks I planted my necklace on you."

"I think so."

Patch frowned, his dark eyes calculating. "If I take you home, can you face Hank and convince him you've got nothing to hide? I need you to make him believe nothing has changed. This night never happened. No one blames you if you aren't ready, least of all me. But first I need to know you can handle this."

My answer to his question came without hesitation. I could keep a secret, no matter how difficult, when the people I loved hung in the balance.

CHAPTER

I SET MY FOOT HEAVY ON THE VOLKSWAGEN'S GAS pedal, hoping my route didn't intersect with a bored cop who had nothing better to do than slap my wrist. I was on my way home, having left Patch with great reluctance. I hadn't wanted to leave, but the thought of my mom alone with Hank, a puppet under his influence, was unbearable. Even though I knew it wasn't solid logic, I told myself my presence could protect her. The alternative was giving in to Hank, and I'd die before I went there.

After dishonorably trying and failing to convince me to stay until a normal waking hour, Patch had taken me to retrieve the Volkswagen. I didn't know what it said about the car that it managed to sit unscathed in the industrial district for several hours. At the very least, I'd expected the CD player to have been ripped out.

At the farmhouse, I jogged up the porch steps and let myself in quietly. When I flipped on the kitchen light, I smothered a scream.

Hank Millar leaned against the counter, a glass of water dangling negligently between his fingers. "Hello, Nora."

I instantly threw up a shield, hiding evidence of my alarm. I narrowed my eyes, hoping the gesture appeared annoyed. "What are you doing here?"

He inclined his head toward the front door. "Your mother had to run to the office. Some emergency Hugo sprang on her at the last moment."

"It's five in the morning."

"You know Hugo."

No, but I know you, I wanted to say. I briefly entertained the idea that Hank had mind-tricked my mom into leaving so he could corner me alone. But how could he have known when I'd come home? Still, I didn't discard the idea.

"I thought it only polite to get up and start my day too," he said. "What would it say about me if I stayed in bed while your mother works?"

He didn't bother to hide that he'd slept here. As far as I knew, this was the first time. It was one thing to manipulate my mom's mind, but to sleep in her bed . . .

"Thought you had plans to sleep at your friend Vee's house. Party's over so soon?" Hank asked. "Or should I say, so late."

My pulse jumped with rage, and I had to bite back the angry words flying to my tongue.

"I decided to sleep in my own bed." *Take a hint.*

A condescending smile hovered at his mouth. "Right."

"Don't believe me?" I challenged.

"No need to make excuses with me, Nora. I know there are very few reasons a young girl would feel compelled to lie about sleeping over at a friend's house." He chuckled, but it wasn't a warm sound. "Tell me. Who's the lucky guy?" A blond eyebrow arched, and he raised the glass to his lips, tipping back a drink.

My pulse was all over the place, but I put every ounce of conviction into faking an air of calm. He was stabbing in the dark. There was no way he could know I'd been with Patch. The only way Hank was going to confirm anything I'd done last night was if I let him.

I gave him an incensed look. "Actually, I was watching a movie with Vee. Maybe Marcie has a history of sneaking out with boys, but I think it's safe to say I'm not Marcie." *Too snide.* If I was going to get through this, I needed to back off slightly.

Hank's superior amusement didn't fade from his expression. "Oh, really?"

"Yeah, really."

"I called Vee's mother to check up on you, and she delivered shocking news. You hadn't stepped foot inside their house all night."

"You checked up on me?"

"I fear your mother is too lenient with you, Nora. I saw through your fib and thought I'd take matters into my own hands. I'm glad we ran into each other, so we could have this little chat privately."

"What I do is none of your business."

"At the moment, true. But if I marry your mother, all the old rules go out the window. We'll be a family." He winked, but the effect was far more menacing than playful. "I run a tight ship, Nora."

Okay, try this on for size. "You're right. I wasn't at Vee's. I lied to my mom so I could go for a long, undisturbed drive in the country to clear my head. Something strange has been happening lately." I tapped my head. "My amnesia is starting to clear. The past several months don't feel quite so vague. I keep seeing one particular face over and over. My kidnapper's. I don't have enough detail to identify him yet, but it's only a matter of time."

He held his face perfectly expressionless, but I thought I saw anger swell in his eyes.

That's what I thought, you abominable prick. "Trouble was, on my way back into town, my piece-of-junk car broke down. I didn't want to get in trouble for driving around by myself late at night, so I called Vee and asked her to cover for me. I've spent the past few hours trying to get my car to start."

He didn't flinch. "Why don't I have a look at it, then? If I can't figure out what's wrong with it, I shouldn't be in the car business."

"Don't bother. I'll take it to our mechanic." In case he didn't catch the hint, I added, "I need to get ready for school and I need to get some studying done. I prefer peace and quiet."

His smile pinched at the corners. "If I didn't know better, I'd think you were trying to get rid of me."

I gestured pointedly toward the front door. "I'll call my mom and let her know you left."

"And your car?"

My, my, he was being obstinate. "Mechanic, remember?"

"Nonsense," he said, brushing me off easily. "No need to make your mother pay a mechanic when I can solve the problem. Car's in the driveway, I presume?"

Before I could stop him, he walked out the front door. I followed him down the front porch steps with my heart in my throat. Positioning himself at the nose of the Volkswagen, he rolled up his sleeves and reached expertly inside the front grille. The hood popped up and he propped it open.

I stood beside him, hoping Patch had done a convincing job. It had been his idea to have a backup plan, just in case Vee's story didn't hold. Since it looked like Hank had overridden Patch's mind-trick by going straight to Mrs. Sky, I couldn't be more grateful for his caution.

"Right here," Hank said, pointing to a tiny fissure in one of the many black hoses coiled around the engine. "Problem solved. It'll hold for a few more days, but it's going to need fixing sooner rather than later. Bring it by the dealership later today and I'll get my men on it."

When I said nothing, he added, "I have to impress the daughter of the woman I intend to marry." It was said lightly enough, but there was a sinister undertone. "Oh, and Nora?" he called out after I'd turned to go. "I'm happy to keep this incident to ourselves, but for your mother's sake, I won't tolerate more lies, regardless of your intentions. Fool me once . . ."

Without a word I walked inside, forcing myself not to hurry or glance back. Not that I needed to. I could feel Hank's perceptive frown follow me all the way through the door.

A week passed without any word from Patch. I didn't know if he'd found Dabria, or if he was any closer to uncovering Hank's motivation for hanging around my family. More than once I'd had to stop myself from driving to Delphic and using trial and error to track my way back to his granite studio. I'd agreed to wait for him to contact me, but I was beginning to kick myself for doing so. I'd made Patch promise not to abandon me to the sidelines while he went after Hank, but his promise was starting to look awfully flimsy. Even if he'd hit nothing but dead ends, I wanted him to call because he missed me the way I was missing him. Couldn't he be bothered to pick up the phone? Scott also hadn't resurfaced, and in keeping with his request, I hadn't gone looking for him. But if one or both didn't reach out soon, all bets were off.

The only thing distracting me from Patch was school, but even it wasn't doing a commendable job. I'd always considered myself a top-notch student, though I was starting to wonder why I bothered. Compared to the immediate need to deal with Hank, getting into college felt like a secondary concern.

"Congratulations," Cheri Deerborn said as we strolled into second-hour English together.

I couldn't figure out why she was smiling so widely. "For what?"

"Homecoming nominations were posted this morning. You're up for junior class attendant."

I just stared at her.

"Junior class attendant," she repeated, stressing each word individually.

"Are you sure?"

"Your name's on the list. Can't be a misprint."

"Who would nominate me?"

She eyed me oddly. "Anyone can nominate you, but they have to get at least fifty other people to sign the nomination form. Like a petition. The more signatures the better."

"I'm going to kill Vee," I muttered, as the only logical explanation presented itself. I'd taken Patch's advice and hadn't called her out on lying to me, but this was inexcusable. Homecoming royalty? Even Patch couldn't protect her now.

Seated at my desk, I hid my cell phone beneath the desktop since our teacher, Mr. Sarraf, had a strict no-phone policy.

HOMECOMING ATTENDANT? I texted to Vee.

Fortunately, the bell hadn't rung yet, and she gave me a prompt reply.

JUST HEARD. UM . . . CONGRATS?

UR SO DEAD, I punched in.

EXCUSE MOI? U THINK I DID THIS?

"Better put that away," said a cheerful voice. "Sarraf is squinting at you."

Marcie Millar dropped into the next desk over. I knew we had English together, but she always sat in the back row with Jon Gala and Addyson Hales. It was no secret Mr. Sarraf was practically blind, and they could do just about anything back there short of lighting up.

"If he squints any harder, he's going to give himself a brain hemorrhoid," Marcie said.

"Brilliant," I said. "How do you come up with this stuff?"

Missing my sarcasm, she sat taller with self-satisfaction.

"I saw you made the homecoming ballot," she said.

I said nothing. The lilt of her voice didn't appear to be making fun, but eleven years' worth of history between us implied differently.

"Who do you think will win male junior attendant?" she kept on. "My bet's on Cameron Ferria. Hopefully they've dry-cleaned the royalty robes since last year. I have it on good authority that Kara Darling left armpit sweat marks inside her robe. What if you had to wear her old robe?" She wrinkled her nose. "If she did that to her robe, I'd hate to see what she did to the tiara."

My mind unwillingly traveled back to the only homecoming I'd attended. Vee and I had gone as freshmen. We'd been newly anointed high schoolers, and it only seemed appropriate to see what all the fuss was about. At halftime, the booster club marched onto the field and announced the royalty, starting with the freshman attendants and ending with the senior class queen and king. Each member of the royalty had a robe in school colors placed on their shoulders and a crown or tiara shoved on their head. Then they took a victory lap around the track in golf carts. High class, I know. Marcie won freshman attendant and soured any desire I had to attend another coronation.

"I nominated you." Marcie flipped her hair off her shoulders, giving me the full wattage of her smile. "I was going to keep it a secret, but anonymity isn't my thing."

Her words whipped me out of my reflection. "You did what?"

She tried on a sympathetic face. "I know you're going through a rough period. I mean, first the whole amnesia thing and"—she dropped her voice to a whisper—"I know about the hallucinations. My dad told me. He said I should be extra nice to you. Only I wasn't sure how. I thought and thought. And then I saw the announcement about nominating this year's homecoming royalty. Obviously everyone wanted to nominate me, but I told my friends we should nominate you instead. I might have mentioned the hallucinations, and I might have exaggerated their severity. You gotta play dirty to win. Good news is, we got over two hundred signatures, more than any other nominee!"

My mind reeled, tottering between incredulity and disgust. "You made me your charity project?"

"Yes!" she squealed, clapping her hands daintily.

I bent across the aisle, pinning her with my most hardened and severe look. "Go to the office and retract it. I don't want my name on the ballot."

Instead of looking wounded, Marcie put her hands on her hips. "That would mess up everything. They've already printed the ballots. I peeked at the stack in the front office this morning. Do you want to be a paper waster? Think of the trees that sacrificed their lives for those reams of paper. And what's more, screw the paper. What about me? I went out of my way to do something nice, and you can't just reject that."

I tipped my neck back, glowering at the water stains on the ceiling. Why me?

CHAPTER

23

AFTER SCHOOL I FOUND A NOTE TACKED TO THE front door: *Barn.* I stuffed the note into my pocket and headed to the backyard. The split-rail fence at the edge of our property opened to a sprawling field. A whitewashed barn was plunked down in the middle of it. To this day, I wasn't sure who the barn belonged to. Years ago Vee and I had dreamed of turning it into a secret clubhouse. Our ambitions quickly died the first time we hauled open the doors to find a bat hanging from the rafters.

I hadn't tried to enter the barn since, and even though I hoped I could say I was no longer terrified of small flying mammals, I found myself opening the door with great hesitation.

"Hello?" I called in.

Scott was stretched out on a weathered bench at the back of the barn. Upon my entrance, he pulled himself up to sitting.

"You still mad at me?" he asked, chewing a piece of wild grass. If it weren't for the Metallica T-shirt and frayed jeans, he might have looked like he belonged seated behind the wheel of a tractor.

I skimmed the rafters. "Did you see any bats when you came in?"

Scott grinned. "Scared of bats, Grey?"

I dropped down on the bench beside him. "Quit calling me Grey. It makes me sound like I'm a boy. Like Dorian Gray."

"Dorian who?"

I sighed. "Just think up something else. Plain old Nora works too, you know."

"Sure thing, Gumdrop."

I grimaced. "I take that back. Let's stick with Grey."

"I came by to see if you have anything for me. Information on Hank would be good. Do you think he knows it was us spying on his building that night?"

I was pretty sure Hank didn't suspect us. He hadn't acted any creepier than usual, which, in retrospect, wasn't saying much. "No, I think we're clear."

"That's good, real good," Scott said, twisting the Black Hand's ring around his finger. I was glad to see he hadn't taken it off. "Maybe I can come out of hiding earlier than I thought."

"Looks to me like you're out of hiding now. How did you know I'd find your note on the front door before Hank?"

"Hank's at his dealership. And I know when you get home from school. Don't take this the wrong way, but I've been checking up on you now and then. I needed to know the best times to contact you. By the way, your social life is pathetic."

"Speak for yourself."

Scott laughed, but when I didn't join in, he nudged my shoulder. "You seem down, Grey."

I heaved a sigh. "Marcie Millar nominated me for homecoming royalty. Voting happens this Friday."

He gave me one of those complex handshakes that college fraternities use on TV. "Well done, champ."

I gave him a look of pure disgust.

"Hey, now. I thought girls loved this stuff. Shopping for a dress, getting your hair done, wearing the little crown thing on your head."

"Tiara."

"Yeah, tiara. I knew that. So what's to hate?"

"I feel stupid having my name on a ballot with four other girls who are actually popular. I'm not going to win. I'm just going to look stupid. People are already asking if it was a misprint. And I don't have a date. I guess I could take Vee. Marcie will come up with a hundred lesbian jokes, but worse things could happen."

Scott spread his arms wide, as though the solution was obvious. "Problem solved. Go with me."

I rolled my eyes, suddenly regretting bringing up the topic. It was the last thing I wanted to talk about. Right now, denial seemed the only way to go. "You don't even go to school," I reminded him.

"Is there a rule about that? Girls at my old school in Portland were always dragging their college boyfriends back to dances."

"There's not a rule, per se."

He considered briefly. "If you're worried about the Black Hand, last time I checked, Nephilim dictators don't consider human high school dances a top priority. He'll never know I was there."

At the image of Hank trolling the school gym, I couldn't help but laugh.

"You laugh, but you haven't seen me in a tux. Or maybe you don't like broad-shouldered guys with muscular chests and wash-board abs?"

I bit my lip to conquer another, harder laugh. "Quit intimidating me. You're starting to make this sound like a role reversal of Beauty and the Beast. We all know you're beautiful, Scott."

Scott gave my knee an affectionate squeeze. "You'll never hear me admit this again, so listen up. You look good, Grey. On a scale from one to ten, you're definitely in the top half."

"Gee, thanks."

"You're not the kind of girl I would have chased after when I was in Portland, but I'm not the same guy I was back then either. You're a little too good for me, and let's face it, a little too smart."

"You've got street smarts," I pointed out.

"Stop interrupting. You're going to make me lose my place."

"You've got this speech memorized?"

A smirk. "I've got a lot of time on my hands. As I was saying— hell. I forgot where I was."

"You were telling me I can rest assured that I'm better-looking than half the girls at my school."

"That was a figure of speech. If you want to get technical, you're better-looking than ninety percent. Give or take."

I laid a hand over my heart. "I'm speechless."

Scott got down on his knee and clasped my hand dramatically. "Yes, Nora. Yes, I'll go to the homecoming dance with you."

I snorted down at him. "You are so full of yourself. I never asked."

"See? Too smart. Anyway, what's the big deal? You need a date, and while I might not be your number one choice, I'll do."

A clear image of Patch appeared in my thoughts, but I swept it aside. Logically, I knew there was no way Scott could read my mind, but that didn't ease my guilt. I wasn't ready to tell him just yet that I was no longer working exclusively with him to bring down Hank; I'd enrolled the help of my ex-boyfriend, who just so happened to be twice as resourceful, twice as dangerous, the embodiment of masculine perfection . . . and a fallen angel.

Hurting Scott was the last thing I wanted. Quite unexpectedly, he'd grown on me.

And while I found it odd that Scott had suddenly decided complacency was the way to go with Hank, I didn't have the heart to tell him he wasn't allowed one night of fun. As he'd said, the homecoming dance would be the last thing on Hank's radar.

"Okay, okay," I said, giving him a playful jab to the shoulder. "It's a date." I put on a serious face. "But you'd better not be exaggerating about how fine you look in a tux."

It wasn't until later that night that I realized I'd failed to tell Scott about Hank's decoy building and the real Nephilim safe house. Who would've thought homecoming would weigh on my thoughts more heavily than stumbling inside a barracks of armed Nephilim? It was times like this when having Scott's cell phone number would have come in really useful. On second thought, I wasn't sure Scott had a cell. Phones were traceable.

At six I sat down to dinner with Mom.

"How was your day?" she asked.

"I can tell you it was absolutely fantastic, if you want," I said, chewing a bite of baked ziti.

"Oh dear. Did the Volkswagen break down again? I thought it was very generous of Hank to fix it, and I'm sure he'd offer to help out again, if you asked."

At my mom's blind admiration of Hank, I had to exhale slowly

BECCA FITZPATRICK

to regain my composure. "Worse. Marcie nominated me for home-coming royalty. Worse yet, I made the ballot."

Mom lowered her fork. She looked stunned. "Are we talking about the same Marcie?"

"She said Hank told her about the hallucinations, and she's made me her new charity case. *I* didn't tell Hank about the hallu-cinations."

"That would have been me," she said, blinking in surprise. "I can't believe he shared that information with Marcie. I distinctly remember telling him to keep it private." She opened her mouth, then slowly closed it. "At least, I'm almost positive I did." She set down her utensils with a clink. "I swear old age is getting the better of me. I can't seem to remember anything anymore. Please don't blame Hank. I take full responsibility."

I couldn't bear to see my mom lost and bewildered. Old age had nothing to do with her inability to remember. I had no doubt in my mind that Patch was right; she was under Hank's influence. I wondered if he was mind-tricking her day by day, or if he'd instilled in her a general sense of obedience and loyalty.

"Don't worry about it," I murmured. I had a piece of ziti poised on my fork, but I'd lost my appetite. Patch had told me there wasn't any use in trying to explain the truth to my mom—she wouldn't believe me—but that didn't keep me from wanting to scream out in frustration. I wasn't sure how much longer I could keep up the charade: eating, sleeping, smiling, as if nothing were wrong.

Mom said, "This must be why Hank suggested you and Marcie go dress shopping together. I told him I'd be very surprised if you had any desire to go to homecoming, but he must have known what Marcie was planning. Of course, you're under no obligation to go anywhere with Marcie," she corrected in a rush. "I think it would be very big of you, but clearly Hank doesn't know how you feel about Marcie. I think he dreams of seeing our families get along." She gave a miserable little laugh.

Under the circumstances, I couldn't bring myself to join her. I didn't know how much of what she said was from the heart, and how much was dictated by Hank's mind-tricks. But it was very clear that if she was thinking marriage, Patch and I needed to work faster.

"Marcie cornered me after school and told me—yes, told me—we're going dress shopping tonight. Like I had absolutely no say in the matter whatsoever. But it's all good. Vee and I have a plan. I texted Marcie and told her I couldn't go shopping because I'm out of money. Then I told her how sorry I was, because I was really looking forward to her input. She texted back and said Hank gave her his credit card and she was paying."

Mom groaned in disapproval, but her eyes crinkled with amusement. "Please tell me I raised you better than this."

"I already picked out the dress I want," I said cheerfully. "I'll get Marcie to pay for it, and then Vee will just happen to bump into us as we're leaving the store. I'll take the dress, ditch Marcie, and go out for doughnuts with Vee."

"What does the dress look like?"

"Vee and I found it at Silk Garden. It's an above-the-knee party dress."

"What color?"

"You'll have to wait and see." I smiled devilishly. "It's one hundred and fifty dollars."

Mom waved this off. "I'd be surprised if Hank even notices. You should see how he burns through cash."

I settled higher in my chair, pleased with myself. "Then I don't suppose he'll mind buying my shoes, too."

I was supposed to meet Marcie at Silk Garden at seven. Silk Garden was a boutique dress shop on the corner of Asher and Tenth. From the outside it resembled a château, with an oak-and-iron door and a cobblestone walk. The trees were wrapped in blue decorative lights. In the front windows, mannequins modeled dresses beautiful enough to eat. When I was little, my dreams of grandeur included becoming a princess and claiming Silk Garden as my castle.

At twenty past seven, I paced the parking lot, scouting for Marcie's car. Marcie drove a red Toyota 4Runner, fully loaded. Somehow I got the feeling her shifter never popped out of its socket. I doubted she'd ever had to smack her dashboard for ten minutes straight before the engine caught. And I was willing to bet her ride never broke down halfway to school. I cast a gloomy look in the direction of the Volkswagen and sighed.

A red 4Runner swerved into the parking lot, and Marcie jumped out. "Sorry I'm late," she said, throwing her handbag up her shoulder. "My dog didn't want me to leave."

"Your dog?"

"Boomer. Dogs are people too, you know."

I saw my chance. "No worries. I already looked around inside. Picked out my dress, too. We can make this real quick, and you can get back to Boomer."

Her face fell. "What about my input? You said you valued my opinion."

I pretty much just value your dad's credit card. "Yeah, about that. I had every intention of waiting for you, but then I saw the dress. It spoke to me."

"Really?"

"Yes, Marcie. The heavens opened and angels sang 'Hallelujah.'" In my mind, I smacked my head against a wall.

"Show me the dress," she directed. "You realize you have a warm skin tone, right? The wrong color is going to wash you out."

Inside, I walked Marcie over to the dress. It was a party dress with an all-over green-and-navy tartan print and a ruched skirt. The saleslady had said it made my legs stand out. Vee said it made me look like I actually had a chest.

"Ew," Marcie said. "Tartan? Too schoolgirl."

"Well, it's the one I want."

She flipped through the rack, grabbing one in my size. "Maybe it will look better on. But I don't think I'll change my mind."

I carted the dress back to the fitting room with a bounce in my step. This was *the* dress. Marcie could huff all night; she wasn't going to change my mind. I shucked off my jeans and shimmied into the dress. I couldn't get the zipper up. I twisted the dress around and looked at the tag. Size four. Maybe an honest mistake, maybe not. To give Marcie the finger, I stuffed the fat at my midsection into the dress. For a minute, it looked like it might work. Then reality set in.

"Marcie?" I called through the drape.

"Mmm?"

I passed the dress out to her. "Wrong size."

"Too big?" Her voice was laced with an overkill of naïveté.

I blew hair off my face to keep from saying something cynical. "A size six will do, thank you very much."

"Oh. Too *small*."

It was a good thing I was in my underwear, or I'd have been tempted to march out and slug her.

A minute later Marcie pushed a size six through the drapes. On its heels, she passed in a floor-length red number. "Not to sway the vote, but I think red is the way to go. More glam."

I hung the red dress on the hook, stuck my tongue out at it, and zipped myself into the tartan party dress. I twirled in front of the mirror and mouthed a silent squeal. I imagined myself descending the farmhouse stairs on homecoming night while Scott looked on

silence

from below. All of a sudden I wasn't picturing Scott. Patch leaned on the banister, dressed in a tailored black suit and silver tie.

I gave him a flirty smile. He held out his arm and escorted me to the door. He smelled warm and earthy, like sun-baked sand.

Unable to control myself, I grabbed his jacket lapels and hauled him into a kiss.

"I could get you to smile like that, and without sales tax."

I whirled around to find the real Patch standing in the fitting room behind me. He was wearing jeans and a snug white tee. His arms were folded loosely over his chest, and his black eyes smiled down at me.

Heat that wasn't entirely uncomfortable flushed through my body. "I could make all kinds of pervert jokes right now," I quipped.

"I could tell you how much I like you in that dress."

"How did you get in?"

"I move in mysterious ways."

"God moves in mysterious ways. You move like lightning—here one moment, gone the next. How long have you been standing there?" I would die of mortification if he'd watched me try to cram myself into a size four. Not to mention watching me strip down!

"I would have knocked, but I didn't want to linger outside and risk Marcie. Hank can't know you and I are back in business."

I tried not to overanalyze what "back in business" meant.

"I have news," Patch said. "I reached out to Dabria. She's agreed to help us run interference on Hank, but first I need to come

BECCA FITZPATRICK

clean. Dabria is more than an old acquaintance. We knew each other before I fell. It was a relationship of convenience, but not too long ago, she caused you a fair share of inconvenience." He paused. "Which is a nice way of saying she tried to kill you."

Oh boy.

"She's over her jealousy, but I wanted you to know," he finished.

"Well, now I know," I said a little tartly. I wasn't especially proud of my sudden insecurity, but couldn't he have told me this *before* he called her? "How do we know she's not going to play assassin again?"

He smiled. "I took out an insurance policy."

"Sounds vague."

"Have a little faith."

"What does she look like?" And now I'd stooped from plain old insecure to superficial.

"Stringy, unwashed hair, doughy around the middle, unibrow." He grinned. "Satisfied?"

I wondered if that translated into curvy and gorgeous with the brains of an astrophysicist. "Have you met with her in person yet?"

"Won't be necessary. What I want from her isn't complicated. Before she fell, Dabria was an angel of death and could see the future. She claims she still has the gift and makes decent money at it from, believe it or not, her Nephilim clients."

I figured out where he was going with this. "She's going to keep her ear to the ground. She's going to eavesdrop on her clients and see what pops up on Hank."

"Good work, Angel."

"How does Dabria expect to be paid?"

"Let me handle that."

I stood hands on hips. "Wrong answer, Patch."

"Dabria has no interest in me anymore. She's motivated by cold, hard cash." He closed the space between us, running his finger affectionately along the inside of my necklace. "And I'm not interested in her anymore. I've set my eyes elsewhere."

I steered clear of his hand, knowing full well the seductive power his touch had of erasing even my most important trains of thought. "Can she be trusted?"

"I'm the one who ripped out her wings when she fell. I have one of her feathers for safekeeping, and she knows it. Unless she wants to spend the rest of eternity keeping Rixon company, she's going to be motivated to stay on my good side."

The insurance policy. Bingo.

His lips grazed mine. "I can't stay long. I'm working a few other leads, and I'll get back to you if they pan out. Will you be home tonight?"

"Yes," I said hesitantly, "but aren't you worried about Hank? These days, he's about as permanent in my house as a light fixture."

"I can work around him," he said with a mysterious gleam in his eyes. "I'll be coming in through your dreams."

I cocked my head, evaluating him. "Is this a joke?"

"For it to work, you have to be open to the idea. We're off to a promising start."

I waited for the punch line, but it quickly dawned on me that he was dead serious. "How does it work?" I asked skeptically.

"You dream, and I insert myself into it. Don't try to block me, and we'll be good to go."

I wondered if I should tell him I had a stellar track record of not blocking him when it came to my dreams.

"One last thing," he said. "I have it on good authority that Hank knows Scott is in town. I wouldn't think twice about it if he were caught, but I know he means something to you. Tell him to keep his head down. Hank doesn't think highly of deserters."

Once again, having a legitimate way to reach Scott would be useful.

On the other side of the drape, I heard Marcie arguing with a saleslady. Probably over something as trivial as a smidgen of dust on the full-length mirrors. "Does Marcie know what her dad really is?"

"Marcie lives in a bubble, but Hank keeps threatening to pop it." He inclined his head at my dress. "What's the occasion?"

"Homecoming," I said, twirling. "Like?"

"Last I heard, homecoming requires a date."

"About that," I hedged. "I'm sort of . . . going with Scott. We both figure a high-school dance is the last place Hank will be patrolling."

Patch smiled, but it was tight. "I take that back. If Hank wants to shoot Scott, he has my blessing."

"We're just friends."

He tipped my chin up and kissed me. "Keep it that way." He unhooked his aviator sunglasses from his shirt and slid them over his eyes. "Don't tell Scott I didn't warn him. I have to roll, but I'll be in touch."

He ducked out. And he was gone.

CHAPTER

24

AFTER PATCH LEFT, I DECIDED IT WAS TIME TO STOP playing princess and change back into my ordinary clothes. I'd just tugged my shirt over my head when I knew something wasn't right. And then it hit me. My handbag was gone.

I looked under the plush bench, but it wasn't there. Even though I was almost positive I hadn't hung it on a hook, I looked behind the red dress. Shoving my feet into my shoes, I flung back the drape and hustled out to the main store area. I found Marcie tearing her way through a rack of push-up bras.

"Have you seen my handbag?"

She paused long enough to say, "You took it into the dressing room with you."

A saleslady bustled over. "Was it a brown leather saddlebag?" she asked me.

"Yes!"

"I just saw a man leaving the store with it. He came in without saying a word, and I assumed he was your father." She touched her head, frowning. "In fact, I could have sworn he said he was . . . but maybe I imagined the whole thing. The whole moment felt so strange. My head feels fuzzy. I can't explain it."

A mind-trick, I thought.

She added, "He had gray hair and was wearing an argyle sweater. . . ."

"Which way did he go?" I cut her off.

"Out the front doors, heading toward the parking lot."

I ran outside. I could hear Marcie on my heels.

"Do you think this is a good idea?" she panted. "I mean, what if he has a gun? What if he's mentally unstable?"

"What kind of man steals a purse from under a dressing room door?" I demanded out loud.

"Maybe he was desperate. Maybe he needed cash."

"Then he should have taken your bag!"

"Everyone knows Silk Garden is posh," Marcie rationalized. "He probably figured he'd score big no matter which bag he grabbed."

What I couldn't tell Marcie was that he was most likely either Nephilim or a fallen angel. And instinct told me he was motivated by something bigger than a potential handful of cash.

We ran into the parking lot just as a black sedan backed out of a parking space. The glare of its headlights made it impossible to see behind the windshield. The engine revved and the car gunned toward us.

Marcie yanked on my sleeve. "Move, you idiot!"

Tires squealing, the car floored past us onto the street. The driver ran the stop sign, switched off his lights, and vanished into the night.

"Did you see what kind of car it was?" asked Marcie.

"An Audi A6. I got a partial on the license plate."

Marcie appraised me up and down. "Not bad, Tiger."

I gave her a look of pure irritation. "Not bad? He got away with my handbag! Don't you find it a little odd that a guy who drives a flashy Audi needs to steal handbags? My handbag in particular?" Which begged the question, what did an immortal want with my handbag?

"Was it designer?"

"Try Target!"

Marcie hitched her shoulders. "Well, that was exciting. What now? Drop it and get back to shopping?"

"I'm calling the police."

Thirty minutes later a patrol car pulled to the curb in front of Silk Garden and Detective Basso swung out. Suddenly I wished I'd taken Marcie's advice and dropped the whole thing. My night had just gone from bad to worse.

Marcie and I were inside, pacing by the windows, and Detective Basso came in and found us. His eyes showed initial surprise upon seeing me, and when he ran his hand over his mouth, I was pretty sure it was to hide a smile.

"Someone stole my handbag," I informed him.

"Walk me through this," he said.

"I went into the fitting room to try on homecoming dresses. When I finished, I noticed my handbag wasn't on the floor where I'd left it. I came out, and the saleslady told me she'd seen a man running off with it."

"He had gray hair and an argyle sweater," the saleslady offered helpfully.

"Any credit cards in the purse?" Detective Basso asked.

"No."

"Cash?"

"No."

"Total value of missing items?"

"Seventy-five dollars." The handbag had cost only twenty, but standing in line for two hours to get a new driver's license had to be worth at least fifty.

"I'll file a report, but there's not a lot we can do. Best-case scenario, the guy ditches the bag and someone turns it in. Worst case, you buy yourself a new bag."

Marcie linked her arm through mine. "Look on the bright side," she said, patting my hand. "You lost a cheap bag, but you're getting a swanky dress." She handed me a dress bag with the Silk Garden logo. "It's all taken care of. You can thank me later."

I peered inside the bag. The floor-length red gown hung neatly inside.

I was in my bedroom, and I was forking down a piece of chocolate cake. I was evil-eyeing the red dress, which I'd hung on the closet door. I hadn't tried it on yet, but I had the distinct vision that I was going to look eerily like Jessica from *Who Framed Roger Rabbit.* Minus the D cups.

I brushed my teeth, splashed water on my face, and dabbed on eye cream. Saying good night to my mom, I padded down the hall to my bedroom, buttoned myself into a cute pair of flannel pj's from Victoria's Secret, and cut the lights.

Taking Patch's advice, I cleared my mind and prepared for sleep. Patch said he could come inside my dreams, but I had to be open to the idea. I was a little bit skeptical, a little bit hopeful. And not the least bit opposed. After the night I'd had, the only thing I could imagine making me feel better was having Patch take me into his arms. Better in a dream than not at all.

Lying in bed, I reflected on my day, letting my subconscious twist the memories into phantoms of dreams. My mind toyed with bits of dialogue, flashes of color. Suddenly I was standing in the dressing room at Silk Garden with Patch. Only in this version, he had his fingers hooked in the belt loops of my jeans and my fingers were mussing up his hair. Our mouths were an inch apart, and I could feel the warmth of his breath.

The dream had almost towed me under completely when I felt my blankets being dragged off my body.

I sat up to find Patch standing over my bed. He was wearing the same jeans and white tee I'd seen him in earlier, and he balled up my blankets, tossing them aside.

A smile lit his eyes. "Sweet dreams?"

I looked around. Everything in my room was just as it should be. The door was shut, the night-light on. My clothes were draped over the rocking chair where I'd left them, and the Jessica Rabbit dress still hung from the closet door. Despite no visible evidence, something felt . . . not quite right.

"Is this real," I asked Patch, "or a dream?"

"Dream."

I gave an appreciative laugh. "Wow. Could've fooled me. It's so real."

"Most dreams are. It isn't until you wake up that you see all the plot holes."

"Talk me through this."

"I'm in the landscape of your dream. Imagine that your subconscious and mine walked through a door you created in your mind. We're in the room together, but it's not a physical place. The room is imagined, but our thoughts aren't. You decided the setting and the clothes you're wearing, and you decide everything you say. But since I'm actually in the dream with you, as opposed to a version of myself that you dreamed up, the things I say and do aren't the work of your imagination. I control those things."

I was pretty sure I understood enough to get by. "Are we safe here?"

"If you're asking if Hank will spy on us, no, most likely not."

"But if you can do this, what's stopping him from doing it? I know he's Nephilim, and unless I'm way off here, it seems like fallen angels and Nephilim have a lot of the same powers."

"Until I tried invading your dreams a few months ago, I didn't know much about how the process works. I've since learned it requires a strong connection between both subjects. I also know the dreaming subject has to be deep under. The timing can get tricky and requires patience. If you invade too early, the subject will wake up. If two angels, or Nephilim, or any combination of the two, invade a dream at the same time, pushing and pulling with their own agendas, the dreamer is far more likely to wake up. Whether or not you like it, Hank has a strong connection to you. But if he hasn't tried invading your dreams yet, I don't think he'll start this late in the game."

"How did you learn all of this?"

"Trial and error." He hesitated, as though meaning to tread carefully with his next words. "I also got a little outside help from a fallen angel who recently fell. Unlike me, she had a strong grasp on angel law before she fell. I wouldn't be surprised if she has the Book of Enoch, a tome about the history of angels, memorized. I knew if anyone had answers, she did. After a little arm-twisting, she told me." His face was a mask of indifference. "She meaning Dabria."

My heart gave an unpleasant twist. I didn't want to be jealous of Patch's ex—obviously I understood there was no way he didn't have some kind of romantic history—but I felt an overpowering aversion to Dabria. Maybe residual anger—she *had* tried to kill me. Or maybe instinct telling me she wouldn't hesitate to betray us again.

"So you met her in person after all?" I asked accusingly.

"We ran into each other today, and while I had her, I decided to get to the bottom of a few questions that have been weighing on my mind. I've been looking for a way to communicate with you undetected, and I wasn't going to waste the opportunity that she might provide answers."

I hardly heard him. "Why did she track you down?"

"She didn't say, and it's not important. We got what we wanted, and that's what I care about. We now have a private form of communication."

"Did she still look doughy around the middle?"

Patch rolled his eyes.

I was acutely aware that he'd dodged my question. "Has she been to your studio?"

"This is starting to feel like Twenty Questions, Angel."

"In other words, she has."

"No, she hasn't," Patch answered patiently. "Can we be done talking about Dabria?"

"When do I get to meet her?" *And tell her to keep her hands off.*

Patch scratched his cheek, but I thought I saw his mouth twitch. "Probably not a good idea."

"What's that supposed to mean? You don't think I can handle myself, do you? Thanks for the vote of confidence!" I said, seething at him and my own stupid insecurities.

"I think Dabria is a narcissist and an egomaniac. Best to stay away."

"Maybe you should take your own advice!"

I started to whirl away, but Patch hooked my arm and brought me around to face him. He pressed his forehead to mine. I started to pull away, but he laced his fingers through mine, effectively trapping me against him. "What do I have to do to convince you I'm using Dabria for one thing, and one thing only: to break down Hank, piece by piece if I have to, and make him pay for everything he's done to hurt the girl I love?"

"I don't trust Dabria," I said, still clinging to some of my indignation.

He shut his eyes, and I thought I heard the softest of sighs. "Finally something we agree on."

"I don't think we should use her, even if she can get to Hank's inner circle faster than you or me."

"If we had more time, or another option, I'd jump on it. But for now, she's our best chance. She won't double-cross me. She's too smart. She'll take the cash I'm offering and walk away, even if it hurts her pride."

"I don't like it." I snuggled into Patch, and even in the dream, the warmth of his body effectively cast away any lingering chill. "But I trust you."

He kissed me, long and reassuring.

"Something strange happened tonight," I said. "Someone stole my handbag from the dressing room at Silk Garden."

Patch immediately frowned. "This happened after I left?"

"Either that, or right before you came."

"Did you see who took it?"

"No, but the saleslady said he was male and old enough to be my father. She let him stroll right out with it, but I think he may have mind-tricked her. Do you think it's a coincidence that an immortal stole my handbag?"

"I don't think anything is a coincidence. What did Marcie see?"

"Apparently nothing, even though the shop was practically empty." I gauged his eyes, cool and calculating. "You think Marcie was involved, don't you?"

"Hard to believe she didn't see something. It's starting to feel like the whole night was a setup. When you went into the dressing room, she could have placed a call, letting the thief know it was safe to come in. She could have seen your bag underneath the drape, and walked him through the theft step by step."

"Why would she want my bag? Unless—" I stopped. "She thought I was carrying the necklace Hank wants," I realized. "He's roped her into this. She was playing fetch for him."

Patch's mouth was set in a grim line. "He's not beneath putting his daughter in harm's way." His eyes flickered to mine. "He proved that with you."

"Are you still convinced Marcie doesn't know what Hank really is?"

"She doesn't know. Not yet. Hank could have lied to her about why he needed the necklace. He could have told her it belongs to him, and she wouldn't ask questions. Marcie isn't the type to ask questions. If she sees a target, she turns into a pit bull."

Pit bull. Tell me about it. "There's one more thing. I got a look at the car before the thief drove away. It was an Audi A6."

From the look in his eyes, I knew the information meant something to him. "Hank's right-hand man, a Nephil named Blakely, drives an Audi."

A shiver chased up my spine. "I'm starting to get a little freaked out. He obviously thinks he can use the necklace to force the archangel to talk. What does he need her to tell him? What does she know that he'd risk the retaliation of the archangels for?"

"And this close to Cheshvan," Patch murmured, a look of distraction clouding his eyes.

"We could try to break the archangel out," I suggested. "That way, even if Hank gets a necklace, he won't have an archangel."

"I'd thought of that, but we're facing two big problems. First, the archangel trusts me even less than Hank, and if she sees me anywhere near her cage, she's going to make a lot of racket. Second, Hank's warehouse is crawling with his men. I'd need my own army of fallen angels to go against them, and I'm going to have a hard time talking fallen angels into helping me rescue an archangel."

Our conversation seemed to dead-end there, and we both contemplated our slim list of options in silence.

"What happened to the other dress?" Patch asked at last. I followed his gaze to the Jessica Rabbit gown.

I heaved a sigh. "Marcie thought I'd look better in red."

"What do you think?"

"I think Marcie and Dabria would be instant friends."

Patch laughed low, the sound of it tingling my skin as seductively as if he'd kissed it. "Do you want my opinion?"

"Might as well, since everyone else seems to have weighed in."

He sat on my bed, leaning back nonchalantly on his elbows. "Try it on."

"It's probably a little snug," I said, suddenly feeling conspicuous. "Marcie tends to buy down when it comes to sizing."

He merely smiled.

"It has a slit up the thigh."

His smile deepened.

Locking myself in my closet, I tugged on the dress. It moved like liquid over every curve. The slit fell open halfway up my thigh, exposing my leg. Stepping out into the low light, I swept my hair off my neck. "Zip it up?"

Patch's eyes made a slow assessment of me, sharpening to vivid black. "I'm going to have a hard time sending you off with Scott in that dress. Just a heads-up: If you come home and the dress looks even slightly tampered with, I will track Scott down, and when I find him, it won't be pretty."

"I'll relay the message."

"If you tell me where he's hiding, I'll relay it myself."

I had to work not to smile. "Something tells me your message would be a lot more direct."

"Let's just say he'd get the point."

Patch took my wrist and reeled me in for a kiss, but something wasn't right. His face grew hazy at the edges, dissolving into the background. When his lips met mine, I hardly felt it. Worse, I felt myself pulling away from him like a piece of tape peeling back from glass.

Patch noticed it too and swore under his breath.

"What's happening?" I asked.

"It's the half-breed," he growled.

"Scott?"

"He's knocking at your bedroom window. Any second now, you're going to wake up. Is this the first time he's come prowling around at night?"

I thought it might be safer not to answer. Patch was in my dream and couldn't do anything rash, but that didn't mean it was a good idea to stir up the competition between them any further.

"We'll finish this tomorrow!" was all I had time to say before the dream, and Patch, swirled into the recesses of my mind.

The dream snapped apart, and sure enough, Scott stood in my bedroom, closing the window behind him.

"Rise and shine," he said.

I groaned. "Scott, you have to stop this. I have school first thing tomorrow. Plus, I was in the middle of a really good dream," I grumbled as an afterthought.

"About me?" he said, flashing a cocky smile.

I simply said, "This better be good."

"Better than good. I got a gig playing bass for a band called Serpentine. We're opening at the Devil's Handbag next weekend. Band members get two free tickets, and you're one of the lucky recipients." With a flourish, he threw down two tickets on my bed.

I was growing more awake by the second. "Are you crazy? You can't be in a band! You're supposed to be hiding from Hank. Going to the dance with me is one thing, but this is taking things too far."

His smile died, his expression souring. "I thought you'd be happy for me, Grey. I've spent the past couple months hiding. Now I'm living in a cave and scavenging for food, which is getting harder and harder to find with winter coming. I have to force myself into the ocean three times a week for a bath, and I spend the rest of the day shivering by the fire. I have no TV, no cell. I'm completely cut off. You want the truth? I'm sick of hiding. Living on the run isn't living. I might as well be dead." He stroked the Black Hand's ring, still snug around his finger. "I'm glad you talked me into wearing this again. I haven't felt this alive in months. If Hank tries anything, he's going to be in for a big surprise. My powers have intensified."

I kicked out of my blankets and stood up to him. "Scott, Hank knows you're in town. He's got his men searching for you. You have to stay hidden until—Cheshvan at least," I threw out, believing Hank's interest in Scott would wane once his full plans, whatever they were, unfolded.

"I keep telling myself that, but what if he's not?" he remarked blandly. "What if he's forgotten about me and all this is for nothing?"

"I know he's looking for you."

"Did you hear him say it?" he asked, calling my bluff.

"Something like that." Given his current state, I couldn't bring myself to tell him where the information had come from. Scott wouldn't take Patch's advice seriously. And then I'd have to explain why I was mixed up with Patch in the first place. "A reliable source told me."

He wagged his head back and forth. "You're trying to scare me. I appreciate the gesture," he said cynically, "but I've made up my mind. I've thought this over, and whatever happens, I can face it. A few months of freedom is better than a lifetime in prison."

"You can't let Hank find you," I insisted. "If he does, he'll put you in one of his reinforced prisons. He'll torture you. You have to ride this out a little longer. Please," I begged. "Just a few more weeks?"

"Screw it. I'm out of here. I'm playing at the Devil's Handbag whether you come or not."

I didn't understand Scott's sudden blasé attitude. Up until now, he'd been meticulous about staying away from Hank. Now he was putting his neck on the line for something as trivial as a high-school dance . . . and now a gig?

A horrible thought struck me. "Scott, you said the Black Hand's ring connects you to him. Is there any way it's drawing you closer to him? Maybe the ring does more than give you heightened powers. Maybe it's some kind of—beacon."

Scott snorted. "The Black Hand isn't going to catch me."

"You're wrong. And if you keep up that attitude, he's going to catch you sooner than you think," I said gently but firmly.

I reached for his arm, but he drew away.

He ducked out the window, slamming it shut behind him.

　　　　　BECCA FITZPATRICK

CHAPTER

I T WAS FRIDAY, AND VOTING FOR HOMECOMING ROYALTY
was scheduled to take place during lunch. At the moment, I
was sitting in health, watching the clock inch toward the dismissal bell. Instead of worrying that hundreds of people I had to
spend the next two years of my life with might burst into hysterics
upon seeing my name on the ballot, and in less than ten minutes'
time, I concentrated on Scott.

I needed to find a way to talk him back inside the cave through

Cheshvan, and as a precaution, I needed a way to get him to take off the Black Hand's ring. If that didn't work, I needed a way to contain him. I vaguely wondered if I could recruit Patch's help. Surely he knew of several good places to detain a Nephil, but would he trouble himself over Scott? And even if I managed to talk Patch into cooperating, how would I ever earn back Scott's trust? He'd view it as the ultimate betrayal. I couldn't even reason with him that it was for his own safety—he'd made it clear last night that he no longer valued his life. *I'm sick of hiding. I might as well be dead.*

In the middle of my thoughts, the intercom above Miss Jarbowski's desk buzzed. The secretary's voice came through, carefully measured.

"Miss Jarbowski? Pardon the interruption. Would you please send Nora Grey to the attendance office?" A touch of sympathy crept into her tone.

Miss Jarbowski tapped her foot impatiently, apparently not appreciating being cut off midsentence. She flicked her hand in my direction. "Take your things, Nora. I don't think you'll make it back before the bell."

I scooped my textbook into my backpack and headed for the door, wondering what this was all about. I knew of only two reasons students were called to the attendance office. For ditching, and for excused absences. As far as I knew, neither applied to me.

At the attendance office, I tugged on the door, and that's when I saw him. Hank Millar sat in the lounge, his shoulders hunched,

BECCA FITZPATRICK

his expression haggard. His chin was propped on his fist, and his eyes stared blankly ahead.

Reflexively I backed away. But Hank saw me and immediately rose to his feet. The deep sympathy etched on his face wrung my stomach sick.

"What is it?" I found myself stammering.

He avoided looking directly at me. "There's been an accident."

His words rattled around inside me. My initial thought was, why would I care if Hank had been in an accident? And why had he come all the way to school to tell me?

"Your mom fell down the stairs. She was wearing heels and lost her balance. She has a concussion."

A tide of panic crashed over me. I said something that might have been *no* or *now*. No, this couldn't be happening. I needed to see my mom *now*. All of a sudden I regretted every sharp word I'd said to her these past couple of weeks. My worst fears came crawling in from every direction. I'd already lost my dad. If I lost my mom . . .

"How serious is it?" My voice wobbled. Deep down, I knew I didn't want to cry in front of Hank. A trivial matter of pride that shattered the moment I pictured my mom's face. I shut my eyes, trapping the tears.

"When I left the hospital, they couldn't tell me anything. I came straight here to get you. I've already signed you out with the attendance secretary," Hank explained. "I'll drive you to the hospital."

He held the door for me, and I mechanically ducked under his arm. I felt my feet carry me down the hall. Outside, the sun was too bright. I wondered if I would remember this day forever. I wondered if I would have reason to look back on it and feel the same intolerable emotions I'd felt upon learning my dad had been murdered—confusion, bitterness, helplessness. *Abandonment*. I choked, no longer able to hold back a sob.

Hank unlocked his Land Cruiser without a word. He raised his hand once, as if to give my shoulder a consoling squeeze, then made a fist and dropped it.

And that's when it hit me. Things were looking a little too convenient. Maybe it was my natural aversion to Hank, but it crossed my mind that he could be lying to get me inside his car.

"I want to call the hospital," I said abruptly. "I want to see if they have an update."

Hank frowned. "We're on our way there now. In ten minutes, you can talk to her doctor in person."

"Excuse me if I'm a little worried, but this is my mom we're talking about," I said softly, but with unmistakable firmness.

Hank dialed a number on his phone and handed it to me. The hospital's automated system picked up, asking me to listen carefully to the following options, or stay on the line for an operator. A minute later I was connected with an operator.

"Can you tell me if Blythe Grey was admitted today?" I asked the woman, avoiding Hank's gaze.

"Yes, we have a Blythe Grey on record."

I exhaled. Just because Hank hadn't lied about my mom's accident didn't mean he was innocent. All these years living in the farmhouse, and never once had she fallen down the stairs. "This is her daughter. Can you give me an update on her condition?"

"I can leave a message for her doctor to call you."

"Thanks," I said, leaving my cell phone number.

"Any news?" Hank asked.

"How do you know she fell down the stairs?" I quizzed him. "Did you see her fall?"

"We'd arranged to meet for lunch. When she didn't answer the door, I let myself in. That's when I found her at the bottom of the stairs." If he detected any suspicion in my voice, he didn't show it. If anything, he sounded morose, loosening his tie and wiping sweat off his brow.

"If anything happens to her . . . ," he muttered to himself, but didn't finish the thought. "Should we go?"

Get into the car, a voice inside my head commanded. Just like that, my mind emptied of all suspicion. I could grasp only one thought: I needed to go with Hank.

There was something strange about the voice, but I couldn't place it through my muddled mind. All my reasoning power seemed to float away, making room for that one continuous order: Get into the car.

I looked at Hank, who blinked benignly. I had the impulse to accuse him of something, but why should I? He was here to help. He cared about my mom. . . .

Obediently, I slid inside the Land Cruiser.

I didn't know how long we rode in silence. My thoughts were a whirlwind, until suddenly Hank cleared his voice. "I want you to know she's in the best hands. I requested that Dr. Howlett oversee her care. Dr. Howlett and I were roommates at the University of Maine before he went on to Johns Hopkins."

Dr. Howlett. I juggled his name a moment—and then it came to me. He was the doctor who'd cared for me after I first returned home. After Hank saw fit to return me, I corrected myself. And now it turned out Hank and Dr. Howlett were friends? Any numbness I felt was quickly eclipsed by anxiety. I felt a swift and instant distrust of Dr. Howlett.

As I was frantically considering the connection between the two men, a car pulled up beside Hank's. For one split moment, I didn't see anything wrong with the picture—and then the car slammed into the Land Cruiser.

The Land Cruiser careened sideways, grating against the guardrail. A shower of sparks flew from the scraping metal. I barely had time to yelp when we were battered again. Hank overcorrected, the rear of the Land Cruiser fishtailing violently.

"They're trying to run us off the road!" Hank yelled. "Get your seat belt on!"

"Who are they?" I shrieked, double-checking that my seat belt was fastened.

Hank jerked the wheel to avoid another hit, and the abrupt movement jarred my attention back to the road ahead; it curved sharply to the left as we approached a deep ravine. Hank stomped the gas, trying to outrace the other car, a tan El Camino. The El Camino gunned forward, swerving into the lane ahead. Three heads were visible through the windshield, and from what I could tell, all were male.

An image of Gabe, Dominic, and Jeremiah flashed to mind. It was pure speculation, since I couldn't make out their faces, but even the mere suggestion caused me to yell out.

"Stop the car!" I shouted. "It's a trap. Put the car in reverse!"

"They destroyed my car!" Hank snarled, accelerating into a chase.

The El Camino screeched around the bend, skidding across the solid white line. Hank followed, veering dangerously close to the guardrail. The shoulder of the road dropped away, plunging into the ravine. From way up here, it looked like a giant bowl of air, with Hank racing recklessly along the rim. My stomach turned circles, and I clutched the armrest.

The El Camino's taillights blazed red.

"Look out!" I screamed. I flattened one hand to the window and the other against Hank's shoulder, trying to stop the inevitable.

Hank jerked the wheel hard, sending the Land Cruiser up on two wheels. I was thrown forward, my seat belt catching hard across my chest, my head colliding with the window. My vision clouded, and loud noises seemed to descend on me from every direction. Crunching, shattering, piercing noises that exploded in my ears.

I thought I heard Hank growl something—Damn fallen angels!—but then I was flying.

No, not flying. Tumbling. Over and over.

I didn't remember landing, but when my mind registered again, I was on my back. Not inside the Land Cruiser, somewhere else. Dirt. Leaves. Sharp rocks biting into my skin.

Cold, pain, hard. Cold, pain, hard. My brain couldn't move beyond three chanted words. I saw them slide across my vision.

"Nora!" Hank yelled, his voice sounding far away.

I was sure my eyes were open, but I couldn't make out any one object. Bright light I couldn't see past stretched from one edge of my vision to the other. I attempted to rise. The directions I gave my muscles were clear, but there was a breach somewhere along the lines; I couldn't move.

Hands grasped my ankles first, then my wrists. My body glided through the leaves and dirt, making a strange rustling noise. I licked my lips, trying to call out to Hank, but when my mouth opened, the wrong words came out.

Cold, pain, hard. Cold, pain, hard.

I wanted to rattle myself out of the stupor. No! I screamed inside my head. No, no, no!

Patch! Help! Patch, Patch, Patch!

"Cold, pain, hard," I muttered incoherently.

Before I could correct myself, it was too late. My mouth was stitched closed. As were my eyes.

BECCA FITZPATRICK

Solid hands grasped my shoulders, shaking me.

"Can you hear me, Nora? Don't try to get up. Stay on your back. I'm going to get you to the hospital."

My eyes popped open. Trees swayed overhead. Sunlight spilled through their branches, casting strange shadows that altered the world from light to dark, and back again.

Hank Millar bent over me. His face was cut up, blood trickling down, blood smearing his cheeks, blood matting his hair. His lips were moving, but it hurt too much to make sense of his words.

I turned away. Cold, *pain*, hard.

I woke in a hospital, my bed behind a white cotton curtain. The room was peacefully, yet strangely, quiet. My toes and fingers tingled, and my head might as well have been strewn with cobwebs. *Drugs*, I mildly noted.

A different face leaned over mine. Dr. Howlett smiled, but not enough to show teeth.

"You took a frightful hit, young lady. Plenty of bruising, but nothing's broken. I had the nurses give you ibuprofen, and I'll give you a prescription before you go. You're going to feel tender for a few days. Considering the circumstances, I'd say you should count your blessings."

"Hank?" I managed to ask, my lips paper-dry.

Dr. Howlett shook his head, rumbling a short laugh. "You're

going to hate hearing this, but he pulled through without a scratch. Hardly seems fair."

Through the haze, I tried to reason. Something wasn't right. And then my memory opened. "No. He was cut up. He was bleeding badly."

"You're mistaken. Hank came in wearing more of your blood than his own. You got the worst of it by far."

"But I saw him—"

"Hank Millar is in pristine shape," he cut me off. "And once your stitches fall out, you will be too. As soon as the nurses finish checking these bandages, you'll be good to go."

Underneath it all, I knew I should panic. There were too many questions, too few answers. Cold, pain, hard. Cold, pain, hard.

The glow of taillights. The crash. The ravine.

"This will help," Dr. Howlett said, surprising me with a prick to my arm. Fluid streamed from the needle into my blood with nothing more than a faint sting.

"But I just regained consciousness," I murmured, a pleasant chemical exhaustion washing through me. "How can I be okay already? I don't feel right."

"You'll make a faster recovery at home." He chuckled. "Here you'll have nurses poking and prodding you all night."

All night? "It's already evening? But it was just noon. Before Hank—health class—I never had lunch."

"It's been a rough day," Dr. Howlett said, nodding complacently.

BECCA FITZPATRICK

Under the layers of drugs, I wanted to scream. Instead a mere sigh escaped.

I laid a hand on my stomach. "I feel funny."

"MRI confirmed you don't have internal bleeding. Take it easy for the next few days, and you'll be up and running in no time." He gave my shoulder a playful squeeze. "But I can't promise you'll feel like climbing into another car any time soon."

Somewhere in the middle of the fog, I remembered my mom. "Is Hank with my mom? Is she okay? Can I see her? Does she know about the car crash?"

"Your mom is making a very speedy recovery," he assured me. "She's still in ICU and can't have visitors, but she should be moved to her own room by morning. You can come back and see her then." He leaned down, as though to make me his coconspirator. "Between us, if it weren't for the red tape, I'd let you sneak in to see her now. She had a pretty nasty concussion, and while there was memory loss at first, considering her condition when Hank first brought her in, I think it's safe to say she'll pull a one-eighty." He patted my cheek. "Luck must run in the family."

"Luck," I repeated lethargically.

But I had an alarming feeling stirring inside me, indicating that luck had nothing to do with either of our recoveries.

And maybe not our accidents, either.

CHAPTER 26

AFTER DR. HOWLETT GAVE ME CLEARANCE TO leave, I rode the elevator down to the main lobby. On the way, I dialed Vee. I didn't have a ride home, and I hoped it was still early enough that her mom would let her rescue a stranded friend.

The elevator eased to a stop, and the doors glided open. My phone clattered at my feet.

"Hello, Nora," Hank said, standing directly in front of me.

Three counts passed before I summoned my voice. "Going up?" I asked, hoping I sounded calm.

"Actually, I was looking for you."

"I'm in a hurry," I said apologetically, scooping up my phone.

"I thought you might need a ride home. I had one of my boys bring over a rental from the dealership."

"Thanks, but I've already called a friend."

His smile was plastic. "At least let me see you to the doors."

"I need to stop by the restrooms first," I hedged. "Please don't wait. Really, I'm fine. I'm sure Marcie is anxious to see you."

"Your mother would want me to see you home safely."

His eyes were bloodshot, his whole expression weary, but I didn't for one moment think it was from his role as the grieving boyfriend. Dr. Howlett could insist all he wanted that Hank had arrived at the hospital unscathed, but I knew the truth. He'd come out of the crash worse than I had. Worse, even, than the crash warranted.

His face had resembled pulverized meat, and while his Nephilim blood had cured him almost instantly, I'd known from the moment he'd shaken me out of unconsciousness, and I'd taken that first blurry look at him, that something had happened to him after I blacked out. He could deny it up and down, but his condition had resembled being mauled by tigers.

He was haggard and exhausted because he'd battled a group of fallen angels today. At least, that was my current working theory. As

I traced my way back through the events, it was the only explanation that made sense. *Damn fallen angels!* Weren't those the words
Hank had sworn viciously a fraction of a moment before the crash?
He clearly hadn't planned on running into them . . . so what *had* he
planned to happen?

I had a terrible feeling churning inside me. One, I realized in
retrospect, I'd been dangling at the back of my mind ever since
Hank had shown up at school. What if Hank *had* in fact set the day's
events up? Could he have pushed my mom down the stairs? Dr.
Howlett said she'd initially suffered from amnesia, a device Hank
could have used to keep her from remembering the truth. Then
he'd picked me up from school . . . for what? What was I missing?

"I smell rubber burning," Hank said. "You're thinking hard
about something."

His voice jerked me to the present. I stared up at him, wishing
I could glean his motives from his expression. It was then that I
realized his eyes were just as fixed on me. His gaze was so intent, it
was almost trancelike.

Whatever conclusion I'd been about to draw swam away. My
thoughts tipped sideways. Suddenly they were all out of order, and
I couldn't remember what I'd been pondering. The harder I tried
to remember, the more my thoughts careened into an abyss at the
back of my mind.

A cocoon stretched around my mind, wrapping any cognitive ability tightly out of reach. It was happening all over again. The muddled,

heavy sensation of being unable to control my own thoughts.

"Has your friend agreed to pick you up, Nora?" he asked with that same laserlike attention.

Somewhere deep inside, I knew I shouldn't tell Hank the truth. I knew I should say Vee was coming for me. But what reason did I have to lie to him?

"I called Vee, but she didn't answer," I admitted.

"I'm happy to give you a ride, Nora."

I nodded. "Yes, thank you."

My mind was jumbled, and I couldn't snap out of it. I strolled down the corridor beside Hank, my hands cold and shaking. Why was I trembling? It was nice of Hank to offer me a ride. He cared about my mom enough to go out of his way for me . . . didn't he?

The ride home was uneventful, and at the farmhouse, Hank followed me inside.

I stopped just inside the door. "What are you doing?"

"Your mom would want me to look after you tonight."

"You're staying the whole night?" My hands started to shake again, and through my cotton-filled head, I knew I had to find a way to make him leave. It wasn't a good idea to let him sleep over. But how could I force him out? He was stronger. And even if I could get him out, my mom had recently given him a house key. He'd come right back inside.

"You're letting cold air in," Hank said, gently prying my hands from the door. "Let me help."

That's right, I thought with a smile at my own muddleheaded silliness. He wanted to help.

Hank tossed his keys on the counter and sank into the couch, kicking his feet up on the ottoman. He angled his eyes at the cushion next to him. "Want to unwind with a show?"

"I'm tired," I said, hugging myself now that the awful quivering had spread above my elbows.

"You've had a long day. Sleep might be just what the doctor ordered."

I fought through the oppressive cloud suffocating my brain, but it seemed there was no end to the thick darkness. "Hank?" I asked quizzically. "Why do you really want to stay here tonight?"

He chuckled. "You look positively frightened, Nora. Be a good girl and go up to bed. It's not like I'm going to strangle you in your sleep."

In my bedroom, I scooted the dresser in front of the door, effectively blocking it. I had no idea why I did it; I had no reason to fear Hank. He was keeping a promise to my mom. He wanted to protect me. If he knocked, I would push the dresser aside and open the door.

And yet . . .

I crawled into bed and closed my eyes. Exhaustion raked down my body, and by now I was shivering violently. I wondered if I was catching a cold. When my mind began to feel heavy, I didn't fight it. Colors and shapes seesawed in and out of focus. My thoughts slid deeper into my subconscious. Hank was right; it had been a long day. I needed sleep.

It wasn't until I found myself standing at the threshold of Patch's studio that I began to sense that something wasn't quite right. The haze scattered from my brain, and I realized Hank had mind-tricked me into submission. Flinging open Patch's front door and dashing inside, I shouted his name.

I found him in the kitchen, slouched on a bar stool. One look at me, and he swung off and crossed to me. "Nora? How did you get here? You're inside my head," he said with surprise. "Are you dreaming?" His eyes flicked back and forth across my face, hunting for an answer.

"I don't know. I think so. I crawled into bed feeling a desperate need to talk to you . . . and here I am. Are you asleep?"

He shook his head. "I'm awake, but you're eclipsing my thoughts. I don't know how you did it. Only a powerful Nephil or fallen angel could pull off something like this."

"Something terrible happened." I threw myself into his arms, trying to dissipate my convulsive shivers. "First my mom fell down the stairs, and on our way to the hospital to see her, Hank and I were hit. Before I blacked out, I think Hank said the other car was full of fallen angels. Hank drove me home from the hospital—and I asked him to leave, but he won't!"

Patch's eyes flashed with anxiety. "Slow down. Hank is alone with you right now?"

I nodded.

"Wake up. I'm coming to see you."

Fifteen minutes later there was a soft rap on my bedroom door. Dragging aside the dresser to clear the entrance, I cracked the door to find Patch on the other side of it. I grabbed his hand and hauled him inside.

"Hank is downstairs watching TV," I whispered. Hank had been right; sleep had done me a world of good. Upon breaking out of the dream, enough of my normal thought process had returned to make me see what I'd been unable to before: Hank had mind-tricked me into submission. I'd let him drive me home without a single complaint, let him walk inside my house, let him make himself at home, and all because I'd thought he wanted to protect me. Nothing could be further from the truth.

Patch gave the door a gentle kick closed. "I came in through the attic." He looked me over, head to toe. "Are you okay?" His finger traced a bandage covering a thin laceration cutting across my hairline, and his eyes blazed with anger.

"Hank has been mind-tricking me all night."

"Play everything back, starting with your mom's fall."

I swallowed a deep breath, then recounted my story.

"What did the fallen angels' car look like?" Patch asked.

"El Camino. Tan."

Patch rubbed his chin in thought. "Do you think it was Gabe? It's not what he usually drives, but that doesn't necessarily mean anything."

"There were three of them in the car. I couldn't see their faces. It might have been Gabe, Dominic, and Jeremiah."

"Or it might have been any number of fallen angels targeting Hank. With Rixon gone, there's a price on his head. He's the Black Hand, the most powerful Nephil alive, and any number of fallen angels want him as their vassal for bragging rights alone. How long were you out before Hank drove you to the hospital?"

"If I had to guess, only a few minutes. When I came around, Hank was covered in blood, and he looked exhausted. He could barely lift me into the car. I don't think his cuts and bruises came from the crash. Being coerced to swear fealty sounds plausible."

A truly savage look sharpened Patch's features. "This ends here. I want you out of this. I know you're set on being the one to bring down Hank, but I can't risk losing you." He stood and paced the room, clearly upset. "Let me do this for you. Let me be the one to make him pay."

"This isn't your fight, Patch," I said quietly.

His eyes burned with an intensity I'd never seen before. "You're mine, Angel, and don't you forget it. Your fights are my fights. What if something had happened today? It was bad enough when I thought your ghost was haunting me; I don't think I could handle the real thing."

I came up behind him, threading my arms under his. "Something bad could have happened, but it didn't," I said gently. "Even if it was Gabe, he obviously didn't get what he wanted."

"Forget Gabe! Hank has something planned for you and maybe your mom, too. Let's concentrate on that. I want you to go into hiding. If you don't want to stay at my place, fine. We'll find somewhere else. You'll stay there until Hank is dead, buried, and rotting."

"I can't leave. Hank will immediately suspect something if I disappear. Plus, I can't put my mom through that again. If I disappear now, it will break her. Look at her. She's not the same person she was three months ago. Maybe in part that's due to Hank's mind-tricks, but I have to face the fact that my disappearance weakened her in ways she'll probably never recover from. From the moment she wakes up in the morning, she's terrified. To her, there's no such thing as safe. Not anymore."

"Again, Hank's doing," Patch dismissed curtly.

"I can't control what Hank did, but I can control what I do now. I'm not leaving. And you're right—I'm not going to step aside and let you take on Hank alone. Promise me now that whatever happens, you won't cheat me. Promise you won't go behind my back and quietly do away with him, even if you honestly believe you're doing it for my own good."

"Oh, he won't go quietly," Patch said with a murderous edge.

"Promise me, Patch."

He regarded me in silence a long time. We both knew he was faster, more skilled in fighting, and, when it came right down to it, more ruthless. He'd stepped in and saved me many times in the past, but this was one time—*one time*—when it was my fight to pick, and mine alone.

At last, and with great reluctance, he said, "I won't stand by and watch you go up against him alone, but I won't kill him privately, either. Before I lay a hand on him, I'll make sure it's what you want."

His back was to me, but I pressed my cheek against his shoulder, nuzzling him softly. "Thank you."

"If you're ever attacked again, go for the fallen angel's wing scars."

I didn't follow him right away. Then he continued, "Club him with a baseball bat or ram a stick in his scars if that's all you have. Our wing scars are our Achilles' heel. We can't feel the pain, but the trauma to the scars will paralyze us. Depending on the damage done, you could cripple us for hours. After stabbing the tire iron through Gabe's scars, I'd be surprised if he came out of the shock in less than eight."

"I'll remember that," I said softly. Then, "Patch?"

"Mmm." His response was terse.

"I don't want to fight." I traced my finger along his shoulder blades, his muscles stiff with aggravation. His whole body was clenched, frustrated beyond measure. "Hank has already taken my mom from me, and I don't want him to take you, too. Can you understand why I have to do it? Why I can't send you off to fight my battles, even though we both know you win in this department, hands down?"

He exhaled, long and slow, and I felt the knots in his body loosen. "There's only one thing I know for certain anymore." He turned, his eyes a clear black. "That I would do anything for you, even if it means going against my instincts or my very nature. I would lay down everything I possess, even my soul, for you. If that isn't love, it's the best I have."

I didn't know what to say in return; nothing seemed adequate. So I took his face between my hands and kissed his set, determined mouth.

Slowly, Patch's mouth molded to mine. I relished the delicious pressure shooting across my skin as his mouth rose and dipped against my own. I didn't want him to be angry. I wanted him to trust me the way I trusted him. "Angel," he said, my name muted from where our lips met. He drew back, his eyes judging what I wanted from him.

Unable to bear having him so close without feeling his touch, I slid my hand to the back of his neck, guiding him to kiss me again. His kiss was harder, escalating as his hands ran over my body, sending hot chills shuddering like electricity under my skin.

His finger flicked open a button on my cardigan—then two, three, four. It tumbled off my shoulders, leaving me in my camisole. He pushed up the hem, teasing and stroking his thumb across my stomach. My breath came in a sharp intake of air.

A pirate smile glowed in his eyes as he concentrated his attention higher, nuzzling the curve of my throat, planting kisses, his stubble raking with a gratifying ache.

He lowered me backward against the soft down of my pillows.

He tasted deeper, holding himself over me, and suddenly he was everywhere; his knee trapping my leg, his lips grazing warm, rough, sensuous. He splayed his hand at the small of my back, holding me tightly, driving me to sink my fingers deeper into him, clinging to him as if letting go would mean losing part of myself.

"Nora?"

I looked to the doorway—and screamed.

Hank filled the entrance, leaning his forearm on the doorjamb. His eyes swept the room, his face contracted in quizzical contemplation.

"What are you doing!" I yelled at him.

He didn't answer, his eyes still roving every corner of my bedroom.

I didn't know where Patch was; it was as though he'd sensed Hank a split moment before the doorknob turned. He could be feet away, hiding. Seconds away from being discovered.

"Get out!" I sprang off the bed. "I can't do anything about the house key my mom gave you, but this is where I draw the line. Do not *ever* come into my bedroom again."

His eyes made a slow scan of my closet doors, which were cracked. "I thought I heard something."

"Yeah, well, guess what? I'm a living, breathing person, and every now and then I make noise!"

With that, I flung the door shut and sagged against it. My pulse was all over the board. I heard Hank stand resolute a moment, probably trying to pinpoint, once more, whatever it was that had brought him up to search my bedroom in the first place.

At last he wandered down the hall. He'd frightened me to the point of tears. I swatted them hastily away, replaying his every word and expression in my mind, trying to find any clue that would prove whether he knew Patch was in my room.

I let five treacherously long minutes pass before I cracked my door. The hall outside was empty. I returned my attention to my bedroom. "Patch?" I whispered in the faintest voice.

But I was alone.

I didn't see Patch again until I fell asleep. I dreamed I was wading through a field of wild grass that parted around my hips as I walked. Ahead, a barren tree appeared, twisted and misshapen. Patch leaned against it, hands pocketed. He was dressed in head-to-toe black, a stark contrast against the creamy white of the field.

I ran the rest of the way to him. He wrapped his leather jacket around us, more as an act of intimate possession than to conserve heat.

"I want to stay with you tonight," I said. "I'm scared Hank is going to try something."

"I'm not letting you or him out of my sight, Angel," he said with something almost territorial in his tone.

"Do you think he knows you were in my bedroom?"

Patch's agitated sigh was barely audible. "One thing's for sure: He sensed something. I made a big enough impression that he came upstairs to investigate. I'm starting to wonder if he's stronger than I've given him credit for. His men are impeccably organized and trained. He's managed to hold an archangel captive. And now he can sense me from several rooms away. The only explanation I can think of is devilcraft. He's found a way to channel it, or he made a bargain. Either way, he's invoking the powers of hell."

I shuddered. "You're scaring me. That night, after Bloody Mary's, the two Nephilim who chased me mentioned devilcraft. But they said Hank had pronounced it a myth."

"Could be Hank doesn't want anyone knowing what he's up to. Devilcraft might explain why he thinks he can overthrow fallen angels as early as Cheshvan. I'm not an expert in devilcraft, but it seems plausible that it could be used to combat an oath, even an oath sworn under heaven. He might be counting on it to break thousands upon thousands of oaths Nephilim have sworn to fallen angels over the centuries."

"In other words, you don't think it's a myth."

"I used to be an archangel," he reminded me. "It wasn't under my jurisdiction, but I know it exists. That's about all any of us knew. It originated in hell, and most of what we knew was speculation.

silence

Devilcraft is forbidden outside of hell, and the archangels should be on top of this." An edge of frustration crept into his tone.

"Maybe they don't know. Maybe Hank found a way to hide it from them. Or maybe he's using it in such little doses, they haven't picked up on it."

"Here's a cheerful thought," Patch said with a short, unamused laugh. "He could be using devilcraft to rearrange molecules in the air, which would explain why I've had a hard time tracking him. The whole time I've been spying for him, I've done my best to keep a tail on him, trying to figure out how he's using the information I've fed him. Not easy, given he moves like a ghost. He doesn't leave evidence the way he should. He could be using devilcraft to alter matter altogether. I have no idea how long he's been using it or how good he's gotten at harnessing it."

We both contemplated this in chilling silence. Rearranging matter? If Hank was capable of tampering with the basic components of our world, what else could he manipulate?

After a moment, Patch reached under his shirt collar, unclasping a plain men's chain. It was made of interlocking links of sterling silver and was slightly tarnished. "Last summer I gave you my archangel's necklace. You gave it back to me, but I want you to have it again. It doesn't work for me anymore. But it might come in useful."

"Hank would do *anything* to get your necklace," I protested, pushing Patch's hands away. "Keep it. You need to hide it. We can't let Hank find it."

"If Hank puts my necklace on the archangel, she'll have no choice but to tell him the truth. She'll give him pure, unadulterated knowledge, and freely. You're right about that. But the necklace will also record the encounter, imprinting it forever. Sooner or later, Hank's going to get his hands on a necklace. Better he takes mine than finds another."

"Imprint?"

"I want you to find a way to give this to Marcie," he instructed, clasping the chain at the nape of my neck. "It can't be obvious. She has to think she's stolen it from you. Hank will grill her, and she has to believe that she outsmarted you. Can you do that?"

I pulled back, giving him an admonitory look. "What are you planning?"

His smile was faint. "I wouldn't call this planning. I'd call this throwing a Hail Mary with seconds left on the clock."

With great care, I thought through what he was asking of me. "I can invite Marcie over," I said at last. "I'll tell her I need help picking out jewelry to go with my homecoming dress. If she's really helping Hank hunt down an archangel's necklace, and if she thinks I have it, she'll take advantage of having access to my bedroom. I'm not thrilled about having her poking around, but I'll do it." I paused meaningfully. "But first I want to know *exactly* why I'm doing it."

"Hank needs the archangel to talk. So do we. We need a way to let the archangels in heaven know Hank is practicing devilcraft. I'm a fallen angel, and they aren't going to listen to me. But if Hank touches my necklace, it will imprint on the necklace. If he's using devilcraft, the necklace will record that, too. My word means nothing to the archangels, but that kind of evidence would. All we'd need to do is get the necklace into their hands."

I still felt a tug of doubt. "What if it doesn't work? What if Hank gets the information he needs, and we get nothing?"

He agreed with a slight nod. "What would you like me to do instead?"

I thought about it, and came up empty. Patch was right. We were out of time, out of options. It wasn't the best position to be in, but something told me Patch had been making the best of risky decisions his entire existence. If I had to get dragged into a gamble as big as this, I couldn't think of anyone I'd rather be with.

CHAPTER

IT WAS FRIDAY NIGHT, A WEEK LATER, AND MY MOM
and Hank were in the living room, cuddled on the couch and
sharing a bowl of popcorn. I'd retreated to my room, having
promised Patch I could keep my cool around Hank.

Hank had been infuriatingly charming the past few days, driving
my mom home from the hospital, stopping by with takeout every
night promptly at dinnertime, even cleaning our roof gutters earlier
this morning. I wasn't foolish enough to lower my guard, but I was

driving myself mad trying to pull apart his motives. He was planning something, but when it came down to *what*, I was at a loss.

My mom's laugh carried up the stairs, and it pushed me over the edge. I punched in a text to Vee.

YO, she answered a moment later.

I HAVE TICKETS 2 SERPENTINE. WANNA?

SERPEN-WHA???

FRIEND OF THE FAMILY'S NEW BAND, I explained. OPENING GIG IS TONIGHT.

PICK U UP IN 20.

Promptly twenty minutes later, Vee screeched into the driveway. I thundered down the stairs, hoping to make it out the door before I had to endure the torture of hearing my mom make out with Hank, who, I'd learned, was a very wet kisser.

"Nora?" Mom called down the hall. "Where are you going?"

"Out with Vee. I'll be back by eleven!" Before she could veto, I raced outside and threw myself inside Vee's 1995 purple Dodge Neon. "Go, go, go!" I ordered her.

Vee, who'd have a bright future as a getaway driver if college didn't pan out, took my escape into her own hands, peeling out of the drive loud enough to frighten a flock of birds out of the nearest tree.

"Whose Avalon was in the driveway?" Vee asked as she sped across town, oblivious to road signs. She'd dramatically bawled her way out of three speeding tickets since getting her license, and was firmly convinced that when it came to the law, she was invincible.

"Hank's rental."

"I heard from Michelle Van Tassel, who heard from Lexi Hawkins, who heard from our good friend Marcie that Hank is offering up a big ol' reward for any police tips that lead to the arrest of the freak shows who tried to run you off the road."

Good luck with that.

But I smirked appropriately, not wanting to tip Vee off that anything was wrong. Ideally, I knew I should tell her everything, starting with having my memory erased by Hank. But . . . how? How did I explain things I could hardly comprehend myself? How did I make her believe in a world teeming with the stuff of nightmares, when I had nothing but my own word to offer up as proof?

"How much is Hank offering?" I asked. "Maybe I can be coaxed into remembering something important."

"Why bother? Lift his bank card instead. I doubt he'd notice if a few hundred walked off. And hey, if you get caught, it's not like he can have you arrested. It would screw up any chance he has with your mom."

If only it were that simple, I thought, a gritty smile frozen on my face. If only Hank could be taken at face value.

There was a tiny parking lot near the Devil's Handbag, and Vee cruised through it five times, but a spot didn't open up. She widened her search block by block. At last she parallel parked along a stretch of curb that left half the Neon hanging out in the street.

Vee got out and surveyed her parking job. She shrugged. "Five points for creativity."

We walked the rest of the way on foot.

"So who's this friend of the family?" Vee inquired. "Is he male? Is he hot? Is he single?"

"Yes on the first count, probably on second, I think so on the last. You want me to introduce you?"

"No siree. Just wanted to know if I should keep my evil eye trained on him. I don't trust boys anymore, but my scary-radar goes off the charts when it comes to pretty boys."

I gave a short laugh trying to imagine a squeaky-clean, dolled-up version of Scott. "Scott Parnell is anything but pretty."

"Whoa. Hold on. What's this? You didn't tell me the old family friend was Scottie the Hottie."

I wanted to tell Vee that was because I was doing my best to keep Scott's public appearance tonight quiet, not wanting any word of it to reach Hank's ears, but I brushed it off with an innocent, "Sorry, I must have forgotten."

"Our boy Scottie has a body you can't forget. You've got to give him that."

She was right. Scott wasn't bulky, but he was very muscular and had the well-proportioned physique of a top-notch athlete. If it weren't for the tough, almost scowl-like expression he carried everywhere, he'd probably attract throngs of girls. Possibly even Vee, who was a self-proclaimed man hater.

We rounded the final corner, and the Devil's Handbag came into view. It was a charmless four-storey brick structure with creeping ivy and blacked-out windows. On one side it neighbored a pawn shop. On the other sat a shoe repair store that I secretly suspected was the front for a thriving fake ID business. Seriously, who replaced their soles anymore?

"Are we going to get tagged?" Vee asked.

"Not tonight. They aren't serving alcohol at the bar, since half the band is underage. Scott told me we'd only need tickets."

We stepped into line, and five minutes later cleared the doors. The spacious layout inside consisted of a stage on one side of the room, and a bar on the other. Booth seating close to the bar, cafe tables near the stage. There was a decent crowd, with more coming in by the minute, and I experienced a squeeze of nervous anticipation for Scott. I tried to pick out Nephilim faces in the audience, but I wasn't experienced enough to trust myself to do a thorough job. Not that I had a reason to believe the Devil's Handbag made a likely hangout for nonhumans, particularly those with allegiance to Hank. I was simply going on the belief that it didn't hurt to be cautious.

Vee and I went right to the bar.

"Something to drink?" the bartender, a redhead who hadn't skimped on eyeliner or nose rings, asked us.

silence

"Suicide," Vee told her. "You know, when you put a little shot of everything into the glass?"

I leaned sideways. "How old are we?"

"Childhood only comes once. Live it up."

"Cherry Coke," I told the bartender.

As Vee and I sipped our drinks, sitting back and taking in the preshow excitement, a slender blonde with her hair stuffed into a messy—and sexy—bun sashayed over. She leaned her elbows back on the bar, giving me a cursory glance. She wore a long bohemian dress, pulling off hippie-chic flawlessly. Other than a swipe of siren-red lipstick, she was sans makeup, which drew my attention to her full, pouty mouth. Fixing her gaze on the stage, she said, "Haven't seen you girls around before. First time?"

"What's it to you?" Vee said.

The girl laughed, and while the sound was soft and tinkling, it made the hairs on the back of my neck rise.

"High schoolers?" she guessed.

Vee narrowed her eyes. "Maybe, maybe not. And you are . . . ?"

The blonde flashed a smile. "Dabria." Her eyes pinned mine. "I heard about the amnesia. Pity."

I gagged on my cherry Coke.

Vee said, "You look familiar. But your name isn't ringing a bell." She pursed her lips in evaluation.

In response, Dabria cast cool eyes on Vee, and just like that, all suspicion dissipated from Vee's expression, leaving her as blank as

BECCA FITZPATRICK

placid water. "I've never seen you before in my life. This is the first time we've met," Vee said in a monotone.

I glared at Dabria. "Can we talk? Alone?"

"I thought you'd never ask," she answered breezily.

I pushed my way over to the hallway leading to the restrooms. When we were out of the crowd, I spun on Dabria. "First, quit mind-tricking my best friend. Second, what are you doing here? And third, you're a lot prettier than Patch led me to believe." Probably didn't need to throw in that last bit, but now that I had Dabria alone, I wasn't in the mood to dance around. Best to get straight to the point.

Her mouth curled into a satisfied smirk. "And you're quite a bit more plain than I remember."

Suddenly I wished I'd pulled on something more sophisticated than boyfriend jeans, a graphic tee, and a military-style hat. I said, "He's over you, just so we're clear."

Dabria examined her manicure before looking up at me through lowered lashes. With unmistakable regret she said, "I wish I could say I was over him."

I told you so! I thought angrily at Patch.

"Unrequited love sucks," I stated simply.

"Is he here?" Dabria craned her neck to search the crowd.

"No. But I'm sure you already knew that, since you've taken it upon yourself to stalk him."

Something mischievous danced in her eyes. "Oh? He noticed?"

"Hard not to when you've clearly made it your life's purpose to throw yourself at him."

Her pouty smirk adopted a hardened edge. "Just so you know, if it weren't for my feather Jev keeps tucked in his pants, I wouldn't think twice about dragging you out to the street and giving you a front-row seat with an oncoming car. Jev might be here for you now, but I wouldn't breathe easy. He's made quite a few enemies over the years, and I can't tell you how many of them would love to chain him in hell. You don't treat people the way he has and sleep with both eyes closed," she said, cold-blooded warning creeping into her tone. "If he wants to stay on Earth, he can't be distracted by some"—her gaze raked over me—"childish little girl. He needs an ally. Someone who can watch his back and be useful to him."

"And you think you're just the girl for the job?" I seethed.

"I think you should stick to your own kind. Jev doesn't like to be tied down. One glance at you, and I can tell you've got your hands full with him."

"He's changed," I said. "He's not the same person he was when you knew him."

Her laughter rang off the walls. "I can't decide if your naïveté is adorable, or if I want to smack some sense into you. Jev will never change, and he doesn't love you. He's using you to get to the Black Hand. Do you know how high the price on Hank Millar's head is? Millions. Jev wants that money as much as the next fallen angel, maybe more, because he can use it to pay off his enemies, and trust me when I say they're snapping at his heels. He's ahead of the game because he has you, the Black Hand's heir. You can get close to the Black Hand in a way most fallen angels can only dream of."

I didn't bat an eye. "I don't believe you."

"I know you want the Black Hand, sweetie. Just like I know you want to be the one to destroy him. Not an easy feat, considering he's Nephilim, but pretend for a minute it's possible. Do you really think Jev will hand Hank over to you when he can deliver him to the right people and receive a ten-million-dollar paycheck? Think about it."

On that note, Dabria raised a shrewd eyebrow and merged into the crowd.

When I returned to the bar, Vee said, "Don't know about you, but I didn't like that chick. She rivals Marcie for the number one spot on my skank-detecting meter."

She's worse, I thought grimly. Much worse.

"Speaking of instincts, I haven't made up my mind yet how I feel about this particular Romeo," Vee said, sitting a little higher on her stool.

I followed her gaze, finding Scott at the end of it.

A good head taller than the crowd, he waded toward us. His sun-streaked brown hair hugged his head like a cap, and paired with bedraggled jeans and a fitted T-shirt, he looked every bit the bass player in an up-and-coming rock band.

"You came," he said with a hitch of his mouth, and I knew right away he was pleased.

"Wouldn't miss it for the world," I said, trying to squash down any uneasiness I felt over Scott's obstinate refusal to stay in hiding a little longer. One brief glance at his hand revealed that he hadn't removed the Black Hand's ring. "Scott, this is my best friend, Vee Sky. I don't know if you two have officially met."

Vee shook Scott's hand and said, "I'm happy to see there's at least one person in this room taller than me."

"Yeah, I get my height from my dad's side," Scott said, clearly not in a hurry to elaborate. Then to me, "About homecoming. I'm sending a limo over to your place tomorrow at nine. The driver will take you to the dance, and I'll meet you there. Was I supposed to get one of those flower things for your wrist? I totally forgot about that."

"You two are going to homecoming together?" Vee asked, eyebrows vaulted, fingers pointing between us in a puzzled manner.

I could have kicked myself for not remembering to tell her. In my defense, I'd had a lot on my mind.

"As friends," I reassured Vee. "If you want to come, the more the merrier."

"Yeah, but now I don't have time to buy a dress," Vee said, sounding genuinely discouraged.

Thinking on my feet, I said, "We'll go to Silk Garden first thing tomorrow. Plenty of time. Didn't you like that purple sequin gown, the one on the mannequin?"

Scott jerked his thumb over his shoulder. "I gotta go warm up.

If you can hang around after the show, find me backstage and I'll give you a private tour."

Vee and I exchanged a look, and I knew her estimation of Scott had just risen several notches. I, on the other hand, prayed he'd last long enough to give us a tour. Surreptitiously casting my eyes about, I hunted for signs of Hank, his men, or anything else troublesome.

Serpentine came on stage, testing and tuning the various guitars and drums. Scott jumped onstage with them, flinging his guitar strap across his shoulder. He strummed a few notes, biting the guitar pick between his teeth as he nodded to his own beat. Looking sideways, I found Vee tapping her foot in rhythm.

I nudged her elbow. "Anything you want to tell me?"

She bit back a smile. "He's nice."

"I thought you were in boy detox."

Vee nudged me back, harder. "Don't be a Debbie Downer."

"Just getting my facts straight."

"If we hooked up, he could write me ballads and stuff. You gotta admit, nothing's sexier than a guy who writes music."

"Mm-hmm," I said.

"Mm-hmm, yourself."

Onstage, a crew from the Devil's Handbag helped adjust the microphones and amps. One of the crew members was on his knees, taping down cords, when he paused to wipe sweat off his brow. My eyes fell on his arm, and I was hit by a flash of recognition so strong it seemed to rock me back. Three words were tattooed like a mantra on his forearm. COLD. PAIN. HARD.

I didn't know the significance of the combination of words, but I knew I'd seen them before. A pair of curtains drew back, revealing my memory long enough for me to remember seeing the tattoo right after I'd been hurled from Hank's Land Cruiser. COLD. PAIN. HARD. I hadn't remembered it before, but now I was positive. The man onstage had been there. Directly following the crash. He'd grabbed my wrists as I'd drifted into unconsciousness, dragging my body through the dirt. He had to have been one of the fallen angels riding in the El Camino.

As I came to this startling conclusion, the fallen angel dusted his hands and jumped offstage, wandering the perimeter of the crowd. He made brief conversation with a few people, slowly progressing toward the back of the room. Abruptly, he turned down the same hall where Dabria and I had talked.

I called into Vee's ear, "I'm going to run to the restroom. Save my spot."

Edging through the crowd, huddled three and four deep around the bar, I followed the fallen angel into the hallway. He stood at the far end of it, bent slightly forward. He shifted, revealing his profile, holding a lighter to the cigarette balanced between his lips. Exhaling a plume of spoke, he stepped outside.

I gave him a few seconds' head start, then cracked the door and stuck my head out. A handful of smokers loitered in the alley, but other than a flick of eyes, no one paid me any attention. I stepped all the way out, searching for the fallen angel. He was halfway down the alley, walking toward the street. Maybe he wanted to smoke alone, but I had a feeling he was leaving for good.

I ran down my options. I could hurry back inside and enlist Vee's help, but I didn't want to risk involving her if I could help it. I could call Patch for backup, but if I waited for him to arrive, I'd risk losing the fallen angel. Or I could take Patch's advice and immobilize the fallen angel, taking advantage of his wing scars, and then call for backup.

I decided to give Patch as much of a heads-up as I could and pray that he hurried. We'd agreed to reserve calls and texts for emergencies only, not wanting to leave any unwanted evidence lying around for Hank to find. If this didn't constitute an emergency, I didn't know what did.

IN ALLEY BEHIND DEVIL'S HANDBAG, I texted in a hurry. SAW FALLEN ANGEL FROM CAR CRASH. WILL AIM FOR WING SCARS.

There was a snow shovel propped against the back door of the shoe repair store, and I picked it up without thinking. I didn't have a plan, but if I was going to immobilize the fallen angel, I'd need a weapon. Keeping an unsuspecting distance behind, I followed him to the end of the alley. He turned onto the street, flicked his cigarette into the gutter, and dialed on his cell phone.

Hidden in shadow, I picked up bits and pieces of his conversation.

"Finished the job. He's here. Yeah, I'm sure it's him."

He hung up and scratched his neck. He let go of a sigh that sounded conflicted. Or maybe resigned.

Taking advantage of his quiet contemplation, I crept up behind him and swung the shovel sideways in a vicious sweep. It smashed into his back with more power than I ever thought I possessed, right where his wing scars should be.

The fallen angel staggered forward, taking a knee.

I brought the shovel down a second time with more confidence. Then a third, fourth, fifth time. Knowing I couldn't kill him, I slammed a fierce blow to his head.

He wobbled off balance, then slumped to the ground.

I nudged him with my shoe, but he was out cold.

Hurried footsteps rang out behind me and I flipped around, still clutching the shovel. Patch emerged from the darkness, breathless from running. He looked between me and the fallen angel.

"I—got him," I said, still in shock that it had been so easy.

Patch gently pried the shovel from my hands and set it aside. A faint smile twitched his lips. "Angel, this man isn't a fallen angel."

I blinked. "What?"

Patch crouched beside the man, took his shirt in his hands, and ripped the fabric. I stared at the man's back, smooth and muscular. And not a wing scar in sight.

"I was sure," I stammered. "I thought it was him. I recognized his tattoo—"

Patch peered up at me. "He's Nephilim."

A Nephil? I'd just bludgeoned a Nephil unconscious?

Rolling the Nephil's body over, Patch unbuttoned his shirt, inspecting his torso. At the same time, our eyes traveled to the brand just below his clavicle. The clenched fist was all too familiar.

"The Black Hand's mark," I said with astonishment. "The men who attacked us that day, and nearly drove us off the road, were Hank's men?" What did it mean? And how could Hank have made such a grave error in judgment? He'd claimed they were fallen angels. He'd sounded so certain—

"Are you sure this was one of the men in the El Camino?" Patch asked.

Rage leaped inside me as I realized I'd been played. "Oh, I'm sure."

ANK ORCHESTRATED THE CAR CRASH," I SAID, deadly quiet. "Originally I thought the crash had upended his plans, but none of it was by accident. He told his men to hit us, and he planted it in my head that they were fallen angels. And I was stupid enough to fall for it!"

Patch transported the Nephil's body behind an overgrown hedge, concealing it from the street. "This way he won't attract any attention before he wakes up," he explained. "Did he get a good look at you?"

"No, I took him by surprise," I said distractedly. "But *why* did Hank need to crash his car? The whole thing seems pointless. His car was totaled, he was severely beaten up in the process—I don't get it."

"I don't want you leaving my sight until we've figured this out," Patch said. "Go inside and tell Vee you don't need a ride home. I'll pick you up out front in five."

I scrubbed my hands briskly over my arms, which prickled with goose bumps. "Come with me. I don't want to be alone. What if there are more of Hank's men inside?"

Patch made a sound that wasn't quite amusement. "If Vee sees us together, things will get messy. Tell her you found a ride home, and you'll call her later. I'll stand just inside the doors. I won't let you out of my sight."

"She won't buy it. She's a lot more cautious than she used to be." Quickly I worked out the only plausible solution. "I'll ride home with her, and after she leaves, I'll meet you up the street from my house. Hank is there, so don't drive any closer than you have to."

Patch pulled me into a brief, hard kiss. "Be careful."

Inside the Devil's Handbag, a loud murmur of complaint spread through the audience. People threw wadded napkins and plastic straws on the stage. A group on the far side of the floor took up chanting, "Serpentine sucks, Serpentine sucks." I elbowed my way over to Vee.

"What's going on?"

"Scott bailed. Just up and ran. The band can't play without him."

A sick feeling settled in my stomach. "Ran? Why?"

"I might have asked him if I could have caught him. He took a running leap off the stage and sprinted for the doors. Everyone thought it was a joke at first."

"We should get out of here," I told Vee. "The crowd isn't going to hold much longer."

"Amen to that," Vee said, hopping off her bar stool and scurrying toward the doors.

At the farmhouse, Vee bounced the Neon into the driveway. "What do you think got into Scott?" she asked me.

I was tempted to lie, but I was tired of playing this game with Vee. "I think he's in trouble," I told her.

"What kind of trouble?"

"I think he made some mistakes and upset the wrong people."

Vee looked bewildered . . . then skeptical. "Wrong people? What kind of wrong people?"

"Very bad people, Vee."

That was all the explanation she needed. Vee shoved the Neon into reverse. "Well, what are we doing sitting here? Scott's out there somewhere, and he needs our help."

"We can't help him. The people who are looking for him don't exactly have a conscience. They wouldn't think twice about hurting us. But there is someone who can help, and with any luck, he'll be able to help Scott get out of town tonight, where he'll be safe."

"Scott has to leave town?"

"It's not safe for him here. I'm sure the men who are looking for him expect him to try to leave, but Patch will know a way around them—"

"Hold up! Back up. You've got that whack job helping Scott?" Vee's volume shot higher and she glared at me accusingly. "Does your mom know you're mixed up with him again? Did you ever think maybe, maybe this was information you should tell me? I've been lying about him this whole time, pretending he never existed, and all the while you were hooking up with him behind my back?"

Hearing her blatant confession, minus any trace of remorse, ignited my temper. "So you're finally ready to come clean about Patch?"

"Come clean? Come clean? I lied because unlike that dirtbag, I actually care what happens to you. He's not right in the head. He showed up and your life was never the same. My life either, while we're on the subject. I'd rather face down a gang of convicts than bump into Patch on an empty street. He's real good at taking advantage of people, and it sounds to me like he's up to his old tricks again."

I opened my mouth, so upset I couldn't untangle my thoughts. "If you saw him the way I do—"

"That ever happens, you can bet I'll gouge my eyes out!"

I strove for composure. Angry or not, I could be rational. "You lied, Vee. You looked me in the eye and lied. I'd believe it of my mom, but not you." I pushed the door open. "How were you going to explain yourself when I got my memory back?" I demanded suddenly.

"I hoped you wouldn't get it back." Vee threw her hands in the air. "There. I said it. You were better off without it, if it meant not remembering that freak show. You don't think straight when you're around him. It's like you see the one percent of him that might be good and miss the other ninety-nine percent of pure psychopathic evil!"

My jaw fell open.

"Anything else?" I snapped.

"Nope. That sums up my feelings pretty adequately on the subject."

I shot out of the car and slammed the door.

Vee rolled down her window and poked her head out. "When you come back to your senses, you have my number!" she called out.

Then she floored down the driveway and sped off into the darkness.

I stood in the shadow of the farmhouse, trying to collect my cool. I reflected on the vague answers Vee had given me when I'd first come home from the hospital without a shred of my memory intact, and my temper threatened to explode. I'd trusted her. I'd relied on her to tell me what I couldn't figure out for myself. Worst of all, she'd collaborated with my mom. They'd used my memory loss to push the truth further out of reach. Because of them, it had taken me that much longer to find Patch.

I was so worked up, I nearly forgot I'd told Patch to meet me down the street. Reining in my anger, I stormed away from the farmhouse, keeping my eyes alert for signs of Patch. By the time his form slowly took shape in the shadows ahead, the worst of my sense of betrayal had died down, but I wasn't ready to call Vee and extend forgiveness just yet.

Patch was parked by the roadside, straddling a black vintage Harley-Davidson Sportster motorcycle. I felt a shift in the air when I saw him; something dangerous and enticing resonated like a live wire. I stopped in my tracks at the sight of him. My heart stammered a beat, almost as if he held it in his grasp, commanding me in his own secret ways. I believed it. Bathed in moonlight, he looked positively criminal.

He handed me a helmet as I walked up. "Where's the Tahoe?" I asked.

"Had to ditch it. Too many people knew I drove it, including Hank's men. I parked it in an abandoned field. A homeless guy named Chambers is living out of it now."

Despite my mood, I flung my head back and laughed.

Patch lifted his eyebrows in inquiry.

"After the night I've been having, I needed that."

He kissed me, then secured the helmet strap under my chin. "Glad I could help. Hop on, Angel. I'm taking you home."

Despite being deep underground, Patch's studio was warm when we arrived. I took the time to wonder if the steam pipes running beneath Delphic helped heat the place. There was also a fireplace, which Patch promptly lit. He took my coat, storing it in the closet just off the foyer.

"Hungry?" he asked.

It was my turn to raise my eyebrows. "You bought food? For me?" He'd told me angels can't taste and don't require food, which made grocery shopping unnecessary.

"There's an organic grocery store just off the highway exit. I can't remember the last time I went shopping for food." A smile glittered in his eyes. "I might have gone overboard."

I walked into the kitchen, with its gleaming stainless-steel appliances, black granite countertops, and walnut cabinetry. Very masculine, very sleek. I went for the fridge first. Water bottles, spinach and rocket, mushrooms, ginger root, Gorgonzola and feta cheeses, natural peanut butter, and milk on one side. Hot dogs, cold cuts, Coke, chocolate pudding cups, and canned whipped cream on the other. I tried to picture Patch pushing a shopping cart down the aisle, tossing in food as it pleased him. It was all I could do to keep a straight face.

I grabbed a pudding cup and offered Patch one as well, but he shook his head no. He perched himself on one of the bar stools, leaning his elbow on the counter contemplatively. "Do you remember anything else from the crash before you blacked out?"

I found a spoon in the drawer and took a bite of pudding. "No." I frowned. "This might be something, though. The car crash happened right before lunch. I originally thought I couldn't have been unconscious for more than a few minutes, but when I woke up in the hospital, it was evening. That means my time line is missing about six hours . . . so how do we account for those missing six hours? Was I with Hank? Lying unconscious in the hospital?"

Something worrisome flicked across Patch's eyes. "I know you're not going to like this, but if we could get Dabria close to Hank, she might be able to read something off him. She can't see inside his past, but if she still has some of her powers and can see his future, it might clue us in on what he's been up to. Whatever his future holds, it's dependent on his past. But getting Dabria close to him isn't going to be easy. He's being careful. When he goes out, he has at least two dozen of his men forming an impenetrable barrier around him. Even when he's at your house, his men are outside, guarding the doors, pacing the fields, and patrolling the street."

This was news to me, and only made me feel more violated.

"Speaking of Dabria, she was at the Devil's Handbag tonight," I said, aiming for a nonchalant air. "She was kind enough to introduce herself."

I watched Patch closely. I wasn't sure what I was looking for. It was one of those things where I'd know it when I saw it. To his credit, and my frustration, he showed no outward emotion or interest.

"She said there's a reward on Hank's head," I continued. "Ten million dollars to the first fallen angel who successfully drags him in. She said there are people who'd rather not see Hank lead a Nephilim rebellion, and while she didn't give me specifics, I think I can figure out the details on my own. I wouldn't be surprised if there are a few Nephilim out there who don't want Hank in power. Nephilim who would much rather see him locked away." I paused for emphasis. "Nephilim who are planning a coup d'état."

"Ten million sounds about right." Again, said with no hint of his real feelings.

"Are you going to sell me out, Patch?"

He said nothing for a long moment, and when he spoke, his words vibrated with quiet derision. "You realize this is what Dabria wants, don't you? She followed you to the Devil's Handbag tonight with one intent: to plant it in your head that I want to betray you. Did she tell you I've gambled away my fortune and the ten million will pose too great a temptation? No, I can tell by your face it's not that. Maybe she told you I have women tucked away in every corner of the world, and I plan on using the money to keep them flocking to me. Jealousy would be more in her taste, which is why I'm betting if I haven't hit the nail on the head yet, I'm getting warmer."

I tipped my chin higher, using defiance to mask my insecurity. "She said you've amassed a long list of enemies and you're planning to pay them off."

Patch barked a laugh. "I have a long list of enemies, I won't deny that. Could I pay them all off for ten million? Maybe, maybe not. That's not the point. I've stayed one step ahead of my enemies for centuries, and I intend to keep it that way. Hank's head on a platter means more to me than a paycheck, and when I learned you share my desire, it only strengthened my resolve to find a way to kill him, Nephilim or not."

I wasn't sure what to say in response. Patch was right—Hank didn't deserve to spend the rest of his life quarantined in a remote prison. He had destroyed my life and my family, and anything less than death was too kind a punishment.

Patch raised his finger to his lips, silencing me on the spot. A moment later there was a brusque knock at the outer door.

We shared a look, and Patch spoke to my thoughts. *I'm not expecting anyone. Go to the bedroom and shut the door.*

With a nod, I signaled I understood. Moving silently, I crossed the studio, closing myself inside Patch's bedroom. Through the door, I heard Patch give an abrupt laugh. His next words were laced with menace. "What are you doing?"

"Bad timing?" returned a muffled voice. Female and oddly familiar.

"Your words, not mine."

"It's important."

Alarm and anger sprang to my chest as the unmistakable identity of the visitor became clear. Dabria had dropped by unannounced.

"I have something for you," she told Patch, her voice a little too smooth, a little too suggestive.

I'll bet you do, I thought cynically. I was tempted to stroll out and give her a warm welcome, but caught myself. Chances were, she'd be more open to talking if she didn't know I was listening. Between my pride and potential information, the latter won out.

"We had some luck. The Black Hand contacted me earlier tonight," Dabria continued. "He wanted a meeting, was willing to pay top dollar, and I acquiesced."

"He wanted you to read his future," Patch stated.

"For the second time in two days. We have a very thorough Nephil on our hands. Thorough, but not as careful as he's been in the past. He's making small mistakes. This time he didn't bother dragging along his bodyguards. He said he didn't want our conversation overheard. He told me to read his future a second time, to make sure both versions matched. I pretended not to take offense, but you know I don't like to be second-guessed."

"What did you tell him?"

"Normally my visions are prophetess-client privilege, but I might be willing to strike a deal," she said, her tone hinting toward flirtatious. "What are you laying on the table?"

"Prophetess?"

"Has a certain cachet, don't you think?"

"How much?" Patch asked.

"First one to name a price loses—you taught me that."

I thought I heard Patch roll his eyes. "Ten thousand."

"Fifteen."

"Twelve. Don't press your luck."

"Always fun doing business with you, Jev. Just like old times. We made a great team."

Now it was my turn to roll my eyes.

"Start talking," Patch said.

"I foresaw Hank's death, and I gave it to him straight. I couldn't give him specifics, but I told him there's going to be one less Nephil in the world very soon. I'm starting to think 'immortal' is a misnomer. First Chauncey, and now Hank."

"Hank's reaction?" was all Patch said.

"He didn't have one. Left without a word."

"Anything else?"

"You should know he's in possession of an archangel's necklace. I sensed it on him."

I wondered if this meant Marcie had succeeded in stealing Patch's necklace from me. I'd invited her over to help me choose the best jewelry for my gown, but oddly, she hadn't taken me up on the offer. Of course, I wouldn't put it past Hank to give her his house key and tell her to snoop in my bedroom while I was out.

"You wouldn't happen to know any former archangels who are missing their necklace?" Dabria asked speculatively.

"I'll wire your money over tomorrow," was Patch's mild answer.

"What does Hank want with an archangel's necklace? On his way out, I heard him tell his driver to take him to the warehouse. What's at the warehouse?" Dabria pressed.

"You're the prophetess." This said with an undercurrent of amusement.

Dabria's tinkling laugh resonated through the studio before turning playful. "Maybe I should look into your future. Maybe it intersects mine."

That brought me to my feet. I strolled out, smiling. "Hello, Dabria. What a nice surprise."

She swung around, outrage blazing across her features as her eyes took me in.

I stretched my arms over my head. "I was taking a nap when the pleasant sound of your voice woke me."

Patch smiled. "I believe you've met my girlfriend, Dabria?"

"Oh, we've met," I said cheerfully. "Fortunately, I lived to talk about it."

Dabria opened her mouth, then shut it. All the while, her cheeks turned a darker shade of pink.

"Seems Hank came across an archangel's necklace," Patch said to me.

"Funny how that worked out."

"Now we figure out what he plans on doing with it," Patch said.

"I'll grab my coat."

"You're staying here, Angel," Patch said in a voice I didn't like. He didn't often hint at his emotions, but there was a clear note of firmness mixed with . . . worry.

"You're taking this one alone?"

"First, Hank can't see us together. Second, I don't like the idea of dragging you into something that could get messy fast. If you need one more reason, I love you. This is uncharted territory for me, but I need to know that at the end of the night, I have you to come home to."

I blinked. I'd never heard Patch speak to me with this kind of affection. But I couldn't just let the matter drop.

"You promised," I said.

"And I'll keep my promise," he answered, shrugging into his motorcycle jacket. Crossing to me, he tipped his head against mine.

Don't think about moving an inch outside this door, Angel. I'll be back as soon as I can. I can't let Hank put the necklace on the archangel without hearing what he wants. Out there, you're fair game. He's got one thing he wants—let's not give him two. We're going to end this once and for all.

"Promise you'll stay here, where I know you're safe," he said out loud. "The alternative is I order Dabria to stay put and play watch-dog." He raised his eyebrows as if asking, *What's it going to be?*

Dabria and I exchanged a look, neither of our expressions remotely pleased.

"Hurry back," I said.

CHAPTER

I PACED PATCH'S STUDIO, SELF-TALKING MYSELF OUT OF running after him. He had promised me—promised me—he wouldn't take Hank down on his own. This was my fight as much as it was his, more even, and given all the countless ways Hank had made me suffer, I'd won the right to dole out his punishment. Patch had said he'd find a way to kill Hank, and I wanted to be the one to send him into the next life, where the deeds he'd committed in this life would haunt him for eternity.

A voice of doubt crept into my thoughts. *Dabria was right. Patch needs the money. He's going to deliver Hank to the right people, give me a cut of the money, and call it even.* Between asking permission and begging forgiveness, Patch held firmly to the latter—he'd said so himself.

I braced my hands on the back of Patch's sofa, breathing deeply to imitate an air of calm, all the while inventing various ways I might bind and torture him if he returned without Hank—alive— in tow.

My phone rang, and I shoveled through my messenger bag to answer it. "Where are you?"

Short, hard breathing sounded in my ear. "They're onto me, Grey. I saw them at the Devil's Handbag. Hank's men. I bolted."

"Scott!" Not the voice I expected, but by no means unimportant. "Where are you?"

"I don't want to say over the phone. I need to get out of town. When I went to the bus station, Hank had men there. He has them everywhere. He's got friends in the police force, and I think he gave them my picture. Two cops chased me into a grocery store, but I got away through the back door. I had to leave the Charger behind. I'm on foot. I need cash—as much as you can get—hair dye, and new clothes. If you can spare the Volkswagen, I'll take it. I'll pay you back as soon as I can. Can you meet me in thirty at my hideout?"

What could I say? Patch had told me to stay put. But I couldn't sit back and do nothing while time was running out for Scott.

Hank was currently occupied at his warehouse, and there was no better time to try and get Scott out of town. Beg forgiveness later, indeed.

"I'll be there in thirty," I told Scott.

"You remember the way?"

"Yes." More or less.

As soon as I hung up, I rushed through Patch's studio, opening and closing drawers, grabbing whatever I thought would be useful to Scott. Jeans, T-shirts, socks, shoes. Patch was a couple of inches shorter than Scott, but it would have to do.

Upon opening the antique mahogany armoire in Patch's bedroom, my frantic search slowed. I stood in place, absorbing the sight. Patch's wardrobe was impeccably organized, chinos folded on the shelves, dress shirts on wood hangers. He owned three suits, a tailored black with narrow lapels, a luxurious Newman pinstripe, and a charcoal gray with Jacquard stitching. A small bin stored silk handkerchiefs, and a drawer held multiple rows of silk ties in every color from red to purple to black. Shoes ranged from black running sneakers to Converses to Italian loafers—even a pair of nubuck flip-flops for good measure. The woodsy scent of cedar lingered in the air. Not what I was expecting. At all. The Patch I knew wore jeans, T-shirts, and a ratty baseball cap. I wondered if I'd ever see this side of Patch. I wondered if there even was an end to the many sides of Patch. The more I thought I knew him, the more the mystery deepened. With these doubts fresh in my mind, I asked myself once more if I thought Patch would sell me out tonight.

I didn't want to believe it, but the truth was, I was on the fence.

In the bathroom, I threw a razor, soap, and shaving cream into a duffel. Then a hat, gloves, and mirrored Ray-Bans. In the kitchen drawers, I found several fake ID cards and a roll of cash totaling more than five hundred dollars. Patch would be less than thrilled when he discovered the money had gone to Scott, but given the circumstances, I could justify playing Robin Hood.

I didn't have a car, but Scott's cave couldn't be more than two miles from Delphic Amusement Park, and I set out at a brisk jog. I kept to the shoulder of the road, pulling the hoodie I'd borrowed from Patch over my face. Cars streamed steadily out of the park as the hour edged toward midnight, and while a few people honked, I managed not to draw much attention.

As the lights leading out of the park thinned, and the road curved toward the highway, I jumped the guardrail and headed down toward the beach. Grateful I'd thought to pack a flashlight, I swept the beam over the craggy rocks and started the most difficult part of the journey.

By my estimation, twenty minutes passed. Then thirty. I had no idea where I was; the landscape of the beach had changed very little and the ocean, black and glittering, stretched on forever. I didn't dare call out Scott's name, out of the horrible fear that Hank's men had somehow tracked him and were also combing the beach for him, but every once in a while I stopped to shine the flashlight slowly across the beach, intending to signal my location to Scott.

Ten minutes later a strange birdcall carried down from the rocks above. I stopped, listening. The call came again, louder. I projected the flashlight in the direction of the noise, and a moment later Scott hissed, "Put the light away!"

I clambered up the rocks, the duffel bouncing against my hip. "I'm sorry I'm late," I told Scott. I threw the duffel at his feet, sinking onto a rock to catch my breath. "I was at Delphic when you called. I don't have the Volkswagen, but I did pack you clothes and a winter hat to hide your hair. There's five hundred dollars in cash, too. It's the best I could do."

I was sure Scott was going to question where I'd managed to find everything on such short notice, but he caught me off guard by taking me into his arms and murmuring a fierce, "Thanks, Grey," into my ear.

"Are you going to be okay?" I whispered.

"The stuff you brought will help. Maybe I can hitch a ride out of town."

"If I asked you to do something for me first, would you consider it?" Once I had his attention, I drew in a breath for courage. "Throw away the Black Hand's ring. Toss it into the ocean. I've thought this through. The ring is pulling you back toward Hank. He put some kind of curse on it, and when you wear it, it gives him power over you." I was now positive the ring was enchanted with devilcraft, and the longer it stayed on Scott's finger, the harder it would be to talk him into taking it off. "It's the only explanation. Think about it. Hank wants to find you. He wants to draw you out. And that ring is doing a stellar job."

I expected him to protest, but his subdued expression told me that, deep down, he'd drawn the same conclusion. He just hadn't wanted to admit it. "And the powers?"

"They're not worth it. You made it three months relying on your own strengths. Whatever curse Hank put on the ring, it's not good."

"Is it that important to you?" Scott asked quietly.

"You're important to me."

"If I say no?"

"I'll do everything I can to get it off your hand. I can't beat you in a fight, but I can't live with myself if I don't at least try."

Scott snorted softly. "You'd fight me, Grey?"

"Don't make me prove it."

To my amazement, Scott twisted the ring loose. He held it between his fingers, gazing at it in silent consideration. "Here's your Kodak moment," he said, then flung the ring into the waves.

I let go of a long breath. "Thank you, Scott."

"Any other last requests?"

"Yeah, go," I told him, trying not to sound as upset as I felt. In an unexpected turn of events, I didn't want him to leave. What if this was goodbye . . . for good? I blinked my eyes rapidly, stalling tears.

He blew on his hands to warm them. "Can you check on my

mom every once in a while, make sure she's hanging in there?"

"Of course."

"You can't tell her about me. The Black Hand will leave her alone as long as he thinks she has nothing to give."

"I'll make sure she's safe." I gave him a light shove. "Now get out of here before you make me cry."

Scott stood in place a moment, a strange look passing over his eyes. It was nervous, but not quite. More expectation, less anxiety. He bent down and kissed me, his mouth closing over mine gently. I was too stunned to do anything but let him finish.

"You've been a good friend," he said. "Thanks for having my back."

I touched my hand to my mouth. There was so much to say, but the right words twisted out of reach. I wasn't looking at Scott anymore, but behind him. To the line of Nephilim scrambling up the rocks, weapons drawn, eyes focused and hardened.

"Hands in the air, hands in the air!"

They shouted the command, but the words sounded convoluted in my ears, almost as if spoken in slow motion. A strange buzz filled my ears, escalating to a roar. I saw their angry lips moving, their weapons flashing in the moonlight. They swarmed in from every direction, trapping me and Scott in a small huddle.

The glimmer of hope drained from Scott's eyes, replaced by dread.

He dropped the duffel, clasping his hands behind his head. A solid object, an elbow maybe, or a fist, came out of the night air, smashing into his skull.

When Scott collapsed, I was still grasping for words. Even a scream couldn't cut through my horror.

In the end, the only thing between us was silence.

CHAPTER

30

I WAS CRAMMED INTO THE TRUNK OF A BLACK AUDI A6, with my hands tied and a blindfold blocking my vision. I'd screamed myself hoarse, but wherever the driver was taking me, it had to be remote. He'd never once attempted to silence me.

I didn't know where Scott was. Hank's Nephilim men had surrounded us at the beach, dragging us off in different directions. I pictured Scott chained and helpless in an underground prison, at the mercy of Hank's anger . . .

I slammed my shoes against the trunk. I rolled side to side. I yelled and screamed—then a choke caught me mid-breath, and I dissolved into sobs.

At last the car slowed and the engine was cut. Footsteps crunched through gravel, a key scraped the inside of the lock, and the trunk popped open. Two sets of hands hauled me out, setting me roughly on solid ground. My legs had fallen asleep on the ride, and an assault of pins stabbed up through the soles of my feet.

"Where do you want this one, Blakely?" one of my captors asked. Judging by his voice, he couldn't have been more than eighteen or nineteen. Judging by his strength, he might as well have been made of steel.

"Inside," a man, presumably Blakely, answered.

I was propelled up a ramp and through a door. The space inside was cool and quiet. The air smelled of gasoline and turpentine. I wondered if we were at one of Hank's warehouses.

"You're hurting me," I told the men on either side of me. "Obviously I'm not going anywhere. Can't you at least untie my hands?"

Wordlessly, they hauled me up a set of stairs and though a second door. They forced me down onto a metal folding chair, securing my ankles to the chair legs.

Minutes after they left, the door opened again. I knew it was Hank before he spoke. The scent of his cologne filled me with panic and revulsion.

His nimble fingers picked at the knot of my blindfold, and it

silence

drooped to my neck. I blinked, making sense of the unlit room. Aside from a card table and a second folding chair, the room was bare.

"What do you want?" I demanded, my voice trembling slightly.

Scraping the second chair across the floor, he positioned it to face mine. "To talk."

"Not in the mood, thanks anyway," I said curtly.

He leaned toward me, the hard lines around his eyes deepening as he narrowed his gaze. "Do you know who I am, Nora?"

Sweat leaked from every pore. "Off the top of my head? You're a filthy, lying, manipulative, worthless little—"

His hand lashed out before I saw it coming. He struck my cheek, hard. I recoiled, too shocked to cry.

"Do you know I'm your biological father?" he asked, his quiet tone unnerving.

"'Father' is such an arbitrary word. Douche bag, on the other hand . . ."

Hank gave a subtle nod. "Then let me ask this. Is that any way to speak to your father?"

Now tears welled up my eyes. "Nothing you've done gives you the right to call yourself my father."

"Be that as it may, you are my blood. You bear my mark. I can't deny it any longer, Nora, and neither can you deny your destiny."

I hitched my shoulder, but I couldn't lift it high enough to wipe my nose. "My destiny has nothing to do with yours. When you gave me up as a baby, you forfeited your right to have any say in my life."

"Despite what you may think, I've been actively involved in every aspect of your life since the day you were born. I gave you up to protect you. Because of fallen angels, I had to sacrifice my family—"

I cut him off with a scornful laugh. "Don't start with the poor-me routine. Quit blaming your choices on fallen angels. You made the decision to give me up. Maybe you cared about me back then, but your Nephilim blood society is the only thing you care about anymore. You're a zealot. It's all about you."

His mouth thinned, tight as a wire. "I should kill you right now for making a fool of me, of my society, of the whole Nephilim race."

"Then do it already," I spat, rage overshadowing any anxiety I felt.

Reaching into his coat, he withdrew a long black feather that looked remarkably similar to the one I'd put in my dresser drawer for safekeeping. "One of my advisers found this in your bedroom. It's a fallen angel's feather. Imagine my surprise upon learning that my own flesh and blood is keeping company with the enemy. You had me fooled. Hang around fallen angels long enough and their proclivity for deceit rubs off, it seems. Is the fallen angel Patch?" he asked bluntly.

"Your paranoia is astounding. You found a feather while pawing through my drawers, so what? What does that prove? That you're a pervert?"

He sat back, crossing his legs. "Is this really the road you want to take? I have no doubt the fallen angel is Patch. I sensed him in your bedroom the other night. I've sensed him on you for a while now."

"Ironic that you're grilling me when you obviously know more than I do. Maybe we should switch seats?" I suggested.

"Oh? And whose feather do you expect me to believe was in your drawer?" Hank inquired with the slightest trace of amusement.

"Your guess is as good as mine," I said, defiance dripping from every word. "I found the feather in the cemetery right after you dumped me there."

A wicked smile spread across his features. "My men ripped out Patch's wings in the same cemetery. I daresay it's his feather."

I swallowed discreetly. Hank had Patch's feather. I had no way of knowing if he understood the power this gave him over Patch. I could only pray he didn't.

Trying to draw attention away from that terrifying thought, I said, "I know you planned the car crash. I know it was your men who hit us. Why the charade?"

The superior glint in his smile made me uneasy. "That was next on my list of things to discuss. While you were blacked out, I performed a blood transfusion on you," he stated simply. "I filled your veins with my blood, Nora. My purebred Nephilim blood."

A brittle silence crackled between us.

"This kind of operation has never been done before, not successfully, that is, but I've found a way to tamper with the laws of the universe. So far things have gone better than expected. Should I tell you that my biggest worry was that the transfusion would kill you on the spot?"

I grasped for answers, for some way to make sense of the horrible things he was telling me, but my head was muddled. A blood transfusion. Why, why, why? It could explain why I'd felt so strange at the hospital. It could explain why Hank had appeared so beat and exhausted. "You used devilcraft to do it," I announced nervously.

He cocked an eyebrow. "So you've heard about devilcraft. The angel figured it out?" he guessed, not looking pleased.

"Why did you perform the transfusion?" My mind raced for the answer—he needed me for a sacrifice, a doppelgänger, an experiment. If none of those, then what?

"You've had my blood inside you since the day your mother gave birth to you, but it wasn't pure enough. You weren't a first-generation Nephil, and I need you to be a purebred, Nora. You're so close now. All that's left is to swear a Changeover Vow before heaven and hell. Upon your vow, the transformation will be complete."

The weight of his words slowly sank in, and it sickened me. "You thought you could turn me into one of your brainwashed, obedient Nephilim soldiers?" I rocked violently in the chair, trying to tear free.

"I've seen a prophecy foretelling my death. I've been using a device enhanced with devilcraft to look into my future and, just to be sure, got a second opinion."

I hardly heard him. I was incensed by his confession, trembling with rage. Hank had violated me in the worst possible way. He'd tampered with my life, attempting to twist and mold me as he pleased. He'd injected his vile, murderous blood into my veins!

"You're Nephilim, Hank. You can't die. You don't die. As much as I wish you would," I added on a venomous note.

"Both the device and a former angel of death have seen it. Their prophecies match. I don't have long. My last days on Earth will be spent preparing you to lead my army against fallen angels," he said with the first hint of resignation.

It all locked into place. "You're running this entire plan on the word of Dabria? She doesn't have a gift. She needs money. She can't predict the future any more than you or I. Did it ever occur to you that she's probably laughing herself silly right now?"

"I rather doubt it," he said dryly, as though he knew something I did not. "I need you to be a purebred Nephil, Nora, to command my army. To lead my society. To step up as my rightful heir and free Nephilim everywhere from bondage. After this Cheshvan, we will be our own masters, no longer ruled by fallen angels."

"You're insane. I'm not doing anything for you. I'm especially not swearing your vow."

"You have the mark. You've been preordained. Do you really think

I want you to become the leader of everything I've built?" he said in a hardened voice. "You aren't the only one who doesn't have a choice in the matter. Destiny claims us, not the other way around. First there was Chauncey. Then me. Now the responsibility falls to you."

I glared at him, putting all my hate behind it. "You want a blood relative to lead your army? Get Marcie. She likes ordering people around. She'll be a natural."

"Her mom is a purebred Nephil."

"Didn't see that coming, but even better. Surely that makes Marcie a purebred too?" A nice little trio of supremacists.

Hank's laugh sounded increasingly weary. "We never expected Susanna to conceive. Purebred Nephilim don't mate together successfully. We understood from the beginning that Marcie was a bit of a miracle and would never live long. She didn't have my mark. She was always small, frail, struggling to survive. She doesn't have long now—her mother and I both feel it."

A burst of memories rushed out of my subconscious. I remembered talking about this before. About how to kill a Nephil. About sacrificing a female descendant who'd reached the age of sixteen. I remembered my own doubts about why my biological father would give me up. I remembered . . .

In that one instant, everything became clear. "That's why you didn't bother hiding Marcie from Rixon. That's why you gave me up, but kept her. You never thought she'd live long enough to be used as a sacrifice."

I, on the other hand, had the full package: Hank's Nephilim mark and an excellent chance of survival. I'd been hidden away as a baby to keep Rixon from sacrificing me, but in a twist of fate, Hank now intended me to lead his revolution. I shut my eyes hard, wishing I could block out the truth.

"Nora," Hank said. "Open your eyes. Look at me."

I shook my head. "I won't swear the vow. Not now, not ten minutes from now, not ever." My nose dripped, and I couldn't wipe it. I didn't know which was more humiliating—that, or the quiver in my lip.

"I admire your bravery," he said, his voice deceptively gentle. "But there are all kinds of bravery, and this one doesn't suit you."

I jumped when his finger tucked a lock of hair behind my ear, an almost fatherly gesture. "Swear the vow to become a purebred Nephil and command my army, and I'll let you and your mother go. I don't want to hurt you, Nora. The choice is yours. Swear the vow, and you can shut the door on this night. It will all go away." He untied the knots at my wrists; the rope slithered to the floor.

My hands trembled as I kneaded them in my lap, but not from lack of blood. Something else he'd said had filled me with icy dread. "My mom?"

"That's right. She's here. In one of the lower rooms, sleeping."

The awful sting returned behind my eyes. "Did you hurt her?"

Instead of answering my question, he said, "I am the Black Hand. I'm a busy man, and I'll be honest, this is the last place I want to be tonight. This is the last thing I want to be doing. But my hands are tied. You hold the power. Swear the oath, and you and your mom will walk away together."

"Did you ever love her?"

He blinked in surprise. "Your mother? Of course I loved her. At one time, I loved her very much. The world is different now. My vision has changed. I had to sacrifice my own love for the interest of my entire race."

"You're going to kill her, aren't you? If I don't swear the vow, that's what you'll do."

"My life has been defined by difficult choices. I won't stop making them tonight," he said, a sideways answer to my question that left me with no doubt.

"Let me see her."

Hank gestured to a row of windows across the room. I stood slowly, afraid of the condition I might find her in. When I looked out the panel of windows, I realized I was in an office of sorts, overlooking the warehouse below. My mom was curled up on a cot, watched over by three armed Nephilim as she slumbered. I wondered if, like me, her perception cleared in her dreams and she saw Hank for the monster he really was. I wondered if, when he was gone from her life completely, no longer able to manipulate her, she would see him the way I saw him. It was my answer to those questions that gave me the courage to face Hank.

"You pretended to love her so you could get to me? All those lies for this one moment?"

"You're cold," Hank said patiently. "Tired. Hungry. Swear the vow, and let's end this."

"If I swear the vow, and you end up living, as I suspect you will, I want you to swear your own oath. I want you to leave town and disappear from my mom's life forever."

"Done."

"And I want to call Patch first."

He barked a laugh. "No. Though I see you've finally come clean about him. You can break the news to him after you've sworn the vow."

Not surprising. But I'd had to try.

I put all the defiance I possessed into my words. "I won't swear the vow for you." I cast my eyes toward the window once more. "But I will for her."

"Cut yourself," Hank instructed, placing a switchblade in my hand. "Swear on your blood to become a purebred Nephil and direct my army upon my death. If you break the oath, confess your punishment. Your death . . . and your mother's."

I locked eyes with him. "That wasn't the deal."

"It is now. And it expires in five seconds. The next deal will include your friend Vee's death too."

I glared at him in rage and disbelief, but it was the worst I could do. He had me trapped.

"You first," I ordered.

If it weren't for the determination etched on his face, he might have looked amused. Pricking his skin, he said, "If I live beyond the next month, I vow to leave Coldwater and never come into contact with you or your mother again. If I break this vow, I command my body to turn to dust."

Taking the blade, I screwed the knife tip into my palm, shaking a few drops of blood loose, as I remembered Patch doing in his memory. I said a silent prayer that he'd be able to forgive me for what I was about to do. That in the end, we had a love that would transcend blood and race. I stopped my thoughts there, afraid I wouldn't go through with it if I allowed myself to think of Patch further. With my heart ripping in two different directions, I retreated to some hollow place within and faced the appalling task at hand.

"I swear now, with this new blood running through my veins, that I am no longer human, but a purebred Nephil. And if you die, I'll lead your army. If I break this promise, I understand my mom and I are both as good as dead." The vow seemed far too simple for the weight of its consequences, and I turned my steely gaze toward Hank. "Did I do it right? Is that all I have to say?"

With a shrewd nod, he told me all I needed to know.

My life as a human was over.

I didn't remember leaving Hank, or walking away from his warehouse with my mom, who was so heavily drugged she could barely walk. How I got from that tiny room onto the dark streets outside was a blur. My mom shivered violently and muttered indistinct sounds into my ear. I vaguely noted that I, too, was cold. Frost hung brittle in the air, my breath condensing a silvery white. If I didn't find shelter soon, I was afraid my mom would suffer hypothermia.

I didn't know if my situation was as dire. I didn't know anything anymore. Could I freeze to death? Could I die? What exactly had changed with the vow? Everything?

A car sat abandoned on the street ahead, its tires police-marked for removal, and with little thought, I tested the door. In the first stroke of luck all night, it was unlocked. I laid my mom out gently in the backseat, then went to work on the wires beneath the steering wheel. After several attempts, the engine sputtered to life.

"Don't worry," I murmured to my mom. "We're going home. It's over. It's all over." I said the words more to myself, and I believed them because I *needed* to. I couldn't think about what I'd done. I couldn't think about how slow or painful the transformation would happen when it finally triggered. If it needed to be triggered. If there was more to face.

Patch. I'd have to face him, and I'd have to confess what I'd done. I wondered if I'd ever feel his arms around me again. How could I expect this not to change everything? I wasn't simply Nora Grey anymore. I was a purebred Nephil. His enemy.

I stomped the brake as a pale object staggered into the road ahead. The car swerved to a stop. A pair of eyes swung my way. The girl stumbled, got up, and tottered to the far side of the road, clearly trying to run, but too traumatized to coordinate her movements. The girl's clothes were ripped, her face frozen in terror.

"Marcie?" I asked out loud.

Automatically, I reached across the console, pushing the passenger door open. "Get in!" I commanded her.

Marcie stood there, squeezing her arms around her middle, making small whimpering sounds.

I ejected myself out of the car, ran around to her, and folded her inside the seat. She stuck her head between her knees, breathing much too fast. "I'm—going—to—vomit."

"What are you doing here?"

She continued to gulp air.

I dropped behind the wheel and stepped on the gas, not having any desire to hang around this derelict area of town any longer. "Do you have your phone?"

She made a choked sound at the back of her throat.

"In case you missed it, we're in a bit of a hurry," I said more sharply than I'd intended, now that I fully realized just who I'd picked up. Hank's daughter. My sister, if I really wanted to go there. My lying, betraying, fool of a sister. "Phone? Yes or no?"

She moved her head, but I couldn't tell if it was a shake or a nod.

"You're mad at me for stealing the necklace," she said, barely coherent between hiccups. "My dad tricked me. He made me think it was a prank we'd play on you together. I left the note on your pillow that night to scare you. 'You're not safe.' My dad put some kind of enchantment on me so you couldn't see me sneak in. He also did something to the ink so it would disappear after you read the note. I thought it would be funny. I wanted to watch you unravel. I wasn't thinking. I went along with everything my dad said. It was like he had this power over me."

"Listen to me, Marcie," I told her firmly. "I'm going to get us out of here. But if you have a phone, I could really use it right now."

With trembling hands, she pried open her purse. She rummaged around, then produced her cell phone. "He tricked me," she said, tears leaking from the edges of her eyes. "I thought he was my dad. I thought he—loved me. If it makes a difference, I didn't give him the necklace. I was going to. I brought it to his warehouse tonight, just like he told me to. But then . . . but in the end . . . when I saw that girl in the cage . . ." She trailed off.

I didn't want to feel anything resembling empathy for Marcie. I didn't want her in the car, period. I didn't want her to rely on me, or vice versa. I didn't want any kind of bond between us, but somehow, all of the above managed to be true despite what I wanted.

"Please give me the phone," I said softly.

Marcie pushed her phone into my hand. Curling her legs up to her chest, she sobbed quietly into her knees.

I dialed Patch. I had to tell him Hank didn't have the necklace. And I had to tell him the horrible truth about what I'd done. With each ring, I felt the barrier I'd thrown up, just to get through this, break down. I pictured Patch's face when I told him the truth, the image freezing me. My lip wobbled and my breath caught.

His voice mail kicked on and I called Vee.

"I need your help," I told her. "I need you to watch my mom and Marcie." I pulled the phone slightly away from my ear in response to the noise on her end. "Yes, Marcie Millar. I'll explain everything later."

31

IT WAS CLOSE TO THREE A.M. WHEN I DROPPED OFF Marcie and my mom, leaving them in Vee's care without any explanation. I'd shaken my head firmly when Vee demanded answers, carefully compartmentalizing every emotion. I'd left without a word, intending to find a remote road where I could be alone, but soon it became clear that my aimless driving had a clear destination after all.

I hardly saw the road as I sped toward Delphic Amusement

Park. I screeched into the parking lot, finding myself utterly and completely alone. I hadn't dared allow myself to contemplate what I'd done, but now, surrounded by darkness and stillness, I couldn't bear to be brave any longer. I wasn't strong enough to hold everything back. Bending my head to the steering wheel, I sobbed.

I cried for the choice I'd had to make and for what it had cost me. Most of all, I cried because I was at a complete and utter loss as to how to tell Patch. It was news I knew I should deliver in person, but I was terrified. How, when we'd finally reconciled our relationship, could I explain that I'd turned myself into the very thing he despised above all else?

Using Marcie's cell I dialed his number, torn between relief and dread when his voicemail picked up. Was he not answering because he didn't know it was me calling? Could he know what I'd done? Was he avoiding me until he could come to terms with his feelings? Was he cursing me for making such a stupid, stupid decision, even though I'd had no alternative?

No, I told myself. It was none of those things. Patch didn't avoid confrontation—that was my problem.

I exited the car and walked solemnly to the gates. I pressed my head to the bars, the cold metal stinging my skin, but the pain didn't compare to the ache of regret and longing burning inside me. *Patch!* I cried out silently. *What have I done?*

I rattled the bars, seeing no way to get in, when a metallic groan jarred me alert. The steel in my hands bent as though made of clay. I blinked through the confusion before it struck me. I was no longer human. I was truly Nephilim, and I had the strength and power of one. A horrifying fascination tingled up my spine at the prospect of my new powers. If I'd been looking for a way to convince myself that I could undo the oath, I was rapidly approaching the point of no return.

Prying the bars wide enough apart to squeeze through, I jogged into the park, slowing when I neared the shed leading down to Patch's studio. My fingers trembled as I turned the doorknob. With heavy feet, I crossed the shed and lowered myself through the trapdoor.

Using trial and error, and relying heavily on my memory, I found the right door. I stepped inside Patch's studio and immediately knew something was wrong. I sensed the lingering traces of a violent confrontation in the air. It wasn't something I could explain, but the evidence was there, as palpable as if I'd read it on paper.

Following an invisible trail of energy, I moved cautiously through Patch's studio, still unsure what to make of the strange vibrations all around. I nudged his bedroom door open with my foot, and that was when I saw the secret door.

One of the black granite walls was rolled slightly to the right, opening to a shadowy corridor beyond. Water puddled on the dirt floor. Mounted torches burned with smoky brightness.

The sound of footsteps echoed from the corridor, and my

stomach tightened. The torchlight illuminated the chiseled lines of Patch's face and the edge in his black eyes, which looked right through me, absorbed in thought. His features were so merciless, I could do nothing but stand, paralyzed. I couldn't look at him, and I couldn't not look. I was filled with diminishing hope and surging shame. Just as I was about to shut my eyes to tears, his gaze shifted and our eyes met. One look from him, and the weight fell away. My defenses dissolved.

I walked toward him, slowly at first, my body shaking with emotion, then running into his arms, unable to be away from him any longer.

"Patch—I—don't know where to begin!" I said, bursting into tears.

He clutched me against him. "I know everything," he murmured roughly into my ear.

"No you don't," I protested miserably. "Hank made me swear a vow. I'm not—that is—I'm no longer—" I couldn't make myself say it. Not to Patch. I couldn't tolerate it if he rejected me. Even the slightest halting in his expression, a gleam of scorn in his eyes . . .

He gave me a light shake. "It's all right, Angel. Listen to me. I know about the Changeover Vow. Believe me when I say I know everything."

I sobbed into his shirt, twisting my fingers into it. "How could you?"

"I came back and you were gone."

"I'm so sorry. Scott was in trouble. I had to help. And I ruined everything!"

"I went out to find you. The first place I looked was with Hank. I thought he'd tricked you into leaving. I dragged him back here and got him to confess everything." He exhaled, a haggard sound. "I can tell you how my night played out, but you should see for yourself."

He tugged his shirt over his head.

Pressing my finger gently to Patch's scar, I concentrated on what I wanted to know. Mainly what had happened after Patch had left the studio a few short hours ago.

I was tugged inside the dark recesses of his mind, a cacophony of voices rushing past my ears, while faces blurred together much too fast to pinpoint. It felt as though I were lying on my back on a street at night, horns beeping, tires whizzing dangerously close.

Hank, I thought with all my energy. *What happened after Patch left to find Hank?* One car veered toward me, and I was plunged head-long into its headlights. . . .

The memory opened on a murky street corner outside Hank's warehouse. It wasn't the one I'd successfully broken into, rather the one Scott and I had first attempted to take pictures of. The air was damp and heavy, the stars hidden behind cloud cover. Patch moved silently down the sidewalk, approaching what could only

BECCA FITZPATRICK

be Hank's guard from behind. He leaped at him, dragging him backward in a punishing embrace before the guard could so much as squawk. Patch deprived the man of his weapons, tucking them into the waistband of his jeans.

To my amazement, Gabe—the same Gabe who'd tried to kill me behind 7-Eleven—strolled out of the shadows ahead. Dominic and Jeremiah followed. All three shared a wicked smile.

"Well, well, what do we have here?" Gabe asked in a mocking undertone, brushing dirt off the Nephil guard's collar.

"Keep him quiet until I give the signal," Patch said, handing the guard over to Dominic and Jeremiah.

"Better not fail me, bro," Gabe said to Patch. "I'm counting on the Black Hand being on the other side of that door." He lifted his chin at the warehouse's side door. "You come through for me, and I'll forget any past grievances. You end up wrong about this, and I'll show you what it feels like to have a tire iron rammed into your wing scars . . . every day for a solid year."

Patch merely answered with a cool, measured look. "Wait for my signal."

He edged up to the small window encased in the door. I followed, peering through the glass.

I saw the caged archangel. I saw a handful of Hank's Nephilim men. But to my surprise, Marcie Millar stood just feet away, her posture withdrawn, her eyes wide and frightened. What could only be Patch's archangel's necklace dangled from her bloodless hands, and her gaze flicked surreptitiously to the door Patch and I hid behind.

There was a loud commotion as the archangel bucked wildly, kicking at the bars of her cage. Hank's men instantly lashed back with blue-glowing chains, no doubt enchanted with devilcraft, sending them whipping against her body. After repeated strikes, her skin adopted the same unearthly bluish glow as the chains, and she crouched in submission.

"Would you like the honors?" Hank proposed to Marcie, holding his hand out to indicate the necklace. "Or if you'd rather, I'll place it on her neck."

By now, Marcie was trembling. Her complexion was ashen and she cowered, saying nothing.

"Come, darling," Hank urged her. "There's nothing to be afraid of. My men have secured her. She won't hurt you. This is what it means to be Nephilim. We have to take a stand against our enemies."

"What are you going to do to her?" Marcie stammered.

Hank laughed, but he sounded weary. "Put the necklace on her, of course."

"And then?"

"And then she'll answer my questions."

"Why does she have to be in the cage if you only want to talk to her?"

Hank's smile thinned. "Give me the necklace, Marcie."

"You said you wanted me to get the necklace as a prank. You said it was a joke we'd play on Nora together. You never said anything about her." Marcie sent a terrified glance at the caged archangel.

"The necklace," Hank ordered, hand out.

Marcie backed along the wall, but her eyes gave her away—they flashed briefly to the door. Hank made a convulsive movement toward her, but she was faster. She shoved through the door, almost running headlong into Patch.

He steadied her, his eyes briefly locking on his archangel's necklace dangling from her hand. "Do the right thing, Marcie," he told her in a low voice. "That doesn't belong to you."

I suddenly realized that the events of this memory must have happened moments after I'd left the warehouse with my mom—and just before I'd picked up Marcie off the streets. I'd missed Patch by a matter of minutes. All that time he'd been busy rounding up Gabe and his crew to go against Hank.

Chin quivering, Marcie nodded and stretched forth her hand. Wordlessly, Patch pocketed his necklace. Then he commanded her in a steely tone, "Go."

Not a moment later, he signaled to Gabe, Jeremiah, and Dominic. They rushed forward, swarming through the door and into the warehouse. Patch brought up the rear, shoving Hank's guard in with him.

At the sight of the band of fallen angels, Hank made a throttled sound of incredulity.

"Not a single Nephil in here has sworn fealty," Patch told Gabe. "Have at it."

Gabe flashed a grin around the room, eyes landing on each Nephil individually. His gaze lingered longest on Hank, burning with something almost greedy. "He meant to say none of you strapping lads have sworn fealty . . . yet."

"What's this?" Hank seethed.

"What does it look like?" Gabe answered, cracking his knuckles. "When my buddy Patch here said he knew where I could find the Black Hand, he sparked my interest. Did I mention I'm in the market for a new Nephilim vassal?"

The Nephilim in the room held their places, but I could read the dread and tension on every one of their faces. I wasn't sure what Patch had planned, but clearly this was part of it. He'd told me he'd have a hard time finding fallen angels who'd help him rescue an archangel, but maybe he'd found a way to recruit their help after all. By offering up spoils of war.

Gabe motioned Jeremiah and Dominic to spread out, each taking a side of the room.

"Ten of you, four of us," Gabe told Hank. "Do the math."

"We're stronger than you think," Hank countered with a malicious smile. "Ten on four. Those don't sound like good odds to me."

"Funny, I was thinking they sounded pretty damn enticing. You remember the words, don't you, Black Hand? 'Lord, I become your man.' Start rehearsing. I'm not leaving until you sing them to me.

You're mine, Nephil. Mine," Gabe finished with a mocking jab of his finger.

"Don't just stand there," Hank exploded at his men. "Bring this arrogant fallen angel to his knees!"

But Hank didn't stick around to shout further orders. He bolted through the door.

Gabe's laughter rang from the rafters. He strolled to the door and flung it open. His voice boomed into the night. "Scared, Nephil? You'd better be. Here I come."

At this, every Nephilim in the building fled through the front and rear exits. Jeremiah and Dominic chased after them, whooping and hollering.

Patch stood in the vacated warehouse, facing the archangel's cage. He approached her and she drew back with a warning hiss.

"I'm not going to hurt you," Patch told her, keeping his hands where she could see them. "I'm going to unlock the cage and let you go."

"Why would you do that?" she rasped.

"Because you don't belong here."

Her eyes, ringed with exhaustion, darted over his face. "And what do you want in return? What mysteries of the world do you want answered? What lies will you whisper sweetly into my ear for the truth?"

Opening the door to the cage, Patch reached inside slowly, taking her hand. "I don't want anything except for you to hear me out.

I don't need a necklace to make you talk, because I think once you hear what I have to say, you'll want to help."

The archangel hobbled out of the cage, reluctantly leaning her weight on Patch, her blue-glowing legs clearly impaired by devil-craft.

"How long will I be like this?" she asked, tears jumping to her eyes.

"I don't know, but I think we can both agree the archangels will be able to help."

"He cut my wings off," she whispered hoarsely.

A nod. "But he didn't rip them out. There's hope."

"Hope?" she repeated, eyes flashing. "You see something hopeful in all this? That makes one of us. What kind of help do you want anyway?" she inquired miserably.

"I want a way to kill Hank Millar," Patch said bluntly.

A dull laugh. "And now that makes two of us."

"You can make it happen."

She opened her mouth to protest, but he cut her off.

"The archangels have tampered with death at least once before, and they can do it again."

"What are you talking about?" she scoffed.

"Four months ago one of Chauncey Langeais's female descendants threw herself off the rafters of her high school gym, a sacrifice that ended up killing him. Her name is Nora Grey, but I can tell by the look on your face you've heard of her."

Patch's words shocked me. Not because what he'd said sounded foreign. In one of his other memories I'd heard myself say I killed Chauncey Langeais, but on coming out of the memory, I'd stubbornly denied it. Now there was no closing my eyes to the truth. The fog in my mind shifted, and in a succession of flashes, I saw myself standing in the gym at school, several months ago. With Chauncey Langeais, a Nephil who wanted to kill me to hurt Patch.

A Nephil who didn't realize I was his descendant.

"What I want to know is why her sacrifice didn't kill Hank Millar," Patch said. "Hank was the most direct Nephil in her line. Something tells me the archangels have their hand in this."

The archangel stared back wordlessly. Patch had visibly cracked her composure, which had been whittled down to threadbare from the start. With a faint smile of mockery, she said at last, "Any other conspiracy theories?"

Patch shook his head. "Not a theory. A cover-up—the archangels' cover-up. I missed it at first, but when I realized what happened, I knew the archangels had tampered with death. You let Chauncey die in Hank's place. Given the problems Hank has created for you, why?"

"You really think I'm going to talk about this with you?"

"Then you get to hear my theory after all. Here's what I think. I think just about five months ago the archangels found out that Chauncey and Hank had started dabbling in devilcraft, and they wanted it stopped. Believing Hank was the lesser of two evils, the archangels approached him first. The archangels would have fore-seen Nora's sacrifice, and they decided to offer Hank a deal. They'd let Chauncey die in his place, if Hank agreed to leave devilcraft alone."

"Your imagination astounds," the archangel said, but her voice came out haggard, and I knew Patch was onto something.

"You haven't heard the end of the story," Patch said. "I'm betting Hank sold Chauncey out. And then he sold the archangels out. Picking up where Chauncey left off, he's been using devilcraft ever since. The archangels want him out of the picture before he passes the knowledge on to anyone else. And they want devilcraft back where it belongs—in hell. That's where I come in. I'm asking for the archangels to tamper with death one more time. Let me kill Hank. He'll carry the knowledge of devilcraft to his grave, and if my theory is as dead on as I'm betting it is, that's exactly what you and the rest of the archangels want. Of course, I'm sure you have your own reasons for wanting Hank dead," Patch added meaningfully.

"Pretend for a moment the archangels could tamper with death. I couldn't make that decision on my own," she said. "It would require a unanimous vote."

"Then let's take it to the table."

The archangel spread her hands wide. "In case it isn't obvious, I'm not at the table. I don't have a way to get from here to there. I can't fly. I can't call home, Jev. As long as I'm cursed with devilcraft, I'm an invisible spot on their radar."

"The power in an archangel's necklace is stronger than devil-craft."

"I don't have my necklace," she said wearily.

"You're going to use my necklace. Talk to the archangels. Present my idea and take a vote." He pulled his archangel's necklace from his pocket and unclasped it for her.

"How do I know this isn't a trick? How do I know you won't force me to answer your questions?"

"You don't. The only thing you have at the moment is faith."

"You're asking me to trust a known betrayer. A banished angel." Her eyes locked with his, searching his face, which was as opaque as a lake at midnight.

"That was a long time ago," he said quietly, holding his necklace out to her again. "Turn around and I'll put it on you."

"Faith," she repeated just as softly. Her eyes seemed to weigh her options. Trust Patch, or tackle her problems alone.

At last she turned and lifted her hair. "Put it on."

MY BREATHING SLOWED AS I REALIZED PATCH'S arms were secure around me. We were sitting on the floor in his bedroom, and I was leaning back against him. He rocked me gently, murmuring soothing sounds in my ear.

"So that's that," I said. "I really did kill Chauncey. I killed a Nephil. An immortal. I killed someone. Indirectly, but still. I killed."

"Your sacrifice should have killed Hank."

I nodded numbly. "I saw you tell the archangel. I saw everything. You used Gabe, Jeremiah, and Dominic to clear the warehouse and get her alone."

"Yes."

"Did Gabe find Hank and force him to swear fealty?"

"No. He would have, but I got to Hank first. I wasn't completely up-front with Gabe. I let him think I'd give him Hank, but I had Dabria waiting outside the warehouse. The moment Hank surfaced, she grabbed him. When I came back here and found you gone, I thought he'd gotten to you. I called Dabria and hauled Hank here to interrogate him. I'm sorry about Dabria," he apologized. "I took her with me because I don't care what happens to her. She's disposable. You're not."

"I'm not mad," I said. Dabria was the least of my worries. I had a much bigger concern hammering inside me. "Did the archangels vote? What's going to happen to Hank?"

"Before they voted, they wanted to talk to me. Given everything that's happened, they don't trust me. I told them if they'd let me kill Hank, they wouldn't have to worry about devilcraft anymore. I also reminded them that if Hank dies, you'll become the leader of his Nephilim army. I promised them you'd stop the war."

"Whatever it takes," I said, nodding impatiently. "I want Hank gone. Was the vote unanimous?"

"They want this mess behind them. They've given me the green light on Hank. We have until sunrise." It was then that I noticed the handgun on the floor beside his leg.

silence

He said, "I promised I wouldn't take this moment from you, and if that's still what you want, then I'll close my argument on the subject forever. But I can't let you walk into this blindly. Hank's death will stay with you forever. You can't take it back, and you'll never forget it. I'll kill him, Nora. I'll do it if you'll let me. The option is there. It's your choice to make, and I'll stand beside you either way, but I want you prepared."

I didn't flinch. I picked up the gun. "I want to see him. I want to look in his eyes and see his regret when he realizes where his choices have left him."

Only the briefest moment passed before Patch accepted my decision with a nod. He led me into the secret corridor. The only light flickered from the mounted torches. The flames illuminated the first several feet down the corridor, but after that, I could see nothing through the suffocating blackness.

I followed Patch deeper and deeper, the corridor gently leading us downhill. At last a door appeared. Patch tugged on the iron ring pull, and the door swung toward us.

Inside, Hank was ready. He lunged for Patch. Manacles brought him up short, catching his fists midair. With a chuckle that sounded too insane for my liking, he said, "Don't fool yourself into thinking you'll get away with this." His eyes gleamed with equal parts approval and hatred.

"Like you thought you could fool the archangels?" came Patch's level response.

Hank's eyes narrowed warily. His gaze fell on the gun in my hand, registering it for the first time. "What's this?" he asked in truly chilling tones.

I raised the gun, aiming it at Hank. I took satisfaction in watching his face cloud with confusion, then hostility. "Would someone tell me what's going on?" he snapped.

"Your time is up," Patch told him.

"We've made our own agreement with the archangels," I said.

"What agreement?" Hank snarled, rage seething from every word.

I narrowed my aim to his chest. "You're not immortal anymore, Hank. Death came knocking after all."

He gave a short, incredulous laugh, but the fearful glint in his eyes told me he believed me.

"I wonder what it will be like for you in the next life," I murmured. "I wonder if, right now, you're second-guessing the life you've built. I wonder if you're rethinking every decision, and trying to figure out where it all went wrong. Do you remember the countless people you used and hurt? Do you remember each of their names? Do you see my mom's face? I hope so. I hope her face haunts you. Eternity is a long time, Hank."

Hank beat against the chains so violently, I thought they would snap.

"I want you to remember my name," I told Hank. "I want you to remember that I did for you what you should have done for me. Showed a little mercy."

His wild, vindictive expression was suddenly etched with guarded speculation. He was a clever man, but I wasn't sure he'd guessed my intentions just yet.

"I'm not going to lead your Nephilim uprising," I told him, "because you're not going to die. In fact, you're going to live quite a bit longer. Granted, you won't be living at the Ritz. Unless Patch intends to upgrade this chamber." I raised my eyebrows at Patch, asking him to weigh in.

What are you doing, Angel? he murmured to my thoughts.

To my amazement, my ability to speak to his mind came naturally. An instinctive switch flipped in my brain, and I channeled my words by sheer mental power. *I'm not going to kill him. And you aren't either, so don't get any ideas.*

And the archangels? We had a deal.

This isn't right. His death shouldn't be our call. I thought this was what I wanted, but you were right. If I kill him, I'll never forget. I'll carry him with me forever, and that's not what I want. I want to move on. I'm making the right decision. And though I kept it to myself, I knew the archangels were using us to do their dirty work. I for one had had enough of getting my hands dirty.

To my surprise, Patch didn't argue. He faced Hank. "I prefer it cold, dark, and cramped. And I'll soundproof it. That way, no matter how loud or long you holler, you'll only have your own misery to keep you company."

Thank you, I told Patch, putting all my sincerity behind my words.

A wicked smile crept to his mouth. *Death was too good for him. More fun this way.*

If the mood hadn't been so grave, I might have laughed.

"This is what you get for believing Dabria," I told Hank. "She's not a prophetess; she's a psychopath. Live and learn."

I gave Hank the opportunity for any final words, but as I expected, he was speechless. I'd hoped, at the very least, for a fumbled attempt at an apology, but I hadn't set my heart on it. Instead Hank's final exchange came in the form of a strange, faint smile of anticipation. The effect unnerved me slightly, but I supposed that was what he intended.

A hush filled the small cell. The tension crackling the air ebbed away. Banishing all thought of Hank, I became acutely aware of Patch standing behind me. There was a distinct change in the air, shifting from uncertainty to relief.

Exhaustion drained through me. Its first casualty were my hands, which started to shake. My knees also trembled, then my legs. The draining sensation swept through me like a dizzy spell. The walls of the cell, the stale air, even Hank seemed to spin away. The only thing keeping me grounded was Patch.

Without warning, I flung myself into his arms. He pressed me back against the wall with the force of his kiss. A shudder of relief rippled through him, and I sank my fingers into his shirt, dragging him against me, needing him close in a way I never had before. His mouth pressed and tasted mine. There was nothing expert about

silence

the way he kissed now; in the cool darkness of the cell, hot urgency bound us together.

"Let's get out of here," he murmured into my ear.

I was about to agree, when I saw fire out of the corner of my eye. At first I thought one of the torches had fallen from a bracket. But the flame danced in Hank's hand, a mesmerizing, unearthly blue glow. It took me a moment to understand what my eyes were seeing but refused to believe.

Realization dawned one piece at a time. Hank juggled a ball of sizzling blue fire in one hand and Patch's black feather in the other. Two vastly different objects; one light, one dark. Moving inextricably closer together. A thread of smoke coiled up from the tip of the feather.

There wasn't time to shout a warning. There wasn't time at all.

In that thinnest of moments, I raised the gun. I squeezed the trigger.

The shot flung Hank back against the wall, arms outstretched, mouth open in surprise.

He never moved again.

CHAPTER

33

PATCH DIDN'T BOTHER DIGGING A GRAVE FOR THE body. It was dark, an hour or two before sunrise, and he dragged it to the coast, just beyond Delphic's gates, and with a nudge of his boot, rolled it off the cliffs and into the raging waves below.

"What will happen to him?" I asked, huddling into Patch for warmth. The icy winds ripped at my clothes, painting a layer of frost over my skin, but the real chill came from within, cutting bone deep.

"The tide will drag him out, and the sharks will have an easy meal."

I shook my head to signify he'd misunderstood. "What will happen to his soul?" I couldn't help but wonder if the things I'd said to Hank were true. Would he suffer every moment for the rest of time? I shook aside any remorse I felt. I hadn't wanted to kill Hank, but in the end, he'd left me no choice.

Patch stayed silent, but I didn't miss that he held me tighter, closing his arms protectively around me. He ran his hands briskly over my arms. "You're freezing. Let me take you back to my place."

I held my ground. "What happens now?" I whispered. "I killed Hank. I have to lead his men, but what will I do with them?"

"We'll figure it out," Patch said. "We'll come up with a plan, and I'll be by your side until we see it through."

"Do you really believe it will be that easy?"

Patch made a short sound of amusement. "If I wanted easy, I'd chain myself in hell beside Rixon. The two of us could kick back and soak up the rays together."

I gazed down at the waves, dashing themselves to pieces against the rocks. "When you made the deal with the archangels, weren't they worried you'd talk? This can't look good for them. All you'd have to do is spread rumors that devilcraft can be harnessed, and you'd incite a black-market feeding frenzy among Nephilim and fallen angels."

"I swore an oath not to talk. That was part of the deal."

"Could you have asked for anything in exchange for your silence?" I asked quietly.

Patch tensed, and I sensed he'd guessed the direction of my thoughts. "Does it matter?" he said blandly.

It did. Now that Hank was dead, the haze shrouding my memory was burning off like clouds under the sun. I couldn't remember entire reels of memories, but pictures were there. Flashes and glimpses that grew stronger by the minute. Hank's power, and control over me, was dying alongside him, leaving me wide open to remember everything Patch and I had struggled through together. The tests of betrayal, loyalty, trust. I knew what made him laugh, what set him off. I knew his deepest desire. I saw him so clearly. So breathtakingly clearly.

"Could you have asked them to make you human?"

I felt him exhale slowly, and when he spoke, there was a raw honesty in his voice. "The short answer to that question is yes. I could have."

Tears blurred my vision. I was overcome by my own selfishness, even though rationally, I knew I hadn't made Patch's decision for him. Still. He'd made it because of me, and my guilt tossed and churned as stormily as the sea below.

Upon seeing my reaction, Patch made a sound of disagreement. "No, hear me out. The long answer to that question is that everything about me has changed since meeting you. What I wanted five months ago is different from what I want today. Did I want a human body? Yes, very much. Is it my top priority now? No." He looked at me with serious eyes. "I gave up something I wanted for something I need. And I need you, Angel. More than I think you'll ever know. You're immortal now. And so am I. That's something."

"Patch—," I began, shutting my eyes, my heart hanging from a thread.

His mouth brushed my earlobe, a searing flutter-weight pressure. "I love you." His voice was straightforward, affectionate. "You make me remember who I used to be. You make me want to be that man again. Right now, holding you, I feel like we have a shot at beating all odds and making it together. I'm yours, if you'll have me."

Just like that, I forgot that I was thoroughly soaked, shivering, and poised to be the next leader of a Nephilim society I wanted nothing to do with. Patch loved me. Nothing else was important.

"Love you back," I said.

He bowed his head into my throat, groaning softly. "I loved you long before you loved me. It's the only thing I have you beat at, and I'll bring it up every chance I get." His mouth, pressed to my skin, took on a devilish curve. "Let's get out of here. I'm taking you back to my place, this time for good. We have unfinished business, and I think it's time we do something about it."

I hesitated, one big question looming in my mind. Sex was a big deal. I wasn't sure I was ready to complicate our relationship—or my life—that way, and that was only top on a long list of repercussions. If a fallen angel who slept with a human created a Nephil—a being that was never meant to inhabit Earth—what happened when a fallen angel slept with a Nephil? Based on what I'd seen of the icy relationship between angels and Nephilim, it probably hadn't happened yet, but that only made me more leery of the consequences.

As much as I'd been content in the past to make the archangels out as the bad guys, a shred of doubt crept into my mind. Was there a reason angels weren't supposed to fall in love with mortals, or in my case, a Nephil? An archaic rule meant to divide our races . . . or a safeguard against tampering with nature and destiny? Patch had once said the only reason the Nephilim race existed was because fallen angels sought revenge for being forced out of heaven. To get even with the archangels for banishing them, they'd seduced the very humans they had previously been charged to protect.

They'd gotten revenge all right. And stirred up an underground war that had been raging for centuries: fallen angels on one side, Nephilim on the other, and human pawns trapped in the middle. Even though it scared me to think it, Patch had promised it would end with the annihilation of an entire race. Which one was yet to be seen.

All because a fallen angel wandered into the wrong bed.

"Not yet," I said.

Patch arched a dark eyebrow. "Not yet to leaving, or not yet to leaving with me?"

"I have questions." I gave him a meaningful look.

A smile tugged at his mouth, but it didn't mask a wavering note of uncertainty. "I should have known you've only been keeping me around for answers."

"Well, that and your kisses. Anyone ever tell you you're an incredible kisser?"

"The only person whose opinion I care about is right here." He tipped my chin up to level our eyes. "We don't have to go back to my place, Angel. I can take you home, if that's what you want. Or, if you decide you want to sleep at my place, on opposite sides of my bedroom with a Do Not Cross line drawn down the middle, I'll do it. I won't like it, but I'll do it."

Touched by his sincerity, I hooked my finger under his shirt, trying to find the right gesture to show my appreciation. My knuckle brushed toned skin beneath, and desire shattered me. Why, oh why, did he make it so easy to feel too much, all sensation, blazing and devouring, and forget reason?

"If you haven't guessed it already," I said, something fervent and resonating slipping into my tone, "I need you, too."

"Is that a yes?" he asked, pushing his fingers through my hair, fanning it out around my shoulders and searching my face intently. "Please let it be yes," he said with a gravelly edge. "Stay with me tonight. Let me hold you, even if that's all it is. Let me keep you safe."

As my answer, I slipped my fingers between his, twining us together. I met his kiss with unrepentant boldness, greedy and reckless, feeling his touch loosen my joints, melting me in places I didn't know existed. Breaking me down, one kiss at a time, reeling me further and further out of control, casting me into solid heat, dark and provocative, until there was only him, and only me. Until I didn't know where I stopped and he began.

CHAPTER

34

THE SUN HAD BURNED THROUGH HALF THE DAY BY
the time Patch parked his motorcycle in front of the
farmhouse. I swung off, a silly smile plastered on my
face, a warm glow permeating every inch of skin. *Perfection.*

I wasn't naive enough to think it would last, but there was something to be said about living in the moment. I'd already decided
to file dealing with my new purebred Nephilim blood, and all the
consequences that were bound to come with it, including how

my transformation would manifest itself and ruling Hank's army, under future concerns.

Right now, I had everything I could ask for. It wasn't a long list, but it was a very satisfying one, starting with the love of my life back in my arms.

"I had fun last night," I told Patch, flicking off my chin strap and handing over my helmet. "I'm officially in love with your sheets."

"That the only thing you're in love with?"

"Nope. Your mattress, too."

Some smile crept into Patch's eyes. "My bed's an open invitation."

We hadn't slept with a Do Not Cross line drawn down the middle of the bed, because we hadn't slept together, period. I took the bed and Patch got the sofa. I knew he wanted more from me, but I also knew he wanted my head in the right place. He'd said he could wait, and I believed him.

"Give me an inch, I'll take a mile," I warned. "You should be worried I might confiscate it."

"I'd consider myself a lucky man."

"Only downside to your place is the disturbingly low amount of extraneous toiletries. No conditioner? Lip gloss? Sunscreen?" I jerked my thumb toward the front door. "I need to brush my teeth. And I need a shower."

He grinned, hopping off the bike. "Now that is an invitation."

Reaching up on my tiptoes, I kissed him. "When I finish, it's

D-day. I'm going over to Vee's to pick up my mom, and I'm telling both of them the truth. Hank is gone, and it's time to come clean."

I wasn't looking forward to the conversation, but I'd waited long enough. All this time I'd told myself I was protecting Vee and my mom, but I was using lies to keep them from the truth. I was forcing them into the darkness because I was scared they couldn't handle the light. Even I knew the logic was messed up.

I unlocked the front door, tossing my keys into the dish. I hadn't made it three steps before Patch snagged my elbow. One look at his face, and I knew something was wrong.

Before Patch could shield me behind his body, Scott stepped out from the kitchen. He made a beckoning gesture, and two other Nephilim moved into the hallway beside him. Both appeared about Scott's age. Tall and muscular with hard-bitten features. They eyed me with open curiosity.

"Scott," I said, dodging around Patch and hurrying toward him. I threw my arms around him, hugging him fiercely. "What happened? How did you escape?"

"Given the circumstances, it was decided I'd be more effective on the front lines than locked up. Nora, meet Dante Matterazzi and Tono Grantham," he said. "Both are first lieutenants in the Black Hand's army."

Patch crossed to us. "You brought these men into Nora's home?" he said, eyeing Scott as though he'd like to snap his neck.

"Easy, man. They're cool. They can be trusted," Scott said.

Patch's laugh was low and predatory. "Reassuring news coming from a known liar."

A muscle in Scott's cheek contracted. "Sure you want to play this game? You've got just as many skeletons in your closet."

Oh boy.

"Hank's dead," I told Scott, not seeing any reason to put it gently, or give Patch and Scott further time to swap testosterone-fueled insults.

Scott nodded. "We know. Show her the sign, Dante."

Dante stepped forward. He was over six and a half feet tall and swarthy, and his Latin looks lived up to his name. He extended his hand. A ring identical to the one Scott had tossed into the ocean fitted his index finger snugly. It glowed blue and wild, and the light seemed to skitter behind my eyes even after I'd shut them. "The Black Hand told me this would happen if he died," Dante explained. "Scott's right. It's a sign."

Scott said, "That's why I was released. The army is in pandemonium. Nobody knows what to do. Cheshvan is almost here and the Black Hand had plans for war, but his men are restless. They've lost their leader. They're starting to panic."

I waded through this information. A thought struck me. "They released you because you knew how to find me—Hank's next in line?" I guessed, eyeing Dante and Tono warily. Scott might trust them, but I had yet to make up my own mind.

"Like I said, these guys are clean. They've already confessed loyalty to you. We have to get as many Nephilim behind you as possible before this falls apart. The last thing we need right now is a coup."

I felt light-headed. Actually, a coup sounded pretty appealing. Someone else wanted this job? Fine by me.

Dante spoke again. "Prior to his death, the Black Hand notified me that you agreed to take on the role of commander upon his death."

I swallowed, not having expected this moment to arrive so quickly. I knew what had to be done, but I'd hoped for more time. To say I'd been dreading this moment was an understatement.

I looked all three of them in the eye in turn. "Yes, I swore a vow to lead Hank's army. Here's what's going to happen. There isn't going to be a war. Go back to the men and tell them to disband. All Nephilim who've sworn an oath of fealty are bound by a law that no army, no matter how great, can overthrow. To go into battle at this point would be suicide. Fallen angels are already planning retribution, and our only hope is to make it clear we *aren't* going to fight them. Not this way. It's over—and you can tell your men that's an order."

Dante smiled, but his expression held an edge. "I'd rather not discuss this with a fallen angel hanging around." He leveled his eyes at Patch. "Give us a minute?"

I said, "I think it's pretty obvious that asking Patch to leave is pointless. I'm going to tell him everything." At Dante's sore expression, I added, "When I swore the oath to Hank, I never said anything about breaking up with Patch. That's right. Your new Nephil leader is dating a fallen angel." *Let the talk begin.*

Dante's curt nod was anything but accepting. "Then let's get one thing straight. This isn't over. Stalled, maybe, but not over. The Black Hand stirred up a revolution, and calling it off isn't going to be enough to settle the dust."

"I'm not worried about settling the dust. I'm worried about the Nephilim race as a whole. I'm thinking about what's best for everyone."

Scott, Dante, and Tono shared a silent look. At last Dante seemed to speak for all three. "Then we have a bigger problem. Because Nephilim think rebellion is best for them."

"How many Nephilim?" Patch asked.

"Thousands. Enough to fill a city." Dante's eyes cut toward mine. "If you don't lead them to freedom, you'll break your vow. In short, your head's on the line, Nora."

I stared at Patch.

Stand your ground, he spoke calmly to my thoughts. *Tell them the war is off and there's no room for negotiation.*

"I swore an oath to lead Hank's army," I told Dante. "I never promised freedom."

"If you don't declare war on fallen angels, you're going to instantly make enemies with thousands of Nephilim," he responded.

And if I do, I thought weakly, I might as well declare war on the archangels. They'd allowed Hank to die because Patch promised them I'd quell the uprising.

I returned my attention to Patch, and I knew we were sharing the same grisly thought. Either way, war was coming.

All I had to do now was decide my opponent.

ACKNOWLEDGMENTS

This is always the most humbling part of writing a book.

First and foremost, a big shout of appreciation to my family for offering up support, encouragement, and most of all patience 365 days a year. Justin, I'm sure calling you my biggest cheerleader isn't the manliest of endearments, but very fitting. You are my better half.

Thanks to the many friends who've helped out in immeasurable ways, from babysitting to reading early drafts of Silence to reminding me that laughter really is the best medicine. Sandra Roberts, Mary Louise Fitzpatrick, Shanna Butler, Lindsey Leavitt, Rachel Hawkins, Emily Wing Smith, Lisa Schroeder, Laura Andersen, Ginger Churchill, Patty Esden, Nicole Wright, and Meg Garvin—I am blessed to know you.

I'd be remiss if I didn't say how grateful I am to Jenn Martin and Rebecca Sutton, the dynamic duo behind FallenArchangel.com. Thank you for keeping my fans in the know, and in a much more timely manner than I'd ever hope to accomplish. Your dedication truly astounds.

Thanks to James Porto, the creative genius behind my books' stunning cover art.

Buckets of gratitude to Lyndsey Blessing, my foreign-rights agent, who has helped get my books into the hands of readers across the globe. Thanks to my agent, Catherine Drayton, for ... everything (including talking me into buying that particularly stunning pair of shoes in Bologna).

As always, I am so very fortunate to have a devoted team behind me at Simon & Schuster BFYR. Thanks to Courtney Bongiolatti, Julia Maguire, and Venetia Gosling for your editorial prowess. Many thanks to Justin Chanda, Anne Zafian, Jenica Nasworthy, Lucy Ruth Cummins, Lucille Rettino, Elke Villa, Chrissy Noh, and Anna McKean for bringing so much excitement into my life. I truly feel that I have the easy job in all this.

A nod of appreciation to Valerie Shea, copyeditor extraordinaire. Without you, this book would be far more humorous. And not in a good way!

A big thank-you to Dayana Gomes Marques and Valentine Bulgakov for christening *Silence* characters Dante Matterazzi and Tono Grantham.

Last but never least, thank you to my readers, near and far. Writing for you has been immeasurably thrilling and satisfying. I've loved sharing Patch and Nora's story with you.

AND NOW . . .

A NEVER-BEFORE-SEEN

LOOK AT THE *REAL*

FIRST TIME PATCH

AND NORA MET . . .

FROM PATCH'S

POINT OF VIEW!

Patch rocked his chair back on two legs, stretched out his arms, and folded them behind his neck. His gaze was nailed to the doors leading inside Enzo's Bistro. He'd asked for a table at the back, in a shadowy corner where the light didn't quite reach. A votive candle flickered on every other table, but Patch had snuffed his between his fingers upon sitting. Across the table, Rixon was sprawled in his chair, eyes tracing the ceiling in overdone boredom.

"*I'll wait for you till I turn blue,*" Rixon sang in a mutter. "*There's nothing more a man can do. Ya drank with demons straight from*"—he broke off and, arching a suggestive eyebrow, pointed beneath his feet—"*hell. They almost nearly won as weeeell.*"

Patch smiled. "Warming up for your *American Idol* audition?"

Rixon kicked him under the table. "When are you going to tell me what you're up to?"

A waitress swept past, dropping off two coffees.

Patch took a drink. "Up to?"

"We've been coming here—Enzo's, is it?—every Thursday night round eight. Five weeks in a row. And you thought I didn't notice."

"Four weeks."

Rixon gave a theatrical eye roll. "The lad *can* count."

"They have good coffee."

"Right, then. Trouble with that is, you can't taste it," Rixon pointed out. "Moving on to lie number two, then?"

"I like the atmosphere."

Rixon's eyes bugged with astonishment. "Every girl in this place is under twenty. What do you say we scam up some birds a little closer to our own age . . . seven hundred, at least."

"I'm not here for the girls." *Just one of them.* His eyes flicked to his watch, then back to the doors. *Any minute now.*

"Not here for the girls," Rixon echoed. "Not here for the gambling, the drinking, the fighting. By all accounts, we're blowing a perfectly good night in a *reputable* establishment. Either you've started listening to the wee little angel on your shoulder, or that iniquitous brain of yours is tossing around some scheme."

"And?"

"And I'm betting on the latter. What I want to know is what worthwhile scheme involves a squeaky-clean high school hangout?" he asked, casting a baleful eye about the place.

Outside, a familiar silhouette jogged past the bank of rain-splattered windows. The girl had her arms crossed over her head, doing an amusing job of trying to shield the rain. She hurried inside, giving the door an extra shove to allow her blonde companion time to squeeze in before it slammed shut. They stood in the entrance a moment, shaking off rain and stamping their feet dry.

Rixon was still poking around for answers, but Patch had tuned him out. He was immensely conscious of the shorter of the two girls, a slim redhead with straight shoulders and a chin she held slightly raised in a gesture that could be mistaken for conceit. He'd watched her long enough to know it was something else. He toyed with words like "cagey," "unassuming" . . . "prudent." She'd raked her hair up into a stringent bun, but a few rogue pieces had fallen loose, and the effect brought the slightest curve to his mouth.

Even if he hadn't memorized her schedule, the black spandex running pants and wide-necked sweatshirt that she seemed engaged in a battle of tug-of-war with—one moment it would slide off her shoulder and the next she'd hitch it back into place—would have told him she'd come from the gym. Among the growing list of things he was discovering about her: She was a fair-weather exerciser. Once a week at most. And only when the blonde, a yo-yo dieter, dragged her along.

The hostess led the girls in Patch's direction. Patch slouched, discreetly angling his baseball cap to shield his face. Every other week he'd watched the redhead from across the restaurant, making sure she never had reason to glance his way. She typically sat with her chin propped on laced fingers, listening attentively as the blonde went off on guys, miracle diets, celebrity breakups, or her horoscope.

The hostess weaved to the side suddenly, seating the girls a few tables down. A slippery feeling of anxiety tumbled inside Patch, and the sensation almost made him laugh. When was the last time he'd felt boyish nervousness over being caught in a reprobate act?

But he *had* to play this safe. When he finally introduced himself to the redhead, creating the illusion of meeting for the first time, it had to appear random. Only after he knew her inside and out would he nail down a strategy to gain her trust.

Then he'd drop the proverbial ax.

Rixon was wrong. The angel on his shoulder had long ago been bound and silenced. Patch was driven by his own highest good, his moral compass a function of utility. He had a plan in everything, but the end result was always the same: to satisfy his wants.

After all this time, he was going to get a human body. Because he wanted it, and he had a plan. And the very heart of that plan sat feet away, stabbing at her ice water with a straw.

"I don't know about you, but I'm thinking we need to start sophomore year off with a bang," the blonde announced loudly to the redhead. "No more ho-hum. This year is gonna be epic. No holds barred. And nothing could make this year more epic than snagging Luke Messersmith as my boyfriend. I already jump-started my this-is-how-I'm-gonna-get-him plan. I Sharpied my phone number on his garage door. All that's left now is to sit back and wait."

"For the restraining order?" The redhead was full-on grinning, lighting up her whole face. Clearly she didn't know the effect it had, Patch thought, or she'd do it more often.

"What, you don't like obvious?" the blonde argued.

"His parents are going to blacklist you. Any way you look at it, seven digits Sharpied on a garage door doesn't make for the best icebreaker."

Patch couldn't take his eyes off her. This week more so than the last. Come to think of it, that had been the pattern from the start. It was inconvenient that she didn't resemble Chauncey's long-lost descendant; killing her would have brought him significantly more enjoyment. He didn't know what he'd expected, but not this. Long legs, but a cautious, reserved stride. Prim features. A laugh that wasn't too loud or too soft. Everything in its place.

Another near smile crept to his mouth. He was seized by the

urge to put a crack in her. To make her carefully constructed world topple. One line was all it would take to make her blush. He'd bet money on it.

"Maybe next time go with a text," the redhead suggested. "'Hey, Luke, here are my digits.' Works for the rest of the population."

The blonde blew out a sigh and plunked her chin on her fist. "Fudge it. Snagging Luke Messersmith was a crapshoot anyway. What we need is to set our sights elsewhere. Road trip to Portland. Man, that would make Marcie blow steam out her ears. You and me hanging out with college guys while she models slutty swimsuits at J.C. Penney in front of drooling, prepubescent freshmen."

Rixon's chair scraped forward. "I give up," he said, drawing Patch's attention. "I. Give. Up. What are you after?"

Patch took another sip of coffee. "Quality time with you."

"See, when you lie to me it hurts," Rixon said, swiping an imaginary tear. "I thought we had something special. I thought our joint eternal sentences of damnation were our bond. I know you're up to something and if I have to, I'll beat it out of you."

"Give it a rest."

"I'd like to. Problem is, I'm not stupid."

"You act stupid."

"Right. Thanks for that. For your information, there's a difference between acting stupid and being stupid."

"It's a fine line, but someone has to draw it."

Rixon flattened his hands to the table with a resounding thud. "What are we doing here other than taking an honest stab at death by boredom? And if you don't come clean in the next three seconds, I'll make good on my threat to make a punching bag out of your arrogant smirk."

Patience. When I bring it up, this is what I'm talking about, Patch spoke to his friend's mind.

Digging up each other's flaws, are we? Tsk, tsk. That's no way to kindle a friendship. As for your flaws, you've forgotten how to have fun. Why don't we go find a group of Nephilim to terrorize? Rixon started to stand.

Patch began to rise as well, but the conversation three tables over penetrated his conscious thought, momentarily diverting his attention.

"Why can't any of the guys at school look like . . . those two guys over there. *Yowza.*"

The blonde's voice hung in the air. Patch barely had time to glance sideways and see that both she and the redhead had their eyes pinned on him, definitely and fully aware of him— when Rixon shoved his fist into his jaw. Patch's head snapped sideways, giving him a direct but swimming picture of the redhead's mouth forming a perfect and astonished O.

Well, this was inconvenient.

"Told you I'd beat it out of you," Rixon cackled, dodging lithely around the table.

Patch was on his feet in an instant.

Rixon barreled into him, slamming him back against the wall and into a picture frame. It hit the ground, glass shattering.

From the edge of his vision, Patch saw the redhead blink in stunned confusion and, if he wasn't mistaken, just enough alarm to bring him a certain satisfaction . . . and encourage him on.

Patch reflexively dipped, and Rixon's next jab passed over his shoulder. With an upward swipe, Patch drilled his fist into the underside of Rixon's chin. He attacked the core of Rixon's body, aiming repeatedly for the ribs and flesh around his stomach, but the moment his friend dropped his arms to protect himself, he went for his head. Once, twice. Twice more. After five direct blows Rixon staggered out of range and flipped his palms up.

"You want me to scream uncle, that it?" Rixon panted, wearing a grin that said he was enjoying himself for the first time all night.

The blonde wended her way through the tables to Rixon. She held out her napkin, gesturing at his face. "You've got a little blood . . ."

"Thanks, sweetheart." Rixon dabbed the napkin to his mouth, then cast a sly wink at Patch. His voice slipped easily into Patch's mind. Said *I wanted a girl closer to seven hundred, did I? I meant seven hundred . . . give or take.*

Patch settled grim eyes on the blonde, wishing he could mind-trick her into obediently going back to her table, but Rixon would pick up on it and ask questions. He let out a slow breath. Twenty-four hours from now, Rixon wouldn't remember her name. She, however, had a slightly longer attention span. A complication.

"So tell me, love," Rixon drawled to the blonde. "Ever ridden on a Ducati Streetfighter? I'm parked out back."

The blonde was already throwing her purse strap over her shoulder. "Does your friend have a bike too? He could take my friend, Nora." To Patch's surprise, she waved at him.

"Vee," the redhead said with exasperation and warning.

The blonde didn't bother listening. She turned to Rixon. "First things first. Someone should clean you up. I took a baby-sitting CPR course this summer. When it comes to nosebleeds, I'm your girl." She grabbed Rixon by the sleeve and hauled him toward the unisex restroom.

True to form, Rixon slung an arm around her shoulder and nuzzled her cheek. "Lead the way, Nurse . . . Vee, was it?"

Patch found himself standing in disbelief beside the red-head. Two minutes ago he'd had things under control. He raked his hands through his hair. He might as well have plowed a Mack truck down the middle of his plan.

The redhead shifted her weight. She stole a look up at him, only to immediately swing her eyes away. She was frightened by him. He wondered if he had this effect on her naturally or if she sensed on some subconscious level what he wanted from her.

A strange war of desires battled inside him, pulling him in opposite directions. He wanted to make her uneasy. Ironically, he was also frightened of scaring her off. Now that he had her close, he wanted to keep her there.

She cleared her throat. "Think you could tell your friend to cut back on the slickness factor? If he gets any oilier, third world countries are going to start looking to him as a supplier."

Patch smiled down at her. She was prettier up close. Cautious but expressive eyes, an aristocratic nose, a few freckles she probably hated, and that hair. Wild and rebellious. He had the urge to snap the rubber band and send her hair cascading around her shoulders. Other than his Nephilim mark on her wrist, Chauncey's genes had done her the favor of sparing her any similarities.

"So," he said. "You're from around here?"

She craned her neck, searching the restaurant, clearly bent on appearing absorbed in anything but talking to him. "It would seem so. And you are . . . ?"

"Jev." He could tell by the slight downturn of her mouth she thought it was an odd name. Most humans did.

"And you?" she asked. "Are you from around here? I haven't seen you before."

"I keep a low profile."

"Why's that?"

"You ask a lot of questions."

She flinched. He'd meant to kill the conversation and it worked. He knew he looked like a jerk, but given what he had in store for her, he could do a lot worse. He realized he should leave it alone, but now that he had her talking, he found himself drawn to her. The banter between them felt natural. And she was responding. Scared of him, sure, but equally curious. He could see it well enough in her eyes.

With conscious effort, Patch turned his body toward her, displaying interest. He smiled politely. "I'm in town on business."

"What kind of business?" she asked after a minute.

"Genealogy. Tracking down long-lost family members."

"Which family are you researching?"

"Langeais."

"I'm not aware of any Langeaises in Coldwater."

He rubbed his thumb across his mouth to quell a smile. "Sounds like I've got my work cut out."

"How long are you planning to stay in town?"

"As long as it takes." He bent his head toward hers as though they were conspirators. "It would speed things up if I had a tour guide, someone to show me around."

Her mouth crooked with a wry little smile, as if she knew what he was up to, but she teased him by saying, "You're in luck. Vee is an *excellent* tour guide."

He recovered his surprise quickly. "But I prefer redheaded tour guides."

She spread her hands in regret. "Sorry. I don't know any redheads."

"Check the mirror this morning?"

She tapped her finger to her mouth, a playful gesture that drew his attention to her lips, prim and sensuous, which he had already had the pleasure of noticing. She was cautiously warming up to him, and Patch felt the restaurant tunnel around them, the background noises dropping away. A part of him that had been locked up for so long loosened. He felt a strange satisfaction being near her. A teasing contact that made him want more.

Not missing a beat, she said, "I did. And I recall seeing a brunette."

He laughed, trying to figure out this game she was playing. "Might need to get your vision checked."

"So *that* explains why you have three eyes, two horns, and one very yellow fang where your front teeth should be." She cocked her head to the side, squinting at him.

He grinned. "Busted. I'm a monster. Jev is my deceptively harmless—and shockingly handsome—alter ego."

"And I'm on top of it," she announced with witty triumph.

"Is that a Freudian slip?"

His bluntness caught her off-guard. A self-conscious blush rose in her face. She stood uncertain a moment, then gestured with impatience at the restroom. "How long does it take to clean a bloody nose?"

He laughed low. "Not sure that's the only thing they're doing in there."

Her eyes widened with shock . . . then narrowed in scrutiny, trying her hardest to figure out if he was teasing. For once, he wasn't. "Maybe you should go knock on the door," she suggested at last.

The suggestion didn't appeal to him. He wasn't in any hurry to end things. The thought of leaving her now left him with an impatient ache. He hadn't felt this way in a very long time. As far as he was concerned, he hadn't felt a spark of interest in so long, it was like feeling it for the first time. "Won't do any good. The only thing that'll grab Rixon's attention is the sound of his bike starting. Someone breathes on it, and he notices the condensation. You want to get him out of there, that's your best option."

"You're saying I should take his bike for a ride?"

"More like be my accomplice." He let the idea dangle.

"And you want me to go with you, why?"

So *I can get you alone long enough to erase your mind.* And if he was being honest, to get her alone, period. His eyes dropped to her mouth, and he enjoyed a secret pleasure of imagining kissing her. "Let me guess. You've never been on a Ducati Streetfighter."

There went that chin again, angling higher. "How would you know that?"

"Ride one once, and that's all it takes. You're hooked." He hitched his thumb at the exit. "Now or never."

"I don't run off with guys I've known all of three seconds."

"And a guy you've known, say, twenty seconds? He stand a better chance?"

To his surprise, she laughed. He liked the sound of it, and

against his own good judgment, he wanted to make her do it again.

"Actually," she said, smiling with more ease, "that guy would drastically reduce his chances. Twenty is my unlucky number."

"And your lucky number?"

She bit her lip, debating answering.

Over the top of her head, Patch saw Rixon emerge from the restroom pressing a folded square of toilet paper to his nose. Patch lifted his hat and scrubbed his hair in frustration. That was quick, even by Rixon's standards.

"Is it between one and ten?" Patch asked on a stroke of inspiration.

She nodded.

"Hold the number behind your back. I'll guess it. If I guess right, you and I go for a ride. Doesn't have to be tonight," he added in response to the skepticism flooding her expression. "Next time I offer you a ride on my bike, say yes. It's that simple."

She held his eyes a long moment, then relented with a confident shrug. "You have a one in ten chance of guessing right. I can handle those odds."

How many fingers is she holding up? he called to Rixon's mind.

Hearing him, Rixon looked up and his face split into a grin. *I leave you alone for five minutes, and you're already chasing skirts?*

Fingers? Patch repeated.

What's in it for me?

Next time we fight, you get to give me the bloody nose.

Get to? Rixon tipped his head back, silently laughing. *I'll happily remind you of an occasion just last week when I nearly punched out one of your teeth.*

"Well?" the redhead prodded Patch. "Telepathy skills getting rusty?"

Tomorrow night you call the shots, Patch bargained.

Anything I want? Even if it includes terrorizing underage Nephilim?

Patch sighed. *Anything.*

All right, mate. You're on. She's holding up eight fingers. But keep the flirting to a minimum, will you? Seven minutes in heaven with Nurse Vee are up. I'm ready to roll.

Patch closed his eyes, tightening his face to suggest concentration. He opened one eye, staring down speculatively at the redhead. "Let's go with . . . eight?" He said it with just enough uncertainty to make it believable.

The redhead's mouth dropped. "No way."

Patch rubbed his hands together, genuinely enjoying himself. "You know what this means. You owe me a ride, Nora." Her name was a mistake. He'd agreed to treat her with cold-blooded detachment, limiting all references to her to *the redhead*. He didn't think he was in danger of an emotional slip, but he was dealing with a beautiful girl. He'd learned his lesson once, hence the safeguard.

"You cheated," she accused.

His smile widened. She didn't sound that disappointed, and she knew it.

He played along, raising his shoulders, a display of innocence. "A bet's a bet."

"How did you do it?"

"Maybe my telepathy isn't rusty after all."

Rixon walked up, clapping him on the back. "Let's hit the road, Jack."

"Where's Vee?" the redhead wanted to know.

On cue, the blonde emerged from the restroom, slumped against the doorjamb, pantomimed her own erratically beating heart, and mouthed ooh-la-la.

"What did you do to her?" the redhead asked Rixon.

"Put a smile on her face. There's more where that came from," Rixon added, and Patch shoved him toward the doors.

"Take it easy," Patch told the redhead reluctantly, not ready to give up talking to her, but not wanting to impress any more of her on Rixon's memory. For the time being, he wanted to keep who she really was to himself.

The redhead blinked. "So I guess I'll see you around," she said, wearing a *what just happened here?* expression. Given the circumstances, he should ask himself the same thing.

"Absolutely," Patch answered. Sooner than she thought. Later tonight he planned on making house calls. First to the blonde, and then to the redhead.

If tonight had happened seven or eight months down the road, the timing would have been perfect. As it was, he had to erase their memories. He felt a jolt of regret at needing to wipe the redhead's memory. He wanted her to remember tonight. He wanted her to remember him.

He imagined sacrificing her—a thought he'd turned over in his head a hundred times before—but the image stumbled. For the first time he looked beyond himself—seeing her. Not only did he plan to kill her, but he had it in his mind to betray her first. What would she think of him if she knew? It occurred to him to drag her outside now and get it over with. The image flared in his mind, impulsive and tempting, but he forced it aside. If he could do it now, he could do it tomorrow.

But his hesitation bothered him. Something told him killing her wasn't going to be easy. He hadn't helped his cause by flirting with her and, worse, enjoying it. More than he was ready to admit.

In an effort to refocus his thoughts, he shut his eyes briefly and pictured the end goal. Once he sacrificed her, he'd have a human body. It wasn't complicated. Anything that stood in his way, including his own inner turmoil, was irrelevant.

Without thinking he turned, stealing a private look at her. He'd only meant to see her face one last time, but to his surprise, she was watching him, too, with a question in those exquisite gray eyes that would haunt him.

Silence playlist

1. **Mad World/**_Tears for Fears_

2. **Trouble is a Friend/**_Lenka_

3. **Paint it Black/**_Rolling Stones_

4. **Always/**_Bon Jovi_

5. **November Rain/**_Guns n' Roses_

6. **The Way I Am/**_Ingrid Michaelson_

7. **Love Walks In/**_Van Halen_

8. **Back in Black/**_ACDC_

9. **Zombie/**_The Cranberries_

10. **All I Want is You/**_U2_

11. **Blinding/**_Florence and the Machine_